Rage for Vengeance

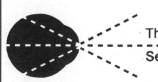

This Large Print Book carries the
Seal of Approval of N.A.V.H.

A BYRNES FAMILY RANCH WESTERN

RAGE FOR VENGEANCE

DUSTY RICHARDS

THORNDIKE PRESS
A part of Gale, a Cengage Company

Farmington Hills, Mich • San Francisco • New York • Waterville, Maine
Meriden, Conn • Mason, Ohio • Chicago

Copyright © 2019 by Dusty Richards.
Thorndike Press, a part of Gale, a Cengage Company.

ALL RIGHTS RESERVED
Thorndike Press® Large Print Western.
The text of this Large Print edition is unabridged.
Other aspects of the book may vary from the original edition.
Set in 16 pt. Plantin.

LIBRARY OF CONGRESS CIP DATA ON FILE.
CATALOGUING IN PUBLICATION FOR THIS BOOK
IS AVAILABLE FROM THE LIBRARY OF CONGRESS

ISBN-13: 978-1-4328-6515-3 (hardcover alk. paper)

Published in 2019 by arrangement with Pinnacle Books, an imprint of Kensington Publishing Corp.

Printed in the United States of America
1 2 3 4 5 6 7 23 22 21 20 19

Dear fans,

Thanks for your support and letters. The Chet Byrnes Ranch series rides on. Life and times of a man and his extended family forced to move from Texas by a bloody feud to the Arizona Territory. In the mid-1870s his family and associates work hard on the empire building of the Quarter Circle Z in the vast region that ranges from the sparse spiny cactus desert to the vast ponderosa pine forests of the high country.

I appreciate your thoughts. There are more of these books coming. Currently all of the books in this series are available.

Your emails are great. If you have any questions, comments, I will sure try to answer your email. If you like it, please rate the novel on Amazon. Helps my sales and I'll write more of these books for those of you who follow me.

Thanks and God Bless
Dusty Richards
dustyrichards@cox.net
dustyrichards.com

This book is dedicated to a great spokesman and author of western fiction

my dear friend Cotton Smith

There's an empty place at the campfire tonight. Cotton lived and breathed the West, and filled the pages of his many books with authentic themes of the life he loved. He knew the desert by heart from endless research as well as long trail rides with the Desert Caballeros. When he was President of Western Writers of America, the organization moved into a modern vision we shared to better serve our many members and readers. Cotton will be there when we get to that great pasture in the sky, welcoming us with his rich voice and telling us the coffee's done. Until then, he will be greatly missed.

God bless his lovely wife, Sonya, his family, and his many fans. A true warrior of the pen has left us. Amen.

CHAPTER 1

The sulfurous smell of gun smoke plus sagebrush stung his nose. Chet Byrnes rose up to look over the upset buckboard bed and with his Colt .45 blazed away at the distant shooters. Behind him, Cole Emerson, the young man who rode with him, was crawling back uphill, attempting to keep low in the sagebrush and bunchgrass after recovering the rifle thrown from their buckboard wreck while they tried to outrun the would-be shooters.

A few infrequent wild shots from the attackers kicked up dust around Chet, and one struck the wood of the bed. They were too far away to do much damage with handguns. Belly-down on top of the rise east of them were the three masked men who, on horseback, had charged the two of them on the buckboard traveling west. Mid-day the glaring sun bore down hot. Their racing buckboard must have struck something, upset and threw both men and the bed off the frame. Their team of horses lost no time heading west with the empty trucks hitting the high spots.

Cole took a seat on the ground behind the upright bed and levered a cartridge in the rifle's chamber. "This gun appears to be all right. Where are they at?"

"There is tall stalk standing up there; one of them is on your right side of that stem and belly-down. Aim low." Chet finished reloading cartridges in his own Colt.

Cole nodded and gained his feet to standing behind the upset wagon bed. He laid the rifle barrel on the wood side, took aim, and fired.

Results were a man screamed in the cloud of dust set off by the bullet on the rim line. "I'm hit, boys. Get them."

Another stick figure rose with a smoking revolver. Cole took aim and his second shot struck the shooter and sent him down. He ducked to reload with a smile at Chet. "You see number three?"

"No, not yet. Bet he won't expose himself now we have the rifle. My dad always said don't send a boy when you needed a man. Good shooting."

"He may have fled."

"Yes. I think he got the hell off that ridge."

Chet listened and could hear a horse running off, no doubt with the last attacker aboard.

Cole handed him the rifle. "I'll go try to catch our horses."

"Meanwhile, I'll go see if they can talk and tell us anything."

Cole gave him a concerned frown. "Watch them. Wounded snakes can bite."

"Oh yes, I know all about that. Wonder why they tried to rob us?" Chet asked.

Amused by the question, Cole chuckled. "We must have looked rich. Damned if I know, Chet."

"Maybe we both should go up there and check on them. I'd bet their saddle horses are up there. That team ran off maybe as far away as Center Point waiting for us by now."

Chet laughed. "How much of these so-called robberies are we going to have when we are up and running this stage line that we're trying to get ready for?"

"This whole road is isolated, and I guess the criminal element holding out up here has no one to stop them until we take a hand in doing that."

"Your brother-in-law at the Windmill Ranch, Sarge, covers part of this route driving contract cattle every month to the

Navajos for us. Does he have much trouble?"

"I bet Sarge just handles them if they are dumb enough to try him. He probably leaves them for the buzzards."

Amused, digesting Chet's words, Cole nodded. "I bet he simply does that. Your sister's husband is a tough quiet guy, and he takes the ranch's monthly cattle drives damn serious."

"He sure does a great job of getting them there on time at it too."

They were climbing up the steep slopes through the knee-high sagebrush and grass-clad slope to reach the ridge. Guns in hand, he and Cole both kept an eye on their destination on the top.

"You hurting?" he asked Cole.

"Not bad. But I bet we're both sore in the morning. Lucky we flew off through the air when that bed overturned in our wreck."

"My wings aren't as good as they used to be for cushioning a landing." Chet's hip was sore where he hit on it.

"Hell, mine too. I can see the first guy, and he looks alive."

Cole started to the left, leaving Chet with the wounded outlaw lying on the ground. He could see their two bay saddle horses grazing through their bits a short ways away.

Good. He was not made for much walking after being tossed out of a wagon. They'd have something to carry them to the next stage stop on the route. He knelt and felt for the man's pulse on his neck. Nothing. The unshaven kid looked pretty ragged. He turned him on his back. Besides, he needed a haircut and a bath, which he'd probably not get before his funeral was held.

"This guy is alive," Cole shouted.

"Coming. This one isn't taking in air anymore."

Cole gave a head toss back to the other. "I made sure he was disarmed and asked him who he was. He said he ain't answering questions."

Obviously, from the bloody shirt, the outlaw'd been shot in the right shoulder. The scraggy bearded man in his twenties looked in pain seated on the ground.

"We can leave you here to die. We want answers or else . . . ?" Chet told him.

"Go to hell."

Bent over, Chet grabbed a handful of his shirt and jerked him up in his face. "How about some pancake cactus spines under your fingernails? I can make you real uncomfortable, and I am not messing around with saving you either. Now who are you?"

"Johnny Duncan — Texas — what are you

bastards going to do to me?"

"Probably cut your throat. What were you three after?"

"A man said he'd pay us well if you two never got back to civilization."

"Who was that man?"

"I don't have a real name —" Pain cut his words off.

"Then how were you going to collect the money?"

"He said he'd meet us Friday and pay us a hundred dollars apiece."

"Where? At Horse Head Crossing?"

"Yeah. Longhorn Saloon. Wore a brown suit coat. Boss of the Plains Hat. Gray mustache. Maybe forty. I think he was a gambler."

"Scars?"

"Top of his right hand been bad burned a long time ago."

"No name?"

"He never gave it."

"How much money was he going to pay you?"

"I told you. A hundred dollars apiece."

"It don't sound like anyone I know," Cole said.

Chet agreed.

"I can catch their horses and ride up to the next station. Get some help and bring back a conveyance for him in a few hours," Cole said.

"You do that. Who got away?" he asked the outlaw.

"A kid named Soapy Jones. I knew he had no guts for this deal, but he made an extra gun. Rod Place over there came up here with me from Texas. Heard they needed cowboys. Hell, there ain't no cows up here. We've about starved."

"How did you meet this guy in the suit?"

"We built some fence for another guy over by Saint Johns. When we met him the three of us really needed a drink and a little loving from a dove. He offered us twenty bucks apiece to start this deal. Paid us that money and promised us a hundred more to each of us if we stopped you and him — that guy just now went after the horses."

"How did you recognize us?"

"Oh, he had good photographs of you and some pretty little Mexican gal all dressed up."

"That was my wife. Was there a name of who made the photo?"

"I never noticed. He had another of that guy with you and another pretty woman holding a boy."

"That was his wife, Valerie, and my son Rocky who she is raising." Rocky was the boy Chet had fathered back in Texas.

"You looked like them pictures."

"Don't guess he ever said how he got those photos?" Chet asked him.

"No, but they were good pictures. He said you'd be coming back through here shortly on horseback or buckboard."

Cole was back leading the horses. "I'll ride on west. Get some help."

"Ride easy. Duncan here saw pictures of us that guy had. The ones taken of you, Valerie, Liz, Rocky, and me that we had made. I guess by the traveling photographer who came by Center Point. What was that a month ago?"

Cole shook his head. "About that long ago. Wonder how he got them?"

"The guy hired them must be moving up and down our stage line. I have a description . . . now we need to find him. He paid them twenty apiece and promised a hundred more for each one of them if we were disposed of."

"Don't tell my wife . . . she may want to collect it for herself."

"Cole Emerson, you know better than that."

He was smiling and nodding while handing Chet the reins to the second horse. No way that that boy's wife would take a reward

16

for killing them. She might shoot the guys who did it but not him.

"There's a pint of whiskey in the right hand saddlebag on the horse you got," Duncan said. "I may need that."

Cole retrieved it, handed it to Chet, and left.

Chet handed it over to the man who used his teeth to get the cork out and then swallowed some of it. Chet loosened the cinch on the horse left behind and then hobbled him so he didn't run off. It would be a long, dreary day waiting on Cole's return and then them hauling the man to the doctor. This no-name man who hired them bothered him — especially how he got to possess copies of those photos from the traveling photographer. But it made sense if he wanted them assassinated to have good pictures of his intended victims.

By mid-afternoon Cole was back with a team of several Navajo boys who worked for their agent, Clyde Covington. They had brought a wagon to reload the bed, plus the truck, team of horses that ran off, and they set in to get things fixed. The spring seat got messed up in the overturn, and the crew of Navajo boys were laughing and having fun while they replaced it with a different one they'd brought along.

The wounded prisoner was treated enough to move, and the dead man's body was loaded in the wagon bed to go back west. Chet rode the other outlaw's horse with Cole and they went ahead of the wagons and team. A crewmember drove their repaired buckboard.

On the way to station number three they talked about Duncan, and Chet told his man again about the photos the man showed him.

"This guy Duncan have our photographs to identify us by?"

"Yes, he described the ones we had made up at Center Point of Liz and I and the one of Valerie, you, and Rocky. Copies of those ones that traveling picture man made of us a months ago. That was how those three knew who we were heading west in the buckboard and got after us."

Cole made a pained face. "That stranger must know us then."

"Or he has some other purpose for wanting us dead."

"Or so we fail to put this stage line in operation from Gallup to the Colorado River together and another party gets the mail contract."

"Call him Mr. X, but I want him and the sooner the better."

"What will you charge Duncan with?" Cole asked.

"Attempted armed robbery and murder."

"That's what they tried. Who got away?"

Chet shrugged. "Some kid named Soapy Jones. No telling where he went if he's smart. But I bet we run into him again."

Cole agreed and they'd reached the number-three station about sundown. Clyde Covington came from the corral area to meet them. A tall somewhat bent cowboy in his forties, he came shaking his head, concerned about their incident.

"You two got in trouble already?" His warm smile and laughter made a good ending to a helluva day. Chet turned to meet Clyde's straight-back proper wife, Iris, who reached up and kissed him on the cheek at the front door of the station.

"My lands. I heard they had shot at you, and you weren't here when expected, so I figured our boss has been killed. Whew, you have had some day. I'm glad too that that pretty wife of yours wasn't along as well."

"So was I. It has been a tough day, but we survived it."

"Why did they do that anyway?"

"I think so we couldn't start the stage line in six weeks."

"Can we still do that?"

"If I have to send all my cow hands up here we will do it."

"We're as ready, I guess, as we can be. They said we'd have the horses here soon."

"Last I had any word from the man in charge, Rod Carpenter, in Gallup, he said his men would move the horses in place in the coming week. There is a tack man coming too, and he will bring you the extra harness you will need."

"Your man Harold Faulk helped finish the corrals," Clyde said. "That is a hardworking bunch of men. Him, his son, wife, and daughter are sure scrappy. Why, they work as hard as the men he works. I never saw the likes."

"I hired them back earlier. He rode clear over to our place asking about work, and I'm proud because he's got all the stops ready over on this side of Center Point. Cole has another crew over west lining things up that are about ready too. You all will be earning your money in a few weeks."

"When will we be getting stages?" Clyde asked, showing them seats at the table.

"Oh, for now buckboards will do. It will take twelve months to move up to stage-coaches."

"I'll be glad to be started. I guess the way

things are the stages must be really coming?"

"Oh, they will. These men I am working with were relying on help that talked big, but it took more than that to put a set of that many stage stops together. No way they'd ever gotten the stages and horses here in time to meet that first mail contract. I am guessing some others folks want that mail contract, so keep your guns handy."

"Who do you think might be bucking you?"

"Clyde, all I have is that outlaw's description of the man who had photographs of both Cole and I with our wives to point us out. We had those pictures made some time back by a photographer passing through. He must have sold more prints he made so that we could be identified by the ones he hired to come after us."

"Ah, you two will get him. I know and read about your law work. Yes siree, you'll get them."

"Wish I was that sure. Your food looks great. I guess Cole is coming."

"He's washing up on the porch," Iris announced.

"Good. We really got thrown off that buckboard when it overturned. I guess when a driver don't show on schedule, you will have to go look for him after some time passes."

"You bet, and we need to get rid of these holdup men," Clyde said.

Chet agreed.

Chet decided, in the morning, the pair of them should head back to Center Point and see what else had gone wrong. Clyde said the Yavapai County deputy at Horse Head Crossing would hold the would-be robber until the jail wagon came to pick him up and haul him for trial in Prescott, the county seat for all that part of Arizona in the 1870s. Of course there were only jackrabbits, a few scattered homesteaders, and ranches spread thin all over that land. Horse Head Crossing, St. Johns, and a few army posts pretty well summed up the whole area.

Maybe the stage line would develop more settlements. That was why Chet felt it so important to make this line work like the Black Canyon Coach Line did from Preskitt to the Hayden's Ferry and Mill. The connection of this new stage route there at the San Francisco Peaks to the military road that led down to Camp Verde was why he called that stop Center Point. All hands were there building houses, barns, corrals to be the central place for the stage operation running from Gallup on the east over to the Colorado River ferry, which made up the territory's western boundary with California.

They arrived at Center Point two days later and were greeted by both wives and his four-year-old son, Rocky. Damn, Liz looked great running to meet him. He hugged her tight and kissed her in a volley of hammers pounding and handsaws cutting boards.

"You have any trouble?" she asked.

"Oh, some. Someone hired three guys to kill us coming back. I can tell you more later. How is the boy?"

"Oh, he's fine."

"Hey, big guy, how are you?" He hoisted his son up. The boy was really growing.

"I am fine, Daddy. They were worried you were not back. What took you so long?"

"We wrecked a buckboard is all."

"I am as glad as they are that you came back. I better go tell Valerie that you are fine."

He set him down. Rocky, on the ground, hurried for his stepmother. Chet laughed. "You tell her I am fine."

"Who was the *hombre* wanted you dead?" Liz asked.

"Some guy in a bar at Horse Head Crossing hired three lost Texas cowpokes. He promised to pay them a hundred dollars apiece to eliminate Cole and me both. Worse yet, that guy had copies of those pictures of you and me, plus Valerie, Cole, and Rocky they took up here a few weeks ago. This guy showed them to those three would-be killers, but where he got them from I don't know."

"I never saw that photographer again, did you?" Liz asked, leading him to the large tent set up as a mess hall.

"No. I never saw him again, but when Jesus and Spud get up here, I'll go find the guy that hired them cowboys and he'll wish he never tried it."

"Now I have to worry about that meeting?"

"No, I'll kill him where he is at. Hell with bringing him in alive even."

"Oh, I am just so glad you are finally at home. I must tell you that the young man Shawn McElroy on the Force has been seriously writing to Reg's widow Lucy Byrnes."

"Well, what is wrong with that?" Valerie brought him a plate of food and bread. He acknowledged her.

"Nothing. But he wants to move up here to be closer to her."

"Lord, I don't know how, but I'll work on it. Maybe Ratchet Thornton could go down there and help Roamer. That Force job is still tough work but not near as bad as when I started it down there."

"Good." Valerie nodded. "I think Shawn would be a good one for her."

"How big is she?" Last time he saw her the second pregnancy showed some. She already had one baby girl who was still pretty young — heavens, him and Liz had been trying hard for over two years to have a child, but she'd pre-warned him she had never been pregnant with her first husband.

His wife frowned at him. "Oh, she's not that big. Besides he must be very serious about her with one child and the baby coming."

"I can say she is a dandy lady, and I'd do anything I could for her. What's next?"

"You said you were going looking for this guy who hired killers to get after you?"

"I need to stop him from harming the real drivers. I've spent lots of time and energy invested in this stage line. Getting it together. So anyone trying to stop it needs to be stopped first."

Liz nodded in agreement.

Chet said, "I thank you girls and the cook for this food. My stomach was sure empty when we got here. Valerie's feeding Cole, I see. Those two are lovebirds maybe worse

25

than we are."

Liz looked in their direction. "Maybe, but they are two great people among the giants in your operations. But you know that well."

She leaned over and kissed him on the cheek. "I will go see about a bath for you."

He put down his fork. "I'd rather talk to you than eat alone. Stay here."

"Go ahead and eat. I will sit here and listen. I like to be with you too. I still shake my head about when I came looking for the man with the gold horses. I expected a grand place and you were staying at some adobe hovel called a *ranchero* under a canvas."

Liz continued, "But there you were, this man, standing so tall, hat off and so handsome — how could I ever impress him that I was thinking very serious about him and wanted to share his life at that first minute I ever saw you." She winked at him and went on. "So he showed me the valley on horseback and I went wading in the river. Oh, it was like heaven I was in such a dream. Alone with him and then like Jesus did the disciples at the last supper — he washed my feet."

Chet shook his head as if amused. "I only dried them. So you could get your boots and socks on."

She jumped up and squeezed his head to her chest hard. "That was the longest day of my life. Even longer than when my first husband kidnapped me and took me off to marry me. That time was never that long as the time I spent with you. Chet Byrnes, you have shown me more than any man on this earth could have and I love being your wife — but that day had to be the grandest of them all. From the time when I arrived at your place down there until at last I slept by myself in that tent set up for me and Anita."

He shook his head at her. "That was after we'd made love — in the hay of all places — under those stars. Afterward when I let you go to your tent I feared so much that you would be gone from my life, like a dust devil whisked away, and when those two letters finally found me I thanked God for holding us together."

"Drink your coffee now and I will bathe you and shave you so we can be man and wife all over again."

"Salute to that." He raised his cup and downed the remains. He noticed Valerie had already left with her two men — Cole and Rocky.

Late that night he lay awake on a cot. Still weary from all the riding and not sleeping

27

in his own bed, he wondered who really was that man who hired the guns and what was his business? He'd find him, he vowed, lying there in the dark holding his sleeping wife tight to him.

CHAPTER 2

Dawn came as Chet slipped outside into the cool mountain air. The sky still shadowy as the pink of morning had barely broken in the east, though some rays struck the mountaintops of pine and above them. His bladder empty, he ducked and went back inside the tent to finish dressing.

"The cook will have breakfast ready at the big tent. These men have worked long hours and they work hard every day. Buildings are really taking shape. There are stacks of hay and more being delivered." Liz pointed out the fodder after they dressed and left for the food tent.

The open-sided large tent was full of workers eating breakfast. Some had said hi to him as they came in. Bill Corbett, the man in charge of them, came by and told him good morning.

"Get your food and set down," Chet said, looking up from his meal.

"Glad you're alive."

"I am too. I see lots of progress going on. We don't need it completed to start the run, but we do need it completed before fall."

"I'd hire some more real carpenters, but if they don't know anything they aren't worth ten cents."

Chet agreed. "This is a big project here. You have all the material you need here, right?"

"Oh, most is here. I'm not short anything right now. That mill tries hard to supply us. My men work hard. I think we are doing all we can."

"Keep up the good work. We will need some buildings at the other stations in the future as well."

"That should be a snap. Again, happy to see you weren't hurt in the wreck."

"I'll survive. You and your boys keep pounding."

Corbett left him and Liz said, "He works hard."

"You should know."

"Oh, I don't see much goes wrong. They all work. He is a real taskmaster. You call him that?"

"Yes. We were lucky to find him."

Chet knew there was no way to know where his man Jesus was at that moment.

Cole sent him west to check on a problem at one of those stations on the western side of Center Point. There would be no telegraph to use like Preskitt had going south, and the route would definitely be harder to manage without a telegraph wire from Gallup, New Mexico, to the Hardeeville Ferry crossing where it met the California Stage Line.

After breakfast he and Liz went south in a buckboard to check on Robert and his wife at the sawmill. It was simply a side trip to get her away for some fresh air, apart from the hammers beating nails going up at the center for support. It was a fresh ride through the turpentine-smelling ponderosa pines that covered the high country in northern Arizona Territory. They reached the couple's nice house, and Robert's pregnant wife Betty invited them in, excited over any company that dropped by.

Chet loved the sweet Mormon girl who married his man in charge of the mill's timber-hauling setup when the mines in southern Arizona hired all their help away and they couldn't get the trees to the mill. Chet set up a log-hauling division, and Robert soon was chosen the superintendent despite his age. Since then things had moved so well Chet feared they didn't worry enough about him. At the dance in Camp Verde, Robert met the tall blond beauty, Betty, and despite efforts by her family and girlfriends for her not to marry him, she did it anyway and later laughed about her place in life living in a large company house with a man who had a real job. Plus she knew he loved her.

Despite the federal law against polygamy, many of the LDS faith ignored the law. Betty told Liz privately she didn't have to worry about Robert finding another wife. He'd told her, many times in the beginning, that one was enough for him. She also could make her husband coffee though she never drank it herself. Her man also saw she got to attend her church of the Latter-Day Saints each Sunday even if he was working on a needed thing. They were looking forward to their first child.

Fred Roach, in his thirties, was Robert's number two man who joined them for the lunch that Betty and Liz spread out on the large table. Chet considered it a congenial visit. Robert reported things were going smoothly, and they were well caught up with the mill's needs. For some time he'd wanted more logs hauled in from distant points and finally they would begin doing that. In a move to get some of the distant logs hauled

in quicker, he hired some oxen team owners without work to bring them in cheaper
than he could, thus solving his biggest concern.

The visit passed and Chet knew what he
knew before he came by — the log-hauling
operation was going smoothly. After lunch
he and Liz drove back to the noisy camp
and she thanked him for her break from the
hammers and saws.

Coming up through the construction zone
of men who were packing boards on their
shoulders, Chet saw the brown face of his
man Jesus Martinez and the shorter Spud
Carnes on horseback coming to meet them.

"Hey, how you two doing?" He stepped
off and handed her the bridle lines to hold.

"Good. Spud and I never rocked over one
buckboard," Jesus said, and shook his hand.
"Elizabeth, is Anita here?"

"No. But I have letters for you at my tent."

Pleased by her promise, he smiled at the
news. "Thanks so much. I'll get them at
supper."

Liz disagreed with him. "No, you get up
here and we will go get the letters now."

Chet smiled at his wife's ways. "Spud, go
with them and put the team up for her. I
am going to check on things and we can all
talk tonight at supper."

"Yes sir. Mr. Byrnes, I mean Chet, like you said to call you. I sure like riding with Jesus. It sure beats herding cows."

"I bet it does." He was still laughing about the short orphan's words. When Spud first met Cole, who had commented he was kinda short, Spud had come back quick with the comment that a short pistol can kill you quick as a long one.

"Your wife all right?" Chet asked Cole, who'd just joined them.

"Oh yes, and so is Rocky. He's doing as good as usual. Robert is getting along like usual at the mill?"

"He is and even better. No baby yet but it must be close. Betty is always cheerful too."

"He's lucky, isn't he?" Cole shook his head, and Chet felt his motion was more over the baby coming than anything else since both he and Cole remained without offspring of their own from their marriages.

"That too. What do you know after a day back here?"

Cole smiled. "Bill's working hard here. I guess they'll start delivering stock from the east to the west at each station, and the tack man is going to be leaving them all supplies, I hope, like Carpenter promised. We will know when they get here, huh? I have some serious questions to discuss with you about our charges in two letters I just received from their auditors. You need to look them over."

"I can do that. What else?"

"Do you have a good enough contract to get our full expenses out of this deal?" Cole asked, walking beside him.

"You think we're in for a raw deal?"

"What have they really done for us?"

"Cole, you know something I don't?"

"They may have left us out here to hang. We made a deal that I thought you'd be repaid for all bills we made building this line in haste for them. They are telling me now we have overcharged them and they won't pay it. Those expenses are all at their actual cost."

"I will send a letter to the man. I can get to the bottom of it."

"We better do something."

"Better yet, I will write a wire to send to Hannagen from Preskitt. And the messenger can wait down there for his answer. Get your letters on the overcharges so after I read them, I will make up a telegram."

Cole nodded. "I hope it is all a mistake. But we are getting close and have run our backsides off to get to here."

Chet found Jesus seated in a camp chair, busy reading the letters from his girlfriend

Anita back at the Preskitt Valley Ranch house.

"Everything all right?"

Jesus smiled and sat up. "Oh yes. You doing good?"

"Cole has some letters from Hannagen complaining we have overcharged him. He wants me to see them. He's gone after them."

"Hey, he'd been really robbed if he didn't have you two. That Carpenter guy could never have done what we've did in that short a time."

"Cole thinks they want to cheat us out of our work and expenses."

Cole, Valerie, and Rocky arrived. Liz joined them.

Chet began reading the letter and then looked at the bottom page. *I have been instructed these costs are too high as per the project person in charge, Rodney Carpenter, and I will not pay them.*

"Carpenter is the problem." Chet felt his hot breath coming out of his nose. He had all he wanted from that entire blowhard at the Windmill Ranch meeting months ago and his flimsy plans for setting up this deal. He went for pen and paper. Liz was beside him.

"What do you need?"

"A pen and paper. I am sending Spud to wire Hannagen my letter to tell them that they can go to hell and we will dismantle all their stops if they won't cover our expenses. This doesn't even have my work in the bill, and that will be big when I get through with him."

He wrote the following:

HANNAGEN
I OPENED THE LETTER FROM YOUR AUDITOR SAYING THAT ROD CARPENTER TOLD HIM WE WERE OVERCHARGING YOU. THAT IS A LIE AND IF YOU HAVE NO PLANS TO PAY ME WHAT IS OWED I WILL DISMANTLE ALL I HAVE DONE AND THE WHEELS WONT ROLL. I WANT THE FULL AMOUNT OF MONEY OF THAT BILLING DEPOSITED IMMEDI- ATELY TO MY BANK IN PRES- COTT AZ. T.

CHET BYRNES

"I want Spud to take this to Preskitt. Wire it and wait at the ranch for the reply and then get back up here with his answer."

"I can go tonight, Chet."

"No, you wait till first light. Get a fresh

saddle horse from Robert. Then at the lower ranch on the Verde you get some shut-eye there and another fresh horse. Then go to the wire office in Preskitt and send it. Wait at the upper ranch for his reply and then get back up here when you get it. But don't kill yourself."

"I won't. I can handle that."

"You ornery kid. I know you can. Where did Rocky go?"

"He's over here," Valerie said. Turning to the boy, she pushed him gently. "Go see your daddy. Go on . . . he's over there."

The boy rounded the table and held his arm up. "I'm here, Daddy."

"Good. Did they bring your pony up here?"

"Shorty is over at the corral. I ride him a lot. But I may need a bigger one."

"Well, we better look for one, huh?"

"I could give Shorty to someone else who needs a short pony?"

"Better wait about giving him away for a while. Daddy is pretty busy building a stage line right now."

"You can find one?"

"Sure, we will look for a bigger one."

"Good. I better go check on Valerie; she may need me to help her."

"You do that." He set the busy boy down,

and he rounded the table headed for his stepmother.

"Mr. Byrnes, there is an Indian woman here to see you. She says she knows you," one of the workers told him.

"Where is she?" he asked, rising. Then he saw the straight-backed Navajo woman Blue Bell coming with her leather skirt swirling around her legs.

"Liz, this lady is Blue Bell."

His wife rose, took her hand, and then they hugged.

"So nice to see you. Your generous husband gave me a horse when mine died and would take no money. His brother-in-law Polanski tells me all about him when he brings beef to our tribal points. I heard today your man was here and wanted to tell him thanks again. I see too why he has you. You are a very beautiful woman."

"Thank you. I wondered at first why such a pretty lady came to see him, but like me you are another admirer of him."

They both laughed.

"Would you have some breakfast? We have plenty."

"No, but I hear you are starting a new stage line across the territory. Could my people help you?"

"We have one of your trading posts as our stop."

"That was how I knew it was you doing this. Several of our men are working for the other stops. Oh Liz, I have told people I know your man, and many times I have to tell the story of how he gave me that fine horse to get home with. Also he recently helped another Navajo woman being held against her will near House Rock Valley. He is a hero among my people and provides us good beef on time. You have a very fine man with you, and if either of you ever need my help call on me."

"Thank you," Liz said.

Blue Bell strolled away.

"You were never tempted by her?" she asked under her breath.

"She told me her people needed her too much to take a man. She is a spokesperson among them, and I respected her for doing that."

"To be honest, I will thank God for her calling. She is a very pretty woman."

"No prettier than you are."

"Thanks. Glad you think so."

"Elizabeth, I don't need another wife."

"Well, I sure met my competition up here today."

Chet shook his head to dismiss the mat-

40

ter. Then he laughed. "All my concerns about this business and a woman outside of my wife is nothing."

"I won't mention her again."

He squeezed his wife's shoulders and spoke to the amused Jesus. "You and I need to go look for this guy who hired the shooters."

"When?"

"In the morning."

"For now, I will need you to pick a man to ride with us tomorrow. Cole has enough to look after about the line. We will need a camp outfit."

"Can I go along?" Liz interrupted.

"I guess. Though it may be some hard riding to find the guy hired those three."

"You have a lead?" she asked.

"Some. I have a description of him and where he planned to meet them to pay them for killing the two of us."

"Where at?"

"Horse Head Crossing. The Longhorn Saloon."

"Who else is going along?"

"I'm leaving that for Jesus to find us a good man."

"Fine. I need to go get a few things ready for the trip. Valerie and I may run in to the store. You going to write Shawn and make that switch?"

"If nothing else happens he can help Cole up here. He can do book work and he writes great letters. I'll send word to Tom to send Ratchet Thornton up to talk about him going down to help Roamer and Bronc Morales on the Border Force of Deputy U.S. Marshals. And when he gets there, Shawn can come north. That all right?"

"I think it is what you needed to do."

"Now I hope that Jesus finds a man, today, that can help us."

She nodded. "Oh, he'll be fussy who he chooses. I am going to change and get ready. There is a boy named Alex at the stables who will hitch us a team."

"I'll go get one for you, then I can write the letters and get ready for tomorrow."

She stood on her toes and kissed his cheek. "I am so glad I have you and Blue Bell doesn't."

"No worry. I'm off for a buckboard."

He found the young man who quickly caught a team, curried them down, and harnessed them with care. They talked about all the things at the base they were doing to get ready. The young man was excited about when the service would be up and running. "If I show how good I am with horses, do you think I could drive some runs?"

"You better ask Cole . . . he's the man to do the hiring."

"I will do that. This is a good team for the women. They're well broke."

"Good. I'll take them down there and load those sisters up."

The women, at last on the spring seat, were sent off to shop. Chet took the paper, pen, and ink to write the letters. The first one was for Tom Flowers at the Camp Verde Ranch. He was to send Ratchet Thornton up to their new headquarters next week so he could talk to him about riding for the Force down in southern Arizona. Chet mentioned things were progressing on the stage line and he'd see him some time, didn't know when, but knew he was handling things well on the Verde River place. Told him to tell his lovely wife, Millie, he said hi. Signed the letter and put it in an envelope.

Then he wrote Shawn a letter. He thanked him for keeping records and all the expense sheets so well. He also noted that he had asked for his help for him to get closer to Lucy Byrnes. He warned Shawn he knew nothing about her desires or future plans, but he understood his reason for wanting to be up there was her. Cole had a place for him working on the stage line. He thought Ratchet could do his job in southern Arizona as lawman instead of the cowboy he now was. Then he closed and signed it Chet Byrnes.

That done, he took a *siesta.* Jesus woke him. He sat up and smiled.

"Who did you find?" He threw his feet off the cot and rubbed the sleep from his face.

"The ex-cowboy-turned-carpenter, Spencer Horne. He's a good horseman and can use a gun. He quit to become a carpenter but misses the horses and riding. I asked Bill and he agreed that he could spare him. Horne will be ready to ride. I'm making sure he has everything he will need."

"I knew you'd find us the right one. Thanks."

Jesus stood up. "I'm going to finish getting us ready to go."

"Good. I have the letters drafted for Tom about Ratchet and for Shawn about my actions."

"Shawn sound very serious about Lucy?"

"She's a great woman. I think he knows that and even with her children he's set his mind to having her."

Jesus made a sad face. "Reg taking his life really hurt lots of people . . . not only his

44

wife. I never thought he would do that."

Chet shook his head. He personally saw no reason for Reg's choice of taking his own life. But he also had learned a few details afterward that he'd never discussed with anyone. There, obviously, were some other things involved that Chet had a hard time accepting. *The notion that Reg had an affair with another woman who later dumped him.* But no one needed to know that. He was dead and his wife, child, and unborn one had no need to know anything about it to smother them in more grief, especially Lucy. His next business to settle was to find this man under the Boss of the Plains Stetson hat who wanted both him and Cole dead.

They would start out early the next morning to find Mr. X. Who hired him? Still lots of questions to be answered on that subject.

CHAPTER 3

They left Center Point in the pink of dawn. He chose the two stout roan horses for him and Liz to ride. Jesus had a bay horse, and the new man, Spencer Horne, rode another Camp Verde Ranch–branded bay named Hondo. Jesus selected three packhorses, and they all left with their horses' heads up and no one being thrown. Nice morning with some saucy jays and camp robbers in the pines scolding them as they rode out early from the night's stay. It would take four long days to reach Horse Head Crossing and the saloon where the hired gunman said they were to meet Mr. X.

Chet brought Spencer up to date on their mission while they rode east.

"I sure am grateful to ride with you three. I hated quitting the ranch, but carpenter wages are twice a cowboy's pay. I hoped to get settled down someday, find a wife and have a family before I'm too old to enjoy them."

"That would be a good cause."

"I would cheer you on," Liz said.

"Thanks, ma'am. I had never met you till you came up here with Cole's wife, Valerie. My, my, the boss man sure has good taste."

"I don't know about his taste, but I have enjoyed riding along with Jesus and Cole, so it is good to have you now as well."

"They say you have a big *hacienda* in Sonora?"

"My brother-in-law is buying it from me. But yes, I had a very large *hacienda* down there. Now I have all these places my man has, and that is more than enough for me."

"And soon a stage line as well I guess?"

Chet answered him. "We may become partners with them in the future. We took the start-up on as a project. So when we are up and running, then we will decide about a partnership."

"You hatched some pretty nice ranches all over this country."

Chet agreed. "Most of them have worked. I have a new ranch over southeast of the Windmill Ranch my land man recently bought me. You don't have a woman picked out, do you?"

"Well, that sounds like I either need to get off my butt or lose a shot at it."

47

He kinda chuckled, then quickly said, "I'm sorry I said that, ma'am."

"Pretty truthful statement, I thought."

"Yes ma'am, it was. But my mother would have scolded me for it."

"My ears aren't that tender. Jesus, Cole, a big man named Hampt, Chet, and I took a large herd of steers to Ogallala with forty black cowboys out of the Canadian River bottoms up there clear to Nebraska, so my ears have heard it all."

"Boss man, I will sure dwell on that offer. Needs lots of work, I bet."

"It has nice enough house, barn, and corrals to start. You'd need to fence some land and make hay meadows, develop water. But it ain't uptown. Maybe over forty miles east from Mormon Lake."

"I've never been in that country."

"We caught some horse thieves up there. My land man, Bo, ran down the owner, and he sold it more to get rid of it than anything else. But it could be a real ranch."

"Indians bad over there?"

"No. This is up on the top of the rim like the Windmill place. Those Apaches stay south of there most of the time. But who knows with them? I own it now and will stock it with cattle in the future."

"I understand. Thanks for the offer; if I

can connect I'd love to be considered to run it."

The ride went on from station to station. But Chet also noticed there had been no extra horses delivered — no tack so far. He hoped Spud would be back with an answer from Hannagen when he, himself, got back to Center Point. The weather held clear, but each afternoon he could see some thunderheads form in the south . . . though none came up on top of the rim country.

Evening on day four they rode into the village on the Little Colorado River in a veil of mild rain. Horses put up at the livery, they checked in the hotel. Jesus and Spencer went to check out the saloon. Chet had baths drawn for both he and Liz at the hotel. Afterward, changed in fresh clothing, they went downstairs to eat in the dining room.

The two men joined them.

"Learn much?"

"Well, we learned the man you want is, I think, named Gerald Hall. He's a gambler, but one man told us he was a hired killer back in Texas."

"I guess we can now wonder who hired him?" He went back to cutting the meat on his plate.

"Hall took a powder, they said, when they

delivered that wounded bushwhacker here who made you wreck the buckboard."

"Funny thing, wasn't it?" Chet said.

Spencer shook his head. "I bet we can check around and someone here can tell us where he went to."

"We will spend a few days checking. I want more information on him and any associates he might have had in the area. He had to be working for someone who wants to stop us from ever starting the mail run."

"I suppose so they could haul it?" Spencer said.

"Yes. In this land of no money and not many jobs, it might be what they want. But unless they kill me, they aren't getting control of it either."

The next day Chet and Liz rode out to the number-two station set up at the Navajo trading post.

A man in his forties, Rob Simon, the owner and their agent, came out and took his hat off for Liz. "You must be the missus?"

"I am, sir . . . he calls me Liz, which is all right. Nice to meet you, sir."

"My pleasure." The man shook his head warily. "Any information on the attackers, Chet?"

"No such luck. I am looking for a man

called Gerald Hall . . . gambler, dresses fancy."

"He's been by here and asked a lot of questions. Said he was going to invest in your deal. Wanted to know all about it. I told him I was to be a stop-over."

"Well, he hired those three bums to kill me and Cole. I want his hide if I can find him."

"If he comes by here, I'll hold him for you. Come inside and have some coffee."

They rode on after having coffee with the man and one of his two silent Navajo wives who stood by. Rob's Navajo-talking wife Louise was gone on a business trip that day. He had this other wife from the tribe, but she didn't speak English. This vast country on top of the rim was far less settled than any part of the territory save the southwest desert region. Mostly Indian reservation land and only a few people had stuck it out on homesteads or tried to ranch. Too far for most to a store or market to sell whatever they grew. However, for Chet, it was an exciting land of tall bunch grass in many places they rode through — though not much water. The Navajos were peaceful when compared to their cousins to the south, the Apaches, who were a lot less friendly.

Covering the rolling country the next day, Chet and Liz found a man and two sons set up in a draw. They had a windlass and buckets to dig a well as well as a tent and canvas shade for their housing. The forty-year-old man introduced himself as Thomas Chase as he worked the winch while he talked to them.

"You sure are pretty, Mrs. Byrnes. We don't get many fine-looking ladies to stop by here."

"Thank you," she said to him, and smiled.

"How deep are you now?" Chet asked the man.

"Close to thirty feet and not much of any dampness either. We dug wells at two other spots to thirty-five feet and got little water. No sense homesteading if there's no water, is there?"

"You're right. I'm looking for a man named Hall."

"I don't recall meeting anyone with that handle. What do you want him for?"

"He hired three men to kill me."

"Boy, that would be a real reason to find a feller. Sir, my two boys are down in that well working. If you have a minute could I reel them up? I know they have not seen a lady as pretty as your wife in a long time."

Liz nodded.

"Sure." Chet was not so amused, but he understood the man's effort and since Liz sounded game he told him to do that. He took the opposing handle and they winched up the first towheaded boy of maybe fourteen.

"Mrs. Byrnes, this is my youngest, Harvey. Harvey, this is Mr. Byrnes's wife, Liz."

"Oh gosh, you sure are pretty. May I ask why and if you're coming back?"

"Harvey, I go lots of places with my husband over there. But I don't suppose I will return here again."

"You don't mind. How long have you been his wife?"

"Two years now."

"Well, he's a mighty lucky guy to have you."

Chet on the crank brought the second one up, and as soon as he saw Liz, he said, "I can sure see that too."

They all laughed.

Everett was a year or so older and Chet could see that he too was struck at meeting Liz. His brother filled him in on the information he had asked about her. All Everett could do was be red-faced and tongue-stuck.

"Did you witch this site?" Chet asked,

recalling how they found water wells in Texas.

"I got some peach limb forks, but I don't have the power." The man shook his head. "Just chose places where I hope there is some. Can you do it?"

"No, I tried before, but she might have the power." He indicated his wife.

"What are you talking about?" she asked.

"Witching water with a peach tree fork."

"I have never done that."

"Get a branch. All you do is hold it with both hands and point the branch out in front and walk until it turns down."

"Why would I have such power? You think I am a *bruja*?"

"Liz, God gives such powers. Just try it. I have a hunch you could find these men water if there is any around here."

Soon armed with the forked branch, she began walking across the ground with the branch held out in front. Nothing happened. Then a short time later she screamed out a short cry, "It moved. Not me. It moved down right here. What did that?"

He had her by the shoulder. "Go over there and come back. I have this spot marked."

She frowned at him. "That is a very strange thing to do."

She walked away and returned. "See it. See it. Does that mean there is water down there?"

"I'd sure bet there is water down there."

Thomas had his old hat off and scratched the too-long hair on top of his head. "I've seen men and women do that before back in the hill country. It works. I thank you for trying to do that. Boys, we've got us a new place to dig and we may even find it this time. Ma'am, I am sure beholden to you."

She handed him back his stick. "I hope it works, sir."

"I bet it does, don't you, Mr. Byrnes?"

Chet agreed and squeezed her shoulder. He knew she was still upset over a power she had with the stick.

"It is simply a power some folks have. Nothing sacrilegious or bad."

"Oh, I am fine. It scared me. A stick twisting in my grip."

"Thomas, we better get riding. I hope we helped."

"I hope it works," Liz added.

"So do I, and thank you, Mrs."

They rode on, arriving at the hotel past suppertime. Both Chet's men were on the porch bench and jumped up to meet them.

"We thought you two got lost," Jesus said. "Glad you are all right."

"I'll put up the horses," Spencer said. "You two get in and eat."

"Thanks," Liz said as he took the reins.

"You learn anything today?" Jesus asked.

"Liz can witch a well."

She looked at the sky for help before climbing the stairs. "We don't know I can. I just did it today."

Chet told her story going into the restaurant. Jesus told her it was a great skill to have and how certain people in his country could find water.

"Well, I never heard of it. But it is very real in your hands when it signals you. I swear the stick twisted in my hands held tight."

"I am not surprised you had those skills."

"Why? Am I a witch?"

"No. But you have a way about you," Jesus said.

Chet agreed. "I saw it too. That first day we met at Tubac, she had a shield around her when she stepped down from the coach. Then it evaporated for me and I could not believe it went away."

"I saw something in her too, so to be a water finder does not surprise me either," Jesus said.

She shook her head at them. "Don't wait around for me to find a drink of it."

The waiter seated them and took their food order.

"You or Spencer learn anything today?" Chet asked.

"This Hall guy spends some time at a ranch south of here, which is owned by a woman named Hodges. Marina Hodges. I don't know if he is there, but the woman is a widow and I think maybe they are having an *affair.*"

"You don't think he's there now?"

Jesus shrugged. "All I know from what we heard is they have something going on between them."

"How far away?"

"Twenty miles."

"Maybe we better go talk to her."

"Spencer and I can go tomorrow and see what we can learn, if anything."

"Fine. But be careful."

"Oh, we know how."

"What will we do?" she asked, ready to eat some soup the waiter brought them.

"Rest and write some letters. I am still sore from that wagon wreck. I hope Cole is healing too."

After supper he thanked the two men and told them to watch their backs.

The two planned to leave early to go talk to this woman. Upstairs in their room Liz asked Chet if his back was hurting him.

"Some."

"Get undressed and on the bed. I can rub that out. Why didn't you ask me before now?"

"We were both busy."

With Liz sitting on top of him, busy massaging him with her hardworking hands, his muscles slowly began to release the tension that had knotted in them. Soon he felt like putty as she continued and smoothed them all out with her handiwork. He knew he'd sleep well after all this care. Damn, he was lucky to have her.

Where was that damn Hall sleeping? He wanted him very badly. And to know who ever hired him.

CHAPTER 4

The day passed quickly. After years of having the telegraph wire hooked to the outside world in Preskitt and most all of southern Arizona Territory, not having a stage line across the northern part left them segregated to having only the mail, which flowed from Preskitt by a private carrier by buckboard to Gallup, New Mexico Territory. Chet had no idea about telegraph companies, but he wanted to learn more about them and he promised himself to do that.

Mail at Blackberry near where Lucy lived went to Hardeeville, then California and back by the Western Pacific train to places east. That mail would soon be shifted to eastbound stuff on their mail run, rather than sent to California and then back. No matter it eventually would be hauled on the Atlantic-Pacific Railroad on this same route as they used but it might be 1900 before it ever ran its future rails through there at the rate he saw them coming.

That evening, Spencer and Jesus returned. Over supper, they reported on what they learned from this rancher woman.

"Was she pretty?" Liz asked.

"Not bad looking, was she, Spencer?"

"No, but at one time she probably sparkled." He nodded as he replied.

Jesus added, "She looked to be about forty. Wore men's clothing and her hair had some gray in the brown, but it looked like straw. She had it pinned back. I told her we were Deputy U.S. Marshals and looking for Hall. She laughed, said she had not seen him in weeks. Had no idea where he took off to. Then she fed us beans for lunch."

"At least you got to eat. Where is she selling her beef?"

"She asked if we worked for you and could she sell you some beef."

"What did you say?"

"I only worked for you, but she could write you a letter and let you know."

"Think she was hiding him?"

"Spencer?" Jesus asked, "What did you think?"

The man shook his head. "I don't believe he was there today. She never acted upset that we had made it there looking for him either. But I don't think much upsets her . . . she would simply have brushed it aside."

Jesus agreed. "I think he dropped out from sight figuring his hired men told you their purpose. Maybe wire Hannagen and see if he knows the man."

"That's good. I can write and get a wire off to him when I get back to the ranch. He may know the man. I guess we can't do much more here. We will head back to Center Point. I need to do some ranch bookwork. This job is close to being finished. I think that all we still need are the horses and tack delivered. I will feel much better when that is handled and in place. That will be in my note to Hannagen that I plan to write tonight."

They rose, shook hands, and Chet told them they would go back to Center Point after breakfast.

"I reckon this means I go back to nailing boards?" Spencer asked.

Chet shook his head. "Cole has a stage line to run. I think you suit the three of us — Liz, Jesus, and me — so you should stay with us. Unless you want to go back?"

"Lord, no. This is the neatest job I ever had. I am impressed with you and Liz. You two work. You aren't just the boss. You really lead this outfit. Jesus is hard to beat. I knew

I was with a lawman when he was talking to that woman down there. No, I love the deal and count myself lucky to be with you."

"Jesus tell you he near froze to death once on this job?"

"I heard about that. Must have been cold."

They laughed and parted. Liz hugged Chet's arm going upstairs to their room. "I think he's a good man."

"Jesus found him. I figure he looked his choices over."

"You are lucky to find such a good man."

"I found you."

"After I found you." She playfully punched him and laughed.

He unlocked their door laughing. She was fun and happy being his wife. Neat way for them to live together. Not many women would traipse all over Hades with their husbands, but she did and she loved it.

The trip back took three hot days, so they stayed and rested for a day at Center Point. Spud had arrived there the day before with the wire from Hannagen. Chet read the wire:

CHET BYRNES
ALL YOUR EXPENSES WILL BE
PAID AS YOU DIRECTED. NO ONE
WILL BLOCK THOSE PAYMENTS

OR THEY WILL ANSWER TO ME. I LEARNED TODAY THE STOCKING OF HORSES TO STAGE STOPS HAS NOT TAKEN PLACE. I REALIZE IT WILL BE EXPENSIVE BUT IF YOU WOULD HANDLE THE STOPS WEST OF CENTER POINT WITH AT LEAST ONE TEAM, I WILL HAVE MORE DELIVERED ON THE EAST ONES AS WE CAN SECURE THEM. IF YOU CAN BUY SOME HORSES AND TACK WORTH THE MONEY BUY TWO PER STATION. I APOLOGIZE FOR ANY INCONVENIENCE YOU HAVE HAD IN ALL YOUR HARD WORK EXPERIENCED. THIS WOULD NOT BE HAPPENING HAD I KNOWN THAT YOU WERE IN CHARGE OVER IT ALL. I AM GRATEFUL FOR THE WORK YOU AND YOUR MEN HAVE ACCOMPLISHED. HAVE NO FEARS I WILL HAVE ALL YOUR BILLS PAID.

HANNAGEN

"What did he say?" Liz asked.

"We need to buy some horses and tack for the west stations. They haven't found enough, obvious now as I expected, when

63

they didn't bring them as promised. I will need to get word to Tom and the liveryman Frye at Preskitt and get someone to find some teams down at the Hayden's Ferry."

"What's happening?" Cole said, joining them.

"We learned why we don't have horses to change. They can't buy them."

"What in the hell have they been doing while we built stations?"

"My friend, more blow and no-go in New Mexico. Read this. He is paying all our bills. Now we need buckboards, horses, and harness for the west and maybe more for the east side."

After reading the telegram, Cole shook his head. "I am glad we know where we stand and he appreciates our blood, sweat, and tears. What should we do?"

"Tom Flowers needs to get on the stage and head south with maybe two men, saddles, and gear and get as many as they can to bring them back. Frye at the livery might send a wire via Yuma to California and find some over there to be delivered to Hardeeville. We will probably overbuy but we will need them."

"I better stay close and keep things moving."

"Right, Cole. Jesus and Spencer may buy

some in the west of here. I didn't see many east on our trip."

"Who will ride with you?"

"I am going to Preskitt and be sure I still have my ranches. Spud and Liz can ride with me that way."

"And Dennis Crain."

"Who is he?"

"A security man I hired to watch the construction site."

"We go south at dawn."

"He will be ready. He can come back when you get to the Verde Ranch."

"You know him?" he asked Liz when Cole left to get his man.

"Yes. They don't steal a board or nail from this job. He's sharp," Liz said.

"Where did Spud go?"

"To put horses up. He will join us for supper." She stood in front of him, swept off his felt hat, and pushed his lock of hair aside. "Go take a nap. I will wake you. Suspense is over. Hannagen will pay the bills and you need horses; it is all very simple."

He bent over and kissed her. "Thanks. I think I have it straight."

Taking his hat back, he kissed her again and he went off to get some rest. On the cot he fell deep asleep, and when she awoke him he threw his legs off the bed.

"Supper is about ready."

"I am ready. This race to find horses will be a busy one, and to get them up here and out to each station will take some doing. I wonder if Rod Carpenter is still ramrodding things from New Mexico?"

"I guess you will learn in the days ahead."

"I will indeed. You look really nice in that dress."

She shook her head. "I wear my riding clothes a lot. But I thought I better be your wife this evening."

"I am proud of you however you are dressed."

Downstairs he met Cole's security man, Dennis Crain.

"Nice to meet you, sir." The man was in his mid-thirties, close shaven, and he had a permanent tan. His blue eyes were alert as he turned to smile at Liz.

"I understand you're Cole's security man?"

"I guess folks, back before I came along, were helping themselves to the lumber and shingles that were lying around waiting to be used. I worked in law enforcement in Kansas cow towns and offered Cole my services. He said he needed security. I almost immediately captured a thief and let it all be known, and we have had little thievery since. People have told me lots about your widespread businesses, so I am glad to be part of this development. I heard about the ambush. No luck finding the guy who hired the ambushers?"

"No. Gerald Hall took a powder when they failed."

Crain shook his head. "I never heard of him. Do you expect many road agent problems with the setup?"

"I didn't. This end of the territory is pretty vacant, but obviously we will have some. A few years ago road agents held up the mail wagon going from Gallup to Preskitt on a regular basis. That was solved by shooting and hanging a few of the felons, and I have not heard of any more robberies of the mail run since."

"I talked to Cole some about the matter, and he told me the same thing. But it will be new and an opportunity for that bad element in society to try it."

"And we hope to haul Wells Fargo business along with the mail in the future."

"Then it will be a candy train."

Liz laughed as the three of them walked through the food line filling their plates. "I never heard that expression before."

Dennis nodded. "Money and gold shipments make it one."

"We have enough problems with securing horses and harness right now," Chet said. "But road agents can be stopped."

"Like I said about the robberies here, someone put their boot down and they stopped."

"I guess all of us have lots to learn and a short time to be ready," Chet said, listening close to this man with law enforcement experience. Cole had hired a good man. "Who will watch things when you ride south with us tomorrow?"

"Drew Cage, he's another old constable needed work. They won't steal anything from him either. I am looking forward to the ride. I have never seen Camp Verde and the river valley before."

Liz agreed. "It is very pretty, looking at all that from high up on the rim. You don't have a wife?"

"She died in Kansas."

"Oh, I am so sorry."

"Well, after that I began kicking a can down the road. Kinda ruined living there when everything reminded me of her."

"It is no fun being the survivor. I hope you find another," Liz told him.

"Thank you . . . I imagine I will. Cole told

me how you and Mr. Byrnes found each other."

"Oh, it has been a fairy tale come true."

Chet set his plate down. "I just saw Cole and he looked troubled. I'll be back."

He caught up with Cole and stopped him. "You look shaken."

"A man just brought me word they tried to burn down station number four and the ranch headquarters there."

"Herman Rothschild, the man with the Navajo wife named Darling, and the kids from his first marriage . . . Are they all right?"

"I think so from the report. I better take Dennis and go check on them. The man, a freighter who brought me the word, said they were all right but said they had had a shoot-out."

"Spud and I can handle the trip south. You have Jesus and Spencer too."

"They heard about a buckboard for sale and went to see about it for me. When they get through I'll send them back to you."

"Dennis is with Liz eating. He sounds like a great man for your team."

"Oh, he's a great guy. I'm sorry. Didn't mean to mess up your meal."

"No problem. This thing is getting rough."

"I didn't expect a picnic lunch. But it will

be a real job keeping it going. I can see that from here. I'll take Dennis along with me and check on this deal if you can find another guard to ride with you."

"We'll be all right." Chet frowned. "We came by there and stopped and talked to them just a day ago."

"It happened last night and I just got the word." Cole shook his head. "You warned me handling this would be one big headache."

Moving back to the table where Dennis and Liz sat, Cole looked down at Dennis Crain.

"If Chet and Liz can go without you, we need to get some saddle horses and go to station number four after you eat, Dennis."

"Meet you at the livery in ten minutes," his man said.

They would damn sure need better communications, and Chet could see it coming. A telegraph line from Gallup to Hardeeville would need to be strung in time. He had lots to learn and maybe more about communications via the wire. What next?

The next morning after they finished breakfast, Liz, Spud, and Chet rode for the south. They needed to be on guard. Chet didn't have his usual escort, but nothing much happened on a summer ride over the route back off the rim to the Verde. The trip brought back memories of his earlier days in Texas, when he rode alone like that cold day checking cows on the south end of the ranch and three men representing the Reynolds tried to pick him off. He had left them for the buzzards.

The three of them arrived at the lower ranch late the second day. Rhea welcomed them to the big house and told them her husband Victor was working with his men on some new fencing. Chet scooped his two-year-old son, Adam, born to him and his deceased wife, Marge, up and hugged him. He and the boy played on the floor while the women went to help the house-keeper Lea.

His ranch foreman Tom Flowers and his wife Millie soon joined them from their house across the field. Rhea came and took Adam so the men could talk.

"How did things go up there?"

"Tom, Hannagen came back to me with a letter that he needed us to find about a dozen teams, harness, and some buckboard replacements. I think that all-talk man Carpenter could not deliver and he wanted us to stock the west stations. So I guess you and a couple of hands need to go south and find some. Then deliver them to Cole at

Center Point. He sent Jesus west to try and find some more. Actually I doubt Carpenter can even cover the east stations with equipment."

"How many do you need?"

"I'd say a dozen or more to be certain."

"Wow, that may be hard to find."

"I know it won't be easy, but maybe we can find them and get set up in the next four weeks."

"I'll leave in the morning for Hayden's Ferry with two or three men and their saddles to bring them back. Ratchet is due in any day. He's been on the west side with a crew repairing our line fence. Those elk can sure be tough on that fencing."

"Can you take the time away?"

"We always manage. This stage line business has been a big drain on all of us — manpower wise — but things are smooth. Victor is here and he can handle the breakdowns. I really think you did the right thing bringing him here as the farm manager. We have worked hand in hand this summer putting up hay or him sending me help for roundup. And he's a better farmer than I am."

The two laughed.

"I got your letter, and I have to say I hate to lose Ratchet. He's a helluva worker, and for a young man he gets lots of work out of my cowboys in a day."

"Shawn McElroy wants to be closer to Lucy, and I don't blame him."

Tom smiled. "She will sure have a good start on a family."

"Obviously he knows about it all."

"She is a fine lady. What will he do?"

"Help Cole run the stage line. He's a good deskman too. Those boys down there will miss him since he does all their bookwork. And I'm sorry about this last-minute deal. As for the stage line deal, we've had some words over Carpenter. He hasn't carried through on the horses and harness, and he even tried to plug some of Cole's expenses that Hannagen had agreed to pay, but I got that straight."

"And after all his big talk he doesn't have the horses already?"

"Part of them for the east stations. But hell only knows what he got for them."

"You think a businessman like Hannagen would have run him off by now."

"He may be kin or an in-law."

Tom laughed. "You may be right. I hope I can buy some buckboards and teams for down there. We have four repaired ones at the shop here. I will send them north with two teams that we can spare from the ranch."

"I want an invoice with all the charges and their worth to send in. That will sure help. We may have some up at the homeplace on the mountain. I'll check up there this afternoon. If I do I'll have Raphael send someone down and one of his *vaqueros* can deliver them with your men."

"Oh, we will make it," Tom said. "But getting them there may be close."

"Thanks. You and Millie want to eat with us?"

"No, we have the kids, and Millie has supper ready down there."

"I understand. Guess I expected more support out of them. Damn mess and lack of any telegraph connection makes operating it tougher than all get-out."

"Oh, you will win in the end."

"It better be a large mail contract with all the money that's gone out so far, and we aren't through. We will need several stage stops built on those sites."

"Well, he'd never have made it the way things were going, and with that map he showed us at that Windmill Ranch meeting, he had no stops completed for where they went — water or no water."

Chet shook Tom's hand and Millie kissed

him on the cheek. "Good luck, Chet. We are all pulling for you to make this work."

"It will. Thanks. Tell the kids hi."

He and Liz spent the night and in the morning rode on to their big house at Preskitt Valley up on the mountain. The large white headquarters house looked good to him, and Spud had a good time teasing them about how safe they'd been with him.

His foreman, Raphael, came to meet him. "Good morning. You have been busy up north, no?"

"Very busy, but it's good to be back home. Everything here going good?"

"No problems."

"I have some. How many buckboards and teams can you spare? The New Mexico side hasn't found enough."

"Oh, I have two older buckboards that run fine, and we could spare you two teams."

"You could replace them?"

"Oh sure."

"We need to send them down to Tom tomorrow. Have your drivers take saddles and bedrolls. They may need to take them to Cole at Center Point."

"I will send good men in the morning. They can handle whatever."

"Good. Tom is going to Hayden's Ferry to find more. I am going to ride in to see

Frye at the livery and see what he can round up."

"I know of two more that you could buy."

"Are they good enough?"

"Oh, they are all right."

"What will they cost?"

"A hundred dollars, and I will buy them with sound horses."

"Try for seventy-five. Pay a hundred if we have to."

"I will get that done. What else?"

"Nothing. Just keep your eyes and ears open, and if you hear of any more buckboards in that class and price buy them."

"Is your wife doing good?"

"Liz is doing great. We have been traveling a lot. She could use some rest."

"Oh, she is such a woman. You found a good one. I loved the first one and miss her, but this one always smiles and means it."

"That's my wife. She is a wonderful woman. And you are a great foreman." He clapped him on the shoulder. His man Spud was bringing him a fresh saddle horse to ride into town.

"You need another rider with you?" Raphael asked.

"No, all my men are busy on this stage deal. Spud's a good hand. I will be safe."

"What will you do tomorrow?"

"I am not sure."

"If you go anywhere, there will be a second rider to accompany you."

"Thanks, Raphael, but I will be fine today."

He shook his head and headed for the barns. Raphael never forgot the time the deputy made him come back instead of riding on to catch up with him and to help him running down the killers he finally caught and hanged. It wasn't his fault, but Raphael carried a great burden for his safety as directed by his first wife.

Chet and Spud rode into town. They dropped by the livery and spoke to Frye. The man was holding his first newborn son. Gloria had been a widow with two children when her husband was killed in a wreck. She took a job in a house of ill repute to feed her family. Frye heard about her plight and took her out of there and married her. After two or more years of marriage, this was their first child.

"His name is Andrew," Frye showed him. "You must need something. I don't see you much anymore."

"Cute baby. I am jealous."

"Oh, maybe they will send you another, huh?"

"No, there are no more of them. I really

have been busy on this stage line business. We have the setups and now they need buckboards and teams. How many could you let me have?"

"Maybe six. That help you?"

"It is a start. How many could you buy in town besides those?"

"Six more."

"How much would they cost?"

"What can you pay?"

Chet laughed. "Seventy-five bucks with a team?"

"How about a hundred and I get you a dozen plus mine."

"Round them up. I need them delivered to Center Point."

Frye said, "That costs more."

"How much? I have cowboys I pay anyway."

"I can find enough men to deliver them all for sixty dollars."

"I need them right away. If you can do this, you have a deal. I can feed them along the way. Have them stop at the Verde Ranch at Tom's house and he will feed them, get them a bunk, and will send enough food to get them up to the headquarters."

Frey's wife came in the office and smiled at Chet. "How is your wife?"

"Doing great."

"Here, Gloria." He handed her the baby. "I have lots of work to do. Chet just bought me out of buckboards."

"Well, that sounds good."

"Nice to see you. I need to check on more things. That is a sweet baby."

"My life is sweet with him too." Frye had already run off to get his help busy getting set up to make the deal.

"You two make a great pair."

"Thank you, and tell Elizabeth hello for me. I really like her."

"I will."

Outside, he joined Spud, who handed him the reins.

"How did you do?"

"About eighteen buckboards that he thinks he can get for us."

"Wow, we are getting going, aren't we? I sure love tracking around with you. You do more than two men can at this business."

"Well, I never started on a deal I didn't intend to win. This is no exception. Let's go home and see what else fell down."

They both laughed and rode out for the Preskitt Valley. Earlier he had not found Bo in his office, so any purchases his real estate man made in his absence were still unknown to him, but Bo would no doubt be back. His banker was cashing in some more

Navajo beef contracts. The cash-in time for them was stretched from eight to ten months or longer, but Tanner thought that D.C. would catch up again in the future.

There was no reason to panic. They had a good cushion in the bank account and cash in the ranch safe as well since even solid banks failed sometimes. He and Liz had discussed managing the money and agreed half of their cash fortune should be in the large safe. Not many knew about its existence hidden in the cellar of the big house. It was a secret. Well kept.

He and Spud rode home undisturbed. Spud asked him how many cows should be on the range with one bull.

"If it isn't real rough country — one bull will get twenty cows bred on. Real brushy country makes it fifteen cows."

"I just wondered. Someday I want to be like Tom and be a foreman."

"One day when we are riding around I'll show you how to tell a good cow from a bad one."

"Chet, I'd be proud to know how to tell that."

"I'll cut you in."

"I'm looking forward to that lesson. How old were you when you took over the ranch in Texas?"

"Sixteen."

"Wow."

"My dad stayed out way too long without enough water and food trying too hard to find my kidnapped brother and sister. When the rangers brought him back to us he was delirious and knew nothing. I took over then. The ranch had to be run and I was in charge. My younger brother got mad — he never agreed to me doing that. But he wouldn't do it, so without Dad someone had to do it. All my first decisions were not the best, but we did move on and I learned a lot about running a ranch, farming, and life in general."

"Then you fought a war with the Reynoldses?"

"Yes. Three in that family and another guy that I knew stole my remuda and headed for the Indian Territory. They planned to sell them for a high price to drovers without enough horses to get their herd up there. I had to have them to drive my cattle to Kansas. We caught them south of the Red River and hung them.

"In time the family learned and one of the mothers said, 'Oh, they'da brought them back.' "

Spud laughed. "That's funny."

"It was, but they brutally killed some good

brood mares. Ran cattle off, and they even had a shoot-out in the cedar breaks with me where I left three of them dead. A couple of them murdered a woman who I had relations with — then shot my brother who was up in Kansas with a herd of cattle. Spud, it was a bloody fight and the only way I could end it was to get out of Texas."

"Thanks for sharing it with me. I heard bits and parts about your life, but it makes more sense now. That cute boy who's with Valerie at Cross Point — you had to leave his mother in Texas?"

"I never even dreamed she had my baby — her parents were older and could not travel here — regretfully she stayed with them and kept the boy a secret. Her daughter wrote me when her mother died of pneumonia and told me she felt if I wanted him she would give him to me. Cole and Valerie were unknown in Texas and they brought him back for me. I was grateful, though I bet that daughter cried. She had taken charge of him up till then."

"Give me your rein. I will put the horses up. What will we do tomorrow?"

"Breakfast is about seven o'clock at the house. Come join me and we will plan it out."

"I can eat with the *vaqueros.*"

"We will eat together."

"Yes sir."

Liz rushed to hug him. And she shouted for Spud to come eat supper. She had enough food for them both.

"What did you learn today?" she asked Chet, heading for the back porch.

"Frye is getting me about eighteen buckboards and teams. Gloria and him have a fine new baby boy. He is very proud. I've already forgot the boy's name."

"I bet Frye is proud. He made a good choice rescuing her. But we knew that was right."

"Almost as good as mine."

She laughed. "This is a real hurry-up business, isn't it?"

"Stupid too because Cole and I could have gotten those buckboards much earlier. Now we all must rush around. When you don't have full control of a situation, things like this happen."

"I know you have other things on your mind. What is that?"

"Figuring out how to build a telegraph line along the route. It would be a good investment. Even after the rail arrives, it would still be in use. They would use it too."

She squeezed his arm. "My man, you never stop amazing me. But if you say you are doing it, I believe you will do that. What do you need for that?"

"A telegrapher who knows the business. We can get the poles, line them out, and string wire. It's how they work and stay on that I don't understand. But I am sure there is an expert I can hire somewhere to handle that part of it."

"The singing wires, huh?"

"Liz, we're still having fun, aren't we?"

"Oh, Chet Byrnes, I have had fun with you since the first day we met at Tubac."

"Good. We're going to keep doing that."

"Well, no wrecks today?" Monica asked, the buxom Mexican woman in charge of the house and cooking.

He kissed her on the forehead. "Your knee must be better?"

"I'm fine. How is your hip and back?"

"I'm all right."

"Good. I have some roast beef and potatoes left."

"Spud is coming too," Liz said.

"I'll fix him a plate. I guess Preskitt is fine?"

"All I learned there, yes it is okay."

"Where is Jesus?"

"He and the new man Spencer Horne are running around looking for buckboards and horses."

84

Monica shook her head. "You get in more fixes than a half dozen people ever could find. What happens to Spud when they get here?"

"We'll find a place for him."

The guardsman entered the back hall, removed his hat, and smiled. "Horses are up."

"Get in here and eat before I throw it out."

Chet grinned at her words. Monica was back to being herself — her knee must be better.

"Yes ma'am, I could have eaten with the *vaqueros*."

"Food might have been better down there."

"No ma'am. They eat good food, but yours is much better."

"You trying to get on my good side?"

"Ma'am, I've eaten lots of places in this territory, and I'd say of them all, you top my list."

"Don't say that too loud or I will have more than I can feed coming up here."

They all laughed.

"You just take care of the boss. I'll do the cooking."

"I will, ma'am."

Monica excused herself and left them.

"Glad she's better," Chet said to his wife.

"At least she sounds better."

"She's not that mean," she said to Spud.

"This is always good food. I've missed some meals being an orphan, couldn't be helped. But I wasn't lying. She is a great cook. I know, compared to lots of things I've had for food."

"I bet that is so too," Chet said. "We are glad to have you."

"Well, Tom is going to Hayden's Ferry and look for more down there?" Liz asked him.

"He said he'd go down there and take some men to bring them back up here."

"That will take some time after he finds them." She looked at the ceiling for help.

"Yes, it will. We start the mail service in three weeks. Frye is sending the buckboards he is selling us north shortly. I hope they have some units for the east side stations to start with by then."

"Carpenter has not delivered anything he was supposed to so far?"

"Not that I know of. I'll wire Hannagen tomorrow and ask for the count of rigs on the east side, and then we better go back up there and help Cole get them scattered."

"Should I wait here for the answer?" Spud asked.

"No. They can send a *vaquero* with the answer."

"Who is in charge of the Verde Ranch when Tom is gone?" she asked.

"Victor. He can handle it. They just need to check cattle this time of year. The west line fence keeps them from wandering too far west. We may need you to take a rig north, Spud."

"I can sure handle that."

"I know you can."

"Breakfast is at seven," she said as Spud excused himself.

When he was gone, she said, "I believe he could turn back an elephant to save you."

"He's a good young man and well-intended too. He's had a rough life, but he appreciates us too."

"You sore tonight?"

"I could use some more of your massaging."

"I'm the gal that can do it." They went upstairs to bed. He lay quietly for a long time after she finished his rubdown, wondering how they'd ever make the first run on time.

CHAPTER 5

The wire was sent to Hannagen inquiring about the number of units that were sent east. He gave his current promised count for the west and the fact he was still buying them. Then he and Spud rode back to Bo's office and found the real estate man buried in paperwork.

"Sorry I missed you, Chet. I was showing a ranch in the south to a new man."

"Business keeps the door open. How is your wife?"

"Big. Any day they say. She never had one before, so we're excited."

"Any ranch purchases in the future?"

"Two places. But it won't happen for six weeks. I sent your brother-in-law Sarge a letter to check on them for us. He'll get to it."

"Thanks."

"How is the stage line business?" Bo asked.

"Pressing. Spud and I are headed back up there in the morning. They didn't get all the rigs and teams we needed in New Mexico, so we're scrambling."

"I understand. Keep us in your prayers. You know I lost my first wife in childbirth. All right?"

"I am certain it will go right but I will. Tell her I sent my best."

"I will. Young man, take good care of him. He's a great guy. He sobered me up and it was no fun either."

"Spud's a great man to ride with."

"Glad to meet you."

When they were mounted up and headed for the livery to check with Frye on how his deals were working, Spud asked, "What sobered him up?"

"Oh, Bo was drinking his head off, and I hired two big bruisers to babysit him around the clock and not let him drink for several weeks. They dried him out and he does not drink anymore. He met a fine widow woman after his first wife died in childbirth and they have a good life. She never had a baby with her first husband, but they are having one now."

Spud shook his head in disbelief. "You simply dried him out?"

"No problem. Those two were with him

all the time, and he had no chance to drink anything. He sobered up and has been off it ever since then. Built a great land office business and helped me a lot."

They dismounted at the livery, hitched horses, and found Frye busy telling his three men what to do with the buckboards and teams.

"How will they get back from Center Point?" he asked Chet.

"I may need them to scatter the buckboards around the stage stops for me. Pay will be good. We will feed them at the Verde place, then at the big sawmill, which is a hard push in a day. They will see my man Robert up there. His wife Betty will feed and put them up. Then they get to Cole or his man at Center Point. In the end we will bring them back home, but that might take some time."

The three young men standing next to Frye and listening agreed they could use the work. They were taking two buckboards apiece and two teams. The second buckboard would be piled on top of the first one and the second team hitched behind. Frye had two more set up that way going out the next day. He hoped to have the rest, more doubles, going out the third day.

That set up, Chet and Spud got the mail

at the post office and went to eat lunch at Jenn's café. Her daughter, Bonnie, was married to JD, Chet's nephew. JD ran the large desert ranch operation south of Tucson. The buxom Jenn hugged him like always when he came into the restaurant, then showed them to a booth.

"How is Liz? You hauling her all over hell with you still?"

"She's fine. We're busy getting the stage line into operation up north."

"I heard all about it. You bought every buckboard in town, haven't you?"

"I guess so. We need them."

"I get letters from my daughter. Their baby boy, Calvin, is fine. But I think she is going to have number two next. I'd never believed that would happen with her, but she is happy — so what the hell, huh? Kids, huh?"

"Great news. How is Grandma Jenn doing?"

"Business is great. Too good at times."

After lunch they rode back to the ranch.

"I sent four units double decked to the Verde," Raphael said, meeting them.

Chet dismounted. "Good. Frye has two more going up there tomorrow, and more going out the next two days after that. With your eight and his eighteen we will be in good shape for the start. Better if Cole found some up there, and I imagine he has."

Things were beginning to look like they would make it. He and Spud could ride north in the morning. He noticed a familiar rig parked by the horse barn. Hampt or his wife and kids were there. The big burly ranch foreman who helped him get the first ranch rolling had married his brother's widow, May.

Hampt came from the house carrying Miles, his own firstborn with May, who had three others by his brother. "Well, you, finding buckboards?"

"We are getting there, thanks to everyone helping us. If they get enough for the eastern division, we will have the west done."

Liz told Hampt, "They tried to kill Chet and Cole."

"A mysterious guy named Hall hired three dumb cowboys to murder us."

"What the hell did he want?"

"I guess for us to fail at getting the line running."

"You need me?"

"Hampt, you have enough to do over there running that East Verde Ranch."

Hampt shook his head. "No, my foreman can do that. I can be up there helping you and Cole."

"Better listen to him," May said, coming up to them and taking the baby. "He won't be happy if he can't help you."

Chet agreed with his again pregnant sister-in-law, who knew her man well. Why couldn't he and Liz have one of their own? Everyone else did, damn.

"Lunch is ready," Liz said. "We can talk about this over a meal. Did your day go well in town?"

Lunch settled the matter. Hampt was going north to help them. That fact even made Chet feel more secure about the whole deal. Spread out over four hundred miles, there were lots of holes in the net they had not found yet. And the men he felt were the toughest would be with him or sharing the responsibility to get things under way.

The next morning, Spud and Hampt each drove the doubled-up rigs and headed for the Verde Ranch loaded with their bedrolls and camp supplies. After Chet kissed his wife good-bye, he set out to catch the pair. His big dun horse, Crow, hopped halfway to the gate crossbar. The gelding made big high bucks and Chet felt amused when he at last pulled his head up and joined them.

Before noon they were at the big house. Victor's wife Rhea and his son Adam in her arms met them. The boy reached out and hugged him. He held and swung him around. Hampt could not get over how much he'd grown since the last time he saw him.

Lea the housekeeper promised them lunch shortly.

Tom came over and they discussed the need for more rigs in case the east side wasn't filled.

"I have it all settled here. Vic is in charge. I will take the stage with two men to Hayden's Mill at midnight tonight. Then do the best I can down there to find some more. How many will you need?"

"I figure to be certain, six if they are down there. I have no idea how many they have found, but the population isn't that great to start with. Frye, I bet, got all that could be bought in Preskitt. They will be here shortly."

Tom agreed. "I sure hope we make that date."

"We will, but this could have been smoother had we known Carpenter was not finding rigs on his part. Hell, that was all he had to do."

Tom laughed. "I knew you already doubted him doing much at the Windmill Ranch when you had that meeting."

"Left up to him he'd never got anything done, but surely Hannagen knows that by now."

"Wish I was going along to help, but we will get some rigs and ship them to you."

Chet thanked him, and Lea waved them in to eat lunch. Rhea took the boy from him and smiled. "You like Daddy?"

The child agreed.

After lunch they headed north. Tom sent along a man with two buckboards and two more teams from the ranch. No way for them to make Robert's house and the Sawmill that day. They'd camp somewhere on top of the rim by dark.

Times like this made Chet want to fly but he had no wings. They could furnish enough buckboards to get by on the west side, but filling the east side concerned him. Having enough horses remained a concern as well.

They were on top of the rim by dark and, at a waterhole, set up camp. The horses received drinks and nosebags of grain and were hitched on tie ropes between pine trees. Members of the crew set in to cook supper. Rhea sent along some fresh beef to cut up and broil. Beans were boiled, and Chet set up a guard order for two men to watch things in rotating shifts.

Seated on a log eating steaks and *frijoles*

off their tin plates, Spud asked him if he feared they'd be raided at night.

"I don't trust anything left to chance. They may be miles away, but they would like to stop us, and they may just be patrolling this road to be sure we fail to connect."

"How many men could he hire?"

"No telling, but there is little employment up here. Those drifters who attacked Cole and me were out of work. They aren't the only ones that someone told them there were jobs up here and they drifted in. The few ranches up here can hire Navajo boys for half the price of white boys to herd cattle."

Spud nodded. "Sarge have any?"

"He didn't last I checked, but I bet he will hire some when he needs more help."

The lookouts armed with rifles began the shift changes of two hours. He and Spud had the last shift in the morning. Chet was soon sound asleep — dreaming about working roundup on the Verde Ranch. Gunshots woke him.

CHAPTER 6

Spud was there in the dark with a rifle for him and hugging the ground.

"You know how many?" Chet asked, seated on his bedroll fighting to pull his boots on.

He took the rifle and heard Hampt say, "They're running for it. Boys, come on."

The pungent smell of pines rode the cool night air. Chet rushed for the horse line, and the shadowy starlight poured down through the high boughs. Ahead of him and Spud, Hampt and another guard were firing their rifles after the fleeing raiders. Chet saw the orange flashes of their gun muzzles when he caught up with them.

"We get any of them?"

"One or two," Hampt said, reloading his rifle.

"Well, the rest escaped, I guess?"

The Verde Ranch cowboy Lester had one by the collar, shoving him along ahead of

him. "I got one of them. Another ain't moving."

"What's your name?" Chet handed Spud
the rifle and when the man stone-faced him,
he jerked him by two hands full of shirt up
in his face. "Stealing horses out here is a
hanging offense. You either tell me who
hired you and what they said for you to do
or I'm hanging you. What's your name?
Let's start there."

"August Danes."

"Tell me about why you raided us."

"He said he'd pay us a hundred apiece to
stop any buckboard deliveries coming out
of here."

"Who was that?"

"I don't know his name."

"What kind of hat did he wear?"

"Fancy Boss of the Plains one."

Chet released his shirt. "How were you to
collect your money?"

"Said he'd meet us at Mormon Lake next
week and pay us."

These men were more of Hall's hands, no
doubt. "He give you and the rest twenty
bucks for drink and cathouse fare?"

"Yeah, how did you know that?"

"He did that same deal with the last ones
who tried to kill me. One's dead. One's in
jail and the third one ran off."

"What you going to do with me?"

"Slap you in the Yavapai County Jail and let you stand trial for manslaughter and horse stealing. Where is the other outlaw at?"

"Dead," Spud said.

"We can bury him at Center Point. Men, this war has just begun in earnest. Keep your gun hand free. He will try again, so be alert at all times. Who was the dead one?"

"Sonny Brooks."

"Where did you hail from?"

"Texas. Him too."

"Handcuff him, Spud. They are in my saddlebags. He's your prisoner."

"Yes sir."

They began making breakfast. They recovered one live saddle horse, two saddles, and a prisoner. After the meal of coffee, oatmeal, raisins, and brown sugar, they washed dishes and loaded up for the final push to Center Point. Taking no chances, Chet kept the cheek strap on the bridle against his left leg mounting the dun horse. In the saddle he had control of the big horse in the cool dark morning, and they rode for headquarters.

When they arrived at headquarters in mid-afternoon a thundershower swept in, but he was under cover when the big droplets of rain pounded the tent roof accompanied with rolling thunder.

Val was there with Rocky, who had lots to tell his daddy about things happening in camp — like the gray cat had four kittens. Val added that Cole and Dennis should be back anytime. There had been another raid on a road stop, but the station people had held them off. No one had been hurt.

Things were getting tougher as the time drew near. Thank God these raiders that, so far, Hall had hired were only itinerant cowboys and not the real bad tough guys. But Chet would have bet he'd be sending for the meaner ones if he hadn't already. They might not get here in time to stall the first run, but no telling when and where they'd start to disrupt service.

Obviously Hall knew the strengths and weakness of every stop. Station operators reported he'd been there at their places looking over them for investment purposes. He'd get that elusive devil somehow. In the meanwhile he had to make the stops more secure against those hired bandits.

Val asked him how the buckboard situation looked.

"We are doing good if we can stop any ambush efforts. No telling how many unemployed hands he's hired to raid us and where. I am concerned he will dump some real bad men on top of us. Poor leadership and inept warriors so far are not hard to fend off. But I am concerned he may have some tougher gun hands coming. His pockets must be deep, and he's determined to stop us."

"Have you asked Hannagen?"

"No, but he may know him and who he works for."

"You're right." Valerie herded him to a table under the peck of hail on the canvas. "The lack of communication compared to Preskitt makes it hard to operate."

"We are learning lots and we will obviously have more to do. When Cole gets back we will send the rigs out to the stations that need them. I will call a meeting of the extra men who brought rigs up here and see if they want to be shotgun guards on the first runs. I think if each buckboard is guarded we'd have less attacks. Unless he gets some real *desperados* to make raids on us."

"You think he can get them?"

"Money. Money can buy him an army if he has that much."

She reached over and squeezed his hand. "You be careful. You know he wants you out of the way."

Cole arrived back that evening. He had

captured three raiders. One was wounded and probably would die. The lack of medical support almost ensured the twice-wounded raider would not live to be put in the Yavapai County Jail down in Preskitt.

"Unemployed ranch hands?" Chet asked him when Cole and his man Dennis Crain sat down with him.

"Yes. They hit two stations in a row and we ran them down."

"They work for the man who wore a Boss of the Plains Stetson with no name?"

"Yes, but one guy knew him as Anson Hall from Texas," Crain said. "Others say his real name is Gerald."

"Get the one knows him up here. I want to know all he knows about him."

Crain stood up. "I can get him. His name is Schroder."

"You want to know more about Hall?" Cole asked.

"He hired the raiders on the military road up from the Verde Valley that struck us too."

Hampt joined them and shook Cole's hand. "You rounded them up, huh?"

Cole nodded. "There were four of them. Hall promised them a hundred apiece if they burned down a station. They were easy to track down, and we have a guy that knew Hall. My man Crain has gone to get this guy that knew Hall from Texas."

"I bet he paid them twenty apiece for whiskey money and a woman."

Cole agreed. "Same as he did the bunch that wrecked our buckboard."

"Cheap help, huh? He has not paid a hundred bucks apiece for any raid yet." Chet shook his head.

Schroder looked to be in his thirties. His clothes were dirty and he was unshaven, standing with hands tied behind his back.

"Oren Schroder, tell my boss Chet Byrnes all you know about this Hall."

"Well, I had not seen Anson Hall since Fort Worth. He had a gang of thugs hired there and they rode roughshod on stores and businesses that all paid him protection money. The police and a judge cracked down on them. The rangers came in and before they could arrest him, he took a powder and ran for his life. Before leaving he cleaned out a safe because they found it empty. I saw him in a bar at Mesilla when I came west. He told me he would have some work for me and to join him at Dead Horse Crossing a month later."

"He give you money then?"

"Twenty bucks."

"Was it worth it?"

"I had some good food, whiskey, and a

103

nice visit with a lady."

"Well, you will find some prison time for you. How many more has he hired?"

"I'm not sure. Curly Bill Snow I think was coming to work for him."

"He's a killer wanted in several states," Crain said.

"You know he's coming?" Chet asked Schroder.

"Hall mentioned him. Snow's a real bad guy."

"Well, thanks."

The man nodded and Crain took him away.

"How would Hall profit from the mail contract if he had it? No way for him to profit from us failing. He is working for someone, and we need to learn who that is."

"Hannagen must know his opposition," Val said, and they all nodded in agreement. "That is the answer then."

"Where are Jesus and Spencer?"

"They rode east to check on a bunch of raiders that struck out there again, and I have not heard from them."

"If it will be all right, Spud and I will go see if we can help them." Hampt offered.

"In the morning if they aren't back, you two can go look for them. But remember there are people who don't want this to succeed and they'll kill you."

"I understand. Thanks. Spud, let's get some packhorses ready to go."

"Okay. We'll find them."

"You two be real careful," Chet told them. "I don't want May to cry over you or Spud."

"I'll be double careful then." Spud beamed because that made him feel like he belonged too.

"I better get over there to New Mexico and be ready for the start," Chet said.

"You want me along?" Cole asked.

"Maybe you better stay here. I don't need you hurt in an attack."

"Who is going with you?" Val asked. "Jesus is not here. Hampt and Spud are going looking for him. I don't want you out there with a price on your head and no guards."

Cole smiled. "You take Hampt and Spud. Crain and I will look for Jesus and Spencer."

"Fine."

All he needed was to have more trouble — what his enemies would try bothered him the most. He went to catch Hampt and Spud and tell them they were going along with him to Gallup, New Mexico.

In the mountain coolness they left the camp. Hampt, Spud, Cole, and Dennis

Crain rode with Chet. They pushed hard and reached the first station in early afternoon. Herman Rothschild welcomed them. His Navajo wife Darling came out to welcome them. She was very excited as were his children when the men dismounted.

Chet saw right off that there were no horses or an extra buckboard at their ranch. One down and no stock or extra wagon there. And in less than a week they were supposed to be ready.

"Mr. Byrnes. How are you, sir?"

"Herman, I think you and Darling know these men with me. Except maybe Hampt . . . he runs a ranch for me down south of here."

He removed his hat and bowed his head. "Yes, and we are very proud you all came by. Is all this raider business going to delay the start?"

"No, it will happen next Monday."

Cole interjected, "We will bring you at least one team and a spare buckboard. I am going to check on the next stop and see if they have any horses. I will ride back after the next stop and bring you stock anyway."

"Cole, we can make it work. They are way behind over there. It will get straight."

"Have you seen our men, Jesus and Spencer?" Crain asked.

"Yes," the stage stop operator said. "They were here yesterday and asked me about the men that told us to leave or they'd burn us down."

"How long ago was that?"

"Two days earlier."

"Those men who threatened you . . . have they been back?"

"No. But we have been ready for them. Darling can shoot."

"Good. We need to ride on. Hear anything about my two men, send word to Center Point."

"The horses are watered," Spud reported, and everyone mounted up.

Chet shook his head and then he hugged Darling and told her they'd keep them safe. They soon were in the saddle and riding east.

He rode, speaking out loud and asked, "I wonder if Carpenter delivered anything he said they would. We have to have three or four teams besides a spare buckboard."

"It was the only thing he and his men had to do," Cole said. "Tomorrow morning when we get to Clyde Covington's station, if he has nothing, I will head back and supply those two, but we have two more stations after that to check on."

"You're right. I have no answer as to why

they don't have it done. I also wish we knew where Jesus and Spencer were."

"I bet they're gathering outlaws," Spud said, booting his horse up to them.

"I hope you're right."

"Oh, I know Jesus. Those two are on their tracks," Hampt said.

Chet rode along. "I never felt over-whelmed before over the vastness of this country since I came here. We simply rode to where we needed to be. But the stops tied us down. Both distance and lack of communication are restraining us. We better trot more." He nudged his horse out as they crossed the great open grass empire east-ward.

They camped for the night at the next water hole. They'd be at Rob Simms's Two Forks Trading Post by mid-morning the next day. He hoped they had stage horses.

They had a short supper of jerky and some soda crackers. They boiled some coffee. Lack of firewood shorted their cooking needs. But everyone was in good humor despite the lack of the usual available in camp. They turned in at darkness and rose early. Horses resaddled, and packhorses also ready, they rode east facing the rising sun.

Heat and dust rose as they went on until mid-morning when they reached the second station. The pens held several horses and even a buckboard stood parked.

Chet blinked. Cole rode in close. "Those horses are paints. Carpenter didn't send them to him. Those came from Navajos."

"I wonder what the situation here is."

Simms came outside joined by his one of his Navajo wives, the lead one of two Navajo women the man had. Chet knew her name was Naomi. She wore white women clothing and looked very proper when she spoke to them. "Welcome to our outpost."

"Thank you. We're very pleased to be here, Naomi."

Chet let the others, aside from Cole, go inside, and asked his agent, "Did they ask you to buy horses?"

"Rod Carpenter is his name?"

"Yes, he is the supply man on this end."

"He asked me to buy a hundred harness-broke horses in a week. I have eighty-five and more coming."

"He have plans to scatter them to other places?"

"I don't know. He said buy them and the company would repay me."

"What did he say to pay for them?"

"Twenty dollars apiece. Is something wrong?"

"No, that is enough. There was no mention of distributing them?"

"No, he said just to buy them."

"What should we do, Cole?"

"Those horses are all broke enough to drive?" Cole asked the trader.

"Yes. Navajos drive their wives and families to the beef distribution and to trading posts like mine every week. Sometimes more often."

"Good. Eight horses per stop, we will have plenty for all the stops. I will need to get them to the places they belong. Are there some Indian boys who could help me deliver them for a dollar a day and food?"

Simms laughed. "How many do you need?"

"Oh, five or six."

"I will have them here in the morning to take the horses wherever you need them. They will have bedrolls and be ready to travel."

"Good. That suit you?" Cole asked Chet.

"Yes. Simms, I will be certain you are paid too. Not that anyone might skip out, but nothing they have done in New Mexico has been on time or correct in my mind. I am also looking for two of my men. Have you seen either Jesus, who you know, and another man called Spencer?"

Simms nodded, to Chet's relief. Then he

said, "They were after some men who had threatened station operators to close or they'd burn them out. Your two stopped and visited with us for a short time, then hit the saddle. They thought they had a hot trail."

"Those other men ever threaten you?"

"No, or I'da had them killed before they could do that or tried it. There were four of them rode through but they didn't stop. My wife saw them and said they must be hard-cases, and when your men came by a day and a half behind them, they told me what it was those men had done back west."

"Any idea where they went?"

"To New Mexico I guess. Those two men of yours bought some supplies from me and rode off after them."

"That sounds fine. Cole and your hired boys will take the horses west, and I will ride on toward Gallup in the morning. Extra buckboards are coming too. Did Carpenter mention the harness coming?"

"Never mentioned it at all. I did not ask either. All he said was buy a hundred sound driving horses."

"You did great."

"I'll put our horses up," Spud said, gathering them.

"All of you, come inside to my dining room and we will eat supper shortly," his woman said. "You come too, cowboy."

Holding several reins, Spud bowed toward her. "I will sure be there, ma'am."

The woman laughed and led the others to the trading post.

Later that night in a guest cabin bed, Spud asked him, "Was Carpenter going to deliver those horses?"

"Damned if I know. We are very close to starting, and he has done little if anything but bitch about legitimate bills."

"How far are we from Gallup?"

"Two days. Why?"

"That leaves little time to start the first one west and east. Does Cole have a man out there for the first drive from that end?"

"I bet he does. I will ask him in the morning."

"You've worried about this end so much — I hope he has someone."

"We will know in the morning." He wanted to shake his head about what next would happen. Where were Jesus and his new man Spencer? Hell only knew. That they were all right was all he could hope for.

CHAPTER 7

"Lucy's brother-in-law-to-be Drew, who runs our ranch at Hackberry, is all set up on that west end," Cole explained to Chet at breakfast. "He's been a big help and he will send the first eastbound buckboard with mailbags next Monday. We have several horses and rigs out there at the stations by now and they're ready. Not enough horse stock, but Drew said he would have enough to get by for a week or so. I'm not worried about him. When we get these paint horses spread out we will be in good shape, except we have little spare harness in case some break. It is all used and it will break. Some soon, some later."

Hampt spoke up. "Chet, while you are checking the next station, I'll start those horses west with Cole and these Navajo boys, leave some at the third stop, and take the rest on to Center Point. Then I'll take someone with me and go see if Hall is hiding around Mormon Lake."

"You be damn careful and take a good man to back you. I'll find out the holdup on that problem too when I get over there to Gallup."

Cole shook his head. "This setup has been a real headache, but we're going to make it."

"Oh yes. If Drew will take the job running the west end for you, maybe we can put Shawn over at the Hackberry Ranch?"

"I bet he would. We can talk later about it. I'd sure love to have him."

They parted after discussing the plan to have drivers ready the next week at the stops that needed them. Chet felt Cole's plan would work if they got it all done. To get things going, Cole, Hampt, and six Navajo boys took the multicolored horse herd westward to distribute them. Chet and Spud rode east, taking two of the packhorses that Cole had given him while the herders led off the other two.

It was a bright sunshiny day. The two headed east across what looked like the top of the world in waving grass, pungent-smelling sagebrush, and meadowlarks. Chet knew they were in for a long day's ride to reach Johnny White Feather's trading post. Johnny had two Navajo wives and a Comanche woman as well. He'd met them in Pennsylvania at the academy where they had been shipped for education. Johnny White Feather had gone there for his education also. White Feather was the tallest Navajo that Chet had ever seen. All three of his wives were hardly five feet tall. Polygamy was a way of life in the far West, and despite government restraints it didn't bother the Native Americans or the Mormons to take several wives.

He could not imagine keeping more than one woman happy at a time. But the farther he went the more he pondered over Jesus and Spencer being out of pocket. He was so busy settling all the things necessary and being sure they started out right, he had no time to go look for them. Jesus was resourceful enough and damn sure tough enough, but who he might be up against bothered Chet more.

Late in the day they reached the first stop west of Gallup. Johnny met them, smiling, and he had an extra buckboard parked at the corral that was full of horses.

Carpenter must have stocked one station right.

"Good to see you, *señor.*"

"Good to see you are ready. How did that rig out there happen?"

"I went to Gallup and bought that buck-board, and I was told to buy ten horses in case I needed them."

"Did they pay you for them?"

"No, but my wife sent a bill for them in the mail."

"I'll be sure you get paid. Good, John. This here is my man Spud. Have you seen my other man, Jesus?"

"The Spanish man who rides with you?"

"Yes. He and another man are after the raiders who threatened to burn down our stations."

"He has not been by here. Three men came one day and told me that I should stop being your agent. I told them to leave. They acted tough, but my men hit them over the head with baseball bats. One guy woke up so we put him on his horse, tied the others belly-down, and then told the dizzy one for them not to ever come back and sent them racing south. We never heard from them again."

Chet was laughing by the end of Johnny's story. The short attractive woman, Josie — Johnny's Comanche wife — took them inside, as the two men continued to be amused by the story.

"That was how to handle the matter," Chet said.

Johnny agreed. "I get enough bossy people coming west. They think I am a tobacco-store Indian. I don't have to be nice to them."

"John, they raised the hair on the back of your neck."

He just smiled.

"I need to get to Gallup tomorrow. That is Saturday, and only two days before we start the first wagon."

"We will be ready."

"I can see that. Cole is taking enough horses that Simms bought for us west to-day."

"Many Navajos sold him horses. They must think I am too dumb to do that for them."

"I don't know about that but I appreciate all you have done. When I get through in Gallup the next few days they will know that too."

"To be very honest I have more schooling than most of them have."

"Exactly. But when I get through some heads will roll over there."

"Come, you must be hungry. Tell that boy to come too that is putting away your horses."

"He's a short man, Spud, and I will tell him."

"I thought he was a boy."

"No. He is a man and he works hard like a man."

Chet went and told Spud to come inside when he was through.

"Thanks . . . I will be there shortly."

"You spoke of your lost man?" Johnny said, walking back beside him.

"I know Jesus and his new partner won't quit trailing down those outlaws. I imagine he is doing that."

"I told my wife what you were doing with this mail run was a huge chore. You and Cole have worked hard to set this up."

"It will work Monday with little or no help from Gallup whatsoever."

"I can see that."

Josie had taken charge, and they ate a good meal in the house part of the post. They provided a bath for both of them and cots in an army tent. By candle lamp, Chet shaved his face as well.

"His wife Josie is a very smart person," Spud said.

Chet was swooshing the lather off the blade in the bowl of hot water to go back for more. "They both are."

"I agree."

"Good idea." Chet nodded.

"You going to blow up when we get to

Gallup? I know they have not done anything they are supposed to have done. But don't explode."

"I will try not to, Spud."

"Good. I don't want you to have a heart attack. I know how you and Cole provided the most to this success of this venture."

The two of them arrived late Saturday night in Gallup. Horses in the livery and what bags they had were at the Grand Hotel. He and Spud had a meal in the dining room. Chet sent Hannagen a note by messenger. They were halfway through their meal when a man arrived.

"Sir, you must be Chet Byrnes?"

"I am." Chet folded his napkin and stood, despite the man's offer for him not to do so.

"Carl Raines. I represent Mr. Hannagen. He invites you to stay in his large home."

"We have rooms here tonight. We plan to bathe and sleep here tonight. Tomorrow we can move. I only contacted him to let him know we were here."

"My boss said to tell you anything you want or need he can provide you. And to tell you that Rod Carpenter is no longer working for us. We know that first stage leaving Monday would never have happened without you and your men's hard work."

"Carl, tell him we can talk tomorrow. I appreciate your acknowledgment of my team's work. Perhaps meeting at breakfast?"

"Oh yes."

"Is seven too early?"

"No sir. He and his staff will join you."

"This is my man, Spud Carnes. We will be available then."

"I will arrange for a private dining room here in the hotel."

Chet shook his hand and thanked him.

When he left, Spud elbowed him. "You forgot your suit."

"That ain't nothing."

Spud suppressed a laugh.

Chet shook his head. "They will know why too."

"At least Carpenter is gone."

"They remind me of ducks without water. They must not have anyone else either."

Spud smiled. "That young feller did not look like he ever got dirty to me."

They both laughed at his comment.

Somehow, someway, this stage line was going to roll on Monday morning and only because his outfit made it work. When they traipsed upstairs to their rooms, he wondered and worried about Jesus and Spencer. Where in the hell were they?

Breakfast came at seven. In the private

dining room, the Hannagen stage line president, with Howard Jefferson, Gladstone Meyer, his lawyer, and Wade Nelson, Hannagen's secretary, joined Chet and Spud.

"You know my staff. The new man Frank Bailey, in charge of horses and harness, is coming later. I want to thank you and your enduring men for all you have done for this organization. Truly we'd never have built this project without you and your men's assistance, especially having to deal with my poor judgment in choosing my ex-employee Rodney Carpenter. He is gone. Your wire regarding his cutting your expense report woke me up. Then, on top of that, I learned he had done little to support your arrangements and setup for the station stops. So anything we lack we will get for you."

"Cole's man Drew over on the Colorado River will start a buckboard of mail east Monday morning."

"Thank God. Gentlemen, we will meet our mail contract dates as planned. That is oh such wonderful news."

"We don't have any spare harness. Cole is spreading those horses the number two station operator Simms bought for you. And by the way, the man at the first stop, Johnny White Feather, is a well-educated man and we are very blessed to have a Navajo in that slot. He has felt slighted by the treatment given him in the past."

"That will be corrected," Hannagen said, and everyone agreed.

"Good. Let's eat before it gets cold. We have rushed getting this setup together and now need to begin to build the setups needed for a stage line. How is stagecoach procurement coming along?"

"We have six used coaches that were purchased from a bankrupt line out of a San Antonio dispersal."

"When will they get here?"

"The buyer is arranging that now."

"Tell him to grease the axles good before coming up here. They probably have been abused. Get a wagon mechanic down there to go over all of them and fix anything that might threaten to break on the trip. That won't prevent all breakdowns, but it could avoid a few."

"Our man down there says he can find some good stage horses we can use that will be worth the money, and he will arrange to get them up here."

"I would suggest that you have two spare teams to have along if you lose some on the way. That is a long trip regardless of the way they come. Have them all well shod too."

"Good. My man has all that written down. Chet, I can't thank you enough. This would not be happening in the morning without your help and input."

"Gentlemen, this is only the start. Someone, and you must know who it is, is behind all the effort to make this venture fail. They have threatened our agents and tried to burn them out. They won't stop simply because we send off the first buckboard. They will make a harder effort to see us fail."

"I have no idea who, but there was competition for the contract."

"Why don't you hire Pinkerton to find out?" Chet said.

"Yes, that is a good idea."

"It might be too much frontier out here for that outfit, but we need more information and to get to the root of it to be able to stop it."

"You have any name of the individuals?"

"A Texas gun hand and gambler named Gerald Anson Hall hired three unemployed cowboys to kill Cole and I returning to Center Point. They chased us in our buckboard. It wrecked and we had a shootout. One dead, one in jail, and another on the loose. Two of my guardsmen are now somewhere chasing other men that threatened our station managers to close down or they'd burn them out. Three more are under arrest for attacking us up on the rim. My man Hampt Tate went to meet this Hall at Mormon Lake, where he is supposed to be to pay off the attackers."

"Anyone here ever heard of this Hall guy?" Hannagen asked.

Everyone around the table shook their heads. That was what Chet suspected. Whoever brought him in and hired him was unknown as well.

"I have his name down and I will start a search today, sir," Wade Nelson, his secretary, said.

"The lack of communication really makes it hard to do much." Hannagen shook his head over the matter.

"We need to talk about that too after we get things rolling," Chet said.

"I will be ready. You staying for the start?"

"Yes, I want to see the first man off."

"Move to my house. We have conveyances to take you back and forth."

"That's fine. Once the first man leaves, Cole has it set up that at every other stop we change drivers. That way, he can return to Gallup the next day. If a driver must go on, of course, that will need to be straightened out and a way found of getting him back to his place. I am certain we will have delays and weather problems. In the winter around Center Point, deep snow will slow us down or cause a stoppage because of the elevation, but that happens all over the West, so I don't think that is too much to worry about."

"And if these attacks at the stops persist — what should we do?"

"We need a couple of teams of enforcers on both ends to stop it. We have any more trouble, we will need to hire shotgun guards. A Greener is a very effective weapon to stop holdups. We may also need them for valuable shipments, but we can't make that a marker for the thieves."

"How is that, Chet?"

"If armed guards only ride with valuable loads, the outlaws will figure which ones to rob. We will need them on all rides."

Hannagen shook his head. "I would never have thought about that. Wells Fargo ships lots of money and gold, and it would be good to have them as a customer."

"I agree."

Frank Bailey arrived. A nice-looking man, he apologized. "I had lots to do this morning . . . a lot needed my attention. Nice at last to meet you, Mr. Byrnes. I have been waiting for this event." He shook Spud's hand too. "Good to meet you too, sir."

Frank was a clean-cut man in his thirties. Five-ten or so, thin built, he wore a six-gun on his side. Maybe he came from law work. Chet felt he sounded like a leader of men and not slack in getting things done. That was a good sign. He hoped they'd hired the right man this time. The conversation went back to readiness.

"The driver will head out at eight a.m. from our headquarters tomorrow morning?"

Chet nodded.

"Your man Emerson will have the relief driver stationed, right?"

"Those are his plans at the second stage stop. Whatever Cole handles he gets the job done. He may even use some of our ranch hands until he finds enough drivers."

"Good."

"The man at the first stage stop west of here is Johnny White Feather. He's a Navajo. He attended the academy in Pennsylvania and is a very smart man. He feels some of your people treated him like a cigar-store Indian. I want him treated better than that. He came here, bought a buckboard and horses when you did not furnish him one. His educated wife has sent you a bill for them. Please pay it."

"I have never met him, but I will pay that bill immediately, and trust me, I won't mistreat him," said Frank.

"Thanks. These station operators are all very involved in our success for a number of reasons. That region out there is isolated. There are few markets to sell their stock or other goods to, and they realize this eventual stage line will help show what they have to the world. Between now and the eventual building of the railroad we will be their lifeline and they ours."

"Chet Byrnes, they told me you were a rancher that got things done. We have studied your cattle drives. They are not some everyday deal, bringing cattle to fulfill a government contract, and you do that ninety-nine percent of the time and on time. Your straight-backed superintendent Polanski is a model distributing those cattle to different headquarters."

"Sarge, we call him, is ex-military. Used to be a cavalry sergeant. Got tired of eating beans all the time and sought work with me. He later married my sister and they have one child. They live at the Windmill Ranch between here and Preskitt."

"The Bureau of Indian Affairs people sure brag on about him."

"We deliver six hundred head of cattle a

month to them. That takes more head than my ranch can provide, so other ranchers make sales to us. One of the station contracts I made was with a rancher that I would buy two hundred head of his cattle each year as long as I could. That will no doubt solve his ranching needs."

"None of my business, but how many ranches do you own?" Hannagen asked.

"Six and starting the seventh one in the next six months."

"How long have you been in Arizona?"

"About four years."

"You've been a busy man, Chet Byrnes, and we are grateful. There was no way we'da made this deadline without you, Cole, and the rest. Lunch is at one o'clock at my house. I will send a carriage for the two of you in an hour if that is time enough?"

"We can ride our horses," Chet told Hannagen, and they all shook hands.

For the first time since he'd started on this plan he felt satisfied that the stage line was under way despite all the problems. Bailey stayed back to speak to him.

"I never thought I slighted that station man, but we won't from here on. There were lots of things I found in a mess. I do have a few extra harness. Not enough to fill all the needs, but I know how important it is we have some at all stations."

"I have a saddlemaker in Preskitt who can make us some harness, enough to fill the west side. Fair enough?"

"Yes sir. I have fired all the worthless help Carpenter had on the payroll. They were drinking on the job and I don't know what else. That Rod Carpenter must have been a pain in your backside."

"Not really because he didn't do a damn thing he was supposed to, and he wasn't around. We just started taking care of everything ourselves."

"I am anxious to meet Cole. He must be a helluva worker."

Chet nodded. He knew he'd never have made this thing go together without him.

He and Spud met Hannagen's wife Vonda at the house. A pleasant, attractive woman much younger than her spouse welcomed them, and Hannagen soon joined them. Vonda showed the two men to their quarters. After settling their bags, all the men went out onto the veranda, as Hannagen called it, and sat in chairs to talk. Chet was amused. He would simply have called it the porch. He hoped Spud did not laugh about it.

"You said you wanted to talk about communication. Tell me your plan for doing this on the station routes?"

"A telegraph line from Gallup to Hardee-ville and joined on both ends. One at each stage stop."

"My, that would be a task to build. I am certain we'd have to face battling competition as to who would get most of those government contracts, and we'd need lots of support in congress to do that. But now may be the time to build it. When and if the railroad ever replaces us, we'd still have a business that would flourish."

"Four hundred miles more or less . . . but it would connect California a lot quicker than the one that goes from Preskitt to Yuma and then back to El Paso."

"You want in on this if I can get federal funds to build it?" Hannagen asked.

"I'd like to look at it."

"We definitely need one for our business."

Spud was laughing.

"What's so funny?"

"Well, sir, I'd be out of a job carrying a wire to Preskitt to send to you and then riding back to give him your answer if you build them talking wires."

The men laughed. Chet felt his idea was planted. Let the man think about it. He knew all about government subsidies, which would certainly work out better than using all of his own money. His mind was on the vast open land spread out between here and California. They'd scrambled hard enough building the stage line to win and on time. Hannagen's new man Bailey sounded like the man to get things done. Cole could handle the rest.

CHAPTER 8

The day started before the heat had evaporated overnight. A large crowd came for the
free sarsaparilla that they were serving in
each person's cup at a bar set up on Main
Street. A shiny team of bay horses was
hitched to the Arizona Territory Stage Lines
buckboard that was all decked in red, white,
and blue ribbons.

The Gallup postmaster, Emil Gaston, carried the canvas bag of mail out of the post
office marked for California. From their
place close by, Chet and Spud stood as a
man readied to fire the pistol shot to send
the driver, on the seat spitting tobacco aside
at intervals, on his way to the Colorado
River.

The gunshot cracked the air and a cheer
went up from the assembled crowd. The two
horses bolted in their collars and sped west
at a pace that if maintained, would kill them
in two hours. Once clear of the town they

would slow to a trot and that would get them to the first station west in eight hours. At Johnny's stage stop they would have fresh horses waiting to replace this team. The dust of the flying wheels made Chet nod in satisfaction. Number one was on the way. The next issue would be to make it safe, and Chet knew that would take some doing.

"Come to the house and celebrate. Soon we will see how successful we are," Hannagen said to them.

"Thanks. We're coming. Makes one feel good to see that rig heading west at last."

Hannagen smiled. "I bet that is sure the case with you."

Chet nodded.

The gathering at Hannagen's house was a party under the roof covering the patio in the backyard — designed more for shading sun rather than rain in this arid land. Several servants ran about with drinks and food on trays.

Chet and Spud met several people who had come to see this new venture off. Obviously there were many curious wealthy people in attendance for the send-off. Spud sipped wine. Chet didn't carry a glass. Plenty of good liquor was served but none appealed to him. The pair moved around and talked with several businessmen and their wives — some from town, others from Santa Fe, and two men from Fort Worth.

"You know anyone considering buying the sections of land that checkerboard the Atlantic-Pacific future roadbed?" a man in an expensive business suit asked.

Chet shook his hand. The middle-aged man in his fine tailored clothes introduced himself as T. J. Rounds from Dallas. In Chet's opinion, Rounds had some interest in the large spread of government land given the railroad to build the tracks across the territory.

"Lots of land and spread over four hundred miles would make a snake-shaped ranch."

"Oh, I never realized it was that long."

"Oh yes, and I would see no use for it. Fencing needed to keep stock off the tracks, and then moving them over the tracks to graze on the other side, would be lots of work. There are some large ranches available, but that one is not one to buy for my purposes."

"How is the cattle business over there?"

"Fine. But few markets and a lack of water sources to move the cattle are things the railroad will bring to us when it ever comes."

The man smiled. "They are slow getting

out here, aren't they?"

"Very slow."

"This country's never recovered from the Civil War debt. These continued recessions are ruining ever recovering to a stable national economy, and it will take that to ever build those tracks out here."

"Maybe my children will see it." Chet smiled at the man.

"Then you would not recommend buying that land?"

"Not for a ranch."

"What part of the territory do you like the best for cattle ranching?"

"I have ranches from south of the Grand Canyon to the border. Managed right, they all are good places to ranch."

"You have no sheep?"

"No sheep."

"I am told they make much more money than beef cattle."

"I am not interested in them."

"You hate them?"

"I simply don't care anything about them." Chet chuckled and thanked him for the visit.

Away from him, Spud asked, "No sheep?"

"No sheep."

Spud laughed and they went for some food. "These people must all be very rich.

But I love your own ranch parties more with everyone. A lot of these people never worked a day in their life for anything."

"I agree. They think it all comes on a silver plate. I like our style better."

"Did that last guy ever attend any of your parties?"

"No, and he won't. There are two kinds of men in this world. Those that do things and those that only talk about them. Thank God we do things."

"Right. I'd hate to have to change."

"I, damn sure, will be ready to ride in the morning."

Chet squeezed Spud's shoulder and smiled. *Thank God for him.*

In the middle of the night there was a knock on his door. Chet put on his pants to go see who was there. A woman in a night-dress held a lamp. "Mr. Byrnes, your wife is here. They had a breakdown and missed the opening start."

Liz was in his arms. "Val and I planned too late, I guess. We passed that driver going west of station number one. We wanted to make the first run start. We switched horses — oh, we couldn't stay home and not be here."

"You all right, Val?" he asked the bedraggled-looking woman standing behind his wife — a woman who always looked dressed up just so and so.

"Sure, I'm fine. Liz came up to Center Point and we took the boy with his wife — I mean his nanny — and like two crazy girls decided we could make the run over here in time to watch it."

"What if Hall's killers got after you?" Chet asked, squeezing his wife hard, so glad they were safe but upset about the dangers they could have faced out there.

Liz gave him a little hard look in the now lit hallway. "We both can shoot. We aren't crybabies."

"But that was a hell of a long trip for you two to make."

"Your people all applauded us at the stations when we stopped. They hooked us up with a fresh horse and gave us food and water."

"You two had anything to eat lately?"

"Yes, and we are very tired." Liz pushed him toward the door.

He said, "I can go sleep in Spud's room."

"There are two beds in there," Liz said, and Val agreed. "You and I in one. Her in the other bed. We just want to get some sleep. Tomorrow we can straighten it all out."

Both women pushed by him into the room.

"Close your eyes," Liz said.

He closed the door and obeyed her. When they were both in bed, Liz said, "You can open them now and get into bed."

They were damn serious about sleeping. Both of them died when they hit the pillow. He had lots of scares, but this was the worst one so far. Two women in a buckboard coming two hundred miles through outlaw country for a grand opening. They were both crazy.

He finally closed his eyes. Damn, he loved them both. They were precious.

CHAPTER 9

At the early morning breakfast, he and Hannagen shared some plans about operations of the line. By spring they would start stagecoach trips three times a week in place of buckboards, and as their business grew they would increase the stage runs. That would make his six coaches work while they looked for more.

"Thanks for your plan to check them out before they left San Antonio. In the next few weeks I want to start a completion report and the cost, so send in your bills so I have an idea about the sum of the cost to this point. Do you still have an interest in investing in the stage line?"

"Keep us informed. We will continue with building stage stops at the sites we have where there is not a ranch or place already there that we can use."

Hannagen's wife found Liz and Val some nice dresses to wear home while the two men had their dusty felt cowboy hats brushed clean by some household help. A fresh team of horses was hitched up and ready to go.

Chet and Spud shook Hannagen's hand. He told his four visitors thanks. With two packhorses the two men trotted along behind the buckboard as they headed for Dead Man's Crossing on the Little Colorado. He aimed to check both stage stops and pinpoint where Jesus and Spencer had gone.

He hoped Johnny White Feather might have a few adventuresome Navajo boys who could tag along and track for him. In the past he'd always counted on Jesus to do that. Now he was going to find those two, and something bad better not have happened to them or he'd find the villains and spill the law book on their heads.

He'd worried long enough about how they could find them and where they went. Spud, he felt, understood his concern, and Liz and Val could manage the buckboard and anything that came their way, but they'd damn sure need to push forward now, and hard. Trails would be cold and might be hard to decipher, but someone knew and he'd get the information out of them — where Jesus and Spencer were, searching for the raiders.

Their horses were well shod and had rested, so he pushed them all day across the northern part of the Arizona Territory. They were accompanied by meadowlarks, bobwhite, and blue quail that scattered through the sage and tall dried bunchgrass at their approach.

Antelopes raised their prong horns to check on them, sometimes ran and other times went on grazing. Mule deer bounded off in stiff-legged jumps, and the elk herds were the most cautious and moved quickly away at the discovery of them. No doubt. Chet decided they were the most shot at by the passersby. Despite some traffic on the road, this was still a very unsettled country with no buffalo, where widespread cattle- or sheep-raising had not even started. A land shared by the Navajos, with red-tailed hawks and bald eagles soaring the azure skies on a hot wind. Buzzards swooped low enough to be sure to find out if anything they saw was alive.

Water or the lack of it made the isolation even harder to stand. The moon lakes or *playas* in places that didn't drain into streams were much more rare there than over in New Mexico or west Texas. For any development, windmills and tank buildings would be the only way to use it. No great farming business would ever be here. The rainfall was too scarce and trees were almost a sacred commodity. A few cottonwoods along where the trickles of creek water ran, and when the elevation rose juniper-like cedar in the hill country of Texas flourished.

But the winters could be snowy enough to cover the grass, so haying became a necessity — some winters none of the white stuff fell and others it stayed on like Montana — except over at Center Point and that was a high enough elevation to have lots of snow every year. That accumulation would block their route too, part of the time, but that was natural. Hall and his hired men were the force he had to stop. There would be enough added criminals passing through to keep a private force busy rounding up outlaws until law enforcement replaced the stage line's effort.

"We've been doing all this riding in silence . . . are you busy gathering ideas how to ranch all this country?" Spud asked, riding in close to him.

"Oh no. We have that new ranch where we went to arrest those horse rustlers that time, and it needs development before I think about other places."

"Boy, it will need lots of work but that down there borders the pine forest. This country would need a lot of work too. There's not a tree in sight out here."

"No, we've hauled in all the lumber and posts to these stations on this side of the midway. I also think it may get more moisture down there on the lip of the Mogollon Rim too where our new place is located."

"Sarge's operation does well and it's up here on the high country."

"The Windmill Ranch works because of the past water development and my brother-in-law Sarge. It is a yearling operation, not a cow or calf form of ranching. Cows and calves, to succeed, need lots of care. Most of the steers we drive up there are two years old, can fight a bear or even a grizzly attack, or they can outrun them — calves can't."

"What will this rim ranch raise?"

"Cows and calves and we may need to thin the stock killers out too."

"What will we do at Johnny's stage stop tonight?"

"I hope he can get some young men to ride with us that can track and if needed, fight while looking for Jesus and Spencer."

"But you still don't know where they went?"

"There is someone somewhere who knows where they went. We find them, we can find Jesus and Spencer. I suspect those two are rounding up those raiders somewhere."

Spud shook his head. "I enjoy being with you, but there sure aren't many places I'd like to live up here. That's cozy country around Preskitt and the friendly people besides your *vaqueros,* their families, and the friends you have made and helped all sum up to a great place to live."

"We simply don't stay around there enough?"

"That's right. Don't get me wrong but I guess I get homesick now I have tasted it." Spud shook his head. "I lived lots of places, but that site is cool when it is hot as heck up here and down at Tucson. The home-place gets my vote."

"Don't tell too many about how great it is. It's getting crowded over there." Chet laughed at his companions' complaints.

Johnny White Feather and his Comanche wife Josie greeted them at sundown at the first stage stop.

"I see those women found you. We gave them fresh horses," he said, laughing. "They were too late for the start with you, but that first driver, coming through here, said he had an affair with a mirage that passed him."

Spud laughed. "I bet it was a pretty one."

They all were amused.

"You have not heard from my man Jesus,

144

have you?" Chet asked.

John shook his head. "You worried about him?"

"It isn't like him not to have come in and checked with me."

"He never came by here. You thought he took after some of those guys that had threatened the other stations."

"I think he did. Do you have some boys that can shoot and track for me for a few weeks?"

"How many?"

"Two or three. I need to leave in the morning."

"I will send for them. They will be here ready to go. They are brothers and have some education. They speak English too," John assured them.

"Good . . . my Navajo is pretty weak."

With Chet and Spud helping Liz and Val off the buckboard, they joined Johnny and his wife heading inside. "So was mine when I came here five years ago."

"I know you met these ladies as they came by yesterday. The dark-headed one is my wife Elizabeth. The brunette is Valerie. She's Cole's wife."

"We gave them fresh horses," Josie said. "They needed them badly."

"I am grateful for that."

Josie laughed. "How long have you had her?"

"Two years. We met down by Tubac."

"She is your second wife?"

"Yes, my first wife died almost a year before and I didn't need — want — a wife."

Liz spoke up. "I was on my way home and I heard that the man with golden horses was at this place. He was a U.S. Marshal and I expected a big building of stone. It was only some *jacales* and corrals and a canvas-covered shade. No gold horses and this big man with his hat in his hand came to meet me. My husband was killed three years before — I didn't need a man. But all at once I felt I needed this one."

"Oh, I know how you felt. I was teaching Indian children when John came back east for me. He said he had two wives because of tribal customs but he needed me too."

"What did you think?" Liz asked.

"He and I dated before he came back here. I always liked him but I had to think long about sharing a husband. They are my sisters now. And we are busy and will be busier with the stage line."

"No children?"

Josie shook her head. "You either?"

"We have not had any. Chet has two sons by two other women. So he has heirs.

146

Maybe someday."

"I hope so too."

Spud joined them and they sat at the large dining table. The wives served them steak and potatoes while Chet talked to John about the stage line.

"We have bought six coaches and are being certain they are in good shape to drive them up here from San Antonio."

"You going to bring them out here?"

Chet laughed. "I hope not."

"I never saw that Carpenter but once."

"They fired him. A man named Frank Bailey took his place."

"I won't miss Carpenter. He spoke to me like I was a dirty-shirt Indian."

"He'd never gotten the stage stops set up. I knew that on my first meeting. The new man Bailey will be better, I assure you. Or you tell Cole and he will stand up for you."

John smiled. "Thanks."

The meal completed, Chet thanked all of them and the four went out to the small hogan that had been set up for them.

"I would think him already having two wives was hard for her to accept?" Liz asked Chet later.

"She overcame it well. I think one woman would be all I'd need."

"Good enough. I am that way too."

He hugged and kissed her.

In the morning he met the Be-Good brothers — Harold, Eagle, and Star. They ranged from eighteen to twenty-three. Short, as most Navajo men were, they smiled big and spoke politely to him. Harold the oldest thanked him and said they had pistols, horses, two packhorses with bed-rolls, and some supplies.

"Go pick up three rifles and cartridges and scabbards from John's stock. We may need them. Spud, go with them and get the food we'll need for ten days."

"Yes sir."

"I pay two dollars a day. This is my wife Liz. The other woman is Valerie Emerson, wife of Cole Emerson, the superintendent. My name is Chet. We are going looking for two of my men. We grain our horses and move."

"We understood. You have a beautiful wife, sir."

"Not sir. Chet. And yes I do and she works too."

"I will get that right too. We are honored to ride with you — Chet."

"You may not be so happy later. We will see."

Spud needed an extra packhorse to carry all the supplies. John fixed them up, and

Chet told him to send the bill to the main house and he'd pay it when he got home. That suited the tall trader.

They made the next station west by mid-afternoon. Clyde Covington came out, met them, and shook hands with his crew. Took his hat off and shouted to Iris she had real company. The woman rushed out to hug Liz, Valerie, and Chet too.

"Well, the first buckboard came by here and went. Will there be more?" Iris asked.

"They will be coming on a regular schedule. The company has bought six used stagecoaches and are having them gone over in San Antonio before they start this way. It will be next spring before we begin our passenger business."

"You two women come inside. Those men always have something to talk about," Iris said, beckoning to Liz and Val.

Alone, Chet asked Clyde if he knew any more about Jesus and Spencer.

"I heard they were tracking them northeast. Rumors had it they had a shoot-out up there and they gunned down one of the raiders. But four more got away. I think they are headed for the Colorado gold country. That four-state country north of here is real tough. People say there are tribes of little people hiding up there and it ain't no place to go. The Navajos avoid it. There's some gold up there too."

"They shot one and the other four ran away?" Chet asked.

"That was pretty straight information."

"I have a man with me. His name's Harold Be-Good. John hired him for me. I want you to tell him what you learned since he might know that country."

"Sure . . . I've met him. How did you hire him?"

"John spoke to him for me. I only met him last night, but those three brothers can find my men."

"They are well regarded in their tribe."

"John spoke of them as good trackers and the right men to look for mine."

"Harold, Clyde says he heard about a shoot-out where one of the outlaws was shot."

"That happened at Pinon Mountain?" Harold asked him.

Clyde nodded. "It happened four days ago."

"I didn't know the officers' names. But yes, the men who ran them off said they were U.S. Marshals and the men they came to arrest had a shoot-out with them."

"How far away did that happen?"

"A good day's ride away."

"We will get up early and ride up there."

"Sure. I am sorry . . . I didn't think they could have been your men."

"No problem. They can't be too far away then."

Harold agreed and they went to eat Iris's food.

"You learn something?" Liz asked quietly at the table.

"Clyde thinks my men had a shoot-out at the Pinon Mountain Trading Post a few days ago. One of the outlaws was shot and the other four escaped."

"Then our men may be all right?"

"We can hope so, but there is no doubt they are in pursuit and may need our help."

"What is up there?" Liz asked Harold.

"Maybe Durango."

"That's in Colorado," Chet added.

"Is it far away?" she asked Harold.

The Navajo nodded.

"How can Valerie get back to Center Point?" Liz asked Clyde.

"My sons are well-mannered men. They know how to defend themselves and the lady too."

"Val, what do you think?" Liz asked her.

"I hate to be a burden, but I would like to get back to my son and home at Center Point."

Chet agreed. "The boys can get you home in a day and a half. They can use fresh teams at the next station."

"That would be great."

He nodded. "Find Liz a horse and saddle. She can go north with us."

"Thank you. Cole may kill me. But it was fun, Liz, even if we missed the grand start." They hugged each other.

The next morning Chet rode north with his posse and reached the isolated trading post with the setting sun a fiery ball in the west. Harold rode up to the log post's door and dismounted. An old Indian came out and hugged him.

"Chet, this is Robert Nelson. He runs this store. He said your men left here two days ago to chase down the four remaining outlaws who tried to rob him. The marshals rode in while the robbery was in progress and they had a shoot-out. Four of the outlaws escaped and rode north. Your men went after them."

"Were any of the lawmen shot?"

The old man shook his head. "Those bandits couldn't hit a fat bull in the ass. They ran like rats from a brush fire."

"They were going to rob you?" Chet asked the man.

"They tried but men arrived, now I know

yours, and told them to surrender. They said, 'Hell no.' There was lots of gun smoke inside and they ran out shooting and got on their horses and run away. One man was shot dead. The Navajo tribal police came later and they went after them too. I had to have some boys bury the dead one."

"We need to water our horses. We have feed for them. Do you have enough food to feed us?"

"Yes."

"I will pay you."

"*Gracias.* Your men paid me. The Indian police had no *dinero.*"

The meal was mutton. Chet managed to eat it but thought it tasted like wool that smelled. Liz tried not to laugh at the faces he made eating it. They made camp later, on the ground, to sleep for a few hours. They cooked oatmeal for their breakfast before dawn and rode on north before the sun pinked the horizon in the east.

The day dragged on. They crossed a very weak stream where they were able to refill their canteens and the horses were able to drink their fill. Chet saw little change in the orange and red barren hill country studded with dusty boughs of juniper brush. They rode after the easy-to-see horse tracks winding north through knobs that studded the country. In Chet's appraisal, a goat would starve in this part of the desert.

How far must they go to find them?

CHAPTER 10

Some quail roosters greeted the first light of the sun pinking the night-cooled air. A joint effort was made to build a fire for coffee and more cooked oatmeal — Spud headed the team. The brothers also saddled and packed the horses. The animals ate corn from nosebags and switched their tails while Chet and his crew ate their breakfast. Then dishes were rinsed and packed. They remounted and moved out in a long trot to try and catch up with his men, who were he hoped not too far ahead.

Mid-morning, Harold said he heard distant shots. Chet agreed and they galloped their horses with Liz coming in the rear in case they rode into a war zone.

At last, on a ridge, Chet could see the smoke from gun muzzles. The steep slope headed toward a ranch headquarters and corrals. The outlaws, Chet thought, must be in the ranch buildings, and he hoped it was his men and the Indian police that were surrounding them.

"Stay back," he said to Liz. "Stop at the next flat on the hillside. We will hobble our horses there. That's out of gun range. You stay with them."

He dismounted on the flat and heard more shots. Quickly he hobbled his horse and then drew his rifle from the scabbard. He saw someone wave a familiar gray hat from the ring.

"That's Jesus," Liz said, swinging out of the saddle lithely. "It is him."

Chet hugged and kissed her. "He looks damn good too. Stay here. Men, grab your rifles and spread out. They need some reinforcement down there."

Spud went left as they jumped downhill, going from place to place. The three hired Navajos were parallel with him. They all scrambled when they hit loose gravel, and in places some of them slid on their butts but recovered fast.

Before reaching gun range they halted and spread out. Chet moved toward Jesus, who was coming to meet him.

"Hey, Chet. How good to see you."

"You and Spencer all right?"

"We are fine. It has been a long trip, but now, along with the Navajo police, they are surrounded. We found them this morning. We ran off their horses first thing so they couldn't get away again. But they won't give up."

"They have any hostages in those buildings?"

"I don't think so. The two Indian police thought that they killed whoever lived here when they took over the ranch. They know they will hang for that and won't surrender. I think we will have to do that job of hanging them."

"Who is the Indian police in charge?"

Jesus pointed to a man standing off to the left. "Sergeant Bull Horse."

"Let's talk to him." Chet got his attention and waved for him to come over.

They met the big Indian in charge, and the officer thanked him for coming. Chet explained he was a U.S. Marshal there to help.

"These are your men?"

"Yes, they are."

"They are good lawmen and I appreciate them trying not to kill, but the bad ones say they will die in there. They won't surrender."

"Let's heat things up if you think the owners are dead. We can burn them out."

"How?"

"Flaming arrows. Harold, we need some flaming arrows."

"Let me find a bow or a thing we can use." He turned to his brothers. "You two find some arrows."

His brothers frowned at his request.

"We need a fire. Build one. Go look in the barn from the back side."

The two laughed and ducked when two shots from the house barked. Then they ran over and tore some of the siding from the barn. They soon came out empty-handed of a bow and shook their head. No such items in the barn from their disappointed faces.

Harold told them, "Make torches and throw them at the house roof."

Spencer came around the side of the house and had joined them. "Good to see you, Chet."

"Better for me to see you and Jesus. When one of you boys gets a fire started, go get my wife off the mountain safely and situate her west on that flat ground. The rest of us can throw flaming torches on that roof. This will soon be over."

The fire started, the younger brother went to take Liz off the mountainside. They used the shed as cover from which to hurl flaming boards over it and onto the cedar shingles. The ranch house soon burst into flames and Chet told them to shoot to kill if the outlaws came out armed.

The posse set on their knees, rifles aimed. The small house was being consumed when a choking man, pistol armed, charged out the door. Rifle bullets cut him down on the porch, and he fell facedown with his vest on fire.

Two more shots inside made Chet believe they were suicide intended. The blazing roof collapsed and aside from the cracking fire — it was over.

He handed Jesus his rifle and went to hug his sad-looking wife coming to join them.

Liz in his arms, he cleared his throat. "They decided that was their way out."

"Hold me. After all this business I am shaking inside worse than outside."

"I can do that. It has been a hard push by all of us to run down this worthless trash. I am taking you back to Preskitt and go find that bastard Hall. He hired them and the others."

"Why can't we live on the ranch and ignore them?"

He held her tighter in his arms. "Because if we don't stop them, they will hurt more innocent people."

"I will try to understand your concern. I don't want to lose you. I lost one man. I don't think I could live without you, Chet Byrnes. So think about me."

He felt her wet tears soak into his shirt and closed his eyes tighter to hold his own back.

CHAPTER 11

The sun came up while Chet sat on the porch swing and sipped hot coffee at the Preskitt Valley house. Hampt had sent him word that Hall never showed up at Mormon Lake, and despite his efforts to find out about any source no one knew anything about him. Had the gang done their work would he have been there to pay them? Probably not.

Hall's activities to suppress the stage line operating hardly proved expensive, no more than the dummies following his orders received. There was a threat he had tougher enforcers coming. Curly Bill Snow's name came up again. The Chief Territorial U.S. Marshal had sent Chet a page about Snow's criminal past and said his whereabouts were unknown.

Snow was reported to be a hired gun and suspected in several murders of prominent Texas businessmen and ranchers who were killed for the money paid to him to exterminate them. Tying him to the crimes had proved hard, because Snow's lawyers were the best money could buy and they out-talked the local prosecutors. Of course, Snow could slip into a territory unreported, eliminate someone, slip away to Mexico, and spend the blood money on *putas* and a good time.

There had to be a way to find him. Had Hannagen, in Gallup, told him all he really knew about competition for the mail run he beat out to get that contract? He wondered. The cool soft wind swept his clean-shaven face and a house wren scolded him.

Someone was coming from the west side of the ranch buildings and pens. Raphael removed his *sombrero* and smiled in the still gray light at Chet.

"I always want to call you *Patrón.* I know better but for so long in my life I called the main man my *patrón.* You look like a man in deep thought about something in your life. May I join you?"

"Of course. You find sleeping in hard?"

"Habit, they say. I like to check things before the day begins. Anything undone can show up. What needs repair is exposed. What needs new paint? What shingle is broken and how attentive my men are about

162

the ranch."

"I know you still have guards at night."

"Oh, *sí*. I just sent them to bed for an hour or so. It has been years since anyone dared even try us."

"Until I solve the matter up north, tell them to be careful. They may be challenged."

"I can do that quietly."

"Good. There should be enough bulls for you coming from our own herd this year. I know you like the shorthorns, but we can cross your roan longhorns with our Camp Verde Herefords and get bigger calves."

"Those cattle down there — I have been there to see them with Tom. They are *grande,* and I won't mind breeding them to the ranch cows."

"Raphael, not that I am planning this, but it needs thinking on. Will you have a special man, someday, to replace you? I don't think you are too old or puny to run this ranch, but when you do choose to stop all this, I want you to have a *segundo* ready to replace you."

He nodded thoughtfully.

"Now tell me what I need to do for you?"

"Oh, Chet, I have no needs not filled. I love your heading the ranch. I need something, you send me to buy it. You trust in me, and I hope I live up to that trust."

"Raphael, you are like a father I never had. Keep doing it your way. I don't know how to make it run better. The *frijoles* you raise here feed not only all of our ranches but also the poor in your church."

"I am proud of that too. So many people eat off that small acreage we raise each year."

"I need to go back to help Cole. Elizabeth plans on staying here. Jesus and Spencer are helping patrol the stage line. Of Jesus, do you know why Anita will not marry him?"

"I have no idea. She speaks well of him."

"If he ever wakes up and decides she really does not ever want to be his wife — she may lose him."

"Some women never know what they should do."

"Sí."

Chet rose, downed the last of his coffee. "God be with you, *mi amigo.*"

"And with you, *patrón.* I will burn candles at my church for your safe return."

CHAPTER 12

When Chet and Spud arrived at Center Point headquarters, he saw Lucy Byrnes talking to Valerie and his son Rocky. Lucy looked further advanced in her pregnancy.

"There is the boss himself now," Valerie announced.

He hugged Lucy carefully and kissed her cheek, then Valerie's as well, before he hoisted Rocky up in his arms. "What brings you over here?"

Lucy smiled. "I got a letter to meet Shawn here."

"I understood he was coming up here. He has Ratchet trained to do his job down there."

With a wry look on her face, she shook her head. "I really look spiffy, don't I, to meet a suitor?"

"Lucy, I want you to be happy. We go back to lots of things and times. You are like a daughter to me, both of you women."

"I felt a little silly, but we have written about all these issues in letters. I think Shawn is very sincere and I know one should wait a few years before they remarry, but we decided the baby in me is no obstacle and he or she, like her sister, needs a father too."

"I am sure not questioning him or you. But my wife will want a festive event. Please her. She is a generous person and very sincere."

"I won't disappoint her. The ranch is secure out there. Our hay is stacked and we have a good calf crop. Drew is working hard for Cole, and they are making it work. I think he wants to do that — run the west end for Cole."

"We can work it out. Are those two ever getting married — your sister and him?"

She nodded. "I think it is set."

"No one drove you down there?"

She shook her head. "I made it fine over here. I can drive over to Preskitt no problem."

"I want a driver to take you. Let me do that?"

"That would be a big job."

"I have some men that can do this. I will find you one. Drive you down to Robert's and next day drive to Camp Verde and stay with Victor and Rhea at the big house. Then drive up to Liz's house."

"I have to have a driver?"

"Yes. I have enemies."

"Don't try to argue with him," Valerie said. "She will be at my house until you find a driver for tomorrow."

He talked to his son, set him down, and went on. Spud had his horse and his own to put up.

When he joined him, Spud said, "She is pretty pregnant, isn't she?"

"Yes. She didn't deserve Reg committing suicide, especially since he knew she was expecting."

"You know folks who do that never think about anyone else but themselves."

"Right. I forgot to ask if Cole was here." Chet looked around for him.

Spud laughed. "Cole Emerson would have already been here if he knew you were here."

"Oh, he's not that way."

"I didn't mean it like that. Cole is your right arm and he likes that position. Like you and Jesus, you three are near to what I call attached people."

"You feel that way?"

Spud gave him a grin and a nod. "It is damn sure growing on me."

"Good. We may see lots more of each

167

other. Let's go check on some food."

The head cook, Lucifer Nigh, came out and greeted him. "Well, the real boss is here. What do you two want to eat?"

"Anything but mutton stew."

He laughed and readjusted his white apron. "They told me not to feed you that. I have some good ham, and I bought some yams from a local man. That suit you two?"

"Fine."

"Cole should be back any time. They had some more trouble on the east side with more holdup men two days ago. But Buck Howard, one of the drivers, blew two of them away with his twelve-gauge shotgun. Cole kinda figured that might quiet them down. I'll get your food . . . you two have a seat. Briley, get the boss man some coffee and his guard some too."

"Aye, sir."

"They must be completing construction here. Lots less pounding and sawing going on today."

Spud agreed. "What're we going to do?"

"Whatever Cole needs us to check on. I bet he has work we can handle."

Spud nodded as their food arrived.

After lunch with all the staff out of pocket, Chet went and took a *siesta* at the cabin that had been built for him and Liz. Things sounded pretty quiet, and he wondered why he even came up there when he was awoken by a knock.

"Chet. Chet, you in there?" It was Jesus's voice.

"Coming." At the door he let Jesus, Spud, and Spencer into his living room. "What's wrong?"

"They struck another driver," Jesus said. "They killed him and shot the horses."

"Get some packhorses and supplies. We better go find the killers. Where did it happen?"

"Over near number three. Clyde sent a Navajo boy with the news. Here is the letter he sent."

Chet read the note. "Anyone know this Billy Green the driver?"

The men shook their head.

"We need to find out if he has a wife, family. I better go check with Valerie and see if she knows."

He met her coming across the yard.

"What's wrong?"

"They murdered a driver over east. I am going to take the men and run them down. His name was Billy Green."

"He was a new man. Cole may know about him. I expect him back tonight. I am glad you are here to handle this."

"We will run them down. Keep your security here on the guard. We're all are under attack."

"Yes. May I ask you a personal question?"

"Sure. What is it?"

"Lucy doesn't want a driver to take her south. What can I do?"

"Insist. Anything can happen. We have no idea about who the enemy are or where they will hit. Want me to handle it?"

"No. I will. You be careful. I love you, Chet Byrnes, and you are so important to all of us. You understand I owe you my life for putting me on that stage to Preskitt that day in Tombstone when my life was hanging on by a thread. Now I have Cole and Rocky, and thank God to you for all of it."

He hugged her. "Insist she has a driver going down there. I'll handle this holdup deal. Tell Cole to double his guard."

"I repeat — do be careful."

"Done." He hurried off to the livery area to get ready to ride out. He knew Valerie was a sincere person since they sent her north to help Jenn in her café. Both Valerie and Jenn's daughter — JD's wife, Bonnie — were wild young girls at the time, gone down to get rich working in a brothel. Valerie could not stand the situation and went to work in a café — lost in the wild mining town. He recalled sending her to Jenn, who needed the help and offered her a respectable place to work. Cole later courted her and they married. Good for both of them.

Chet, Spud, Jesus, and Spencer saddled up and, with loaded packhorses, rode east before Cole made it back. It would be over a day's travel to reach the station, but they'd make part of the way there before sundown. The four-man team felt they would run these killers into the ground in a few days. Maybe others would be ready to quit their killing, raiding, and trying to stop the mail run if these ones were made an example of.

In a day and a half they were at Clyde Covington's stop. The fresh grave had a cross on it not far from the stage stop. Grim-faced Clyde met them.

"The Navajo boys said there were four or five men who killed him. One of the killers was riding a mule. Don't ask me. The boys said it."

"You see anyone riding a mule who came by here?" Chet asked, dismounting and shaking his hand.

"No. But those boys can track and they said there was one at the death site."

"No idea who did it?"

Clyde shook his head. "He didn't come in

on schedule so I sent some boys to find out if he broke down. They came back and said they found him shot . . . him and the horses too. Probably the only way to stop him."

"The mail gone?"

"Yes."

"Water our horses and maybe one of those Navajo boys of yours will show us the site. We have some hours of daylight left to track them."

Clyde spoke to one of his men, "Black Hat, go get a horse for you and me."

Turning to his wife, who was standing there, he leaned forward, kissed her cheek, and said, "Sorry, Iris, but I am going with them to show them the site."

"I understand. I hope you run them down, Chet Byrnes," she said as they all mounted up.

Chet waved that he heard her and rode on to the windmill tank to water his mount. There he dismounted and introduced himself to Black Hat, Clyde's man.

"You think they are still in the country?"

"I am not certain. We never saw them. From what we could see of the tracks, they stopped the driver and killed him and the horses. Then they fled I think."

Chet nodded that he understood. "But they came from somewhere, and robbing mail is not very profitable — opening all those letters for any money."

The Navajo nodded. "I have heard they have many men coming to stop the mail run."

"From Texas?"

"Maybe."

Chet nodded. "Wherever they can hire them from, I'd bet."

Black Hat agreed.

Everyone mounted again, and with Black Hat in the lead, they rode out. A flock of bold buzzards half rose when they approached the attack site. The birds were feasting on the dead horses with many of them simply walking around to avoid contact but not flying off in their brash ways.

Spud quickly agreed with Jesus that there had been a shod mule there. The raiders had ridden north into more of the Four Corners country, bringing back the memory of those other outlaws, inside the flaming cabin, the shots still ringing in Chet's ears.

Where would this chase end? No telling.

There was no reason to stay here. Killing the horses was a cruel exercise to show how mean these men were or thought they were. Western people didn't slaughter horses. They rode them — cared for them — more than folks cared for their dogs. These were warped-minded individuals, worse than border bandits. Worse than Apache warriors and their acts of war. He led the way from the site.

"Jesus, are we two days behind them?"

"Yes."

"Let's trot and find them before they kill someone else."

The others agreed.

They found where the outlaws made camp in a canyon their first night. Jesus said, when they searched it, there had been four men and a woman. He pointed out her smaller moccasin tracks.

"She does the cooking. All those prints around the fire ring are mostly hers. They probably left before dawn and rode north some more from the tracks leaving out."

"Fire's working," Spud said, getting off his knees from the blazing pile of dry wood and standing up.

"Put the grill on it. This is the coffee water." Jesus handed him the pot. "We'll cook the beans in the other pot."

"I'll get it right," Spud said. Chet smothered a laugh over hearing the directions Jesus gave his helper.

He went off to begin a letter to Liz before the sun went down and he had no light.

Dear Liz,

We found their first camp — the horse killers. You would have hated that scene. Real men don't slaughter good horses. I'd never even have thought about that in my life. It was really bad to see how those great matched geldings had been slaughtered. Tomorrow we will pick up their trail and one day ride up on them. There is always a conclusion to these chases and the bad are in the end stopped. How many days away can that be? I have no idea. But we will track them down. I will close now and write more later. The sun has slid away.

I love you, darling —

"Beans are about done, Chet," Spud said.

"I'll put this in my saddlebags and join you all."

"You've been awful quiet all day. I guess you miss her not being here with you."

"Oh, we've been apart before. She spoils me I guess."

"I thought so too. But she is one great woman — your wife. But, hell, you know that too."

"Thanks, Spud."

"I don't mind doing all this. I have all of you. I been in places I had no one. Nothing to eat or drink for days and then it was garbage. I do appreciate this job. And I am not bragging either. I will do this as long as we need and maybe we can catch them in a few days."

Chet hoped so too while eating the brown beans. But two days later they were deeper into the Four Corners badlands and still tracking a day or so behind them.

Jesus had scouted ahead of the main party that day and came back in late afternoon on a sweaty horse. "They are camped at a well about three miles north of here. They are resting, thinking and acting like they have no one on their tail. We can surround them tonight and wake them up with our guns in their faces."

Everyone agreed to the plan. Chet felt much better with their capture close at hand at last.

For supper they ate dry beef jerky and drank canteen water while they rode under the night sky until they were close enough to the camp. On Jesus's command they stopped. He quietly gave them a description of the campsite, over the hill, which was sparsely clad in juniper bushes. Dismounted, they hobbled their horses and, under the stars, quietly went armed, with rifles, to arrest the killers.

Chet made his men shed their spurs and chaps. The metallic ring might signal the bad guys and the chaps might hinder any chase they could need to do on foot.

The deep sage smell of the cool dawn in his nose and Winchester in his hands, Chet set out to arrest the band of men. The slow quiet climb and descent off the mountain would put them all in place. On a picket line the gangs' horses complained some. One pony kicked another and a squeal went up that made Chet and his men moving like shadows hesitate — but no one stirred in their bedrolls, and they went on until — before the pink of dawn cracked the eastern horizon — everyone was in place as planned.

An unaware man in his underwear sat up and began cussing. "Get your lazy ass out of bed and get to cooking some food and coffee."

Chet stepped forward. There was enough light, by then, for him to order all the men to put their hands up. "You're all under arrest. Anyone moves for or draws a gun will be shot. I have a large posse with me, so get your hands in the air."

A protest groan came from the gang members. His rifle set aside by then, Chet fired a round of his .45 in the air. "You want to die out here, just make a move for a gun."

They stumbled around half-dressed while Spud and Jesus handcuffed them in pairs. The woman with them looked to be a teen. In the bright sunlight, she appeared dirty and her brown hair greasy. Dressed like a boy, she seemed fear-struck, but still Chet made her sit on the ground until all the gang was handcuffed and seated too.

"Jesus, you need her to start breakfast?"

"I can use a hand."

"Get up, young lady, and help him."

"What the hell am I supposed to do?" She made an angry face at him.

"You want to be handcuffed with the men?"

"No — no sir."

"Then listen to what he tells you." He had no time to baby her. "Spud, take one of their horses and go get ours. They just need to be unhobbled and bring them over here. Then we will decide how to get these killers to Preskitt."

"We aren't taking them to Horse Head Crossing?" Spencer Horne asked.

"No. They need to be incarcerated in the Yavapai County Jail. This will be a murder and robbery trial to draw attention to others that you can't rob and kill stage drivers and horses on the new line and get away with it. Let's start with the first one in your line. What's your name?"

"Me?" the bucktoothed redheaded teen asked.

"He ain't talking to anyone else, stupid," Spencer told him with a poke from his rifle barrel in the belly.

"Jerry Van Dame."

Chet wrote it down. "How old are you?"

"Seventeen."

"Next."

"Give the man your name," Spencer told the short man in his thirties.

"John Smith."

"He asked you for your name not your alias."

"Thurber Holland."

"Better. How old are you?"

"Thirty-two."

The next prisoner was a lean cowboy. He had bowed legs and was standing in his gray long handles. He gave his name as Slim Eubanks, his age as twenty-three.

The big last man wore a black beard and a head of too-long curly black hair, obviously was blind in his left white eye, and called himself Wolf Rotenberg. He said he was thirty-five. Finishing his list, Chet felt certain many of them were wanted in other places for previous crimes. That meant nothing. He had the stage holdup gang that shot and killed a man, the horses, plus stole the mailbag.

"Now stay seated on the ground. If you make a break for it we will shoot you. Any form of threat to my posse men will get your teeth bashed in. I have little qualms about you or your lives, so remember that. Any infraction of my rules or disobedience will get you bruises and death.

"What did you find in the mail?"

The redheaded kid laughed. "Fourteen dollars and seventy-five cents."

"That all?"

"Yeah."

"What did Hall pay you to do that?"

No one said a word.

"Rotenberg? What did he pay you and all the others?"

"A few bucks apiece is all." He shrugged as if that was nothing to him.

"Where did you meet the man hired you?"

"Saint Johns in a saloon."

"I say you are lying to your men about that amount he paid you to do this."

"How the hell would you know?"

"Because he paid others that he hired, like you, twenty bucks apiece for drinks and a treatment at a house of ill repute."

"Ha," Slim said. "Did he pay you that

much money for each of us, Rotenberg?"

"I got each of you a bottle of whiskey and a woman . . . you'd had none of that if I hadn't got it for you."

"Did you also collect the hundred dollars apiece for each man from him after the guard was murdered?"

"I don't know what you're talking about," the big man muttered.

"You must have met Hall after the robbery and collected that hundred dollars a man on your team and pocketed it. His pants are over there by his bedroll. Spencer, check them for the money."

"That's my business."

"Stay put or else."

Rotenberg obeyed and Spencer soon came up with the cash and showed the money to his crew. "You boys were cheated. He collected it like the boss said he did."

The girl, busy bent over the fire and stirring the oatmeal with a large wooden spoon, said, "Look in his gawdamn boots right there. He's got more in them."

"Bitch. You shut your mouth or I'll stop it for you."

She shook her head and glared back at him. "No, you won't 'cause they're going to hang you by your bull neck till you are dead. And I'll be there to laugh and clap 'cause you ain't going to beat me up ever again."

"You better shut your mouth, bitch. I ain't hung yet."

Chet took immediate offense at his threat. "Rotenberg, I can gag you and will if you threaten her one more time." He meant what he said, and would do it to the outlaw if he persisted.

Spencer held up the money. "Chet, there is well over eight hundred dollars, counting the money in his boots."

Chet nodded at his discovery. "Split three ways with you deputies that might be enough money for Jesus to marry Anita when we get back."

Jesus looked at the sky for God's help, then continued pouring coffee into tin cups set out on the ground. "It isn't money keeps me from getting married to her. She won't agree when to do it."

They all laughed.

They'd saved Spud some oatmeal to eat when he brought back their horses. The outlaws were fully dressed by then; their horses were saddled with bedrolls tied on.

The girl, Lisa Foster, was the one who had been riding the mule, and she never complained nor said much of anything. She kept herself private, and that suited Chet. It would be a long trip back to Center Point, where he could put the prisoners in a buckboard and take them back to Preskitt. He with his crew would be at least a week completing that.

He continued the letter to his wife:

Yesterday we made lots of miles. At dawn today we captured them. The young woman Lisa claims that Rotenberg never married her. He kidnapped her in Texas somewhere and she had been his "common-wife" since then. She said her parents would not take her back — she feels very certain about that so that is not an option.

I want you to meet this female. Her name is Lisa Foster. She needs some habits corrected like her cussing and personal habits like not brushing her hair, but she is neither stupid nor dumb. I know I can find more orphans quicker than anyone else, but I believe in a few months she could be transformed into a worthy person under your guidance. I am now, slowly, making my way back to you.

He could only imagine the two of them meeting when he brought her by the ranch to introduce her. Oil and water or a cat-and-dog deal. Someone would be treed. But in the end, his wife would win and save this girl from a life of prostitution and bad treatment at the hands of worthless men. Time would only tell.

His crew kept the scowling leader handcuffed by himself. Each time he dismounted, one of them — Jesus or Spencer — unlocked the cuffs from the saddle horn and let him dismount. Time and again, Chet pointed out they had a savage tiger and if he ever saw even a slim chance to escape — he'd use it. So the two took turns making him their only responsibility for the day.

Lisa and Spud did the cooking and camp chores. The outlaws chopped wood and gathered it, watered and put feedbags on the horses, all under supervision, but the trustee jobs carried a strict sentence for disobedience. They would ride belly-down over a saddle for every day left in the trip. That threat was enough to make sterling help out of them.

The crew at Center Point had word from a buckboard driver who had passed Chet and his group that they had found the killers of their partner driver and were bringing them in. Two bugle players in a company buckboard met them and escorted them up the dirt main street, past the log stores and shops — all one dozen or so. Reservation

Indians, buckskin-dressed teamsters, and shopping women all stood at attention when the American flag went by them and the song "My Country 'Tis of Thee" was sung and the horns accompanied them.

Cole was dressed up and had on a new blue silk kerchief around his neck and a white starched shirt.

When Chet stepped down, Valerie ran in and kissed his cheek and, almost out of breath, she said, "Don't send a boy when you need a man for a job. God bless you again, Chet Byrnes."

The crowd applauded and Chet held his hands up to stop them. "Not for me but clap for the three great U.S. Marshals with me who brought these killers in to stand trial for the murder of Billy Green, our employee and a good man. Bow your heads please.

"Dear Lord. We are grateful for your protection of us on this long trek to capture these outlaws and return here. And, Lord, please continue to protect our men and women so busy making this stage business work. Thanks for the food we eat, the rain that quenches the earth's fever, and being in all our hearts as we ride the long trail of life. Amen."

"Amen," came his chorus.

Valerie clutched his arm and Cole's too to lead them to the tables all set up. "Take a seat, gentlemen. The help will feed you and I will return. The rest can fill their plates in line. Guards are watching your prisoners. Your men will be seated with you. What about the woman you brought in?"

"Lisa. She's helped Jesus and Spud cook. It is a long story. But she holds up her part."

"May I bathe her and find her some clothing after the banquet?"

"You certainly may. I see Rocky is coming with his babysitter."

"Your son asked me if Stella, the young girl I hired, could be his wife since he had none like you and Cole had."

They all laughed. When his son was climbing on his lap, he stopped and said to his dad, "Find a place for Stella. She needs to eat too."

"There is room on our bench for her," Jesus said. "That all right?"

"Yes, but you can't have her. She is mine."

Chet shook his head. They weren't getting his son's new wife regardless.

"Her name is Stella Riviera. She is his nanny and just came to work with us."

Everyone gave her a bow of their heads.

Valerie rose. "That young lady's name is Lisa. Guys, make room for her too."

186

They did. She sat down. "I know Liz has no idea about this girl." She lowered her voice. "But I will clean her up more tonight. She was very polite to me and we brushed her hair some."

"I think she can be a part of society. She needs some breaks and she is smart enough to take them."

Valerie nodded. "She said she rode a mule?"

"Her captor, I think, gave her that mule so she couldn't outrun his horse trying to escape."

"She tell you that?"

"Didn't need to. She held a slave's position in that camp before we arrested them."

"She's a child."

"Like two girls not much older who ran off to Tombstone, huh?"

"I believe she's smarter than we were back then. She was forced. We weren't."

"Not much difference."

"Just put her on a stage and send her to someone like Jenn. You know both those women you brought back from that horse rustler roundup are married and living a good life."

"I did something right then, huh?"

Cole heard him and leaned over. "Chet, you've been doing good things for years and

Val's my prize from all of that."

"Good. I think we have it all handled up here, so in two more nights, I can sleep in my own bed in my own house with my own wife."

CHAPTER 13

Chet and his crew finally reached home. Liz was out on the porch waiting to greet him. After hugs all around, the boys went their way and he went for a bath and private time with Liz.

When he finally came downstairs again, his foreman took him aside. "You were successful in capturing the murderers. Now what must you do?"

"Find the man who hired them. His name is Hall. Sometimes Anson, other times Gerald. He moves around a lot, hires these unemployed cowboys to do his dirty work, and tries to stop the stage line's delivery. I guess to secure the mail contract."

"How will you catch him?"

"I need a better idea how he goes around to all these places."

"On horseback?"

"Maybe. I know he has been to all of our stations asking questions. Some never knew who he was when he went by there, just that he was a man interested."

"Like a shifty ghost, huh?"

Chet smiled. "I will get him in the end, but I need the end to be now."

Raphael nodded. "This woman Lucy is going to have another baby by Reg?"

"Yes, and she told me that Reg knew it."

His foreman made a sad face. "And he did what he did anyhow?"

"We don't know all the answers. We never will, but I considered it as wrong, if only for that reason alone."

"*Sí, mi amigo.* A baby."

"What a sad thing. We, the living, must continue our lives. Lucy is a strong woman, and she and Shawn will have a good life. They are getting married soon. Here at the ranch. The women will be arranging it, and you know how Liz loves to do these things."

"You always find and fix the lost. That cowboy Hampt, he was lost when you hired him too. Now people seek him out to learn his secrets about his farming. He makes hay so much easier than any other man. Victor came and talked to him. Then Victor told me it went back to the seeding of the alfalfa. He is replacing the old fields in this way and I have seen them — they yield twice as much as they did before. How could a cowboy like Hampt figure that out?"

"He knew nothing, so he had no bad habits. He started like the replants and did them right."

The man shook his gray-topped head. "Sometime get him to explain it again to you and then you to me."

"I know the story. There is a powder available that you put on the seed when you first plant it. That is the secret. You can't add it later. It must cover the seed and then they can live in harmony."

"I think I understand."

Back in the kitchen Chet sat with Liz and Monica having coffee.

"I heard all about the big welcome ceremony at Center Point. The new girl Lisa said she cried it was so touching."

"I think she must have been raised in the backwoods of Texas somewhere."

"Probably, but she reads and writes. I have to admit that Wolf whoever must have treated her very badly, but he never reached her soul no matter the battering she took from him and his nasty animal abuse."

"Good. I saw the same thing."

Seeing that the ranch was in good order, Chet decided to go see Hampt and see what was happening there, perhaps even ride to some of the other places to check them out as well.

He checked with Liz to see if she wanted to come along, but she decided to stay at the homeplace. He would be back soon.

In the cool predawn of the next day, he saddled the big gray horse JD caught on the desert ranch for him. The challenge of, again, riding the high-headed big horse made him aware of how to approach the wild desert mount. Jamming a boot-toe into the stirrup, he quickly swung his chap-coated leg across the cantle. He had to find the other stirrup before this devil from the wild beyond leaped off into Satan's arms for a helluva bucking contest.

The fight began immediately. Chet knew when the gray surged into the air off his hind legs he was headed for the fluffy cloud formation passing over the mountains at that moment. The devil came back down on his front legs and kicking his hind ones, each jump feeling like a paddle-wheel boat reel landing high on Chet's shoulder blades. The jars to the ground piled his body down to the base of his spine and reduced his height two inches. The only saving thing about the whole event had been the horse headed for the open gate trying to discharge his passenger en route. The white-painted board fencing lining both sides kept him from deviating from his course, so the straightaway charge made him easier to ride.

Not any less pain filled . . . there were things like jerking his head up with the bridle that suppressed the height of the next explosion the horse tried. They passed under the crossbar that held the Quarter Circle Bar Z brand sign overhead. But despite it being high enough to clear a high-stacked hay wagon, Chet could read it real plain, at near eye level. When he hit the road going east to the north-to-south route, the gray flapped his body around in crow hops. Chet began pouring steel rowels to his sides at every jump to punish him for bucking. He cross-whipped him with the long reins to pain his belly too. *Run, you devil . . . I'm still in this saddle and you ain't tough enough to pitch me off — so far.*

They raced past the scattered pines and flew by farm vehicles on the main road no doubt headed for some business in town. In congested places he swung the gray through and around them to let him run. His speed was so fast he knew few horses large or small could match the fleetness on the dirt ruts his hooves ate up. Soon it became the animal's awesome strength that propelled him.

With the wind almost burning his eyes, he bent low speaking to the horse most of the time out loud. "Go man go. Today you could have won that new race called the Kentucky Derby, but you never would have gotten out of the gates for a fair run at it, with all that bucking you did."

Chet had never seen a Kentucky horse-race, but he'd seen plenty of dirt-track horseraces in Texas. People led great horses, ugly horses, and others there to compete.

One Saturday morning, as a youth, he saw a farm boy in overalls ride up on a gaunt-looking bay horse to the track west of Kerrville. He drew a few laughs and they teased him how he ought to fill that greyhound out with some more feed. No one knew him or the horse. But they were getting up the bets with a field of five horses to make the long track run.

"I ain't got but twenty dollars . . . would that get me in the race?"

Sam Finney said, "Son, that horse won't get out the gates let alone run the whole track. You can get in but you will look funny coming in tomorrow morning to the finish line."

They laughed. Red Horace didn't laugh much but he laughed that morning and placed a ten-dollar bet on the bay horse against a hundred dollars if he won.

That boy bet his twenty with two guys. Chet's dad suspected there was a deal cooking. All he had was ten dollars, but he got good odds on the bay winning on that money. Chet was a boy then and he remembered it well. His paw wasn't supposed to add any more on that grocery account, and his mother expected them to bring home grocery items that she needed to feed the family.

Sitting high in the saddle on his runaway horse crossing the mountaintop, that race was as vivid in Chet's imagination as the day they ran it. They had put the bay on the outside so he didn't get in anyone else's way on the track.

The starter gun went off and they were off. Bay was last, but coming down the opening stretch, his dad elbowed him. "That damn bay is beginning to run."

Chet's hopes for their grocery money had almost evaporated. But he agreed on the second turn, the bay was running wide and halfway up the field.

He borrowed the Kline boy's field glasses and coming around the last turn, he saw that farm boy laying his whip to the bay. He never had touched that horse before. This time he was going after the three leaders.

First he passed the Rio Ranch dun, then he crept up on Spotted Horse, a good horse to bet on. Sam Finney's hot-blooded black thoroughbred Kentucky horse, Sampson, began to drop back like he had run his all, and the farm boy pushed his horse hard and he won that race by a length.

The track wasn't any quieter than the South was when Robert E. Lee signed the surrender document. Dad swore him to secrecy that day. They got the groceries and paid off the bill they'd owed at the store for years. Chet's mom never knew how it got paid but she accepted it.

Chet tried to turn the gray into the road that led to Hampt's house. Instead he flew over the wooden gate into the alfalfa. He must have cleared it by two feet, landed in the powerful sweet-smelling legume field. Chet managed to circle him around and back to the gate. Then he dismounted and led him out, closing Hampt's gate. In a circling motion he remounted his hard-breathing sweaty mount, and the gray single-footed all the way down the long lane to the two-story farmhouse set among the pines trees.

Hampt was waiting for him on the front porch.

"You're up early." Turning his head to the

house, Hampt yelled, "Ray, get out here and lead your uncle's horse around to cool him off. He rode him hard." Now looking at Chet, he asked, "Anything wrong?"

Chet shook his head to show he had no worries. "I wanted to trot. Gray wanted to run. He won the battle."

Hampt clapped him on the shoulder. "Any more trouble up north?"

"No. Just thought I'd come over and take some humps out of his back. And see how things were over here."

"I bet you had a real wild exhibition on him, cool as it was this morning." Hampt laughed out loud. His wife joined them, hearing the last, so Hampt continued talking to May. "May, he's so caught up he's breaking horses for a living these days."

May had been married to his younger brother who was shot in Kansas, by the Reynolds clan, while on a cattle drive. This is what had forced him to leave Texas over four years earlier. His brother married her to be a babysitter when his first wife died. He already had three sons and a daughter born around the time his wife died. He found and and married May, the chubby backward-acting — they thought — daughter of a rich banker family who had disowned her for marrying him. After his brother's tragic death she had a girl.

Then she came west to Arizona with the entire Byrnes family. They never knew May could play piano or sing. Even Chet's sister Susie didn't know about it. When May married Hampt he found out she sang and made her sing for everyone. She taught the children how to play the piano. Now they had a baby son and another one on the way.

Her second stepson, Ray, was going to attend an academy the next year in St. Louis to prepare him for college. He'd be the first Byrnes to ever go to college and Chet was excited about it all. As for May's family fortune, when both her parents died, Chet hired a very expensive lawyer in San Antonio to fight her exclusion from the will and won half the inheritance for her.

He was glad after the large settlement the couple stayed on and ran this ranch for the family, but in reality they could buy and own several of their own. A big stout unemployed cowboy, Hampt helped Chet carve out the Verde River Ranch from a crooked foreman the out-of-state ranch owner feared.

Chet could recall the early timid dates between May and Hampt. His sister-in-law had been very bashful and Hampt, despite his open give-'em-hell ways, turned into as quiet a suitor as she was a backward date. Hampt feared his usual manners would run her off and they might have, but when she saw his honesty and dedication he soon won her heart. She also gave him the backbone to become a foreman and a great ag man with his alfalfa.

Their story was a great one.

"You spoke about stringing a telegraph wire," Hampt said, "across the territory where there isn't one?"

"You interested?"

May brought the coffeepot over to refill their cups.

"Honey, I've asked him about the telegraph business," Hampt said.

She sat down and smiled. Prettiest smile in all the land, May could melt an iceberg with it. "Chet, we have lots of money in the bank. It only makes three percent. I told Hampt we'd follow you if you'd let us in on it or the stage business, if you'd let us."

"What if you lost it all?"

"We'd start over again."

Hampt nodded. "I know things can go belly-up, but you've been making good decisions and we kinda wanted to piggyback with you."

"This money business is a lot like quicksand. It can swallow you in a hurry. I will keep you informed of any progress I make on the deal. Right now I need a telegraph man to talk to."

"What about your stage line?"

"It isn't done yet, and they are tallying up expenses. I will tell you what I see when the paper comes out."

"We'd take part of it or both if we can get in."

"If I do you will too."

May rose, gathered up her dress some, and leaned over to kiss him on the forehead. "God bless you, Chet Byrnes. I told Hampt you were the best guy we knew. You convinced Ray to go to college. I think your brother would say the same if he could come back from his grave. You saved the family and many of our lives coming out here. You know I almost didn't come with you. Susie said to me, 'May, that damn brother of mine can do anything he sets his mind to do. In a few years he will have us expanded bigger and better than Texas.' And here we are. I have Hampt who spoils me. Children of my own now with him, and we have no bills or owe anyone."

"Nice ain't it, May? I saw this land had a future, but I never expected for things to get in shape as fast as they did for all of us."

"I know you are happy with Elizabeth, and

I love her. But do the past women in your life cross your mind very much?"

"They murdered one woman I loved. I barely recall our illicit meetings. She planned to divorce him, but I tore up that note when I found her body. I once stood holding another crying woman who could not move her parents because of their poor health. I had no idea she had Rocky in her belly, and whether she knew it or not at that time I will never know. Then my first wife, who waited for me, knowing full well I might bring a wife from Texas. My conscience got so struck I married her and she really didn't expect me to do that. Two husbands and no children and bang we had one — a son that was already born and came to us. May, I always had a strong foreboding feeling about her horses. Even this morning when Gray jumped the field gate instead of reining into your lane — I remember her jumping. She loved it so much I could not deny her that one passion. I lost her and about lost my own way."

"You found Elizabeth."

Chet nodded. Smiling, he said, "Did you wake up one day and see your husband as the neatest guy who ever held you in his arms?"

"Yes, he came to the big ranch house one

day on the Verde. Oh, I had kissed him a time or two but they were small 'thank you for putting up with me' kisses. I was upstairs making beds in the big house on the Verde and saw him dismount his horse at the backyard gate and come up through that great garden and said to myself — that big rascal is coming to propose to me. I threw down the sheet, ran down the stairs, met him at the back door, and we really kissed. I mean he kissed me so hard I swooned and got out of breath. I finally huffed, 'Yes, I will marry you.'

"I thought he'd asked me to marry him — so I supposed he had said it. I told him fine and that no one was here, that I have a bed made upstairs and let's go honeymoon on it."

"He said, 'Ah, honey, I need to shave and take a bath first.' "

" 'No excuses,' I said. 'I told you yes. That is what you wanted. Then let's settle it right now. We can't always have the nicest conditions. We are simple people and that is what we need to do to seal this deal about it right now.' "

They all three were laughing.

"Were you shocked?" he asked Hampt.

"I was so dizzy-headed I wasn't sure we'd done it. So we did it again."

She held up three fingers and nodded. "I thought I was about to marry a billy goat. Susie came home shortly after the third time, and I think she knew something had happened. We told her we were going to get married. Then I told the kids and they mobbed him."

"So you know all about it now," Hampt said.

"So see," May added, smiling, "I answered his question before he asked me."

"Better yet, you hauled him upstairs and you two did it then."

"I didn't want him to back out." She blushed some more.

"I was so dizzy the first time, I wanted to remember it, so we did it again."

She shook her head. "Boy, I said to myself, this was going to be real fun, and we laid there and kissed for a long time until we did it again."

"Jesus or Cole probably told you about Liz and me?"

They both shook their head.

"Well that night after the foot-washing deal. We slipped away after a big meal and made love in a hay pile. That was her plan so if I smelled hay I'd recall her."

May ducked her head. "Oh my goodness. She did that in a hay pile to you."

"It worked. She probably never told you, but her first husband kidnapped her and a priest married them before they went to bed.

"He never courted her. He had his mind made up, swooped her up. Married her and then consummated the marriage in his great *casa*. Two years later some bandits came to his front door, killed his guards, and shot him down in the front doorway. She grabbed a pistol and came to the head of the great stairs, shot two of them dead as they were coming up the stairs. Then she saw the third one coming back inside the front door way and blew him away. She said she never looked for another man. Came to buy some palomino horses from a *gringo* and said this handsome cowboy met her and swept her away."

With the stories told, all of them smiling, Chet said it was time for him to leave.

Hampt got down to the serious. "If you are going home, leave that damn gray horse here. Ty has broken six horses to ride for folks. I think breaking horses is his calling. He isn't the book reader his brother is, but he has a good way with crazy broncs. He can get them out of it."

"He can have him. So he doesn't hurt the boy is my only concern."

"Honey, tell Ray to get Chet a horse to ride home. I have one more story Chet may not have heard, but none of you can tell Susie that I told you."

"I won't."

"After her husband died, Sergeant Polanski came to see her and sat on the couch. You know, I think, that he was very serious about her even before she married number one, but he never thought he was good enough for her. Right after the boy's death, Sarge came back time and again, always clean-shaven, polite, and prim-acting, sat on the couch, and talked about small things.

"No one was there. Susie and him were alone. I think she'd gotten weary of this straight-backed suitor. So she finally asked him if he had a purpose being there.

"He answered her red faced. 'I want to marry you?'

"She asked him right out . . . 'Why?'

"He said he loved her. He always had even before she married her dead husband.

" 'If you loved me, why don't you put your arms around me?'

" 'I can,' he said. So she went over, sat down beside him.

"He put his arm around her shoulder, not special like.

"She spoke up and said, 'Men do that to

each other. Can't you hold me or are you afraid my pregnancy might jump on you?'

" 'Susie, I am not afraid of anything but hurting you.'

" 'You can't hurt me. You can't hurt my baby. Just remember, if you get me you get the baby too.'

" 'I'd love it like my own.'

" 'Then what are you waiting for?' she asked him.

" 'Damned if I know.' They made love on the couch and they became inseparable."

Going home on a young blue roan horse that Ty said had the makings of a real great cow horse, Chet reflected on the day and all he had learned. Whenever the pony saw a cow nearby or far away he acted interested like a good cutting horse acted facing a critter. In Texas he knew about some real hands at training cutting horses. Maybe the boy was a real horse expert. Like peach-tree-limb well finders, horse training was a trait most folks who did it were born with — some trained to be that, but you needed traits born in a man that showed you could try to do it and win at it.

"The night boy said I missed the best bucking competition ever held here this morning," the groom Adriano teased him when he got back to the homeplace. "You sell him today?"

"No."

"Big shame. That is one wild sumbitch."

"When Ty brings him back, you will beg to own him."

"That stem-winder? Never. Who owns this horse?"

"Take the saddle off this horse and ride him with your knees bareback."

"Is this a trick, *señor*?"

"No."

"I can do that, but no boy taught him that."

The saddle piled on its nose, the youth leaped on his back and soon had the roan backing and then short loping in circles without a bridle. "Who did this?"

"Ty Byrnes, my nephew."

"I can't believe this. Who owns him now?"

"My wife. I am making him a present to her."

"Whew, does he have more?"

"In the future we will see. He has the big gray horse next."

The groom shook his head. "Never."

"What do you want to bet with me?"

"That he can make him that gentle?"

"Yes."

"Five dollars."

"If he can't I will pay you ten."

"You can pay me now."

Chet shook his head. "Put her horse up. I need to get up there or she will think I abandoned her."

"I won't abandon her, *señor.*"

"Me either."

On the porch, he put his hat on the peg, rolled up his sleeves to wash his hands and face.

"You did come home. How were they?"

"Funny. I can tell you some amusing private stories later."

"Good."

"My nephew sent you a wonderful blue roan horse. We may run down and see my son tomorrow at the Verde and you can ride him."

"Why me?"

"You needed this one."

"I am ready to go north."

"How is your project girl Lisa doing?"

"I sent her to town today with one of the *vaquero*'s wives, Marana. The doctor told her she probably was not pregnant. That made her happy. Me too. She works hard at what tasks you put her to do, and if she sees something wrong she tells me."

"I knew you could find her a place eventually."

"I know men reckon she is very fragile, but she does things well and she is bright. We better eat . . . Monica will be upset."

He bent over and kissed her on the mouth. "Good to be back."

She hugged him by grasping his shirt-sleeves and pulled him close to her face. "Always, big cowboy. Always good for me to have you with me."

CHAPTER 14

Next mid-morning Chet found his son Adam at the big house at the Camp Verde site. His nanny Rhea opened the front door and from behind her, Adam hollered, "Daddy."

Liz was laughing. "He sounds just like his father."

"Big man, Daddy is here." On his knees he scooped up his son and kissed him. "How are you doing?"

"You eat lunch?"

"Sure, we can always eat."

"Rhea will fix some."

"I bet she would."

"Oh, Chet, how are you?"

"Fine, Rhea, my son grows so fast I can hardly believe it."

"Señora Byrnes, why are you all in the hall? Come in the dining room, please?" her housekeeper asked them.

Chet, holding his son, told them to go

ahead. He and Adam were coming.

The front door flew open and Victor came hurrying in. "Is everyone all right?"

"Most of us," Chet said. "What is wrong?"

"There is a messenger from Center Point looking for you over at Tom's. They have more trouble up there."

"I'll go up to Tom's," Chet said, and handed his son to Rhea. "I plan to be back for lunch."

Liz followed him out. "I'll stay here and wait for you."

Halfway across the dry short grass span, Tom and another man hurried to meet them.

"What is up, Tom?"

"This man works for Cole. He says they burned down a stage line station."

"Which one?"

"Number three," the young man said.

"Was anyone hurt or shot?"

"The man's wife is dead."

"That's Clyde Covington's wife Iris —" Chet felt he had been struck in the heart by a spear. The lovely woman who always pecked him on the cheek for visiting was dead.

He nodded he heard. "Tom, you send for my men to join me up there. I am going to ride for Center Point."

"What about Liz?"

"She will probably go along with me. I want packhorses and supplies. We'll go after them and hopefully find the raiders."

"What is wrong?" Liz asked, coming from the house.

"Iris Covington was murdered."

Her beautiful face crumpled into sorrow. He reached out and hugged her tight. "I am sorry, but their station was attacked. I have no more details. I am sending for the men and packhorses. They can catch us up there. Jesus, Spencer, and Spud can all meet us at the station. Tom will get word to them."

"I hate to leave the new girl."

"Tom can get a guard to take you back. I understand your concern."

"Oh, Chet, I hate it worse you going ahead alone. It may be a trap."

"I'll send two cowboys with him that can fight," Tom said.

"I'm sorry. Time counts."

Liz wiped the tears from her cheek. "You take care. I will burn candles for your safety at my church."

Tom said, "Chet, I'm going to get your boys to ride with you."

"Thanks. Your name is?" Chet asked, turning to face the messenger.

"Oh, I am Clay Whitson. I'm a driver.

Cole took some men and went up there. He told me to find you and you'd know what to do."

"You can ride back with me. Go up to the big house and tell them I said to feed you. I'll be along in a minute."

Whitson looked a little taken aback.

"Knock on the door," Liz said to him. "They won't bite you.

"Good. I was afraid —"

Things looked set. Chet took Liz back down to the big house, assuring her that he would be careful. He hurriedly ate lunch, held and kissed his son, then hugged his wife hard, kissed her good-bye.

"I'll be back as soon as I can."

"I will be waiting."

He went to join the assembled men.

"These are my best men, Buck McCray. Dooley Hansen. They know and understand the danger and are ready to go with you," Tom said.

Chet shook their hands and thanked them. He noted they had bedrolls on their saddles and rifles in their scabbards. "I hope we have no problem, but it will be a tough ride. I want to join Cole and his men if they haven't already collected the raiders."

"Tom explained they killed a woman in

the raid."

"I hate that. She was a lovely woman and mother. But we will run them into the ground."

"We've heard how hard everyone worked on that stage line. What is wrong with these people?" Buck asked him.

"If I knew all that I'd probably be rich," Chet said.

He nodded, mounted the roan horse, and swung him around. "Ready?"

The two men were already mounted.

"I have sent a man to get your helpers," Tom said. "Victor and I can send more if you need them."

"I think this will be enough. But I appreciate your concern." With that done he set the roan into a long trot for Camp Verde and the road north. The notion that he could have ridden the big gray but probably would have wind broke him getting there went through his mind. No need to kill a great horse — Ty might make him a better one.

Still struck hard with the sad notion that paid raiders had murdered Iris Covington, he wondered how many more killers Hall could hire.

Past midnight they awoke Robert and his wife. Chet apologized and explained their need. They slept a few hours in bedrolls on the floor in the house. The very pregnant Betty made them breakfast and brushed off their apologies for disturbing her sleep.

"Land sakes fellows, Robert and I live in this wonderful Byrnes family house and we have a great life. I will share it any time you need it, and when my baby comes you can help me entertain it."

"Boy or girl?" Clay asked.

"Ten toes, ten fingers, and a smile is all I want."

They all gave her a small hug going out the door and she beamed. Chet kissed her cheek and shook Robert's hand. "Jesus, Spencer the new man, and Spud are coming tonight, I imagine."

"No problem. We hope you find the guilty parties," Robert said.

"We will," he promised the bright young leader of his timber-hauling operation.

They paused, shook hands again, and both had a moment of powerful silence. Chet felt certain his man knew the pressures he faced. Both knew the strong influence each had on the other.

They were, after a few hours' push northward, entering a vast high open meadow. A single shot rang out from somewhere nearby, sending Clay's horse stumbling and throwing the others into a scramble. Off the stricken horse Clay made a quick move to get behind him. Gun in his hand, he, like the others still in the saddle, searched around for the shooter.

"The puff of gun smoke came from over east on that hillside," Buck said.

"Get for cover," Chet shouted, and pointed to the timber behind them. The words were barely out of his mouth when a shot stung Dooley's horse and he left bucking but headed for cover. The rider soon got him under control. In the meantime, Chet swung Clay up behind him and they rode for the pines a quarter mile away.

The four men reached the edge of the woods and removed their saddlebags, bedrolls, and meager supplies. Horses were driven away from the shooter side of the area and hobbled while two of them with rifles studied the faraway site of the shooter on a pine-clad hillside.

No more shots were fired in the next thirty minutes. No pursuit from the ambushers. Time clicked away.

"Dooley and I are going to check that side out. We won't look too hard 'cause I figure he's long gone. Clay can ride double, but use the road, we will rejoin you north of here. We can send someone back to get your saddle, Clay."

He nodded.

Chet and Dooley, armed with rifles on their horses, rode around the meadow close to the pine-clad slope and drew no fire. Saw no sign of anyone or anything.

Chet felt lots of searching would not prove anything. They'd not find a needle in the haystack from where the sniper had been. Chet counted them all lucky the gunman had not done any more damage than destroy a horse. They'd send back others to take the saddle off the dead horse, which might require turning him over to get it free.

Satisfied, they gave a two-shot all-clear message and headed north.

The two riding double soon joined them. Chet hurried his mount to get them all quickly to the stage line operations area. When they arrived, Chet saw Valerie come running across the grassy ground to meet them.

"You got the word then what happened? Cole took four men and went to track them down. Lots of folks are steaming mad up here about them killing poor Iris." She bent over to catch her breath.

"Easy, sister. We'd have been here sooner but a sniper shot at us down in that meadow south of here. Killed one of our horses."

Her blue eyes opened wide and she frowned. "You see the sniper?"

"No, he was a long ways away. Probably ran off after he shot at us."

Valerie broke down and cried in Chet's arms. "Damn. Should I go down to the Verde River Ranch with the boy for our safety or what?"

"No. Stay here. You have enough men to stop any attack. We will get this bunch of murderers and slam them in jail."

"Where are Jesus and Spencer and Spud?"

"They were at one of the other places checking things out. When we got the word of the attack, Liz and I were at the Verde place playing with Adam."

"If anything happened to Rocky I don't know what I'd do. I sure am attached to him."

"You are safe enough here. When my men get here we will go find Cole. Now we could eat."

"Oh, I am so sorry. Come on. The crew at the tent will feed you. I guess with Cole gone — it doesn't help my fears."

"No help to have him gone. Valerie, you are one cute, pretty stepmother concerned about way too much." He herded her toward the tent knowing his compliment made her blush.

"I can go get your little man but he is sleeping and his nanny or wife, or whatever she is to him, is watching him." She laughed a little about Rocky telling them he needed a wife too.

"That business he needed a wife is too cute. I won't leave till the crew catches us. I hope they don't snipe on them."

"It is getting crazy . . . this killing business."

"That's why I'm here. This has to be stopped."

"Any idea who the sniper was?"

"I didn't have my best trackers with me. It would have been a needle in a haystack to try and find. It was a long-range shot that was done, I am sure, from a special sniper rifle with a telescope sight."

"I hope Cole doesn't get hurt. He has three good men with him, but he isn't you."

"Me? He's as good a man as any I know."

"No, Chet Byrnes. God put a shield around you."

"Then how come I got shot down at Tombstone then?"

She shook her head. "I don't know."

"Val, we are both lucky we have survived the scraps we have been in. You have Rocky and Cole. I have the head men jobs over the ranches all set, the rest is all good, plus

219

I have Elizabeth. We can work out anything else that comes our way, can't we?"

His arm around her shoulder, they went to the tent and the crew there fed them.

"What are the plans?" Clay asked him over the meal.

"When the others get here we will go help Cole. He's left word where he is going. Arrange for some packhorses and supplies. This may be a long chase."

"I wish I knew who that sniper was," Clay said.

"We'll get him before this is over."

"You need to take a nap?" Val asked him.

"I have our cabin. I may do it. Next few days I figure won't support much sleep. Has anyone arranged to get Clay's saddle?"

"Three guys just left here well-armed to go get it," Buck said.

"Good. Get some rest. There won't be much time for that in the days ahead."

They agreed and went off to find some shade and spread a bedroll. Once in the cabin setup, Chet shed his boots and pants. The interior was cool from the night before's low temperature. Stretched out on the bed, he wished Liz had come along and he had her there to hug and love. Soon his eyes fell shut and all the stage line problems dissolved in his sleep.

Later in the day he dressed and went back to the commissary tent for supper. About then the rest of his crew, Jesus and the others, arrived. They must have come after him at breakneck speed. They arrived in time to eat anyway. He rose and shook their hands.

"We just got word they shot at you south of here?" Jesus began with.

"Some sniper shot a horse out from under one of the men. The shooter was a great distance up in the pines, and our chances of finding him were small. We looked a little, but then rode on."

"We saw the dead ranch horse and I knew he wasn't one you rode."

"Clay was the man who rode him. And I'm grateful that we only lost a horse. But someone knew we'd head north, and someone intended to kill one of us or more."

"Is Cole looking for the men who murdered Iris?"

"He and several men are out there now, and I hope on their tracks. I want you and Spencer to stay here and be the backup force in case there is more trouble."

"Who rides with you then?" Jesus asked.

"Spud, Buck, Dooley, and Clay, the new man whose horse was shot. That's enough."

"What do the two of us do?"

"I want a team here, because he may have

221

another group to attack us."

"Where do you think he will strike again?" Jesus asked.

"Jesus, if I knew that I'd go there myself."

"Fine. We can wait here, but if you need us send word."

"I will. I promise. Now let's eat."

"Do you have any word who they are that killed the woman and burned Clyde's head-quarters?"

Chet shook his head. "All I can do is suspect our past individual who hired all the others where things have happened."

"When you get ready, I want to go with you and find him when you get back."

"Fine . . . we will first capture these kill-ers. Then you and I and whoever can go look for Hall. It may be the only way we can settle this business. I asked Hannagen to hire the Pinkerton Agency to find him. But who knows about them."

Jesus agreed and sat down. "I wonder if that will be who we need. These stupid hired hands Hall hires need to be found and jailed, but we won't ever settle this until we get him."

"Do you have any idea where to find him?"

"He has to have been here to hire those other men. Let me and Spencer go spy on that woman we found who had some kind of an affair with him."

"I don't want you two killed."

"We won't get killed. But I think he has some people hide him out. It may not be her, but he's stayed before and may pass through there going back and forth to observe us."

"Maybe? But if someone he doesn't know, part of us, went undercover and searched for him they might find him making his trips and get a notion how to trap and catch him."

"Who is that?"

"Maybe while you two are trying to track him you will find that individual."

Jesus nodded and Spencer agreed. "How much should we offer him?"

"Five hundred dollars and no one will know who did it for us."

"I know we will have to be careful. But that might get him nailed down too."

"Okay, so you don't stay here as backup. Do your search, but I don't want you to stay gone without any contact for more than ten days."

Jesus made a disappointed face like he'd asked too much. "I hope you get them. I'd like to get back to normal again."

Chet smiled. "What is that?"

"Chasing down everyday criminals and ranching."

"Everyday law enforcement was bad enough."

"Yes." Jesus shook his head.

Valerie and her nanny for Rocky and the boy joined them for supper before the men had finished eating. Chet had Rocky on his lap feeding him between his own bites, and they had a private conversation about the taller pony that he wanted.

"That may have to wait until we get the stage line running without these bad men."

"Who are they?"

"Rocky, if I knew that I'd arrest them all."

"Good. When this is over, find the pony."

"I will do that."

Satisfied, he went to sit on Val's lap and she shook her head over him.

"He's fine. Just a boy is all."

"Like his father — he's going to be in charge."

Everyone laughed.

Chet shook his head and went back to eating his supper. No winning that argument.

Things in order, he fell in bed early and had the plans to ride out at predawn with his men. Maybe Jesus had the right idea. Catch Hall sneaking around and bring him in alive if they could. His eyes closed shut

— maybe sleep would solve his deepest concerns.

In the cool predawn, Chet rode at the head on the swinging roan horse while his team followed with five packhorses. They made the first big rise and left the pines for the rolling hills, the air clad in a pungent juniper scent. A few spooked mule deer pounded away stiff-legged from the invaders.

Two days away from the attacked stage stop, he saw a construction crew, with lumber, so the reconstruction to start rebuilding was on that way. But still it would never be the same without Iris to greet everyone with a smile and nice words. She always made everyone feel they were special when they visited her.

Her husband Clyde Covington could never replace her. But who knew what? He had thought that about his first wife — and not looking he found his current one. A very different woman but heavens what more could he ask for than her. He would have to see what tomorrow brought.

Things appeared to be all right at the number-four station. Herman Rothschild greeted them and his tall Indian wife Darling came on the run to greet him. She hugged him and told him her friend Blue

Bell told her he was doing fine when she came by going home.

"Any problems?" Chet asked him.

"We have been lucky. Just threats. I ran them off. But we stay ready and have some dogs to bark at night if anyone comes around."

"There is a man dresses fancy and has a new Boss of the Plains hat named Anson Hall. Has he been around?"

"Not lately, has he, Darling?"

"No. Not lately. Who is he?" she asked.

"The man who hires these killers."

"I'll arrest him if he ever comes back."

"Be very careful. I don't want you killed. He is a very elusive man."

"We will," she promised him.

She fed them some fry bread and meat she had cooked, and they rode on to make more distance that day.

They slept at a small waterhole and rode on early the next morning to reach station number three about midday. A red-eyed Clyde met them and shook their hands. He hugged Chet and shook his head. "It is killing me, Chet. And them getting away, I can't run their sorry asses into the damn ground."

"Cole may have already done that. We plan to join him in the chase if he hasn't."

"She was the light of my life, Chet. Smart woman, she could pinch a penny and she'd feed the mangiest dog came by hungry. Never had a bad day in her life. She said when we made the cattle deal with you our troubles were over — we'd make it up here at last. That and with the stage line business we wouldn't need to worry anymore. But damn it to hell, she ain't here to enjoy any of it."

"Nothing will bring her back. She would expect you to carry on. We will get her killers and they will be punished. Life goes on."

"I know you've had some bad deals happen to you. I heard the stories. I'll try to be like you . . . face them and move on."

"There is no other way, Clyde. They don't come back. I am so sorry. I too share your loss, but things will go on."

He saw the grave out front of the stop and wished his friend had buried her farther away. Not hide her but to a better setting — private-like place. But that was not his decision on how to do it.

They ate a quick meal, Chet shook his hand, and he rode north to find Cole.

Larks and killdeer scouted ahead for them. A Navajo woman with little children and a small flock of sheep told them the riders were three days ahead of them. Him and his team ate dry jerky and canteen water to wash it down with and rode on past dark.

Coyotes howled and silent owls swooped over them with winged bats hunting bugs to be seen against the starlight. When they did stop, he did not sleep soundly or wake up rested. They pushed on across the Painted Desert. The next night they stopped at a trading post. The man's wife fed them *tortillas* and *frijoles.* They thanked her, slept on the ground, and after her breakfast of their own oatmeal rode on.

Chet was convinced they would soon find Cole. Two days later at Chama, high up in the pines of northern New Mexico, they found him and his hard-eyed men in a saloon drinking beer.

"Any luck?" Chet asked.

Cole shook his head. "They vanished up here."

In a whisper, Chet said, "Then they are close."

"What do you mean?"

"They came all this way for a purpose. They got here and are now in hiding. Offer a reward for them. Tell this bartender you will pay for their whereabouts."

"How much?" Cole asked.

"A hundred dollars. There are men who

would sell you their mother for that amount."

Cole went over to the bar and waved the bartender down. "You ever hear of a guy named Anson Hall?"

"Yeah, he's a gambler. He comes in here. What you need him for?"

"A friend of mine wants to talk to him."

"I'll tell him. What is his name?"

"No, he knows that Anson don't want to talk to him. But he'd pay a hundred bucks to find him and never say a word about who sent him. Savvy?"

The bartender nodded. "I'll see what I can do. I could damn sure use the money."

"Couldn't we all." Cole said.

He rejoined Chet. "He said he'd try to find him."

"Good. You say they disappeared near here?"

"Pretty well. They simply evaporated close to here, after we left Durango. They probably split up, but we couldn't find any familiar hoof tracks."

"You have identities on any of them?"

"Nothing makes sense. An Indian squaw said they were white men. No Mexicans or Indians. One had freckles all over his face. Two had black beards. How easy would they be to identify? It was dark when they made the stage stop raid and no one saw them clearly. They wore flour sack masks. They avoided everyone in all those miles, but that one Navajo woman who saw them. Now they must be split up."

"Maybe go back to Durango and ask more questions?"

"We thought we covered it. But you may have a better idea how to do that."

"Cole, someone knows them and saw them somewhere. We have to break that person or find some whore even who knows all about them."

"I don't know how you or I are going to find out anything from one of them."

"You are right, but let's you and I talk to Spud. He's had to exist in some pretty grimy places; there is a chance he could learn some things we didn't even think about."

"Would it risk his life?"

"I don't want that. Let's find him and talk."

"He's out at our camp by now."

"We can talk to him there."

Cole agreed.

Leaving the bar, they joined up with Spud and the others at the camp.

As soon as they got there, Chet, Cole, and Spud went off by themselves, away from the fire. In the cool night they sat on some logs in the dark timber.

"Spud, Cole and his bunch lost those killers between here and maybe Durango."

"No one knows who they are, still?" Spud asked, surprised.

"We may not, but someone does. A handful of guys came up here and they dispersed. We hope there is some dove knows all about them, or some guy that sells them liquor. Some connection. They are hiding but we don't know where or who they are."

"What can I do?"

"Can you go secretly and see what you can find out and not get killed?" Chet asked him.

"I think so. You need to find us the identities of these guys who you chased up here."

"All we have is one had freckles and two had beards according to a Navajo woman."

In the dim light, Chet noted the shake of Spud's head. "Too tough?"

"No. Chet, I have not been back in that gutter since I went to work for you. I don't mind going back, but I dread doing it. If there is an answer I will find it."

"How much money do you need?"

"Fifty dollars in coins or old money. I may not need it all, but it will loosen lips or buy cheap liquor to help them talk."

"You can have all you need. I will leave you a fast horse at the livery and a code to get him and ride the hell out if things fall in."

"I can do that."

"Don't risk your life. We need you, but what you find may solve our search."

"Hey, thanks. I am going to shed my cowboy clothes. Start here or down at Durango?"

"Durango. Higden's Livery. 'Strawberry Hill' is the code word to get the horse I leave for you."

"How do I find you or Cole?"

"The Brown Hotel desk. Leave a message in a sealed envelope. How do you want to get back there?" Chet asked.

"I will hitch a ride on some freight wagon. Give me a few days. If there is any word on them I will know who and where they are at by then."

"Spud, if it gets too tough, get your backside out of there."

"I promise."

Chet worried about the short man. He had been in a tough world, and going back there might get him killed. But he knew not if Spud could prevent it from happening. The wait would be the big hard thing for him.

While the team members scattered looking for leads on the raiders, Chet wrote Liz a letter telling her they were all fine, but at a dead end up there in southern Colorado. He did not tell her about his effort that sent Spud in as a spy to find the men.

They let a few days pass. Then, apart, they quietly drifted into Durango. Cole did not like his boss riding alone, but Chet told him that guards would draw attention. After the long day in the saddle, he felt stiff when he put the horse in the stables and told the man who ran the livery his secret word for the man who might need him.

He went by the hotel restaurant for lunch and soon found himself seated with a woman wearing a veil, black gloves, and the black dress of a widow.

She didn't bother to lift the veil but began to shed her long gloves. "You are the man from Prescott, Arizona Territory?"

"Yes. My name is Chet Byrnes. I live there. What may I do for you?"

Gloves off, she raised the veil and then unpinned the black hat and set it in the empty chair. "My name is Wanda Hampton. I am the widow of the deceased Carlton Hampton and I want to speak to you about some important matters."

"I am a rancher. I can't imagine what I

could do for you."

She shook her head while the waiter asked for a drink order.

"I will take a red wine. French if you have some."

"I'll take some coffee."

"You don't drink?"

"No ma'am. I ordered the coffee. Now what do you need from me?"

"I have a large ranch and men are stealing my cattle."

"Have you reported the thefts to the local law officers?"

"Yes. They do nothing. They say they can't catch them or are too busy to go find them."

"I am here on business, Mrs. Hampton. I fear I have no facilities or men to solve your problems here."

"Mr. Byrnes, I am desperate. The law won't help me. These outlaws are taking my cattle. Is there not any justice left in America?"

"There is and I will inquire tomorrow and see what I can do to help you."

"Thank you. You are a very handsome man and I was told you help people like me who are at the obvious reckless abandonment of the law."

"I will try, Mrs. Hampton."

"My name is Wanda; please call me this."

"Yes, if you wish. Do you wish to share supper with me?"

"If I am not interrupting anything?"

"No. I just arrived in town."

"Oh, that is why it was easy to meet up with you. I had expected you would be harder to find."

"Someone tell you I was in town?"

"Yes. Carl Skinner at the law office of Thurman, Collins and Greener."

"Is he a resident of Durango?"

"Now, I believe he is. He just came from Arizona to work for Mr. Collins."

"Wanda, I must ask you tell no one about our meeting. Not many people know I am here, and my purpose is to arrest some murderers of a family friend who are in hiding here."

She put her hands to her face. "Oh, I am so sorry, I merely thought about my own problems."

"Fine. I will have my man Cole Emerson investigate your case. But no words about it to anyone."

"My dear. I won't tell a soul."

He almost shook his head. This woman in her thirties held no interest to him. She lived in the same world as his aunt. Louise, JD's mother, who was married to Harold Parker, had that Southern aristocracy touch.

That same touch that his first wife Margaret discarded to attract him.

"Maybe we can find a solution."

"I am imposing on you?"

"No. My mind is very busy trying to solve another problem without any connection to yours."

"You have a wife?"

"Yes. A very lovely lady. Her name is Elizabeth. She was a widow who lost her husband in a robbery-murder and was looking for some horses I raise. We met and I courted her, and she agreed to marry me and move to my ranch."

"You lost another woman?"

"Yes, in a jumper accident."

"Oh, that is very sad."

"She wanted to ride her jumpers. She had done it all her life and I could not tell her what I feared the most. But it happened and God took her from me."

Upset that some attorney in town had known about him and the fact that he was in town, he had forgotten that they had ordered food until it arrived. They quietly ate.

"I am sure Mr. Skinner had no malice in pointing you out to me as a person of significant power who would be able to help me."

"I am sure about that too, but I will ask him for less help."

She smiled. "I imagine when you are not caught up in serious business there is some humor in you."

"Some, Wanda. I have some."

"Is this matter that brought you here that serious?"

"Yes. In a raid some vicious men killed a man's wife. She was a very outstanding lady and my friend."

"Do you know the killers?"

"No. But I will find them."

She nodded, picking at her food on the plate with her fork. "I feel very fortunate to have met you, Chet Byrnes. I must say I am a little envious of your wife — she must really miss you."

"She usually rides with me, but this was going to be a hard situation until we found them and I asked her to stay behind."

"Really. She rides with you?"

"Last year we found a huge lost herd out in west Texas and drove them around Kansas to Nebraska."

"Really?"

"It is too long a story to tell you the details, but she rode on horseback all the way from Arizona to west Texas and then to Ogallala, Nebraska, with me."

"Oh, she must be athletic."

"She is a very pretty lady and a sterling person. In payment for her helping me I took her by stage to Denver and we attended an opera."

With the napkin she swept her face and smiled. "You, sir, are a husband deluxe. I'd give a lot to have attended an opera."

"No, just a Texas-born cowboy."

"No. You are much more than that. May I give you my card to give to your man so he may find me?"

"That would be enough."

"May I pay for my meal?"

"No, I invited you to eat. Cole will find you. He is very resourceful."

"Would it disturb your wife if I wrote and told her how kind you were to me and how much I appreciate you?"

"Elizabeth Byrnes, Post Office Box Thirty-Four, Prescott, Arizona Territory."

"Here is my card."

He rose, accepted the card, and thanked her.

He was to meet Cole at breakfast in a café back room the next morning. He also needed to go by and tell Attorney Skinner to not point him out.

In his hotel bed he tossed and turned all night. What was Spud doing? Late into the night, he closed his eyes at last and slept for a few hours.

CHAPTER 15

Chet awoke and couldn't shake his bleary mind. He dressed and went to find the café's back door. The smell of bacon frying and fresh biscuits coming from the kitchen's oven woke him a little more, pushing inside.

"You must be Chet?" the tall buxom blonde in the apron asked.

"That's me."

"I'm Hope. That table and the chairs are for you. I guess your friend will join you soon. How do you like your eggs?"

"Over and done."

"Got it. New coffee is coming."

"You sound busy?"

"We do a good business. I understand your buddy's wife helps a woman who has one in Preskitt."

"His wife used to do that."

"He kind of explained she now has a boy to raise."

"My son."

"There you are, Hope. I said he'd beat me," Cole said as he came into the room.

"Chet, Cole told me all about you and I am pleased to have you as special company. After breakfast, you can use this table for your office and anything else we can do, we will try to help." She set down two cups of coffee. "It is very hot."

"Thanks, Hope. Glad to meet you."

Cole took a seat across from him. "I wonder how our man is getting along?"

"Too early to know. I didn't sleep last night. But I guess we will settle all this someday, hopefully soon."

"What else?"

"I volunteered you to help a lady who says they are rustling her cattle and the law won't stop them."

Cole frowned. "Who is that?"

"Wanda Hampton. A widow woman. Here is her card."

"Hey, Hope?" Cole asked her. "Wanda Hampton?"

"Oh, she is very rich. A little dramatic but I think she is all right."

"Cattle being rustled?" he asked.

Hope turned her palms up. "How should I know?"

"Well, I will go see about her problems."

"Good. I need to go find a lawyer who

recognized me."

"Huh?"

"No problem. He knows me from Arizona, noticed me, and sent Wanda to me."

Cole shook his head between bites of breakfast. "You are, maybe, too famous."

"Not that bad. I'll look at real estate today. It may be a long visit."

"Or Jesus and them will find something over there at Chama."

"You can always hope."

After breakfast, Chet went to the real estate office of Gurley Golden. The short near bald fat man in his forties was showing him ranch maps.

"This place is really great. It has water and good summer range."

"How many cows will it run?"

"Eighty."

"That won't pay cowboy wages."

"Mr. Byrnes, how big a ranch do you want?"

"Five hundred head of mother cows."

Golden slapped his forehead and gave an exhausted sound. "That ranch would cost thousands of dollars."

"That ranch would pay some bills."

Golden shook his head. "I don't have a listing like that."

"Who has such a ranch?"

"The Mendoza family over in New Mexico."

"Would they sell it?"

"I don't know, but I can go down there and ask the old man."

"When will you know?"

"I will know and be back by Friday."

"Good . . . now we are getting somewhere."

"Thank you, Mr. Byrnes. I will have a price for his ranch."

Chet next went by a stationery store, wrote Liz a letter, and sealed it. The man behind the counter stamped it and promised he'd post it before the stage left with the mailbag.

Cole came back from his meeting, shaking his head. "That woman needs a foreman. All she has are some mere boys to herd her cattle, and the foreman is a good field worker, not a ranch foreman. If she doesn't hire some tough cowboys and a real boss over them, she won't have a ranch left."

"What do you think?"

"All those boys she has are field help to hoe weeds. I don't blame the sheriff for not doing anything. He can't stay out there and keep the rustlers off the ranch. The boys she has need to have someone to show them how to do things."

"Who have we got could do it?"

"Spencer. He's damn tough, loves cowboy work, and he might even satisfy her."

"Send word. Wait . . . what about Buck McCray?"

"He's one of Tom's best men. He could run anyone's ranch."

Chet thought the same but was thinking more about Spencer. "Come to think on it, I don't think Spencer wants himself such a sophisticated woman like her."

"Then, what about Buck?"

"He does have the experience to handle whatever comes along."

Cole laughed. "If we take Buck, I bet we'd lose Dooley too. He likes Buck, goes where he goes, and he would make a good jingle bob."

"You are right. He'd back Buck good and they'd be a super team. Send word for them to meet us at her ranch the day after tomorrow. That should be enough time for them to get there."

Cole agreed. "Nothing is happening here, so I'll go get them two myself, and by Thursday we'll be at her ranch. You tell her what we are doing?"

Before going to see Wanda Hampton, Chet found the lawyer Skinner. Chet explained the situation and Skinner had promised him no more advertising he was in town. Next, Mrs. Hampton. He could not imagine keeping her entertained for as long as it would take for the boys to come back here, but at least he had her problem settled. The deal was fixed. He left lawyer Skinner's office and went to find her and tell her what they planned. At least he had not heard about any more attacks on the stage line. But they were a long ways from home to hear anything.

He located her in the rose garden of her town house. She had some snippers and was cutting the roses and putting them into the tissue paper she held in her other arm.

"Ah, where is that man, Cole, who works for you at?"

"Why? You fall in love already?"

"You said he had a wife and your son."

"He does. Cole has gone to get a man to be your ranch foreman. He also will bring his assistant, a man named Dooley."

She rose to her feet. "I have a foreman."

"He can go on being your foreman of the men who work around the house. Buck, Dooley, and a handful of cowboys they hire will take over and maintain the cattle herd and will run off the rustlers."

"Come into the house." Carrying the roses she had cut in her arm, she moved toward the house. As she got closer, a maid opened the double doors for them.

"This is Señor Byrnes. Mary Anna."

"Good day, sir. Aren't her roses pretty?"

"Very pretty."

"You, my dear, may arrange them today. Señor Byrnes and I have business to discuss about the *ranchero.*"

The office held a great polished dark wood table and some straight-back chairs. She showed Chet to one and took another.

"Now how will this work? Your plan?"

"As I said, the Mexican boys you have now can do farming and your hay operation. For your cattle operation, I have a great ranch foreman and his *segundo.* They will take care of the cattle portion with a few cowboys they will hire. With them in charge no one will rustle another head of stock. Buck is his name and I will drive you out to your ranch on Thursday to meet him and Dooley."

"How old is he, this Buck?"

"Forty-two I'd say. Smart man."

"Does he dance?"

"Never knew a Texas cowboy couldn't dance some. You can tune him up a little. He'll dance with you."

"Has he ever been to an opera?"

"Doubt it, but I bet he'd take you to one."

"If he doesn't, I'll expect it anyway."

"He is a good man and knows the ranching business."

"Skinner was right. He said you could solve my problems."

"Thursday. You have a buckboard?"

"Of course. I will have breakfast ready at seven."

"I will be here."

"May I kiss you?"

"No."

"Why not?"

"I don't need you writing my wife that I am running around kissing widows in Colorado."

She broke out laughing. "I would not be that indiscreet."

"I don't trust you."

"Thursday morning at seven?"

"Yes, and know that I think this man is the best one I know available for the job."

"I have no objections."

"Good." He left her rearranging the girl's work at setting up the roses.

No word from Spud. Maybe there was nothing to be found. There had to be.

Thursday, the housekeeper, Mary Anna, cheerfully answered the door for him in the cool morning mountain air. She welcomed him and showed him to the dining room.

"She said your wife was Hispanic?"

"Elizabeth comes from Mexico."

"You like Mexican women?"

"Only my wife."

With a mischievous smile she said, "Well, forgive me . . . I had to ask."

"I forgive you. Thanks . . . I can seat myself."

"Ah, Mr. Byrnes, you made it." Wanda appeared in the doorway.

"You look lovely."

She wore a divided riding skirt and a white silk blouse. A much more attractive outfit than her other clothing. She thanked him, taking her seat across from him. "I am excited about today. Will they be at the ranch when we get there?"

"Cole will have them there."

"I know you are here on business and I am hoarding your time."

"No problem. Glad to help."

"I am grateful and wish I could help you solve your problems. I fear my husband left me thinking to just go on running the ranch with my present foreman."

"How long ago did he pass on?"

"Almost two years now. He had a heart attack and died that evening."

"I understand such a loss."

"Of course. You have such faith in this man that you are bringing me. Tell me why?"

"Tom, my large ranch foreman, told me he could run any ranch. Buck had been running a ranch in southeast Arizona, and the ranch was sold to a man from the east. He came to the ranch and told Buck that he considered branding inhumane. They would no longer brand his cattle. Buck quit, never found another foreman job, so Tom hired him to help him."

"How would that other man find his cattle?"

"Wanda, I have no idea. But Buck can straighten out your problems and make you money."

"I have no doubt you know your business. Is the breakfast satisfactory?"

"Excellent. We need to leave here shortly."

"Oh, I am ready to go when you are."

"Let's go." He finished his coffee and Mary Anna brought him his hat.

The drive in the buckboard went smoothly. The hipshot horses at the hitch rail were familiar. The house wasn't as large as her Durango residence, but it was not a typical ranch house. Three men stood up on the front porch and removed their hats for her.

Chet introduced them to her, then a woman came out of the house and spoke to her. "I will have dinner at noon for all of you. Meanwhile I have made fresh coffee since the men told me they didn't drink whiskey until evening."

"Very good, Louise. This is Mr. Byrnes. He has these men on his payroll."

She curtsied. "Nice to meet you, sir. We can go inside and you can explain this to me."

The meeting soon became more relaxed and Chet let Buck lead the conversation. By then she had him calling her Wanda.

"Wanda, it will take me a few weeks to hire the men I want to ride for me. I have been here long enough to know there are some good men looking for ranch jobs doing lesser jobs than that."

"Oh, I understand. This will be your job. Chet says you can handle it."

"I have stopped rustling on several ranches I worked for. I looked around a little before you got here, and I saw that your ranch needs some better bulls. Many are old, a few even crippled. But we can handle that."

"I will count on you to make such decisions. Anything else you see?"

"Dooley and I left our winter clothes at home."

"No problem. I can get you the clothes."

"You want anything shipped?" Chet asked Buck.

She waved away any concern. "Send their personal things. I will handle the rest."

"Thanks."

They had lunch after settling on Buck's salary at a hundred a month and a bonus on cattle sales. Dooley moved up to sixty and the hands to be hired at thirty dollars a month. When she excused herself, Buck turned to Chet. "It was sure nice of you to think of us. I hope Tom can find some new men."

"He can find men to sit in saddles, but I bet they aren't you two. Good luck. Oh, and if you ever get a chance, take her to an opera. When we came back from Nebraska through Denver I took my wife to one. It really impressed her."

Buck smiled. "Thanks. I'd have never thought about that."

Dooley laughed. Chet knew they could handle this job.

He drove her back that afternoon and delivered her to her front door. She thanked him, kissed his cheek, and told him she appreciated him. "I also will not tell your wife I kissed you. May God go with you."

Back in the lobby of his hotel, the desk

clerk handed him his key and a letter. Not a posted mail one. He waited until he was in his room to open it.

Chet, I found the guy with <u>frackles.</u> He came in late last night to use a <u>hore</u> named Beth Ann. I am finding out where he lives. Pretty secret-like deal. I will have more info after today. Spud

This guy must really be in hiding. He wondered when Cole would be back. The café might be the best place to meet him. Going out, he left the key with the clerk, hurried down the back street in between two buildings to see if anyone tailed him. No one showed up. He ducked through the back door of the café, said hi to Hope, and took a seat at their table.

She brought him some fresh coffee. "You get Mrs. Hampton settled?"

"Settled? No, but now she has some good men to run her ranch and that made her a lot easier to help."

"You are the good fairy."

"Sometimes. Cole was the one who figured out her needs."

"I am learning how much he thinks like you."

"He was my right hand for a couple of years."

"Now he runs the stage line and you helped him find his wife."

"That is close to the truth."

She laughed. "I really thought at first he was on the lookout to find a woman. He isn't."

"No, he isn't. But he is a sharp man and everyone likes him."

"You want to eat. I have some chicken-fried steaks, mashed potatoes, and gravy."

"I'll start. He should be here soon."

She nodded. Hope reminded him so much of his first wife, Marge. Tall enough to kiss standing up. A good woman who treated him well. He wouldn't trade places with his present wife, but he had had a good time with Marge. She also left him a fine son, Adam. He had been real lucky in all of his life. At this moment, though, all he wanted was Hall and his boss arrested so he could get on with his life.

Cole arrived and he handed him the letter from Spud. His man read it quickly. "What next?"

"He has to tell us what he finds."

"I hope he isn't in any trouble. This guy really has stayed hid."

Chet agreed with both items. They had to be close to finding at least one of them.

CHAPTER 16

The cool breeze fluttered the hotel room window's curtains. Someone was knocking.

Chet threw his legs off the bed with an "I am coming."

Still dark outside. What was so important?

"I am sorry, Mr. Byrnes; this guy insisted I let him wake you up." The desk clerk apologized again, pointing to the man standing behind him.

"No problem. I know what he wants. Thank you."

"Yes sir. But it was unusual."

"You did the right thing. You can go back to your desk now."

As the man left, Chet pulled Spud's arm. "Get in here and close the door. I will light a lamp."

"I found their hideout. There are three up there. It is at an old mine in a canyon. They have some Mexican girl cooking for them. But three is all that are there. Their horses

255

look wind broke. They couldn't go any farther on them. Both of the others have beards. I can't find number four."

"We need Cole and the others here to help us arrest them."

"Where is Cole?"

"He's around. We set up Buck and Dooley to run this rich woman's mismanaged ranch yesterday."

Spud chuckled. "You had to help her."

"Had to help her. But that you found them — this may be the best thing we've done."

"This freckles guy has a name. It is Herschel Tones."

"What else?"

"Wanted in Texas for murder."

"Nice guy, huh?"

"He slapped around a whore last night for no reason at all. She'll be all right, but he's a mean bully."

"He came back for her?"

"Yeah, but I bet after what he did to her this time she will lock her door."

"We need him in custody and his buddies too."

"What next?"

"We'll go to the café and have breakfast. Cole should be along."

Hope welcomed them and Chet introduced Spud. They were started on breakfast when Cole arrived. At the sight of Spud he really brightened up. "Well?"

"We have them," the short man said, and went back to eating.

"Three of them. The redheaded one is who he found and trailed."

"There were how many originally?" Cole asked.

"I have no idea."

"Five was my thought, though Spud knew of a fourth but couldn't find him."

"What are they waiting for?" Cole asked.

"Their money for making the raid. I think they are waiting on Hall to come and pay them. They need fresh horses; they had no grain to feed them when we chased them."

"Where is the other guy?"

"I didn't learn anything about him."

"The three of us?"

Chet nodded. "I don't want to lose them."

"When?"

"Texas Ranger–style at dawn."

"I'll be ready."

Spud nodded.

"You don't need to go back," Chet told him. "We will arrest them and get one to spill the beans on the others to spare being hung."

They both made affirmative nods.

That day passed slowly. Word was sent to bring the others, but they'd come too late to help in the roundup. Once his crew had the killers secure, Chet was planning to take stages to get back to his wife. First one to Santé Fe and then another to Gallup and a buckboard ride to Center Point.

Chet needed to be home. Period. So he'd take Spud and Cole back with him. Cole needed to be back to run the stage line while Jesus and Spencer could bring the raiders in.

Predawn they were on foot headed up the rocky road for the mine through the fir and pines deep in the canyon. Spud led the three and stopped at times to listen. They reached the site and moved at the edge of the timber. The two-story-shaft building in the starlight showed no lights were on.

Crossing the open area bedded in discarded material, when he reached for the side door, Spud held his gun barrel to his mouth for silence. Eyes adjusted to the light filtering in the shadowy room, then each man stood over a person under blankets.

Chet stuck his pistol in the face of the outlaw, waking him. "Don't move wrong. It is cocked and ready."

Spud and Cole did the same to the other two.

The three were put on their feet and chained together. Then they were marched outside with the freckles guy complaining they had legal rights.

"Yes, and you are under arrest now."

"You can't arrest us in Colorado."

"Yes we can . . . we are U.S. Marshals."

"Go to hell."

"I want your names."

"Herschel Tones."

Chet wrote it down on his small pad. "What's your name?"

No answer.

"I can improve your memory."

"John Doe."

"Reconsider it."

"John Doe."

"I'll be back. What's your name?"

"Tom Blue, but I am not with these guys. I live here. They said they were broke and out of money, so I let them stay here."

"What is his real name?" Chet pointed at Doe.

"I don't know."

"Spud, is there a rain barrel outside?" Chet asked.

"I am not certain."

"John Doe, I hope you are a river otter. Submerged in it and you might remember your real name."

259

"Clarence Seers."

"Take them out and search everything in here."

They found little of anything of value. Chet decided it was time to make a deal. After his offer to save one witness they sat around stone-faced and never said a word. He told them they would walk back to town leading their horses. He was as good as his word. They marched into town and after leaving the still-spent horses and their saddles at the livery, Chet fed them bean soup in the alley.

Then he marched them to the county jail. Jesus and Spencer arrived, and after Jesus looked them over he shook his head. "Never saw them before."

Chet stopped at the cell bars. "When is Hall due here?"

"Wouldn't you like to know?" Seers said.

"I'll get him. It may take me a long time, but you can count on it. I will apprehend him."

"Never." Seers laughed.

"You thought that of yourself — that I'd never get you. And I did." Chet left with his men. That smug outlaw needed a bigger lesson, and he might get one going back to Arizona.

"No sign of any others?" Jesus asked him.

"Tones slipped out to visit a dove. Spud followed him and learned about the three."

"Two more weren't there?" Jesus asked.

Spud shook his head. "There seems to be nothing to point to them."

"Spud, you did a real good job even finding them."

"There is nothing on any more of them."

"How many horses did they ride into Durango?"

"Six," Arthur, one of Cole's men, said.

"We need three more then?" Chet said.

"Three we don't know or haven't even a description of them."

"Any ideas?"

"If someone could play Hall and try to break them out of jail."

Chet shook his head. "He might hire others to do it, but he won't put a hand in it."

"Bigger question is where is he?"

"Let's find lunch," Cole said. "I am tired of thinking. Spud, there was no others you can think of involved?"

"If they were, I never caught the freckles guy talking to anyone when he came down to the parlor house. And he went straight back to the mine afterwards. But all I had were his freckles to point him out to me. Those other two I'da never found. Except they were with him."

Half was better than none and he had no more sources to ask. Lucky for them Spud saw him and made the connection.

After lunch, Chet decided to take a nap. His plans were on hold as to when he was going home. He was sound asleep when someone knocked on the door. Still dressed, he got up saying he was coming and rubbed the back of his sore neck.

"Hello." It was a woman wrapped in a blanket, and she looked shaken. "I need to talk to you — sir."

He looked up and down the hall and whisked her inside when he saw no one.

"I am pretty desperate. They know I know who they are. I think they would kill me if they could find me. I held the horses on that night of the raid."

"You came here with them?" He looked hard at her. "That Navajo woman never saw a woman."

"I was dressed as a boy to hold the horses."

"Why didn't they kill her? The squaw?"

"I don't know. They killed some others and dumped their bodies so they could not identify them."

"How are you alive?"

"I have been hiding since they split up. In all the confusion I slipped away and I think they thought I was with the other group. I got word that you had arrested part of them this morning. I came to see if you'd protect me if I furnished you the information on the other two."

"What is your name?"

"Shirley Douglas."

"Shirley, I need all their names and all you know about them."

She agreed. "One's name is Alfred McNeal. His father is Haver McNeal, who owns many ranches including a big one east of here. Alfred is twenty-six, and his sidekick Jules Goldman is the same age. They joined Wallace in Arizona on a spree with me along."

"Wallace?"

"Kent Wallace is the freckled son of bitch that led them. Alfred told me he'd marry me, and not share me with his outlaw buddies. So I ran off with him. Not only does his family have ranches, but also lots of money. I thought I would be good with him. Jules was his hang-around buddy. In New Mexico, near Gallup, Alfred met Wallace and they kinda sidled up to each other. He kept telling me we'd have fun harassing the stage stops and make some big money. I told him he better not. He never listened. He quickly went back on his promise, so I don't have to tell you they all used me on that dreadful escape we made for here. I knew if I protested they would simply kill me — I had no choice. I slipped away when we got here and they broke up. I think they each thought I was with the other bunch. I had no one to help me, and then a woman told me you were a U.S. Marshal and had arrested three of them this morning."

"Shirley, I need to find my men and arrest those other two as swiftly as possible before they run away or hide again. Can you wear that blanket to conceal yourself? A friend of mine will hide you in her big house."

"Who is that?"

"Mrs. Hampton. But you must stay hidden there and not run off. I will get my men, take you to Mrs. Hampton, and get things going to arrest those two."

"Mr. Byrnes, my life is really in your hands. They would kill me in a wink of an eye."

"You're safe. I assure you. But don't run or they will find you before I can save you."

Trying not to cry, she asked, "How can I ever repay you?"

"No need. Stay here. I am going to get my men. I will lock the door. Don't open it for anyone but me."

She quickly nodded.

He put on his hat and gun belt. She was seated on the bed and had shed the blanket wrap. No way she could be out of her teens. But at last he had a witness and names he needed for their prosecution. That amounted to arresting the last two and then for him to get back on with his life. Tired of the long-running chase, he found Spud and Cole at the back table of the café.

In low voices he told them he had number six, a young woman, and the names of the other two and their location. Cole was pounding the table with his fists. "I will go get those others."

"I need to hide her now. I believe our friend Mrs. Hampton will keep her until we can arrest those other two."

"I'll get a wagon and we can sneak her out of the hotel and take her over there."

"Get the wagon. She and I will meet you in the alley behind the hotel."

"Spud, you know where her house is at?"

"Yeah."

"She knows you work for me. Explain this girl needs to be hidden and we are coming. It is all to be kept a secret."

"I can do that."

"Despite her ways, Wanda Hampton is a good woman and has to hold up her position."

Spud laughed. "It will go all right."

Chet went back to the hotel and unlocked the door. She sat up wide-eyed. "Is it all right?"

"Things are getting into place. It will work. You'll ride in a wagon to our hiding place, which is at a rich lady's house. She is very — well, sophisticated."

"I sure appreciate all you are doing."

"No. I owe you. We will have those two in jail in the morning. They can't know where you are or they'd already have tried to find you here. We are secret enough for now." They waited inside the hotel's back door until Cole drove up the alley with the big horses and wagon.

Chet undid the chains that opened the back tailgate. Then he easily hoisted her in the back. "Lay down till we get there."

"Sure."

Tailgate rechained in place, he ran around and climbed up with Cole and gave him directions.

"I sent Spud to break the news we were coming."

"Is she real rich?"

"I have no idea, but I suspect she is very rich. She needed Buck and Dooley. I think her husband ran that ranch and when he died, the foreman that he had was only the man who was in charge of the yard crew and farmhands. She needed a ranch superintendent. I think all the ranch hands left because he was not a leader and the leader was gone. Buck was really excited and even more when he saw it."

They stopped in the circle drive and Chet got down. "Get the others and we can meet here. She has a meeting room."

"I can do that. Need help getting her out?"

"No," Chet said, undoing the tailgate. She scooted to the edge and slipped over into in his arms.

"I can smell roses," she said, giggling as he set her down.

"Oh, she has hundreds of them. Let's get inside. That is her at the doorway. Her name is Wanda."

"Thank you so much, Wanda."

"Wanda, this is Shirley. Let's get her inside."

"Of course. Now, my dear, let us remove that old blanket. I understand they want to kill you. You are safe here. Mr. Byrnes is my dear friend and he is very efficient, and his men are more so."

"I had no one to turn to. Thank you for accepting me."

Wanda couldn't hold back and hugged her. "I am pleased I can help you."

She turned back to Chet. "We will get her a bath and some clean clothes. How long will she stay?"

"A few days. I may leave Spud here to keep things safe."

"He seems an intelligent young man. He is welcome to stay."

Chet leaned in and kissed her on the cheek. "Thanks, Wanda."

"Take me along if you plan to attend any operas?"

He nodded, and she rushed Shirley away to clean up and dress her.

Cole had the entire outfit there in no time. They knew where the ranch was located and made plans to surround it at sunup. Being at a good distance from Durango, he told them they were going to leave at midnight. He wanted to be set up there at dawn so as to take the house and hope those two were there.

Wanda offered them supper and told them she had enough beds for all of them. The meal put out was more than some of the posse had ever seen, and they had a ball teasing her. She laughed until she tears ran down her face.

At the end she stopped Chet. "I thought all lawmen were very stoic and never laughed. These men have real fun. I am pleased I shared the meal with you and them."

"Well, it beat sand-flavored beans to all get-out."

"Oh, that would be too gritty for me. Bless all of you."

CHAPTER 17

Everyone had gathered at Mrs. Hampton's house. Cole and Chet's three men — Jesus, Spud, Spencer — plus Clay, the stage line driver. Chet explained about Shirley and how her safety was absolutely essential to the conviction of the raiders. Also about the man who lied to her and mistreated her during their escape from the raid and who they were to arrest in the morning at his father's ranch.

Chet emphasized that there might be resistance to making the arrests and that the man's father had lots of money so he would no doubt fight his son's extradition tooth and nail. With as many riders as they had, they should split up and meet near the large McNeal Ranch headquarters and be in place at sunup. When they had those two men in custody they would split up again and some would take the two prisoners on to Four Corners so no lawyer could forestall their extradition to Arizona. The others would get the three who were in jail, head south, and meet up near Ship Rock. If no connection was made there, then both parties were to bring their prisoners down to Preskitt and jail them there.

"Make certain Shirley Douglas is with that group that takes Wallace. That is his real name, and those three need to be under twenty-four-hour surveillance. Plus Miss Douglas is not to be abused by anyone. I promised her complete safety. She is the star witness we will need to prosecute Iris's murderers and why we rode this hard and far.

"Jesus, you and Spencer be sure we have the needed supplies and packhorses for both teams so we have a swift return home. And thanks to all of you. It would never work otherwise."

Cole told them how to split up. Chet felt they'd have plenty enough men to take over the ranch unless McNeal had army-like fortifications. More than likely he did not. The location was described and the time to meet up was discussed further.

Chet had a chance to talk to Shirley. "I am assigning Spud to look after you on the trip. He's short but a very intelligent young man."

She agreed and he let her go help Wanda and her house staff prepare to feed the men. The men ate and bragged on the large beef roast and all the trimmings being served to them. They were all awed by the spacious house and getting to eat there again.

They also teased Wanda about hiring Buck and Dooley.

Then, with his two men getting supplies and packhorses for the two forces' return trip, the rest rode for the McNeal Ranch. Chet was never certain how they made it there on the moonless night and were ready to awaken the large two-story house. Three men were assigned to cover the bunkhouse and contain the crew.

No guards were found. Two men quietly moved the remuda out of the corral save two horses for the prisoners to ride. They drove the rest of their saddle and buggy horses down a lane to a back pasture and sent them packing. Their recovery would slow any pursuit.

When dawn pinked the sky, Chet and Cole opened the front door, stepped in the shadowy living room, and shouted they were federal law. To not go for a gun as the house was surrounded by marshals and they would be gunned down.

He heard a shot in the backyard and

someone shout, "They're all around."

"What in the hell do you think you are doing?" A red-faced man in his fifties dressed in pajamas shouted from the second-story balcony.

"Get down here, McNeal," Chet ordered. "Before I arrest you for hiding two felons."

"Before I am through I'll have your ass and your badge and your life." A younger woman accompanied him in a silk robe, cautioning him to take it easier.

Then two sleepy young men came out hands high.

"Alfred McNeal and Jules Goldman, you are under arrest for the murder of Iris Covington and your raid on the Northern Arizona Stage Line office."

"You can't prove that." Alfred scoffed at him.

"No? I have the sworn testimony of Miss Shirley Douglas and the confession of your best friend Wallace."

"He never told you anything."

"You two sit down," Chet ordered his father and wife. Then he told two of Cole's men who joined them. "Take those two upstairs and get them dressed. One at a time and they make one move to try anything — shoot them."

"Who in the hell are you, anyway?" the

old man asked as one of the deputies brought the trembling house servants into the living room at gunpoint. Chet made them sit on the floor.

"My name is Chester Byrnes, Deputy U.S. Marshal, and I have the authority to be here and arrest these two and take them back for trial."

"You won't extradite them from Colorado."

"They won't be in Colorado. They will be in Arizona in a few hours and will be held in the Yavapai County Courthouse for trial and execution."

"You ain't got there yet."

"I can take you along as allegedly hiding them out."

"You wouldn't dare."

"When Clay brings the second one down, have him take Mr. McNeal up and dress him. He wants to ride to Arizona with us."

"No, Haver. Don't be foolish . . . your heart won't stand it. Tell him you won't fight this. I don't want you dead."

He put his face down on the wooden table and clenched his fists. "Claudia, he is my oldest son."

She rose and waved her hands at Chet to get his attention. "He has a very bad heart. He cannot ride to Arizona or anywhere. It would kill him. I swear I won't let him do anything foolish."

"Then, Mrs. McNeal, you convince him not to try and follow us. If he does, I will damn sure make him my prisoner and he can cross the Navajo land barefooted with a rope around his neck."

She hugged the bent-over man's shoulders and tears ran down her cheeks. "Tell them you won't. For God's sake, Haver, tell them."

"No. No."

"He is upset. He won't trouble you, I promise."

The two men assigned to dress the pair came down the stairs with them. Chet nodded. "I want those two shackled and on horses. Did we run all the horses off?"

"No sir," Spud said. "We saved two for them to ride, sir."

"What about his ranch hands?"

"We took them a good distance away and they are all barefooted. They will be picking cactus spines out of their feet for a month. And we collected their shooting irons."

"You guys may make real deputies any time now. Let's load up those two and get out of here."

"You are leaving my husband here with

me?" she asked, sounding desperate.

"Anyone tries to break these two loose will pay with their lives."

Mrs. McNeal nodded that she understood. "Thank you. He is a very sick man. I hope this will not kill him."

Chet started the prisoners for the door. "And if you two don't stop grumbling I will gag you all the way home. Savvy?"

The pair loaded on horses, they left for Durango at a trot. It would be a long day but at last they had the killers. They might have escaped arrest, but their sorry treatment of Shirley Douglas had really came back to haunt them.

Three hours later Jesus and Spencer met them outside of Durango with Shirley, the packhorses, and supplies, plus the other three prisoners.

"Let's push to be in Arizona before the old man and his lawyers can get up a posse to stop us."

Everyone agreed. They swung south. Chet, Cole, and his three men, Jesus, Spencer, Spud, and the stage driver Clay Whitson, who made a real hand, were all riding hard with the five prisoners for the Four Corners that marked the border.

Later in the day they dropped off into the hotter desert that made them sweat, but no one complained, except the prisoners. The two mouthy ones were told to shut up. Everyone else was anxious to get home. Chet even daydreamed, in the saddle, about the cool days at Center Point and Preskitt. To be back in his wife's arms and sleeping in a real bed summed up a future welcome he knew would be heavenly. They would be five days to a week to get down there — but this whole mess was now over save the trial.

They pushed across the desolate Painted Desert that the federal government gave back to the Navajo people after letting them go home on foot from their prison camp down on the Rio Grande River. Many had died in the malaria swamp prison, and many more perished walking home after their release. There must have been some better places in all this land they called home. He recalled Blue Bell had once told him about heaven in the mountains in the midst of this land where many people and small flocks went in summer. But they came down in the fall to winter in places where the peach trees thrived, like Canyon Desha.

She explained to him if anyone ever died in a hogan, no one used it again and it remained deserted until it fell in. The front door always faced the rising sun. No one knew where this pattern came from and, in their small flocks, they even had four-horned goats. The origin was unknown. The Spanish had taught them how to weave the wool and hair into their famous blankets, and make silver-turquoise items. Both the metal and the semi-precious stones came from their land.

But crossing so much barren land day after day told Chet the Navajos had gotten no bargain deal. Some mined the coal that stuck out on the surface and sold it for heat to the white men. They told him that in some parts, the surface coal had caught on fire and these places were the land of smoke and red-hot ground.

The most precious thing in the land was the scarce water, but Chet and his crew found it under the guidance of herder women who showed them where the next source was. They were well-rewarded for the information. He paid them in combs and hairbrushes, items they did not have.

Chet's eyes felt burned to the core but when, at last, he saw the peaks above Center Point a day and a half before they would actually arrive there, he felt much better. When they came in sight of the company's sprawling headquarters, he could see they had hung a hand-painted WELCOME banner up strung between two tall pines and an

American flag that waved.

He led the procession into camp on orders from Cole. Standing in a beautiful dress and under a wide-brimmed black cowboy hat, his wife beamed coming from the crowd to greet him. When he dismounted to hug her, his sea legs almost gave out, but she hugged him tightly so he did not fall over.

"I've got the roan," Spud said, and took the reins. "I must say, Miss Liz, you are looking wonderful."

"Thanks, Spud. Good to see all of you. Those are the men who did that?"

"Yes, and that young lady helped us. Hey, Shirley, come meet my wife."

The girl smiled and swung her horse around to face her. "Mrs. Byrnes, if my legs could stand I'd get off this horse and hug you to death. Your husband saved my life."

"He is a great guy, my dear. Can we help you?"

"No, he assigned Spud to take care of me. He can help me down. But thanks again. I really mean that."

Liz turned and squeezed him again. "You always find them."

"Like I found you?"

"I guess similar."

"Good."

"You want food or a bath?"

"I have Navajo sand in every pore of my body. These whiskers are like cactus. A bath is best."

"I have a tub full of hot water waiting. A driver told us late last night you all were coming and I almost took a horse and went to meet you, but when they made that welcome sign I said, I shall wait until he passes under it. How far did you go?"

"Colorado. And had they not treated Shirley so badly we might never have caught them all. Oh, besides that, Tom may kill me."

"Why?"

"I gave a widow woman two of his good men to run her large ranch. Buck and Dooley are both on her payroll as superintendent and main man now."

"Was she rich?"

"I think so. Both her house in Durango and the big one at the ranch were mansions."

"Was she pretty?"

"I guess. She helped me and she made me promise if I ever take you to another opera she has to be invited."

"She must be a neat lady."

"A little too much for me. Buck will settle things down up there for her."

Alone with her help in the tent he peeled

off the dirty clothing and settled himself in the tub. He closed his eyes and savored the warm water. Armed with a brush, she worked on his back, laughing as the water sloshed on her dress while she stole kisses.

"I wished, many times, you had come along. But the last six days were gritty as hell. Sandstorms and glare about wore out my eyes. I would have hated putting you through all that."

"I am sure happy you came back."

"No, I am the happy one, and we managed to arrest the raiders. I really thought that without some help we'd never have found them all."

"What about Hall?"

"He's still on the loose. Shirley never saw him. A prisoner named Wallace made the deal, according to her, and he had all those others already when he got her onetime boyfriend and his buddy to help them. They all abused her going back to Colorado. She feared for her life so badly she couldn't dare run away. Separated in Durango from the others, she heard I had arrested three of them and came for my help. I don't think we'd have ever found the other two if she had not came forward."

"After I shave you, you sleep a while unless you are hungry."

"I could sleep. Maybe in your arms?"

She shook her head but smiled. "Oh yes."

He closed his eyes. *Thank you, Lord, one more time, sir.*

Everyone was there for supper. The wives were dressed up, and so was his son Rocky. He didn't forget to ask if his father had found a larger pony. Chet told him he was still looking for it. Then he watched the boy report back to Valerie across the table, who winked at him, listening to his son's side.

"They make a pair, don't they?" Liz asked him.

"A real good one."

"I was relieved those two men were helping you. And I guess we've had no other problems with raids. I came up here and Tom accompanied me to be sure nothing else broke out. Sarge came over while Tom was here. He has two of his men checking on any undercover business going on. So you and Cole have had help while you were gone. Mail ran smoothly and so all seems to be good."

"We all are on a team."

"We have made plans once you were back to have the Lucy and Shawn wedding at the ranch."

"Good."

"Val and I have it all planned. She really is a smart person, and I love her like a sister. So we will proceed to host it in like a week."

"Fine. I plan to get back to running my own business now we have settled this raid business."

"Do you think Hall has quit?"

"No. But he has gone underground since we will be charging the men he hired with murder. It will be in all the papers and he will know he can be implicated, so I figure he's going to go hide."

"So this matter still lacks a lot before being done?"

"A whole lot. I need to tell Cole about his stage driver, Clay Whitson, who went with us. I spoke to him briefly the night before and promised to put in a word for the man. He wants to join Cole's guardsmen rather than being a driver."

"I think Cole went to check on something. Tell me more about this rich woman who helped you."

"She is a very fussy lady. You know the type — upper-class snobbish women. She came and sat at my table at the hotel and began questioning me about how to get the law to stop the rustlers from stealing. Her husband, who died I guess a year or so before, ran the ranch, and his foreman was head over the farmhands. So she had no one there who could stop the thieves. Her foreman was not up to running them off. The law was shorthanded and told her to hire some men to do that. I saw the ranch and the operation and told her she needed a superintendent and that Buck and Dooley could do it.

"She agreed and they took over. When I needed a place to hold a meeting to plan on how to arrest the last two station raiders, she opened the doors of her expensive home, fed us, and sheltered Shirley for us while we went to get the last two killers."

"How did she ever learn about our trip to the opera?"

"She wondered about your going along with me. I told her the benefits. She didn't forget despite her money, because she has never been to a real opera."

"I am so glad you are now back. We will complete plans to have the wedding."

He was proud of her strength while he was away, and was anxious to sleep with her in his arms that night. Some things were not replaceable — she was one of them. If he only had Hall's whereabouts he could close in on him — and close the circle. Nothing about the man was on the horizon.

CHAPTER 18

The stage line was running. No reports of any more trouble. Chet sent a letter to Hannagen saying that all was well — business as usual. He also told him he was going home to work on his own projects and that Cole could handle matters for the stage line. Nothing was said in the letter that he'd be there for any extended period, but several things needed to be examined.

Plans were for Valerie, Rocky, and Liz to go back to the ranch with Chet. Spud could escort Shirley in a buckboard to the Preskitt Valley Ranch. Jesus and Spencer were to take the prisoners to Yavapai Jail.

Their trial in the future would require a lot of his time. He needed to meet with the prosecutor and be sure Shirley was available for her testimony. His last meeting with Cole was over them starting to build the stage stops. He knew that would take the longest time, but Hannagen said to go ahead and get them ready.

Robert and Betty still waited for their baby, and the second day the group camped for the night so they could arrive at the Camp Verde Ranch operation the next day. Victor's wife, Rhea, met them at the big house front door. Adam and Rocky soon were busy on "boy" things.

Jesus and Spencer took the prisoners on to the jail in Preskitt, where they would await trial. Chet explained leaving Buck and Dooley in Colorado to Tom. "It really was a mess and those two could do the job," he finished with.

"Well if they couldn't do it, no one could. I understand your concern and needs, but I will miss those two rascals. I guess I am the college for the outfit. Ratchet is down helping Roamer at the force. Shawn is up with Lucy."

Tom smiled. "Betty had her baby yet?"

"Any day. Any day now. Those two are on pins and needles waiting for it to come. We are hurrying home to get set up for the wedding."

"I better go get Millie . . . she will want to help on the wedding."

Chet smiled. His prisoners were already on the march to jail. It would be wonderful to have that part of the mess over with.

Where had the summer gone? It was slipping by fast. He went back to the big house where Rhea and her housekeeper Lea were preparing lunch.

He told Liz that Millie was coming to help with the wedding plans. She agreed and Chet went off to talk to Victor about his farming plans.

"I need more hay land. I could use another eighty acres in alfalfa down here."

"Is there a farm for sale close by that has that much irrigated land?"

"I have been looking and Tom has too. The Rileys have a place east of town a short ways that they have on the market."

"What is their asking price?"

"Three thousand dollars they told Tom."

"That may be high. But it has the farmland you need that can be watered?"

"Oh yes."

"I will put Bo on it then and see if he can buy it. How much alfalfa does it have now?"

"A hundred and twenty acres and several stacks. He sells some but there is no big money in the Verde Valley to buy the rest of his hay."

Chet understood all about the economics of northern Arizona. Access to markets to sell things was what it lacked. Down at Hayden's Ferry in the Valley dairy farmers would buy it. Up here there were small sales only. Population and development would help that situation, but it still might take years to reach it. Victor thanked him and went to see about a broken-down mower one of his hands brought in to be repaired.

He made a note in his herd book to see Bo about the Riley place. Then he joined the women in the house. A shame that Susie was such a distance east at the Windmill or her voice would be in their plan making. He'd remind Liz to have her informed about the wedding plans. There were lots of things to do and a short time to get it all done. His ranch crew and their wives at the big house would all pitch in and do the groundwork. They loved *fiestas* and weddings.

He saw to it that Shirley was a part of the family group. Liz had her under her wing and the girl acted much happier. Good. She had a life to live despite her past treatment, and hopefully some guy would sweep her away that deserved her. After lunch, he and Liz set out for the mountain and home.

"When you were trying to get control of this lower ranch, did you ever expect this to become such a big deal?" she asked, on the spring seat beside him.

"I wanted another ranch like we had in

Texas. But no, I never thought I'd be involved in so much or have this much property and money."

"I had once met Margaret at a social event in Tucson," Liz said to him. "She was a widow then too. Or she had been a widow twice at the time so we shared some of the things in our life. My loss had recently occurred and hers sounded over for her. But I guess you had not met her by then?"

"My nephew Heck and I met her on our first stage to here from Tucson. She seemed very excited about me searching for a ranch and wanted to help me. At the time I was committed to Kathren in Texas, who later could not move here because of her family's bad health. And I had no idea she was carrying Rocky then or maybe she found out she was pregnant after I moved out here. I would have found a way to be with her and the child if I had known. But that is spilled milk now. Margaret began to pay all my bills to help this poor Texan. I was neither poor nor as rich as she was, but I could afford what I spent. So I finally had to make her take back the money and told her how I had a woman in Texas. She said that made no difference, I would be good for the society up here. Keeping her at arm's length, I bought the ranch but had to fight a war to recover it. Then I started back to Texas on the stage and it was held up. The outlaws took my nephew Heck as a hostage. I went after them on a stagecoach horse with one of the driver's rifles. I found the outlaws in a shoot-out with each other up near Horse Thief Basin. One of the dying outlaws said they'd cut Heck's throat and threw him off into a canyon. I shot him and then took his saddle horse to ride back and look for my nephew's body.

"I found him in a canyon where they dumped him off and I carried him up to the top in my arms. One of the worst damn days in my entire life. I met the posse on the road. They offered to help me but I said no and rode on carrying him in my arms. I was in a bad state of shock. That boy, my dead brother's son, had in Arizona made a big turn to his life. Instead of the crazy wild youth who drove his stepmother May beside herself — and that's why I took him along with me — became a thinker and doer. But he was dead in my arms and I was the one brought him out there.

"Margaret heard about the robbery and drove down there to help me. When we met on the road, she made me put him on her buckboard wrapped in a blanket to take to the funeral home. She saved my life over the next week knowing full well I had a woman I planned to bring from Texas. At the funeral so many folks came. The headstone and her personal help were always there, but I was fighting myself at allowing her to get to me. Margaret was a wonderful guiding force at that point, but all my family was back in Texas.

"When I came back to Arizona with the family she teamed up with me, and there is no doubt she felt relieved I had not brought a woman back with me. I wanted to go see the high country north of the rim, and she wanted to go along. I told my sister Susie my plans and she said, *Marge won't go along.* Sis said she was too correct to go gallivanting around over the country with a single man. She didn't know Marge. When I asked her to accompany me she said she'd love to. Victor was coming to do all our cooking and promised to make music every night. I got to feeling guilty and married her before we left. We met up with Lucy and since she knew the area, she showed us the country as a guide and became a good friend."

"Marge had never been pregnant before in her other marriages?" Liz asked.

"She said no and she warned me quite openly before we married that a child might be impossible for us to produce. That's why she was so shocked when she learned she was going to have a baby with me. Happy but shocked. She gave up her horse jumping . . . carried him full term. But after Adam came she went back to riding. It was her one deep love to do. I couldn't say no though I worried. And then that happened."

"This was her ranch?"

Chet nodded. "Her father built the house and the rest, and gave us this ranch as a wedding present. He was, and still is, a very smart businessman. Someday it will belong to Adam. I promised him that."

At the ranch, they got a warm reception from the workers and Monica came out on the porch to welcome them home. It felt good to be back. He remembered those hot days crossing the Painted Desert as the cool breeze that smelled of the pines swept his face — he was at home again.

That night in bed she told him very guardedly that she had missed two periods and felt she might finally be carrying a child. She'd held back telling him because she couldn't be absolutely certain. After her second period time went, by she couldn't resist sharing the news and they celebrated.

Later on his back in bed staring at the ceiling, he said, "Liz, no matter how things turn out, I am, as always, terrifically proud to have you as my wife."

"I know that, big man. I know that very well."

CHAPTER 19

The two of them worked hard together on the books the next morning. Liz showed him how Hannagen's payments trailed the billing but not by much more than could be expected at that distance. He still owed them twenty thousand dollars.

"I think he will pay that. It is near the final amount before we start building stage stops," she said.

"I have no idea how much mail contracts pay the contract holder, but men like him don't invest in such things that don't pay. And after all of Hall's efforts to stop us, I decided that it must pay very well."

"Probably does. I think Tanner at the bank told you the government had slipped to longer terms on your scrip for the cattle they hold, and Tanner cashes them when they are available."

"Nothing we can do about that. It is how the government does business."

"In Mexico if the government owes you money, you are unlikely to ever get it paid back."

Chet laughed. "We won't do business with them, then."

Things were still working. Robert's log hauling made a substantial profit. The Diablo Ranch showed sales of cattle. JD promised him that they would expand such sales and while they didn't cover all the expenses, which were in development, things were beginning to gain. The Hackberry Ranch worked well with more cattle coming from sales of the Navajo deal. Tom had made some great cattle sales now that he finally had two- and three-year-old steers to sell. The home ranch and Hampt's place looked successful. The saddle shop was selling new saddles, so that worked. The Force even showed a small profit, so despite the stock market's bouncing ball in New York and economic failures — their whole operation functioned well.

The outlaws were in jail.

That evening after supper, Jesus and Anita sat on the living room couch in private conversation. Anita originally came from Mexico as Liz's maid. She worked in the house for Monica and helped Liz too. That evening she'd fixed Shirley's hair. The other new girl, Lisa, was sewing a dress — all part of his extended family.

He thought of it all as "the women's dormitory," but he kept that to himself and went out to rock on the porch swing in the cooling night. Liz joined him and they talked about the small things in their life. Did he have any plans to go see about anything?

"Nothing that sounds pressing, but since you are in the family way I want you to ride in a buckboard when we go out anywhere."

"Fine, I am like you . . . I don't want anything to spoil it."

"Good. I was afraid to tell you since you like to horseback ride so much."

"I like most of all being with you. Horseback riding is my second love."

"The wedding plans are going well?"

"Shawn is bringing Lucy down here by a slow train in a buckboard. They will soon be here. They can honeymoon at the Oak Creek Ranch. Her youngest sister, Hannah, has her baby girl, Carla, and will keep her all week."

"Sounds planned out to me."

"You would expect that . . . we are pros at these things."

He slumped down in the swing. "I never worry about the celebrations we have. The ranch women get all excited and do tons of work with the rest of you. It is a real *fandango* for everyone."

"We have invited all the people you know, and Shawn's kinfolks will be here too."

"Great job. Maybe you and I should go upstairs and celebrate ourselves?"

She kissed him. "Sounds wonderful."

They went off to bed. While he undressed he wondered where Hall was staying at that night and what he planned to try to do next.

CHAPTER 20

The ranch schoolhouse bell clapping awoke him in the middle of the night.

"What's wrong?" Liz clutched his arm before he stood up.

"They don't ring it like that unless we have trouble. Stay here. I'll go see about it." His pants pulled on and the Colt in his hand, Chet took the stairs under the many questions shot at him from the women above.

"All of you stay down and in the house. I am going to see what's wrong."

He stopped at the back door of the kitchen and saw armed ranchmen running about.

He shouted for his foreman, Raphael.

"*Señor,* some armed men approached the house from the road. My men are saddling horses to chase them."

Chet shouted, "Bring me a horse. I want to go along."

"They can handle it."

"I know that, but I want information from those men. I'll go get dressed."

"Of course, *señor.*"

Chet knew damn good and well if those *vaqueros* ever caught those raiders they'd hang or shoot them. They'd eliminated invaders who tried to raid the ranch before, and they did that with them. This time he needed all the information he could learn from them. He almost ran into Liz going back in the kitchen.

"What happened?"

"Just a few minutes ago armed raiders rode in the gate. The night guard rang the bell to roust the crew. They've fled. Now the men are going after them."

"What will you do?"

"Dress and join them."

"What if you get shot? All of us depend on you."

"Liz, they can't run over me. I need that stopped and with my men along as well — we will stop them. I'm going upstairs to dress —"

"Chet," Jesus shouted, running into them in the dark room. "Spud and I have your horse and a rifle in the scabbard. Sorry, ma'am."

"Go dress," she said to him. Turning to Jesus, she touched his arm. "And you men must bring him back alive."

"We will, ma'am."

She shook her head like she could not believe this was happening. "I am going to get dressed and go burn some candles for all of you at the church."

"Elizabeth?"

"Yes, Chet."

"Take an armed guard along so we don't worry about you."

"I will consider that."

"No. For your husband's sake, take an armed man with you to town."

"I will do that. Thank you."

Chet, coming back down, heard Spud come in the back door. "Anything wrong?"

Jesus answered him. "No, he is dressing upstairs. Is Spencer up?"

"He's out there on horseback waiting."

"Let's go mount up; he will be right out."

Chet, ready, squeezed his wife's face in his hands and kissed her hard. "I love you."

"The same."

He realized, out in the starlight, they had saddled the big gray horse for him. His boot in the stirrup, he swung in the saddle and sat down, expecting the war to begin. The horse waited for him to give him rein and then started out in a quick walk.

God bless Ty. He has made a better hand

with a horse than his deceased father ever could have done. That boy'd sure tamed the big horse down to the using variety. Past the gate bar he and the others short-looped to catch up with the *vaqueros* ahead of them in the cool moonlit night.

They raced past the dark houses and through the business streets of Mayer, and the *vaqueros* felt certain they were on their trail. Chet had talked to Ramón, one of the top hands, who told him that they would catch them by daylight.

The sun had not pinked the eastern horizon of mountains yet. They must be headed for Bloody Basin, a region he knew well from years before chasing the horse thieves who stole Margaret's horses and who, later, killed the two top men who managed the ranch for her and her father.

It would be a long chase until they closed in on them. There were plenty of places to ambush his posse where they headed. But that all depended on the outlaws' leadership and who guided them. By daylight they'd be far enough south and at a lower elevation where the *saguaros* flourished, but with tougher and steeper mountains to climb.

Chet tried to recall the place where they shot the foreman and his second man. It was on a steep mountain-face trail dotted with the tall cactus all around them. He'd caught up with Raphael there back that first time. He was standing above both bodies in tears.

He told Raphael that a posse was coming. When the posse got there he told Raphael to come and join him in the hunt, but the dumb posse leader would not let him ride after Chet, and his man never forgot that.

Chet couldn't either because he hanged the two remaining outlaws at Rye. And later someone wrote an account of the lynching without his name mentioned in a Globe paper. Nothing ever came of the article, but later Cole told him that was how he heard about Chet Byrnes and why he came to work for him — a tough man who by himself found and hanged those two killers and rapists.

When the sun came up they were deep in a canyon surrounded by volcanic rocks. When Chet looked to his left he recognized the steep mountain face covered in tall-armed cactus. Ahead was the cow-face-sided trail that wound up to the next high-above plateau.

"Men, be ready to dismount. They may try to ambush us. This is the place where another bunch killed two good men."

"Raphael told us to watch for this place." Then the leader took his horse in great cat hops up the mountain. In the line, a man's horse scrambled, lost his footing, but his rider was able to shake loose before his mount spilled over backward. There was lots of confusion. Horses were barely reined enough aside to miss being in the tumbling horse's fall. The animal screamed in pain from the force hurling him downward as he rolled over and over again. Meanwhile the others hurried to the top, where they gathered.

Ramón gave the order, "You, Tomás, stay with Santos. And take your time going home. Be quiet when you shoot that horse. They don't need to know where we are. Take care of yourself, *mi amigos.*" The lead man crossed himself and others followed.

"You did the right thing," Chet told him, and they pushed across the grassy flat mesa. "That is one of the worst trails around here."

"It was too steep, but we had to gain it."

"Right. We should catch them now that is behind us."

"Thank you, *señor.* I can tell by the droppings we are getting close to them."

Chet nodded and he felt proud that the gray never slipped a hoof.

Two hours later at a spring site developed into a tank, they watered their sweaty horses, filled canteens, and ate some jerky. They were in the tall juniper country. They would reach a ranch that he knew of in about an hour. He wondered about the woman whose husband worked in the Horse Thief Mines, way to the west, and had been raped by those last outlaws he had chased through there.

They found her place boarded up but someone had kicked in the door. Only some dusty furniture remained and whoever had not stayed there long, so Chet and the posse pushed on. He calculated they were four hours from the next ranch, and when they finally reached a spot near the place, Chet surveyed it with his field glasses. There were a half dozen spent horses hitched in the yard near the house. It had to be the outlaws and they were still there.

"Remember, John Hart and his wife Mary plus two children are in that house. We need to surround the place and on signal take them before they can hurt the hostages. If they have any guards on rooftops, shoot them first and then we will cover the house. Be very quiet and try to not be exposed. The closer we can get the better we can bring them down. If they have weapons in their hands, shoot to kill. It will be them or us who wins this war.

"If one of them breaks and you can't hit the rider, shoot the horse. We need them stopped."

His posse had enough men to contain the outlaws. His purpose was that and that this was to be the last stand those raiders ever make. The men spread out to surround the place.

The afternoon temperature had heated up more than it would have at his house. Advancing with Jesus and Spud through the junipers, they came to a barbwire fence and crossed over it. Sweat trickled down Chet's ribs. Soon they were close enough and waited for the signal from Spencer that the others were in place.

Chet, with his rifle in his hands, stood less than fifty feet from the front porch behind a bushy juniper. The outlaws' hitched horses stomped at biting flies and snorted a lot in the dust — a sign they were tired.

A shot rang out. He heard someone shout and then tumble off the roof on the opposite side of the house.

"We have you surrounded. Hands high. We are U.S. Marshals. We will shoot any opposition or armed persons."

Half their horses had broken their reins

and looked wild-eyed on how to escape. Chet rushed for the cover of a still tied one where he rested the barrel on the saddle seat. Obviously the pony was gun broke.

He spoke softly to settle the horse and drew a bead on the front door. There was lots of shouting going on inside. A woman screamed — damn, they were going to use Mary for a shield. He hated that. But instead a desperate man came to the front door with his two six-guns blazing.

He crumpled down in the doorway . . . shot by three rifles. Chet's horse remained and he kept his watch on through the buck-horn sights for another fool.

The next one must have broken out of the back door. The volley of shots left him screaming, then silent. A pistol shot from a front open window, bullets were returned and a man cussed that he was hit.

"Surrender or die!"

A shooter showed himself at the upstairs window, breaking it out with his gun barrel, and they cut him down.

"You had enough?"

"Hell no. You hold your fire. I have the woman and I'll kill her if you don't let us get away. Stand back."

A man emerged holding a cocked gun at her temple. He had a hold of long blond curls that fell to his shoulders. She looked pale, scared, and was shaking her head in disbelief at being dragged toward the remaining horse, the one Chet was standing behind.

Who was that fancy *hombre* holding her hostage? He was some famous figure and what was he doing in the middle of Bloody Basin running with these killers? Chet had slid the rifle off the seat of the saddle but had not given it up as the golden-haired man brought her out the yard gate.

"Get back from that horse," he ordered.

Chet didn't move at first. The other two bad men who came along with him had handguns that they swung around, threatening the posse members in sight.

"Catch me that horse," the head outlaw ordered.

His man caught the rein and the hostage holder swung his gun away from the woman's head. As he did so, a great knife struck him in the back and he fell to his knees. The other two wilted to their knees as they were shot down.

Chet quickly handed his rifle to a posse man close by, and caught the woman in his arms before she collapsed.

"Oh, thank you, dear God — and you came to save me again, Chet Byrnes, God bless you." With wet eyes she rose up and kissed him.

He blushed. "I am sorry they had to come here."

"No. No. Not your fault that they came here, but you followed and you did the right thing one more time."

"Her family is all right in the house," Jesus said.

"Good. You hear that?"

"Yes." She hugged him again. "I kept thinking, when they arrived, if only Chet Byrnes is chasing them we will somehow survive this day. When I heard your voice, I began thanking the Lord and you ever since."

John Hart appeared at her side. "Honey, let the poor man go. You are embarrassing him."

"I don't care, he saved our lives. Again. Do you men know how great he is?"

"Yes ma'am," Spud said. "That's why we ride for his brand."

She sighed and let go of him, then dropped her shoulders. "I thought the last time would be the last time. You know who that outlaw is, Chet?"

"No."

"That is Curly Bill Snow, the Texas outlaw who will ride no more." She gathered her

308

skirts. "It will take me about an hour, but I want to feed all of you before you start back. Thank God John and my kids have survived."

"Thanks so much. We will pile up the outlaws and see about the wounded ones. Jesus and Spud, you two can help her fix some food."

They agreed and both smiled. Then, shaking their heads, the two men herded her in the house, talking a mile a minute about the whole deal.

"Empty their pockets," Chet said. "We will split that money between all of you men, and any wanted reward paid on them will be split equal ways. Are any alive?"

"Not for long," Spencer said. "Bloodiest deal I ever saw. They had it coming, but it was sure a bad one."

"They were like some rustlers we tried to arrest up on the rim who fought to the last man rather than linger in prison."

"All I can say is that they asked for it."

The lead man for the Preskitt Ranch, Ramón, spoke up. "No one has ever entered our ranch with murder on their mind and lived to talk about it later. My orders from my boss were not to bring them back. I know, Chet, that you wanted them alive. I tried, but I won't fret over them. The earth is a better place today without that blond-haired son of a bitch."

Chet watched the head *vaquero* walk away. He'd said what he believed and that was enough. *Amen.*

CHAPTER 21

In the cool morning after they buried the outlaws in a common grave, Chet said a brief prayer. Then he held Mary by her arms and kissed her forehead.

"I hope I never have to come back here again for any bad reason. God bless you, your husband, and your children. Come stay at my house when you need supplies from Preskitt. My wife, Elizabeth, may have our baby by then. We are excited — it will be her first one."

"I hope she does well, and tell her how much I appreciate her lending you to save us again."

He turned to the posse. "Men, there is a big wedding coming. We need to get home in time for it."

They mounted up, leading the five extra horses and saddles plus guns and anything of value to sell. One horse was too badly wind broken to bother with and was led off to be destroyed far enough away from the house to not smell him.

The return trip took two long days in the saddle. From a distance Chet could see the great white tent was up. Thank God, they'd gotten back in time for the wedding.

Liz in a grand dress ran to greet them, holding up the hem. He dismounted, gave Spud the reins, then caught and swung her around before even thinking about her condition. But he realized the baby was there and growing. They kissed like long-lost lovers and finally came up for air.

He swept her up in his arm and went on kissing her. "Are you doing all right?"

"Yes, and we are still in the baby business. I cannot believe it; I never carried one this long ever before."

"Good mountain air must be the difference."

"Maybe. Or God willed it this way, so I did not have a child to hobble me from finding you."

"No, my dear. A child would not have stopped me."

"But being vulnerable might have made me much more cautious."

"Hell, it has worked well. I thank God a lot for him and you."

"It may be a girl. You have two boys."

"So that it is all there and healthy . . . I don't care."

"Tell me all about the men you went after."

"After I have a bath and you can shave me. It was not a pleasant trip. But they won't ever come back here again."

"It must have been difficult."

"I don't know if Hall hired those others, but rumor has it he'd hired that blond-haired outlaw."

"Who was that?"

"The Texas killer Curly Bill Snow."

"Oh my."

"He's dead now. He won't bother anyone on earth again."

"Thank God you are back here and all right. What comes next?"

"Back to ranch finances and Lucy and Shawn's wedding coming up. How we are doing?"

He set her down at the foot of the back porch stairs.

"Welcome home, mister." Monica stood at the back steps. "It is time you got back here. You cut these days close, don't you?"

The woman never waited for his answer, and he decided she probably didn't want to hear one. She had her say and that was enough.

Lucy and Shawn greeted him inside the house. Of course she was showing, but he could tell she was like Susie was in the same condition when she married Sarge, happy to be wed again.

"Sure proud you made it. Lucy wants you to give her away."

That meant her father was back in the bottle again like he was the last time when she married Reg. He'd had so much faith that last time too, but Shawn surely was smarter than Reg. He'd talk to him some about things before they left. Damn it was hard being the head of a family at times. So much for him to do and so little time to accomplish it all.

Later he spoke to his foreman, Raphael, and told him how well they all worked on the chase. The man nodded and said, "They are all good men. They appreciate the jobs they have here. In Mexico most ranches have no place for wives nor do they worry about them. Here they have *fandangos* and *fiestas.* They have wonderful Christmases, and your wife buys the men dress-up clothing. She buys cloth for their wives to make dresses, and the children go to school. Several boys can now make saddles. You have christening parties for the boys and girls. Besides that, it is a lot cooler here than in Mexico."

"Not a bad climate. A few cold days, some snow, but it melts and the rest of the time wonderful weather. I like it much better than Texas when it rains enough here."

"But the stage line headquarters may have polar bears in winter."

"You've seen pictures of them?"

"Oh yes, and they read me the words for how big they were too."

"Thank God they aren't here."

"I heard a story that the Navajo, a long time ago, came from up there, and their leaders once wore white bearskin coats."

"I will have to ask Blue Bell about that."

"Tell me one thing. Why does she not have a man?"

"Navajo men like to run things. She couldn't help her people if she was such a man's wife. I understand she is educated and those men don't like that either."

"Did you once think about her?"

"Who wouldn't? While she traveled with us coming west she and I had many long talks. She had a tribe to save and I had a ranch to build from a very bad start."

"Now I understand. Thanks for explaining. Nothing is wrong with your choice of women. I loved Margaret and this one is a darling, but I knew you helped the Navajo woman too — and I wondered why. Thanks for sharing that with me."

"We are all doing good — ranching better than I ever could have exactly planned it. Tom is a good leader. Robert loves his job hauling logs. Sarge was the man for the Windmill and the monthly cattle drives. Hampt is a great ranch foreman. He will have a top ranch in a few years. JD's Diablo is going to be another asset. We may some-day drive the Mexican cattle he has grown up to here to fill future needs. He has started oranges and lemon orchards that he waters. When the train tracks get to Tucson in a few years he can ship citrus back east no problem.

"Lucy and Shawn will run the upper ranch. They found enough cattle to stock it for free. It will be a huge operation in time. And this place pulls its part too. You have done wonderfully breeding up the cow herd on this place."

"Not many ranches are this big are they?"

"That Captain King family has a larger one in south Texas. I have never been there, but I understand it is huge."

"The new ranch you just bought over east of here. How big will it be?"

"As large as this one or larger when we get through."

"Who will run it? Have you decided?"

Chet shook his head. "It must be forty to fifty miles east of Mormon Lake. I may not find a family man to run it. Susie is a real ranch-raised woman or she wouldn't make it on the Windmill. This ranch is beyond that place."

His man chuckled. "Everyone can't live in town."

Chet agreed and went back to the house for supper. The women had made the two new girls dresses for the wedding. They were excited. Anita had fixed all their hair to see how it would look for the wedding. Liz made sure the outfits everyone wore were all sewn together right. He lounged in the kitchen while Monica was busy making supper.

"We may start a girls' school here. The two new ones have little education. Many of the *vaqueros'* wives cannot read or write. Liz has worried about it, and she is going to ask you if she can do it here."

"I have no complaints. But will she feel like teaching when she is further along with her pregnancy?"

"Chet Byrnes, that will not hinder a thing in that girl's life."

"If you say so, Monica."

"When did you become so agreeable?"

"I am not going to argue."

"What comes next?"

"I purely hope nothing. I have been to hell and back this summer trying to get that stage line going and putting down the raiders. Right now I am going to take a *siesta* before supper and forget all about everything."

She laughed. "You can't do that. Your mind won't let you."

"I can damn sure try." Chet rose, walked through the dressing party with his eyes half closed, and went upstairs to lie down on his own bed.

Took him forever to get to sleep. Damn Monica. She was right. But he finally slept some.

The wedding day began at sunrise. He let his wife sleep in. They had worked on outfits until late, but they had them complete. Women were putting tablecloths on the tables. The *vaquero* wives were always excited about being a part of any and all the ranch events. And they were fussy about how things went. One of the head women saw a stain on one cloth they laid out and made them replace it. He savvied enough Spanish to know what she had said — *not at our ranch.*

The fires had barbecued all night and the

mesquite smoke aroma hung in his nose and made the saliva flow in his mouth. They used a paddle to stir the cooking — ranch-raised *frijoles.* Two huge pots of them simmered, one was for *gringos* and one for real Mexicans laced with hot peppers.

A three of the women crew sang folk songs while making flour *tortillas.*

"*Señor,* we love your traditions. I know we say this often, but every time I go to church, I say thanks to God. I tell him our *patrón* understands us and appreciates all of us."

"Thank you. This ranch is for all of us."

They crossed themselves and laughed, going back to work. It was this sort of thing that he understood. Out after criminals in barren places, he could always think warm thoughts about his ranches and the fine people who populated them.

He'd talk to Tom about the blacksmith shop making barbwire for his new place. Maybe Raphael knew some young men who needed work that he could enlist as a fencing crew as well as cutting the brush out of the future hay meadows.

They would need to be armed. While Crook had the Apaches on reservations, the threat still hung with the wild ones who ran off to the Madres, then returned to the

United States to raid isolated ranches and homesteads. While he considered the matter, no one came to his mind right off to move over there. That person would come to him.

He had a conversation with Shawn. Drew wanted to be Cole's man on the west end of the stage line, so he would be leaving and they'd shook hands on the fact that Shawn would take over the upper ranch.

"I understand there are over four hundred cows up there with the ones you added from Hampt's?"

"That is right."

"Reg must not have done much in his herd book before he — well — left us. Drew said he had tried to straighten it, but he didn't have the time with only two cowboys and the rest of the boys putting up hay."

"You know I have been busy with all my things. I did not realize he needed more help. Why didn't he hire more?" Chet asked.

"Told me, and I'm being straight with you, that you didn't want to spend the money."

"That's a shame. I may have neglected him."

"He said half his bulls were cross-breed ones. I saw several of them."

"Did he ever tell Tom?"

"I don't think so. But as we are sitting here being honest . . . I need six more cowboys to get that cattle deal straightened out before winter. Ten bulls. The local boys will put up the hay, but the hay equipment needs going over. It is broke all the time. Some of it was abuse. They mowed patches of sagebrush to clear land. That should have been hand done but it wasn't."

"I'm sorry. I can fix that."

"Drew said Reg told him you never got them all the bulls they needed and the ranch did not get one new windmill this summer."

"Well he never asked for any of this. In the early years we were short on bulls and had to freight them up there, but I thought that we had that all fixed."

"I have not seen enough to know how many bulls we will need."

"Spud knows that country. He's wise beyond his years. What if I loan him to you as the jingle bob boss for a while and we see how that works out?"

"The guys are pretty high on him. They say he's tough."

"Yes. He has some knowledge of that high country and could work a roundup crew to get your deal straightened out. He also has enough education to keep a logbook."

"Chet, I'd bet half this year's calf crop has

not been worked. Spud is fine with me and any other help you can find."

"Spud will know some men up there who need work and would be happier up there than anyone I could send. It is pretty isolated. After the honeymoon, you send me a list concerning the equipment, the number of windmills you could set up. Appraise all the places up there that Bo has bought and what you think we could do with them."

"You know they once had an alfalfa place?"

"Yes?"

"Reg shut it down. Said it was too far from the main ranch to use. The range stock has eaten it up now and ruined it."

"Shawn, sounds like we have lots to do. But I believe you and Spud can handle it."

"Lucy wouldn't tell you but I learned he got awful abusive before he took his own life. He threatened her if she complained one word to you about the damn ranch operations being all wrong. Said it was his ranch to run. She was to take care of the baby and not mess with it in any way. I found that very sad."

"I missed that part. After his horse wreck he was in pain a lot, and I found him to be like a wounded bear."

Shawn looked around to be certain they

were alone. "The men told me his reckless-ness caused that wreck. He was so mad that day about some woman that had quit him that he drove that horse after a cow where he knew no horse should go."

"I knew a little about her and don't doubt that. She must have been a hell of an attrac-tion."

Shaw shook his head. "I wouldn't trade Lucy for her. Someone pointed her out to me in the store in Hackberry. I didn't know you knew about the deal."

"I learned after he died."

"Chet, I know she's had hell and didn't deserve it. But I am excited. I loved her since the first time I met her and never dreamed I'd have her for my bride. But I won't mistreat her. I promise you."

"Good. Maybe the Lucy I knew can re-emerge."

"She will. So I get Spud and how many hands?"

"Half dozen to try. Tom may have some but the rest need to come from up there. Like I said, I think Spud knows the good ones to hire."

"Should I tell him?"

"I want to talk to him first. He will go. He wants a job like that. His size has nothing to do with what he can handle."

"I understand. I have a lot to tell my bride and she will be pleased."

"God bless both of you."

"Thanks. I feel a hundred percent better."

Chet looked all over and finally found Spud and Shirley on the front porch swing.

"Hey, you two look nice all dressed up. Shirley, I need to talk to Spud in private for a few minutes."

"Oh, sure. I'll go into the house. Talk to you later." She smiled big at the man and left them alone.

"I see you and her are getting along."

"I really like her. We sure got acquainted riding home together. She got a real raw deal. How long will the trial take do you think?"

"Oh, to get set up and complete it all three months."

"When it is over I want to marry her."

"If you two want to do that, you'd better ask her if she'd be your wife on the upper ranch then."

"What do you mean?"

"Shawn needs a man to be his *segundo*. Things are in less-than-good shape up there. Reg let a lot of things slide and Drew might not have been the right man to fix it. All the spring calves didn't get worked and branded. I imagine there are lots of cull cows need cut out and half-breed bulls rounded up."

"Wow, I'd be the under-foreman, huh?"

"Spud, you and Shirley would have to live on one of the places we've bought until they could build you a house. You know that country. Be sure she understands it isn't living in town up there. You will need more men, and I told Shawn that you could pick the good cowboys."

"Could they have their wives and a place to live like you do here?"

"I don't see why not."

"Chet, I know several good men up there. If they had a roof over their heads for their families they'd jump at the job."

"That's why I am picking you to go help him."

"If she agrees to move with me, I would keep her safe and after the trial marry her."

"Before or after I don't care. Just so she knows about the isolation is all I want to warn you about."

"I will take the job. Thank you for trusting me. I came on as your tracker and now I'm going to be an assistant ranch foreman. Better than that, I am a part of the Chet Byrnes Ranches and his family. I never had any family in my life."

He looked close to tears. "By God, Chet,

thanks, thanks a lot. I'm going to talk to her now before I cry."

"I'll tell Shawn he has you," Chet said after him.

His wife in her fancy dress came across the living room frowning at him. "Whatever is wrong with Spud? He was crying when he took Shirley out of the room."

"He will be fine. Those two struck up a relationship coming home. Spud's going to the top ranch and help Shawn. They have lots to straighten out. He asked to take her along. I said that was not my decision but to warn her that it is real isolated up there."

"Will they marry?"

"Not my problem or decision. I told him do what they wanted to do, but he talked about doing it."

"Kind of short notice."

"I'd have married you the day after we met."

She nodded, amused. "Yes, I think I would have too. But while the wait seemed very long, it was a great union and remains one."

Liz squeezed his arm. "They are coming back and now she's crying."

Spud spoke first after clearing his throat. "She is going north with me. We can decide about wedding plans later."

"Oh, how nice." Liz hugged her and him too.

The rest of the room had a bunch of people milling around and they all, including Lucy, hugged Shirley and told her they'd get along fine.

After all the hugging was over, Shirley came up to Chet. "Chet, I am sorry I am crying — but I am so pleased to be — with him and your wonderful family. I thought when I got to Colorado my life was over. I can't tell you what all of you have done for me."

"Shirley, you are a part of us," Liz said. "Now it's time for the wedding. Girls, let's go over there."

"See you there." Chet headed out to tell Shawn before the walk down the aisle.

He caught up with Shawn outside the tent. "Spud is excited. He's taking the witness girl, Shirley, up there with him. They can live in a homestead house while we build one. He also knows good men who will work for you if you provide them houses. They can also stay in homestead houses until we get some built."

"That's great. Take a little time but we can do it."

"Enjoy yourself some too. The ranch falling apart didn't happen overnight, and it will take planning and time to repair it."

"Chet, with Lucy for my wife I am going to enjoy living."

"Good enough."

The Preskitt Valley house was ready for the wedding. Their reputation for having weddings and other events made them the thing to do and where to appear at in Preskitt society. There would be a story in the *Miner* newspaper about who wore what.

The tent was up and the ranch force cooked enough fresh beef *frijoles* with ranch-raised beef and all the trimmings that went with. Spud thought that the giant frosted lemon cakes looked mouthwatering good. Ice cream had been churned for the occasion.

Everyone was there. The guest list included all the family members, ranch workers, and over half the Preskitt city population.

JD and his wife with baby came from the border ranch by stagecoach. Drew, Fern, and Hannah all came. Lucy's dad was unable to come. Lucy whispered to Chet that he probably went out and got drunk. Lucy's ex-mother-in-law, Louise, and her husband, Harold Parker, were there. Cole sent Valerie with Rocky and her nanny. He wanted to stay and be certain the stage line held together. Chet's banker Tanner came. Bo, his wife, and new baby boy Lawrence were there.

Susie and her son Erwin couldn't come — Sarge was on his way to Gallup with the month's herd, but Hampt Tate and May plus their tribe came, the Verde Ranch bunch; Tom, Millie, Victor, and Rhea with Chet's son Adam all came. Shawn's family and neighbors who knew him as the boy growing up beside them were in attendance as well.

Lisa Foster wore a new dress. Her hair had been washed, cut, and fixed. She still acted as if she were in mild shock. But Liz told Chet not to worry; the girl was a fighter and would make it. Jesus escorted Anita to the event. Someone needed to push that girl, but who could do that? His wife wouldn't. He wasn't certain why not. Maybe he'd solve that problem, himself, one day.

The music began and Chet took Lucy's arm. She looked up and smiled with the bouquet in her hand. "Thanks."

They talked softly as he led her down the aisle.

"Did it shock you when I told Liz I was serious about Shawn?"

"No. It is a new day and a new start. Life's

too short to sit around waiting for the perfect day to do anything."

"He swears he has no objections to me being pregnant. If he'd accept me like this, things will get better for him later." She winked at Chet.

"You are getting a good man."

"I know that."

"You two have crossed all the bridges in your lives."

"Most of them. He knows we will have babies too. They all will be his. He is very honest. I was very honest with him. I am more a ranch hand than a little woman. You know me. That is no concern to him."

"There is no reason for people to wait around for some things to pass. They won't ever pass. Good luck, daughter."

"Thanks, Dad. You know I love you like a father. One more thing?"

"Yes."

"Tonight after the ceremony, do a blessing for us like you —"

"I will. God bless you now."

Leaving Lucy at the head of the aisle with Shawn, Chet joined Liz.

"They will make a strong couple."

"Your sister did the same thing?"

"Yes, and that may have made a stronger marriage. Nothing wrong with the first one, but Sarge and her have molded a good life together."

When Shawn kissed the bride, he saw Spud kiss Shirley in the outer ring on the east side of the tent. Oh well. The food was coming next, and the best wine made in Mexico would be served as well. He joined Liz in the handshaking line as family with both of Lucy's sisters, her baby girl beside them, and Shawn's mother and father.

Meet and greet. Things were shaping up to a big evening celebration.

Rocky had wiggled out of Val's arms and ran to his half brother Adam, who told him something. Too far away to hear but they talked a lot.

He recalled Ty and Ray when they were growing up and May herding them. Ray is back east to prepare for college in a few weeks. He needed to thank the boy for the broke gray horse. And talk about the amazingly short time the job of conquering such a high-headed animal into a model horse took.

Hampt came by. "What will Shawn do now?"

"I am putting Spud with him as his foreman. Shawn will be the superintendent. Things had slipped on the ranch and Shawn saw that in the few days of being up there.

Drew had never been in charge of much and it may have overwhelmed him. Reg had his own problems and he dropped the deal. I guess I never was clear enough to Drew he could hire and do what he needed. He thought two cowboys was all we could afford — lots of work was left undone. He never got a windmill this summer, never put in for one. They hired boys and let them mow sagebrush to clear meadows, which tore up the machines."

"Oh, was it his mental condition — I mean Reg? He got so gawdamn know-it-all before the end I had to tell May to forget about him."

"He had problems in his life."

Hampt nodded. "But he got so he didn't appreciate anything."

Chet nodded. "Yes, even living."

"Amen. I hope Shawn and Lucy will be as happy together as we are with our wives and lives."

"They will be. And I am not sure you know, but Liz and I are looking at a baby coming."

"I heard. I wanted to tell you congratulations. And to warn you that when they start coming they may not stop."

"Thanks. I better move about."

Moving off and finding Tanner, Chet

shook his hand. "Well, we cashed some more paper this week. Sort of shocked me but it moves us closer to five months now," Tanner told him.

"That sounds wonderful. I guess we have one of the best moneymakers in the north half of Arizona?"

"Most people would have to borrow money to exist. You are fortunate. But you planned it that way. Answer a personal question for me? Am I too old to become married?"

"How old are you?"

"Thirty-nine."

"Have you ever been with a woman in bed?"

"No. I have been tempted but no. Is that part hard?"

"Has she been married?"

"Oh yes."

"Then don't worry. Let the cards fall. A woman can be the backbone of your life. You must accept the good and bad things. Don't dwell on things you don't like."

"The lady is a widow. And she is very nice."

"Why didn't you bring her here tonight?"

"I should have, shouldn't I?"

"Yes, you should have."

"Thanks. I will proceed."

"Good luck. I hope it works out."

Tanner smiled. "So do I."

Who in tarnation was she? Maybe Liz knew. Poor man had never made love to a woman in his entire life. That may be a shocker to her.

When Chet told her, Liz had no idea who she might be but she planned to find out. She snickered too about his lack of experience. It would be interesting. Tanner had never had to adjust to whatever would fit a woman in his bland life. He could hardly wait to see results.

Liz looked around and saw people were finishing eating. "We need to move. I know she asked you for a blessing before she cuts the cake."

"Let's go.

"You have the blessing written down?"

"No. Never do. I let Him position the words and hope they come out like He'd have them."

Liz blinked her brown eyes in disbelief to shake her head. "Go ahead."

"Folks, as we have gathered here for these two fine people just married let me say a few words to God about this event. Our dear Lord, we come to you today to introduce Lucy and Shawn. They joined hands together out of the love they found surrounding them. Even at a distance from north to south of perhaps three hundred miles they started a step-by-step march in private letters. They'd met several times at family affairs such as this in the past. So in a friendly way they knew each other. Shawn had no wife. Unfortunately for Lucy her man went to be with you, sir. So two lonely hearts, miles of desert and mountains between them, began to share things that moved onto more personal things — how could they get closer? How could they squeeze each other's hand and let the energy flow back and forth and make this friendship grow richer and deeper? Both of them, Lord, were struck by the same lightning bolt and they came to the ranch here for the real visit.

"Lord help them through the hard days — hold them firmly in the palm of your hand and let them have many years of peace, children, and success until you need them in that great pasture in the sky. We pray in your name. Amen."

"Amen."

Lucy came in her full dress with Shawn on her heels.

"Oh, wonderful. Thank you."

"No problem. You two must have the Oak Creek cabin reserved for tonight?"

Shawn blushed. "We do, sir, and her sister has the baby Carla. She said come back when we get ready."

"Tell my great farmers up there at Oak Creek hi. And drive carefully."

Lucy clutched and kissed him hard. "I owe you a lot."

"No, you owe life your best and remember others . . . that is what it is all about."

Shawn shook his head. "Thanks; if I hadn't had the experience I had working for you and the force, I'd never made a place for me in her heart either."

The couple rode off in the buckboard loaned for the Oak Creek trip.

Liz, hugging his arm quietly, asked him, "What's next?"

Right now I don't know, dear.

CHAPTER 22

The morning after the newlyweds slipped off, his wife woke him up sick and vomiting. He knew it was just a sign of the times, but with the rising sourness in his nose he held her up standing over the thunder mug.

"My dear God, Chet, I have never been this sick in my entire life."

"It ain't just you, dear. You never reached this point before right?"

"Never."

"And I can assure you, it too will pass in, oh, the next four months."

"Was she sick too?"

"Yes, I think it is part of the entire business of pregnancy."

"Oh Lord. May asked me if I had been sick yesterday. Maybe that triggered it?"

"Sit on the bed if you feel weak."

"I won't pass —" And she did. Fainted right into his arms.

He lay her back down on the bed, dressed,

and went downstairs to ask Anita to help him. She hurried upstairs with him. Liz was sitting up and holding her head.

"I am so sorry."

"No problem. Anita will help you."

Back downstairs, he drank some coffee standing at the back door and looking at things taking place all over the ranch.

"She got sick today?"

"Yes, Monica. She did and never did that before."

"Won't be the first time or the last time now she's moved into the fertile side of her life."

"You sound like Hampt."

"How is that?"

"He said when you start having babies you will have more."

"That is what I am talking about."

He wondered at that. First you want one, then you are not sure you need one, and then it's too late. He laughed and shook his head. Life was strange.

He needed to talk to Tom about bulls for Shawn. He and Millie had gone home right after the ceremony was over. He said they had some family problems that needed to be settled. Chet offered to do anything he could to help them. Tom said it would be all right.

Liz came down after a bath. She had dressed but still looked peaked. When both Monica and Anita went out to get something, Liz filled him in on Tom's situation. "I didn't want to tell you, but I think Tom and Millie's daughter wants to elope with some boy."

"How old is she? Fifteen?"

"Same age as Millie was when she married Tom."

"Your own examples can hurt you."

"Yes, they can. Millie said her life was so tough at home and she wanted to escape it and did. But their children have had a good life, were educated and live under a good roof."

"What will they do?"

"Try to make them wait a few years."

"Good luck. I need to go see some people. You feel good enough to ride to town with me?"

"Of course."

"I'll get a buckboard ready and we will go."

An hour and a half later he pulled up near the bank and saw a blue parasol and Tanner coming out of the front door. They were so busy, the two never noticed him. His heart sunk. That woman was the same one; a friend of Marge's who divorced her husband for ignoring her, got together with JD, and then broke his heart by marrying an older rancher. He had died a few months ago. What was her name? Kay, that was it.

"What is the matter?"

"It is too much to tell you."

"Was that Tanner's woman-to-be?"

"I guess so, but he's in for a painful life if he does marry her."

"What can you do?"

"No one can do a damn thing but lump it. Let's go see Bo."

"Fine. Can you tell me more?"

"Later I will try."

"Good. Sounds juicy."

"More like lemon sour."

Bo was at home helping tend his newborn boy, Lawrence. They went by and saw the excited pair.

They both looked exhausted but happy.

"See what you can expect to happen to you," Bo said to him, showing him his son.

Chet nodded. They talked a while, then Chet and Liz headed home.

He decided to go to the lower place in the morning to talk to Tom. He told Jesus his plans that he and Spencer were to meet him at seven in the morning. They'd probably spend the night down there unless things got settled. He also told Jesus to bring Spencer for breakfast. He'd tell Monica they were coming. Jesus said they would be there.

His alarm woke him and after he dressed he kissed his sleepy wife good-bye. She mumbled she was fine but didn't feel like going along so he went downstairs.

Monica had the two men drinking coffee and he joined them.

"Nice day outside?"

"Cool," Spencer said. "It will be hotter downhill today."

"Good part about this country you can go ten miles and be in a new climate. In Texas it was the same all over."

Jesus laughed. "Same all over in Sonora. Hot."

"We are going to speak to Tom about the upper ranch today. Either out of Reg's stubbornness or an oversight we missed making sure everything was good there. They are still using some half-longhorn bulls and don't have enough help. I am holding off any roundup until Shawn gets back from his honeymoon. He said they ruined some of the horse-drawn mowers cutting sagebrush with them. I made him superintendent and Spud the foreman. The boy knows those people and who to hire that will work. Reg didn't order any windmills. Bo has bought several homesteads up there with good dug wells. Easy to make windmill set-ups.

"Shawn and Spud will make a good team. Now I need to get their machinery working. The hay season is over, but I hope they have enough stacked forage for the cattle if we get a snowy winter." His men agreed.

"We may have to go up there and inventory things. Those small farmers with extra hay would welcome us buying some, but we need to do that now, not when the snow is hip deep."

"I hope we don't have to," Jesus said.

"We added two hundred cows to help out that place of Hampt's."

Jesus said, "I know about those cows going up there, and that will double the hay needs."

"First you guys have bandits, now you need hay." Monica left the room shaking her head over the matter.

"She's funny at times," Spencer said, sipping more of the hot coffee she recently poured into his cup.

"She's not a bad cook either," Chet said.

"She's had two husbands. She must know how to be a wife," Jesus said, looking at Spencer.

Spencer made a face at them. "Hey, guys, I don't need her."

"Well, Jesus, we tried."

"Aw the devil with you guys. I want a real pretty woman for my wife."

"Everyone wants them," Jesus said.

"Well, you ain't getting close to marrying Anita," Spencer told Jesus.

"I'm close."

"How close?"

"Maybe by Thanksgiving."

"Congratulations," Chet said, and they got up from the table.

"She know that for sure?"

"Sort of."

Spencer gave him a friendly shove. "Ha, you're daydreaming."

Jesus shook his head, put on his hat, and went outside. "You will see."

Chet smiled. Those two had a way to gouge the other guy until it was humorous.

They rode to the Verde Ranch and dismounted at Rhea's big house. She wasted no time welcoming them and holding her stepson Adam back from running to meet his pap-paw.

"What's wrong?" she asked.

"Need to talk to Tom, see my boy, and bother you."

"I understand. Tom may have rode off about something this morning. He mention anything to you about their daughter?"

"You think he went to find her?"

Rhea made an unhappy face. "I can't say. I don't know."

"I'll go ask Millie. Not your fault. Adam, you look after Rhea I until I get back."

The boy went over to her as she invited the men inside for some fresh coffee.

As quickly as he could, he hurried across to Tom's house and knocked on the door.

When no one answered, he opened it. "Anyone home?"

Red eyed, Millie came from the kitchen. "I'm sorry, Chet. Tom isn't here."

"He gone looking for his daughter?"

"She wasn't here when we got back from the wedding. I told him he'd never find anything in the dark. He never slept. I have no idea where they went."

"Your son say she went with the boy?"

"He didn't know where they went either. They wouldn't tell him."

"What is Tom going to do about it?"

"Bring her home I guess. She'll probably have his child. Oh, Chet, I don't know."

"Millie, I want to go help him. I know children can be real trials. You recall JD and his problems."

"I know my momma cried her heart out when I told her I was going off with Tom. I don't know why. It was one less mouth for her to feed."

"But Sandra has not missed doing much in her life she wanted to do."

"Maybe we've been too nice. She doesn't know what it was like sleeping with four kids in one small bed. We ate lots of things I'd not eat today, to save from starving. East Texas cotton patches was the worst place in the world to grow up in."

"I'm going to go look for them. I bet I can find them." He hugged her tight.

Jesus picked up horse tracks and the three rode east. They went past the place Bo was going to buy for him for more hay ground. It looked decent. They crossed the shallow Verde and, in a clearing, under some cottonwoods sat a lean-to. Chet spotted a good bay horse grazing. He looked as polished as a mahogany desk in the midday sun.

Two other horses raised their heads, a paint and a dun, unsaddled, and grazing nearby.

"You stay here. If I need backup you can come in. I figure they are arguing in there. Maybe I can help settle it peacefully."

His men nodded and dismounted. Chet pushed the good red roan forward, swung off by the bay, hitched up his pants, and settled his gun belt.

Short of the lean-to he stopped and called

out, "Has there been any killing so far?"

A red-faced freckled girl stuck her head out. "Not yet, sir."

"Good . . . I came in time." He removed his hat and joined the three sitting cross-legged on the ground.

"He's Cody Day. This is my kinda uncle . . . Chet Byrnes."

"Yes sir, I've seen you before. Nice to meet you." They shook hands.

"Tom, how far have you gotten?"

He shook his head. "They won't listen to anything I have to say."

"You're pretty calm for you."

"What can I do? Let them lose their lives. They have no work. No home. That horse she brought is yours and must go back to the ranch."

"You tell her how hard her mother cried last night?"

"She has no feeling for us as parents."

"I do too. Mother married him when she was fifteen and left that cotton farm," Sandra said.

"She was starving on a cotton farm. You left a pretty nice house yesterday and all the food you wanted — right?" Chet asked her.

"Yes sir."

"Then you were not leaving them out of abuse or hunger?"

Both of them shook their heads.

"Cody, you have any work to pay you a living?"

"No sir."

"You tell your parents what you were going to do?"

"I left them a note. They were gone to town."

"That wasn't very brave, was it?"

"No sir."

"Did you ask Tom for her hand in marriage?"

"No sir."

"That was not very brave either, was it?"

"No sir."

"Well, you ask him now."

Cody shook his head.

"I'll ask him for you. Can Cody marry Sandra?"

"When he has a paying job and a roof over her head and not this damn tepee."

"How are you going to do that, Cody?"

"Mr. Byrnes —"

"Chet," he corrected him.

"Chet, jobs are hard to find. I don't know how far I'd have to go find one."

"How were you going to support her?"

"Shoot wild game and do day work."

Chet shook his head. "That won't feed and clothe her. She lives in a nice house.

Does some housework and can cook, but she's never had to do without anything."

"I don't know how that would be. Sandy and I want to be together as man and wife. Yeah, she's young. Yeah, she's living at home. But we want to be man and wife."

"What if I offered you a job?"

"I'd take it."

"This job is mucking out stalls and pig lots for the first six months. Then you move up to exercising young horses, riding and training them. Then if you don't quit I'll move you up to a herd drag rider and calf flanker at roundup. By then if you learned how to rope good enough you will become a horse wrangler. You would be working for Tom, here."

"I would do that, sir."

"You quit short of that wrangler job, I'll find you and spank you harder than your daddy ever did."

"I savvy. Thanks for the job."

"Now, ask him."

"Sir, may I marry your daughter?"

Tom dropped his gaze. "You can get your things and come to the house. You may not sleep with her or have any relationship with her until you are married."

"How is next Saturday going to work for you two?" Chet asked all of them.

"Why then?" Tom asked.

" 'Cause it will take me all week to get ready for another wedding and the honeymoon suite at Oak Creek won't be empty till then either. Sandra, you and your mother come to town tomorrow. Liz will take you to get a wedding dress."

"Tell me one thing, Chet Byrnes, how did you figure all this out?" Tom didn't look pleased.

"Tom, you and me didn't have many options. Life is too damn short to be in conflict. Anyone asks you about it, blame me. Now let's ride back home. I have some things you can solve —"

Sandy dove over, knocked Chet on his back, and smothered him in kisses. "Thank you so much, Chet."

He struggled to get up laughing. "Now I have to go tell your mother what I did. Oh yeah, Tom, how many windmills do we have ready?"

That conversation went on all the way back to the Verde Ranch. He had things straight about that by the time they got back there.

"You brought her home," Millie shouted, running off her porch.

"Hold up before you hug her. I made some tough deals here. You may be mad

349

enough to shoot me."

"What for?"

He started on his little finger. "I hired Cody to work here. Tom agreed they could get married next Saturday. He is getting his things to move over here and they can't have any relations this next week. You and her are going with Liz to buy a wedding dress tomorrow. Saturday they are getting married at my house."

She looked repulsed. "He's going to live here?"

"We will get them a place to live."

"I don't know if I can stand him living under the same roof."

"You will." He turned her around to face the house. "Because someday you will want him to share the grandbaby that you will want to hold and spoil. So, grandmother-to-be, bite your tongue. My negotiations were hard won and you will be civil. Get her the dress with Liz, and be there beaming on Saturday."

"You are a good man, Chet Byrnes. I never thought I'd accept, but you're right . . . I will." Millie kept nodding and sniffing.

"We need to ride home and make plans. All my *vaqueros*' wives will moan and in the end do it right."

That night in bed, his wife Liz asked, "Millie agreed, huh?"

"Clenching her teeth. But I knew she never saw her mother again when she rode off with Tom. Losing Sandra would be a bigger heartache than she could bear."

"You think there is a grandbaby involved in this?"

"Might be. Might not. There will be someday, and Millie don't need to miss that. Her mom never saw her kids. I bet Millie don't know if that woman is alive or dead even. Why miss it all? It was the way to go."

"Oh my, big man, you sure get in some tight places."

Real tight at times. Where was that damn Hall hiding at this night? He wanted to nail his hide to the outhouse wall.

CHAPTER 23

The week flew by. It was getting to be a
weekly occasion at the ranch to have a wedding. He sent word to Susie, and word came
back she was coming with her boy and
Sarge.

He posted one to Cole and the answer was
if he could get away. Lucy and Shawn would
be headed home; he was anxious to get up
to the ranch. Spud and Shirley were already
there. He felt good. Maybe in this week he
could go up and look at the hay storage situation. Riding to look at the cattle could wait.

In town he met with the prosecutor, John
Moore, about the many trials coming up
and when they might have them. It looked
like a public-provided defense lawyer would
have to be appointed for all but the rich
son. He had expensive lawyers demanding
bond. No territorial judge would issue a
bond for a prisoner held with murder
charges on him.

He set in to planning future cattle sales and which of his ranches would have them. They would need seventy-two hundred head at six hundred head per month. He had lots of room for bought cattle. Shawn's father, at the wedding, asked him to buy three hundred head. He had him on the list. That meant fifteen hundred dollars to the McElroy family. Tight as money was to people in the times, this would pay all their bills and even have money leftover to pay on their loan. The ranch cattle purchases were a relief to many and made the small ranchers self-sufficient. It was also why, when he needed a posse from time to time, everyone showed up to help him; like his contract with Clyde to set up a stage stop. He got to sell two hundred head of cattle meeting the high standards needed. He recalled how proud Iris was that they'd have that income. She was the dear woman the raiders killed, and her death weighed heavy on his conscience. When the mail came from town he skimmed through it. A private letter in a neat penmanship stood out. He opened it as his wife came by and kissed him on the face.

"Anything needs tending here?"

"I have the usual reward posters they send me, a letter from the Chief Marshal in

Tucson, reporting on court trial dates. And this letter came from El Paso, Texas. I'll read it to you.

Dear Marshal Byrnes,

I was recently shown a wanted poster of a man sought by you named Anson (Gerald) Hall. That man is working in a saloon at Mesilla, New Mexico, as a faro dealer. I am not a lawman nor do I wear a gun, but I can't understand why the local law is not arresting a felon when he is in plain sight. It would seem there is a big payoff going on between criminals and enforcement. If he was over in Texas, the rangers would arrest him on sight. However I have talked to the head ranger for the El Paso district, Captain Tom Proudy, and he says he can't step over there and arrest him in New Mexico.

We have come to a sorry state of affairs when known criminals walk our streets behind state and territory boundaries. Good luck capturing him.

George R. Bryan

Chet put down the letter.

"What will you do about it?"

"I am going to wire the head U.S. Marshal

in Santa Fe and have his men arrest him and hold him for someone from Arizona to bring him back here."

"Will that work?"

"Damn right or heads will fly somewhere."

"How did this man find you?"

"My name was who to contact about the reward I imagine."

"His arrest would be great. It might stop you from walking the floor about capturing him."

He stood up and hugged her. "I have not been that bad, have I?"

"Oh yes, you have. I thought those Colorado arrests would settle you down. They didn't. Hall's running loose planning more trouble for the stage line has been on your front burner the entire time."

"So maybe I can rest now." He hugged and rocked her in his arms.

"Lord, no. You will have a new fire in you before the sun comes up."

He kissed and rocked her some more. She was right. He really wanted the man out of the picture. Then things might get back to normal in his life — whatever that was.

"Oh, Chet, I'm fine. Part of that spirit that drives you is why I am your wife. I just wonder sometimes if you realize how risky your life is. Your world is so expanded from just being a rancher and surviving a feud in Texas to managing an overflowing empire. But keep your head down. I sure think you are going to have yet another family member — the one that is inside of me."

"That will be good in some ways. Others maybe not as swell."

"I know. I may have to become the wife and mother that stays home."

They took a seat on the leather couch. He tucked her under his arm. "Is that going to kill you?"

"No. I, like all women, dreamed of having children of my own. I loved the trailing along with you. Oh, sometimes those trips brought back memories from the past that were sad for me, but I got to see lots of country and more than that I was with you. Whatever it takes for me to be a mother to your children I will do."

"Something new I have been thinking about. I want to find a man who builds telegraph systems. I think a telegraph from Gallup to Hardeeville would be a good investment. Maybe not on the start-up but in time as that corridor up there becomes a national highway, even before the railroad comes, it would serve the stops and connect to the outside world."

"Where is this man at?"

"New York. Washington, D.C. The government built the original wire from Yuma up here to help the army fight the Indians. Today a company runs it for both government and private mail. The original telegraph station was out at the fort."

"Who are these people?" she asked.

"I am going to find out today. You want to go to town?"

"I'm sorry. But the wedding is my top item."

"Sandra has a dress?"

"Oh yes, and Millie cried the entire time they fitted her like I will someday."

"They're young. But they will make it if it was meant to be."

"A job is nice. So he has a start, thanks to you."

"Not thanks to me. Tom and Millie are like my own children."

She agreed. "They built the ranch with you, I know, and they are good people."

"Absolutely. I'm going to find Jesus or Spencer and go to town. May not learn a thing, but I will take the first step."

She kissed him. "Good. Don't fall off the spring seat."

"I may ride in."

"We can talk some more later."

"Sure."

He found his men in the barn adding saddle racks to the expanded tack room. His ranch foreman, Raphael, knew Spencer was a carpenter and was using his skill while they were there.

"Jesus, let's saddle some horses and do some business in town. Spencer has plenty of help, and the addition looks great."

"You two don't get in any mess I have to pull you out of," Spencer teased with the hammer in his hand.

"No, not that deep," Chet promised, giving the saddle he had taken off the old rack to the stableboy, who took it from him saying, "That's my job."

He and his foreman shared a big smile. With Spencer around lots would be fixed or repaired.

"You and Anita planning anything?" he asked Jesus when they were on the road to town.

"I think she is simply afraid. Two of her sisters died in childbirth in Mexico. I don't know if she will ever get over it enough to marry me."

"Would Liz help by talking to her now she is pregnant?"

"She might be mad at me for saying something to Liz about her fears."

"My wife will know how to tell her. Heavens, she's worked for her for years."

Jesus shook his head. "You know I love and I respect her. But I may have to give up on her if she is so afraid of dying over it."

"Maybe the priest could talk to her?"

"I would like some help, that's for sure."

"Let me think on it."

"If anyone can fix it, I trust you most of all."

"I am running out of good men to run ranches."

"You sure are." Jesus twisted in the saddle to look back at a fast-moving rig coming up from behind them.

Chet reined up the horse to the side of the road. The driver standing up on the buckboard reined the team in.

Chet did not recognize the driver.

"Mr. Byrnes, sir. I reckon you don't know me . . . I'm Toby Evans. That's my dad, Harrison, in the back — he's been shot. We've got the HG-Bar Ranch."

"We better get him to the doctor's house. Jesus and I will meet you there. Who shot him?"

"Aaron Cargill, sir."

"Go on. He needs medical attention. We'll talk later."

"Yes sir." The boy charged off.

"He was still alive?" Jesus asked.

"I think so. Who is that man shot him?"

Jesus shook his head. "I don't know him. But that boy has come a long ways from the white sweat on them horses."

"We better see what we can learn. Let's lope."

They rushed after the fast buckboard. Arriving at the doctor's house shortly after the youth, they ran up onto the porch to beat on the door.

While they waited for the doctor to open the door, Chet leaned over the buckboard. "Mr. Evans, can you hear me?" Chet asked the wounded man, who was obviously in a lot of pain.

"Yeah. The boy stopped you back there — I guess we are here, huh?"

"What was the shooting over?"

"My ex-wife —"

The doctor and his male nurse were out there by then to examine him.

"We can talk later," Chet said to him.

Harrison nodded.

"Nasty shot, huh, Doc?" the assistant said.

"Yes, it is. All of us can carry him inside. Then I can see more about it. Now be easy, boys."

Doc Henry and his assistant, Oliver, were soon undressing the patient lying on a table.

"Chet Byrnes, you know about this?" Doc

asked him, busy scissoring the shirt apart.

"No sir. His son stopped and told us who shot him."

"Perhaps we should get a deputy over here to take his statement?"

"Yes, we should. Jesus, go get a deputy."

"I can do that." He left for the arm of the law.

Chet took the boy out onto the porch while the medical team worked on his father.

"Toby, tell me more about this."

They sat on the porch bench side by side. Toby began nodding his head and talking. "Talley is my stepmother, I guess. I say that not in no bad way about her. My real mother Agnes died when I was ten years old. Dad raised the three of us. Bucky and Phyllis and me. Dad met Talley Bunch at a dance. He was lots older than her but that didn't matter to her, she said. So he asked her folks for her hand and they agreed. I'm telling you all this so you understand."

Chet nodded. "I'm listening."

"Well, it wasn't a pleasant marriage like they thought it would be. Dad sent us kids outside when they fought. Their wars got so bad and they really wasn't about anything. Petty stuff but they both bristled up and away they went to shouting and cussing at each other.

"They finally agreed to a divorce. When my sis, Phyllis, turned fourteen she married a Mormon guy and they moved down to Saint David. Bucky went to work over in the Bill Williams mining area. We ain't heard from him in a long time.

"Talley moved back home and the court awarded her a divorce. She took up with this guy — Aaron Cargill — and I heard lots of bad things. I know Dad heard things about how bad Cargill was treating her. It all came to a head this morning. I guess that Talley had run away from him the night before — they were in the road when we started in the buckboard to go to town.

"They were on foot coming up the road. He had her by her hair, well, really dragging her, and she had a black eye. I don't care who it really is, nobody should be treated like that." He shook his head like he'd been repulsed by the whole thing.

"Dad told him to let go of her."

"Cargill blew up. He said, 'This ain't none of your damn business . . . she's my — well — whore.' That was all it took. Dad flew off the seat and they got into a bad fight. Talley was screaming for him to stop . . . she'd go along with him if he quit. Just so he didn't kill Dad.

"Dad knocked him on his ass and that made him so mad he drew this gun and shot him. Dad didn't have a gun on his hip. I didn't have a gun either. Then he drug her off. Really hurting her. A cowboy who works for the RTP outfit come by and helped me load him in the buckboard.

"We find out the condition of your dad, and then I want you to take me and Jesus up there if the deputy doesn't offer to do anything. We will get her out of that situation."

"Aside from their arguing I've really liked her. She really doesn't deserve being treated like that."

"No. Just remember what I promised you."

Jesus agreed when Chet told him the story. When the deputy came out he scowled at Chet and asked, "You in on this shooting business, Byrnes?"

"No."

"Good. I've got a whole jail full of them bastards you've arrested now."

"Fine . . . don't let any of them out."

Chet never heard the cuss words the lawman added when he turned back to talk to Toby.

Jesus shook his head in disapproval. "He don't appreciate our hard days in the saddle

363

to get them. All he wears out is the seat of his pants in a chair."

Toby said to them, "He says they will send word for Cargill to come in. That deputy said it might be called self-defense. Damn it. Dad had no gun."

"I am not the law here. But we can go get that lady out of his place if she wants out and then let the law handle it."

Toby was still fighting mad and stalking the wide porch. "I heard people all my life say, we ain't got no law but a rope."

"No. We have law and we will carry it out later. Jesus, put his team up, rent him a horse and saddle from Frye. After Doc tells us something about his dad's condition we will go see this guy."

"I'm on my way."

Toby stopped and swung on a porch post. "I hope Dad's all right after this."

"How's that?"

"Maybe she, Dad, and I can go some-where and start over. I know Talley's had enough of that mean sumbitch, and if we get her away I bet she'd go away with us."

"Where would you go?"

"I don't know but we'd find someone needed a ranch foreman. I bet the three of us would make him a good hand. We've never had any money. Maybe us working for someone, Talley'd have enough money not to skimp on every little thing and she'd be all right too."

"Toby, that's a lot of ifs." The boy's thinking how to iron out things amused Chet.

"I heard you're from Texas. If you had not come here you'd never found your pretty wife or that big ranch or none of the rest."

"True. We will go get her out if she will leave and we can find out her wishes."

"I would certainly appreciate that, sir."

"I'm just Chet. My men call me that and so does my wife."

"I won't forget it. Someday I'd love to hear your life story if you'd tell me."

Chet smiled. "Might take a week."

"That would be fine."

Doc came outside to talk to them. "We have the bullet removed. If he doesn't take an infection he should be good as new in a few weeks. I want to keep him here for a while. Is that good enough? It wasn't near his heart or vital organs. The bleeding has stopped."

"Doc, Toby will be back to check on him. Thank you and I will pay the bill."

"Chet, you don't have to pay the bill," Toby said after the physician went back inside.

"Toby, I know what I have to pay and not

pay. Let me do this."

"Yes sir — Chet."

"Jesus is coming."

"How much do horses rent for a day?"

"I do lots of business with Frye. He probably won't charge me in this case."

"Boarding our team either?"

"I can handle it."

It was close to evening when they approached Cargill's cabin. They had stopped at a crossroad store for some fresh rye bread and a bowl of beans from the woman who ran it. Beans had been cooking on her stove. A congenial thickset woman in a wash-worn Mother Hubbard dress, and when she learned he was Chet Byrnes, she shook his hand and said, "My name's Annie Cross. All my life I wanted to meet up with you. And I finally have."

"Nice to meet you, Annie."

"What brings you down here?"

"Looking for a man that shot Toby's dad this morning."

She looked shocked. "Who shot him?"

"Aaron Cargill."

"Lands, he's worthless as wormy bread."

"I understand that too."

"If you've done half the things I've read about you doing, then kick that guy hard on the backside for me. I've run him off from here twice with my sawed-off shotgun and should've shot him both times."

Chet chuckled. "He must have done some bad things."

Her blue eyes went to a squint. "I ain't telling you out loud, but I should've *kilt* him for it."

"Annie, we get a chance we will throw in a kick from you."

"Put his back parts right up between his shoulder blades."

"Hey, thanks for thc food. We need to find him before dark." He left three silver dollars for the food on her counter.

She came out on the porch. "Good to meet you, boys. Come back any time. I keep a pot of beans hot all day long."

Then, smiling, she gave a big kick of her petticoats from her button-up shoes for him.

Toby said the next side road went up a canyon to Cargill's. Chet twisted in the saddle to look back at the store. Cargill didn't live far from the lady and if he messed enough with her, she'd shoot him.

Cargill's place was a mess. But he expected no more. The shack had a cowhide for a door. A haggard-looking black-eyed girl came out and stood back against the wall. A bearded man in his thirties came out hatless.

"You didn't get enough of me this morning, boy?"

"Cargill, we come to get one thing straight," Chet said.

"Who the hell are you, mister?"

"My name is Byrnes. Chet Byrnes, and I am here to ask the lady if she would like to leave your abusive custody. Talley, what do you say?"

"She ain't leaving and if'n she opens her mouth, I'll knock all her damn teeth out. You hear me, bitch?"

Cargill whirled at the distinctive sound of Jesus's Winchester levering a cartridge in the chamber. "Move away from her or die. My finger itches badly."

Jesus pushed his horse in closer and with his gun barrel waved the man farther away from her. "You better stand over there or die. Chet, you and Toby take her away and talk to her. He ain't doing anything but counting his blessings that I have not already shot him."

"Who are you anyway, *Messican*?"

"The man that's going to send you to hell. Shut up."

Chet herded her off to a good distance. "Toby has some things to say to you."

She swept her greasy hair back and nodded. Her left eye was swollen shut and looked black, blue, and even had some yellow around it. Her lower lip was badly bruised and when she talked, Chet could see it hurt her. The top of her right cheekbone had suffered a hard blow. No telling what else was wrong with her.

"Talley, listen to me. Dad's going to live. I don't want you to stay with Cargill any longer. He will kill you and I couldn't stand that."

"Toby, he would only come get me and kill you too."

"No, he won't do that, Talley. I can promise you that."

"Who is he?" she asked, pointing at Chet.

"That is my friend, Chet Byrnes."

"Oh, I have heard about you."

"Trust me then. Do you have any things that you want out of that cabin?"

She shook her head and both eyes began to tear.

"Catch her," Chet said to Toby. "She's going to faint."

He did and they both set her down on the ground.

Coming to quickly, she swept her hair back and managed to sit up by them bracing her. "Oh, I am so sorry I did that."

"Nothing to be sorry about here. We are

all going to my ranch. We can sort the rest out some other time. Can you ride double and not fall off from behind Toby?"

She gave a quick nod of her head.

"Set here a minute and I'll help load you up." Chet rose to his feet and went toward the house.

"Cargill, if you aren't gone in twenty-four hours I am charging you with attempted murder. Some of my men will be here to be sure you have fled by tomorrow afternoon. You aren't gone clear out of the country, you will be arrested by a warrant I swore out on you that will be on the Yavapai County sheriff's desk. You savvy?"

The man bobbed his head and collapsed to his knees. Jesus set the hammer on safety and put it back in the scabbard. Chet went back and hoisted the girl up behind Toby and they left.

On the road, he said, "We will stop and eat again at Annie's store. Then it is a four-hour ride back to our ranch."

"I need to go by our place and turn some horses out to graze," Toby said.

"We can do all that on the way I figure. Be lots of riding under the stars, but we'll get there sometime. My wife will think I left her."

"Don't worry, Talley. She's used to him

and his wild-goose chasing," Jesus said.

She cleared her throat. "I have never met her."

Jesus checked his horse to get even with her as they came up the two ruts called a road. "Well, she's a good one and she's pretty too."

"I am sure a mess to meet anyone."

Chet put his horse beside them. "Don't worry, she's used to me bringing in women I find."

They all laughed.

CHAPTER 24

When they rode into the ranch, lights began to come on. Chet put Talley down off the horse and she tried to straighten her clothes. "I wasn't expecting a castle."

"Just where we live. Toby, you two come on and meet my wife."

"We need to do anything tomorrow?" Jesus asked.

"Yes, we still don't know anything about the telegraph."

Jesus agreed with a smile.

Chet headed for the house. Several of the stableboys were leading off the horses. He stopped to thank them.

He saw Liz was already talking to the girl and Toby.

His man with the *sombrero* in his hand smiled at him. "I see from here you rescued more people. God bless you."

"Good night, Raphael."

"Same to you."

He caught up and kissed his wife and nodded. "You met them. They tell you his father was shot earlier and is doing fine? Talley was being held as a hostage by a mean man, so after we got him to the doctor, we had to go get her away from the man. It all took time and then we had to go to Toby's place to turn out his horses."

Liz hugged his waist. "Just so you're in one piece. I will draw this Talley a bath. Then fix her with some clothing to sleep in. Toby can sleep downstairs in the little bedroom. I will be upstairs after I have her settled. Did the mean one do that to her?"

"Yes, that's why we went and took her away from him."

"I hope she recovers from all that." She kissed him and he took Toby to the lower bedroom.

"I can't thank you enough," Toby said.

"No thanks needed. Tell me one thing?"

"What is that?"

"Who is going to marry her when this is settled? I am curious."

"I hope it is me."

"I thought so. Just needed to know. You two could make it."

Toby nodded. "My dad and her'd only fight like they did before."

"Good night. Breakfast is early. Monica is

the cook in the kitchen. Expect a lot of questions from her."

"I will be ready."

Chet was asleep when his wife finally joined him.

She gently woke him. "Did you kill him?"

"No."

"You should have."

He went back to sleep.

In the morning, he left his wife to sleep. In the kitchen he joined Anita and Monica who were seated eating breakfast. Both had met the latest visitors.

Lisa and Sandra, who was staying there that week, were also at the table. Then Toby and Talley joined the room and they were introduced to the table.

"Where do you find all these strays at?" Monica asked.

"Oh, I ride up and down the road looking for them."

Everyone laughed.

Anita said, "He's not kidding. Don't forget these other two," pointing to Lisa and Sandra. Then, looking up from her plate of fried eggs, hash browns, and bacon, she continued. "And we are all a part of the Quarter Circle Z brand."

"Where were you branded at?" Monica asked.

"I can't show it."

They all laughed about that.

Jesus joined them for coffee.

Then Liz came in. "Everyone know each other?"

"They have all been introduced," Chet said.

"Chet, you don't leave today. You will get back way too late. We have Sandra's wedding coming tomorrow and I need your help."

"Tom will take her down the aisle, won't he?"

"He better or I will shoot him," his daughter said.

More laughter.

"Just put it all off until next week for me," Liz told him.

"I will do that, my dear."

"I better go be a carpenter," Jesus said, ready to leave.

"No. You can stay here and help us," Anita said.

Things were off and rolling. The day was spent doing the last of the decorating the women wanted. Toby rode to town and back with a report his father was awful sore but thanked them for saving her. Anita spent the day working on Talley's hair, her bruises, and a wardrobe she could wear. The other two girls helped Monica make apple pies for the meal since they were turning ripe on the large orchard trees.

Later on every female was busy setting each other's hair and ironing their dresses for the next day. Chet stayed out of their way.

Hampt and May came over with their family to spend the night and visit. Chet had a chance to thank Ty for working the gray over and tell him how much he was enjoying the horse. Then alone with him he broached the subject of horses to him.

"We all have different things we'd like to do. Ray is attending the academy this fall. I know books are not your thing. I know a man in Texas who is a great horse trainer and could add to your knowledge. I'd sponsor you going back there for six to nine months so you can learn all he can show you."

"That would be neat. I'd love that."

"Then, if you want, I'll get a ranch for you. You can have the gold horses plus you can fill our needs for working ranch horses. We have sold several of those yellow ones, but I think well broke they'd bring even a steeper price. What do you say?"

"Only one thing concerns me."

"What is that?"

"There is a girl in Preskitt I am, well, pretty sweet on. Her name is Victoria Currents. Do you know her?"

"No, but go ahead."

"Her father has the other bank in town."

"Oh, I have met him."

"I guess he's a little down on our family because you don't do any business with him and First Arizona Bank and Trust."

"Well, simply tell him he never asked for any of our business."

"How would that go over?" Ty dropped his head. "Me spouting off at him, when he has a dislike for me now."

"All right. On Monday morning, you invite him to go to the Verde Ranch in a buckboard and have him look over the Barbarossa horses. Then ask him if he has a place up here around Preskitt for sale at a good price where you can set up a horse farm to breed and show them off. And to also set up a bank account at his bank for that operation."

"Aw shit, Chet, he will know it is all your money."

"Hey, if you need to be set up, he won't care."

Ty was rubbing his hands and so bent over he looked ready to bust.

"Do you trust her enough to go over it

with her first?"

Ty rose up in the chair and straightened his shoulders. "Oh, she'd like for things about us being together to go smoother. Yes, I think she'd be in on it."

"If he eases off some, I bet we can even get your stepparents to deposit some money over there. That might be another carrot for the donkey."

"I had never thought to ask them, but yes, they have money now too. Chet, I have never done anything like this money deal in my life. I hope I don't mess it up. Victoria and I are on the very up and up about waiting to become a couple, and that is damn hard to do when you love each other."

"Something good is worth waiting for."

"I guess if it doesn't work we could run off and get married."

"And miss all the fun of a big ranch wedding and a hideout in Oak Creek."

"We're both older than those two getting married tomorrow. You arrange that?"

"Sort of."

"You amaze me. Actually all of us in the family. I would love that ranch you are talking about. I think I could make it work."

"I don't just think so, I know you have all the potential to do it."

"Boy I am ready. Show him the horses and

then get him to find me a show ranch deal, huh?"

"Step by step."

"Whew, now I can worry about that until it is over."

"Wedding is tomorrow, bring her."

"Oh, she is coming. I'll introduce her to you."

"Good."

Chet wrote a note about the deal and added their names to it. He slipped it in under some other less valuable things in the drawer. Then he went out into the living room mob. He stopped when he saw a black patch to cover Talley's black eye.

She stopped him. "Makeup would not hide it. This has been the greatest twenty-four hours in my miserable life. Thanks to you, sir."

"You realize who really wants you?"

"Yes sir."

"What do you think?"

"Harrison and I never got along. I am older, wiser now and yes, I think Toby and I would be good for each other. If he wants a soiled woman."

"He was your biggest defender."

She nodded. "I hated Harrison was shot over me, and I appreciate you and Toby doing all you did."

"Tread water. Things will work out."

"I do believe they will."

He caught Millie putting out dessert for the evening meal. "Things finding a place?"

"Everything. But at thirty-one, why do I have to become a grandmother?"

"You're a pretty one." He put an arm around her shoulder.

"Liar."

He smiled and went to find Liz.

"Well, I saw you and Ty talking. I had thanked him for my roan horse even if I can't ride him right now. He is precious."

"The horse or the boy?"

She pushed him for saying that.

"Tomorrow Ty is bringing a lady friend to the wedding. Victoria Currents. Meet her and make a small fuss."

"More weddings?"

"I was just informed they both were older than these two getting hitched today."

Liz shook her head and was off to see about more things. Sarge, his sister Susie's husband, was there already. He went over to talk to him.

Sarge jumped in first. "My Navajo buddies tell me you have been crisscrossing their reservation."

"I damn sure hope I have seen the last of that. The county jail bulges with prisoners."

"They sure rained like hail on you for a while. You ever get that guy Hall that you asked me about?"

"Not yet. I wired the U.S. Marshal in Santa Fe to send someone down to Mesilla and arrest him. I understand he had a faro game going on in a saloon down there."

"I bet they miss getting him. They say he's like a cat and has lots of lives. Say, I heard of another guy you helped."

"Who is that?"

"Elizabeth witched him a super well a short while back."

"Oh, Thomas Chase. He has two teenage boys. The boys came out of the dry well to get to see Liz."

"Right, and now he has a Navajo wife he just married."

"Wait until I tell Liz. That water witching bugged her nigh to death."

"She needs to use it more often. That is a real strong well they brought in."

Susie came by and hugged him around the waist. "Hey, how are you? What is this wedding?" She lowered her voice. "A shot gun one?"

"No. But necessary. They planned to run off if denied it. I found him work."

"My big old brother keeps finding people to help. Well, I have to say, you found my

Sarge, Hampt, Tom, plus many more. Is Lucy doing all right?"

"I would say very good."

"Sarge was gone so I couldn't come over here. I wanted to see her."

"She's a dear person. She is showing. What . . . five months? Shawn is like Sarge was about you. He was a longtime admirer of her. Babies don't scare him either. He wanted her like you, Sarge, wanted Sis."

"I always wanted Susie until I got her." Sarge quickly hugged his wife before she beat him in public.

"Sarge, you have added one more feature to yourself since you've been married to her. You've gotten to be funny."

"He damn sure did that. He was an old somber guy, and after he married me I got all that stuff out of him." She went off shaking her head.

Sarge nodded. "I was not having fun before I married her, and boy, I had to learn fast how to be that way. I know you have to leave your wife a lot. I miss mine so much each time, I could about cry. There is not another woman in the world like her."

"Buddy, she was my secretary and mother for years. I missed her for a long time too. Now that you have your man picked, why don't you two take a trip or two off? That crew knows how to handle things."

"I will do that. Someone told me — is Liz going to have a baby?"

"Seems so. She's been all right so far. Not riding horses, which is best. We've got our fingers crossed. Now I'd better make rounds, but before I do, I'll ask you like I asked Robert, do you need anything?"

"I don't need anything. Robert's youngest, isn't he running an operation?"

"He and JD. And they are both doing well."

"I see your reports. We're all are doing good."

"The cattle drives are the most important. I am glad you have so many Navajo supporters."

They parted. Valerie was there with "big man" Rocky.

"Cole has not had another raid, but he is on pins and needles and decided to stay up there. Clay drove me down. You know him . . . he's part of our security force."

"He's a good man."

"Yes, I found it very interesting, talking with him coming down here."

Clay joined them. "I guess I didn't mess her up making our wild ride over to Gallup. You know sometimes you just have got to do something out of orneriness."

Chet laughed and shook his head. When Val asked about Liz, he replied, "She's making it fine. She never has done this baby business before, and by now, she told me, she'd always lost them."

"That teaches you not to brag too soon. Maybe someday one will catch and I can have one too. But Rocky must be like you were. I have to take him away from the others here. He has to be the boss or else. I try to make him get along."

"Just a spell. He should outgrow it."

"You never did," Valerie replied.

"Really?"

"Oh, others stand around and think. You move in and separate them to really get things done. Like that day in Tombstone where I was chiding myself for not staying at the house of ill repute and you told me to 'get on that stagecoach, girl.' Excellent advice, but if it hadn't been you who told me to I'da never come up here."

She shook her head in disbelief. "Then I got my best buddy. I know you and Cole are like two brothers. You stamped him as your brother. I think sometimes when he talks he sounds just like you, Chet Byrnes. God, I love that man, and I can't hardly stand to be separated from him."

■ ■ ■ ■

Wedding morning, he got up early on and was drinking coffee with Monica.

Their housekeeper sounded whimsical telling him, "I was fourteen. First time I was married."

"Did you ever sleep with a man before that night?"

She made a face at him. "You're not supposed to ask that question."

"I am not the man who was cheated. I simply asked."

"No."

"Was it nice?"

"My wedding night?"

"That and the marriage?" He blew on his hot coffee.

"It was very bad and abusive. And I started my plans to divorce him right then and there."

"Catholic women don't divorce their men."

"Took me five years of abuse to get out of it. I looked like that Talley girl the whole time I was his wife."

"Why didn't you kill him and say the devil did it?"

"You don't think I wasn't tempted?

Brother, those were bad days. But I managed to get out of his clutches. The good thing was we never had any kids."

"You got married again, didn't you?"

"Yes."

"Was he any better to you?"

"Some. He was bossy. But we loved each other. Bandits shot him one night in a *cantina* —"

When she quit talking he looked up at her. Her brown eyes were wet and she was chewing on her full lower lip. Damn, she must have been a real pretty woman back then.

"I am sorry that I got so deep personal asking about your past," he said.

"No need for me to cry, but I did that day and many more. I woke up one morning and started walking north. I couldn't stand Mexico any longer. It was hot, dry, and dusty, plus it reminded me I had no man. A widow woman in Mexico is just free bait for horny men. I walked and walked, finally crossed the border, and made it working as cook and doing whatnot in Tucson.

"A man wanted to marry me. But I had one bad one and one good one, so I didn't marry him, but I moved into his *jacale* to live with him. Three weeks of that and I was really glad I had not married him. Then I heard how cool it was in Preskitt in the summertime. I talked to this man who was freighting goods up here about hitching a ride with him and his two men.

"Hale Townsend outright said I'd have to sleep with him if I went along and I'd also have to cook too. What did I care if I had to sleep with him? He was just another male who'd use my body. I was used to that. But I did the wrong thing . . . I found I liked him. It turned out he was not abusive. Polite to me and we talked a lot in those slow passing days as we traveled up here. He even found me domestic work at a big house in town when we got up here. He said he was coming back for me. But a few weeks later I heard that Apaches killed him, his men, and burned his two wagons while they were going back down to Tucson. The Indians were real bad that year."

"Margaret hired you to come out here?"

"Yes. I almost turned her down, but she told me she had *vaqueros* and they had wives so I would be among my people. I didn't miss the crime, the abuse of Mexico, but I missed the music and the friendship of my own people. I didn't need a man. Every one of them had been such a bad chapter in my life, so figuring I could find other work if I needed to leave, I came out here."

"Yes, and I came along."

"Oh yes, but that second husband had really scarred her. He cheated on her and I never figured out why but maybe other women bent over for him — she would never bend. You know. You were married to her. She was beautiful and set in her ways, but she couldn't resist you. You know that?"

"Yes, I always felt she had been a little snobbish but changed for me so I would like her."

"She paid your bills. And warned me not to say a sharp word to you because she wanted you — no matter what it took."

"I loved her. We had a good life. I wished I'd talked her out of jumping horses."

"No. She gave up a lot marrying you. That was her thing to do and excel at."

"What did she give up?"

Monica laughed. "She gave up those formal meals we always had before you came here for your style of *fandangos*. She dressed to please you. She stopped going to those snobbish events for the rich in town and became a rancher's wife."

Chet nodded.

"I don't think she ever wanted to have children until you came along. Adam was a big thing for her to do. But he'd been enough."

His wife arrived.

"Good morning. I've been rehashing life. How do you feel this morning, Liz?"

"Oh, I'm fine this morning. Ready for the wedding." She shook her head. "You know I missed having a wedding like this — not with you but with him. That first one of mine was held in a little walled village with a well, and a small chapel.

"He carried me all night on his lap riding there. I was sleepy and heady both. I didn't know what this big powerful man intended to do with me. I was hardly more than a child — no instructions either."

"Were you afraid?" Monica asked.

"Afraid, yes, he was such a big man. Like Chet here." She hugged him and then took a seat. "But what men and women did together I really had no idea. His men awoke the priest when we got there before dawn. He must have bribed him to marry us. It was over in a wink and he carried me off to his *hacienda.*"

"No white dresses and all the music?" Chet asked her.

"Better yet, after my first night, I told myself I was going to have a baby. These ladies who waited on me hand and foot shook their heads at me, babbling about how my breasts were going to be too small to feed it. Their words brought me back into reality — I was not pregnant that fast and my breasts would fill up when I needed them."

"See, until I married Chet I never had a normal Mexican wedding."

"Tell us one more thing. When your husband kidnapped you, did you think he planned all that to happen?" Chet asked her.

"Yes. He said he saw me three times from afar at events with my parents. I don't think he even bothered to meet my father who would've told that winemaker to go to hell if he'd asked for my hand. He planned and executed it all. But no one was there when the *padre* married us, but after, five of his hired *pistoleros* gently kissed my forehead at the end and blessed me."

"Oh dear, that was a storybook wedding, wasn't it?" Monica clapped her hands.

Liz laughed. "My whole life has been one. From being kidnapped to this man washing my feet. I don't know which one was the highest honor."

"I do."

She narrowed her eyes at Chet. "Which one?"

"Making love to me in a hay pile."

Monica clapped her hands again. "You two are so much fun. I forget about everything bad and count my blessings being here."

They ate her breakfast and then dressed for the day's activities. He knew she'd dress up more for the ceremony. Since Tom was walking his daughter down the aisle he had no plans to change his clothing.

Among the guests, Toby came by and talked to Talley. Then he reported to Chet that his dad was finally resting and Doc was pleased how he was doing. He thanked Chet, who invited him to stay for the festivities.

Cole looked tired when he finally made it there. No trouble so far up or down the line he'd heard about. Valerie took him into the house to rest for a while.

Hampt and Chet found a spot to sit on a bench and visit.

"You've got that Ty wound up. I knew he was sweet on that girl, but he is kind of close-mouthed. Ray talks. Ty listens. After you got through with him yesterday he was talking to May and I all about your plans. We told him we'd help. He'd never asked for nothing before, but he's on a fast horse today. Went to get her for this event with a buckboard. That banker better get ready to like him, huh?"

"I kind of planned it that way."

"I wonder what them Reynoldses, in Texas, you used to live by want for Christmas?"

Chet was halfway between mad and amused. "Why the hell do you want to give them a Christmas present?"

"I owe them a lot for forcing you to come out here."

They both laughed.

Tanner showed up with his woman. Chet saw them drive in.

"Ain't that the gal, Kay, you used to dance with when you were with Marge at them Verde Valley dances?"

"Yes, she is. She's also the one that ruined JD. That's her."

"What is that old devil getting himself into?"

"When I saw her and him coming out of the bank together I asked myself the same thing. He don't know what to do with a woman."

"He don't?"

"Told me he'd never touched one in his life."

"How old is he?"

"About forty."

Hampt started laughing. "I figure he is going to learn a lot in a short time with that sister."

"I better get up and act like a host."

"I see Ty, her, and his in-laws-to-be are coming in the gate in two rigs."

"I can't wait for what Ty's said and done."

"You are kind of a devil if you set your mind to it. May said Millie told her that that damn Chet Byrnes is making a grandmother out of her."

"What did May say?"

"She said I told her she better count her blessings. If Chet Byrnes hadn't come back here we'd all been starving and Millie agreed. Oh, anyone says anything bad about Chet Byrnes, and my wife will get in their face. I love her. She's the best thing ever happened to me, and you know it too."

"Ty's girl is really pretty."

"Hell, he's like his uncle. Never seen you with an ugly woman either."

"We better act friendly." Chet was holding in his amusement.

The wedding went fine. Afterward the groom fed her cake and got frosting all over her face, and that made everyone laugh. When things settled down, the groom found him and took him aside.

"Mr. Byrnes —"

"I'm Chet to you, Cody."

"Yes sir. I told Sandy I was going to thank you and I mean it. For the job too. I didn't figure this would have happened if you hadn't rode out there and, well, settled it all. I won't ever forget what you did for two dumb kids. We'll make you proud."

"Cody, just remember when you and her have problems you need to list the good things you have in your life and get over the bad."

"I promise I will. And the week at Oak Creek . . . well, I'll measure up, sir — Chet."

They hugged.

Chet was about to leave and Cody stopped him. "Would you wait there a minute? I'll get her. She really sent me to get you to say a blessing on our union."

They and several others gathered and he began, "Father in heaven. Sandy and this young man Cody are going to take a walk together today that will last the rest of their lives. Bless and keep them through that journey. If you can, Lord, give them children to enrich their lives and let them always be as much in love as they are today. Amen."

Liz was there and held him. "Very well done. I met Ty's young lady. I hope your plan works."

He smiled and told the pair leaving to have fun.

Millie came in on his other side — sniffing. "This was so much better than losing her."

"I hope Tom was convinced."

"He was. She is his favorite. Men expect too much of their sons sometimes and let the girls get by with anything."

"Cody came by and thanked me. I didn't need that but I consider him as having his boot soles on the ground."

When Millie faded away, Liz asked if he had met Victoria's father yet.

"No. Should I?"

"Sure. He's a businessman . . . I am certain he'd like to visit with another one."

"I'll try not to cross swords with him."

"Oh my. That might be funny or a serious thing."

He stopped Currents when the man was crossing the space.

"I guess we should talk," Chet said.

The man gave him a cold stare. "We have damn little to talk about in my book."

"I am open-minded here. You might open that book. I understand your daughter is eighteen. At that age she can make choices herself. I think we can do better than have a war. You could lose."

"I don't care what age she is — she'll not marry some wet-behind-the-ears cow herder in my lifetime."

"Hold down your tongue. I came here to talk sensibly with you. I understand you don't like me because I don't bank with you. I was in your bank a few years ago. No one in that bank wanted to do business with me, so I crossed the street and began doing business with Tanner. You bought that bank two years ago and moved to town. Not one time did you ever shake my hand and ask for my business. Man don't want my business is one thing — but you never asked for it."

"Why don't you keep running his gawdamn bank? I'll run mine."

"That is not a property I own. They supply the banking services and run it. I don't have a penny in the bank ownership."

He folded his arms over his expensive suit. "Why, you are in there all the time ordering them around about all your deposits and them kissing your ass. I hear all about you."

"Bring a witness. I want him to testify."

"And that little son of a bitch is not taking her home. She is going home with me and my wife, and that's final."

"Only if she is willing."

"Of course she's willing. She lives under my roof. You can't stop me. She is my daughter."

"Keep your voice down."

"I won't, gawdamn you."

"Currents, if I buy a full-page ad in the *Miner* next week and tell folks to get their money out of your bank 'cause you're going under, do you have the cash on hand to stand the run?"

He looked taken aback. "You wouldn't do that."

"Ty Byrnes is my nephew and his desired future I approve of. If you interfere in any way with him and that girl's plans, I will call for a run on your bank that will close you down. We are not playing chess here. One swing, I can knock all the game pieces off your board."

He swore under his breath.

"Now I want you to go look with him at the Barbarossa horses at Camp Verde. He is going to be in charge of them. They are the only horses of that breed in the United States. They sell very high. Then you find them a nice ranch around here, at a bargain price, that they can live on and so you can see your grandchildren in the future."

The man was breathing hard. His hazel eyes would have killed a rattlesnake. "You son of a — they said you were tough. I underestimated you. I won't ever do that again. And if I do all these things like you want done, how do I know you won't blackmail me again?"

"I am only enforcing one thing on you. Ty will treat your daughter as good as any man on earth could, rich or poor. He's hardworking, educated, and I bet in time he will become a real depositor in your bank. Now get your wife and in thirty minutes we will meet in the living room of the house privately. I will have his stepparents there along with my wife plus Ty and Victoria. You will explain your change of mind, agreeing to what they want to happen."

Currents said nothing.

"No one will raise their voice. We will hear everyone. And then proceed."

"You know I don't like it?"

"I also know what they want. I have played a little chess and someday, when I get used to playing it again, I'd like to play against you. But in today's game you are in checkmate. Act like a good loser. You will win in the end."

"Never."

"Hey, you heard me. I can do what I said, and I will, if you act tough with me."

Currents went off to find his wife. Chet went to find Ty and Victoria.

He found them and they walked down to the jumper pen to not be overheard. Ty introduced her.

"Nice to meet you. My father looked mad."

"He threatened me. He said he'd take you home. Not let Ty be with you. I told him he wouldn't. That is why I am here."

"Boy, I am so sorry I got you into this situation."

"We're going to meet at the house in a bit, but before we do, I need both of you to tell me what you two expect and want to do. I will do whatever that is. I told him he would not take you home if you wanted Ty to."

She nodded. "I would like it that way."

"Now. What would you two like to do?"

Ty spoke first. "I want to marry her."

"Yes, I do too."

"Now? Tomorrow?"

"Chet, how about at Thanksgiving?"

She nodded.

"Two months?"

"Fine," they both said together, and he squeezed her hand.

"You must have held a gun on him?" she asked.

"I was very blunt. I threatened to ruin him financially. Don't ever mention it. No matter whatever comes, neither of you ever say what I did today. In twenty minutes we meet in the living room. Just you two, his folks, your folks, Liz, and I."

"Oh, Ty, you told me he could do it." She kissed Chet on the cheek and then the two of them went to kissing like mad lovers.

"You two go find May and Hampt. I'll get Liz and we will meet in the living room."

Jesus caught him. "Need any help?"

"I am holding a meeting in the living room. You and Spencer guard the house doors until we come out. Hampt and May, the Currents, Ty and Victoria, and Liz will be with me."

"Will there be any fighting?"

"The fight is over."

Jesus grinned. "He looked pissed off bad when you left him."

"Pissed off or on. He will listen."

"The house will be secured. You tell me what you did sometime."

"I will. Have you seen my wife?"

"She's with the cooks. I can get her."

"Good. I will clear the house."

When Liz got there, he had everyone out of the house and enough chairs set up in the living room. May and Hampt arrived smiling. Ty and Victoria were next and her parents followed. Her mother's name was Viola, his Arthur. All introduced, Chet began the meeting.

"I want Ty and Victoria to sit in those two

chairs and tell us what they would like to do."

Seated beside each other and holding hands, Ty began, "Victoria and I want to pledge our lives to each other on Thanksgiving."

Viola sucked in her breath loudly enough that all heard. She held her chest. Arthur hugged her in a comforting way.

"Tell all of us why," Chet directed.

Ty said, " 'Cause we love each other and want to have a family of our own."

Next Victoria spoke, "Those are my words too. He is a very hardworking young man. If he already isn't now, he will be one of the greatest horse trainers in the country. Chet is entrusting us with the Barbarossa horses and stallion on our new horse ranch."

"Don't worry one minute, Mrs. Currents. I will take good care of her."

"How can you?" Currents hushed her, frowning hard at her.

Chet spoke, addressing him. "Will you stand up and announce their wedding plans at supper tonight?"

"I will." He stood. "Is this meeting over?"

"Anyone else want to say anything else? No? Then we are adjourned."

The kids were kissing their faces off. Liz offered Viola a room to freshen up in and she agreed. Chet walked by, patted the two lovers on the back, and went to dismiss his guards.

"No fight?"

"No, Jesus. I had that settled before we went in there. It was just getting everyone to agree."

"Boss man, you get more deals settled than any five men could have."

"Monday we go look for a telegraph man."

"Trying again, huh?"

At supper Arthur Currents rose to the occasion to announce his daughter's wedding plans. And then he asked if this gracious host and hostess would hold it on their ranch.

Chet stood up and waved his arms. "We will have it here."

Late that night, his wife asked him in bed, "Was he poking you about holding it here?"

"No. He is still wondering how he can get me back for cutting him off at the knees."

"What did you threaten him with?"

"I got so damn mad I threatened to advertise a run on his bank in the *Miner*."

"Oh my God."

"He was going to take Victoria home and cut them apart. He and I played word chess for a while and I checkmated him."

She hugged and kissed him. "I knew you'd

pointed a gun at his head."

"He'd not have listened to me otherwise."

"Hug your fat wife. You did the right thing. I am glad."

"Those two will do well. So will Sandra and Cody."

"What about Talley and Toby?"

He chuckled. "If his father gets strong enough to help them, I'd put those three over on the Rustlers Ranch and give them a crew and a chance."

"Will they all get along over there?"

"I think so."

"Well, you know best."

"Darling, I am the blind helping the blind."

CHAPTER 25

Breakfast Sunday morning went pleasantly and afterward the rest of the people went home. Talley stayed.

Chet took his wife to her church and after Mass the priest shook his hand. "We are always grateful for all your charity and certainly the sacks of beans you donate."

"You know if you get a clear need send word, Father."

"That is so generous. Thanks and bless you again."

They took a meal at the Palace Saloon. Then drove by to see Bo, his wife, and the family.

The women were feeding the baby while the men, in the living room, talked about telegraph systems. Bo said he heard about a man who strung them. He'd write him for ideas and a possible meeting.

With the baby asleep, the women joined them.

"We're settling down," his wife said. "I am looking for a nanny we can trust so we can attend the next *fandango* you have."

Chet and Liz drove back to the ranch and decided to take the day off from business. She told him that she felt better than she had in ten days. That was good news to him. He'd fretted about her morning sickness, and if she felt better maybe it had, finally, passed.

Talley and Toby were holding hands on the porch swing, swinging slowly, conversing. The nice cooler weather was telling them fall wasn't far off.

"Her eye is going to heal."

"That's good. She looks lots better."

"You would too if you had escaped that madman."

"Maybe turning Cargill loose to leave was wrong."

"He's gone?"

"Raphael sent two men to check, and I told them to bring him back if he was around. They say the neighbors told them he had left."

"Good."

"I am waiting on a report about Hall's arrest from Santa Fe."

"You doubt they will do anything?"

"If not, then the Washington bureau can

get on them."

"Do you think they can?"

"They'd get on me if I didn't do what they asked me to do."

"You never ignore them either."

"I guess not, but he is a reason to do something."

She came over and sat on his lap. "I am not arguing. I am glad to have you here. I realize you want him in prison."

He kissed her. Forget the SOB and savor his wife. It was a rest day and they might even get lost later.

Lisa came in the room and stood before them. "I came to ask you if I could go riding with Miguel today."

"Is he here?"

Lisa nodded.

"Tell him I am watching out for you."

She smiled. "I will and be back in a few hours. Thank you both."

Chet nodded.

When she was gone he smiled. "Your daughter is becoming a lady."

"Raphael said the boy had serious intentions. Is that all right?"

"I simply want her to be off to a better life than living with Wolf."

"She has become a big helper. The ranch women have worked hard on drying apples and making cider with our record apple crop. She's been down there working long hard hours and she is part of those women. They look out for her too."

"All some people need is a chance and they will try. She was only with those killers because she could not escape them."

"Just like me held in chains," she said.

"Let's drag those chains upstairs and sleep."

"Sleep?"

"Well, try."

"I like you at home."

He herded her to the stairs.

Monday morning, he met with his guards over breakfast and told them they needed to prepare to go look at the Rustler Ranch. Toby could ride along with them.

"I want to actually see what assets we have over there. Both of you have seen what works for us on our other ranches. I want your thoughts on the prospects of what we can apply to that place. Also that young man can see if he even wants to move there. He and I will discuss that later today. It must take about two days to simply get over there, then days to look over the entire holding and then two days back. Figure it will take ten days in all."

"What else we need to do?" Jesus asked.

"You were with us, Jesus. That road into the ranch from Crook's Road needs some clearing, and in places some bridges must be built to get a wagon in there over the washouts. It never was a good road. I don't know how they got the material in there to build it in the first place. So the entrance road needs serious work and then we can talk about how we can make it an operational ranch."

"You plan to get the road fixed before winter?" Jesus asked.

"That is why I am making the trip. We didn't ride in there to examine a ranch when we went to get the rustlers hiding there. So let's go see it now."

"What if Toby backs out?" Spencer asked, getting up.

"He is only a candidate. There will be others who will want the job."

"Just curious."

"Sure. I don't have many secrets. All you have to do is ask me. Right, Jesus?"

"That's right. We better take some long handles. I figure the wind may switch and come out of the north any day."

"You may be right."

They broke up and he found Toby at the horse barn to explain they were going to make a decision about the ranch and give him a chance to see it.

"I will be ready to go, sir."

"You may need a jacket and some underwear before we get back."

"I'll go get some. May I ride a ranch horse up there? Mine aren't shod."

"Sure. Pick him out."

"I know I am kind of a pest but thanks. I do have the team home so they aren't on your livery bill."

"You've had lots to do. Get your clothes and we leave at the crack of dawn. Monica will feed us breakfast before we leave."

"Thanks, Chet."

"No problem."

He told his foreman his plans too. Then he went to lunch with his wife in the kitchen. Anita was there. Talley attended and he told her where Toby went and their plans. Lisa was working with the apple crew and would eat down there.

"Maybe you can shoot a fat elk," Monica mentioned.

"That would be good, huh?" he asked her.

"I like elk. So do these women. And it would be a treat."

"I will take a large gun to shoot one for you."

"I hope there is no one out there to shoot at you."

"I bet there are no shooters over there that want me."

"I hope not."

"Thanks, Monica."

The women laughed at his words.

CHAPTER 26

It didn't frost the next morning. Toby drew a horse that bucked. Chet sat aboard his Ty-broke gray and the three of them, along with stableboys, cheered the boy on. Toby's Roman-nosed horse had his head down and bucked over several acres in the driveway and area where they put up the big tent until the youth got his head up and the action was over.

One of the stableboys offered to catch him a new one, but Toby, while using both hands to keep the horse in check, told him, "No. I just got this one broke to ride. I bet your next choice would buck harder."

Everyone laughed. Chet gave the gray the go-ahead and he left in a long walk to lead the procession. Jesus rode in and gave Toby the lead line to an eight-head pack string.

"Since you are lowest man on seniority you get to lead them."

"Thanks."

"Oh." Jesus turned in the saddle. "Don't get that lead rope under his tail. He'll buck harder than he did before. I seen a *vaquero* do that trick on him and he got into the clouds."

"You did great, Toby. Your stable buddies set you up on him. He's solid enough. Just a little goosey."

"Thanks, Chet. I'll get them back if I live long enough."

"You have plenty of time left to do it. Let's trot a while."

They rode on, went through the small village of Camp Verde and down the valley to where the Crook Road split off. They began to climb the mountain to the rim top. At noon break they had some jerky and water, and rode on. There were some thunderheads gathering across the great gap of the Verde River covering almost the whole top of the north rim side. A vast country spread off to the south and he knew they might get rain from those formations later in the afternoon. Good thing they had slickers.

Thunder rumbled across the land, and Chet, after observing what he could of the storm through the veil of pine trees, recalled there was an old barn up a mile or so.

"We'd be dry in it. Let's hurry. Jesus, you and Spencer drive the packhorses some. So we'll make it."

They came at a pretty good clip — the two men slapping the packhorses into a lope and they charged down the road through the trees.

Big cold raindrops fell on their shoulders and thumped on their hats. Coming to a sliding stop at the open doorway, they filed in under the shake roof of the black log barn as all hell broke loose from the sky. They dismounted inside away from the blinding flashes of lightning and waterfall off the eaves.

"It will pass in thirty minutes," Chet said, and pulled out his latigo strap to loosen the girth on his saddle.

"Where we going to camp tonight?" Spencer asked, standing in the doorway and observing the downpour.

"I know a rancher a few miles east of here who might feed and shelter us."

"I bet that would beat our cooking."

"That would not be hard."

Toby had gone around, very methodically, checking all his girths and the loads on the pack string. Chet noted that and never said a word. At least the boy was serious about what his job was with them. The rain stopped, so they mounted up and rode on in the drippy world with rainbows in every droplet of the pine needles. The pungent turpentine breath of the ponderosa pines filled the fresh air, and the horse hooves splashed water in the puddles.

Any time moisture fell in this desert climate the effect produced smiles on men's faces. Chet's outfit was not an exception. In two hours they reined up at the T-Bar-W Ranch, and the tall, broad-shouldered woman in her thirties with thick blond braids wearing a man's tan shirt and jeans came and stood in the doorway of her log house and shouted, "Where is your darling wife Elizabeth?"

"At the house," he said, reined up, and removed his hat. "You know Jesus. That's Spencer, who replaced Cole, and Toby is the pack train wrangler. Boys, this is Chrystal Hayes."

The three men nodded the introduction.

"Why didn't she come?"

"She quit riding."

"Having problems?"

"Well, she's waiting on a young'un."

"My, my. Isn't she lucky? Get off them broncs and come in. My husband Cecil and his brother Burl are checking cows and won't be here till dark if they get back then. She all right?"

"She says about February or March she'll

be better."

"Well." She hugged him and then shook the others' hands. "What brings you up here?"

"We bought that rustlers' hideout up on the rim. Going to see what it takes to make an outfit out of it."

She shook her head. "Elizabeth complained to me when you were up here last that she wished she was going to have a baby and never had one before. I guess she got her wish."

"Yes, she never carried one this long before. So I hope she does."

"Wonderful news. You were setting up a stage line last time. How's it working?"

"The stage line for now is buckboards and mail, but after lots of pestering trouble we are running smoothly."

"You had trouble, huh? Sit down."

She went on directing the guys. "Boys, put them horses in the pen and hay them. There's water in that tank."

"When you come in, bring her some of the apples we brought, Jesus."

"You have a good crop?"

"Yes. A big one. Come on to Preskitt . . . I can load you up on them."

"You know how I hate to travel."

"I have plenty of apples and we will have

some, I bet, past Christmas stored in bushel baskets in a cellar."

"Coffee. Let's drink this and I'll make more for them." She poured him a cup. "I'd have been off with the men but I am babysitting our Jersey cow. She's supposed to calf any day. It's her first calf and you how that can be."

"Yes, I know all about heifers calving."

"You still being a marshal?"

"Yes. Things are much quieter down south. Roamer and two others are handling it."

"Boy, I sure have enjoyed going to your place. I guess when you lost Margaret, I couldn't face going back up there. Your new wife is very nice and smart. Before I married Cecil, Margaret and I rode all over and had a big time. Her second husband wasn't worth the powder to blow him up, and she never lost a thing when he broke his neck. But she really was happy with you. And, well, I thought she'd live out her entire life in earth's heaven — those damn jumpers . . ."

"Aw, I couldn't tell her not to do that."

"Oh hell, you couldn't tell her much of anything. She was the only woman I ever met I could look eye to eye at, but tall as you are you know that."

"I knew how tall she was."

"Well, I like Elizabeth. When you stopped by, going up there to stop them rustlers, I told Cecil that night that your woman is a powerful lady. She told me she wasn't out looking for you that day. All she wanted was a yellow horse, and she found you. I am so glad. I bet you are happy with her?"

"I am very settled."

"Boy you earned it. I guess Cecil don't mind me. He married me when I was an old maid and I keep his house. And work his cattle when he needs me."

"How old were you when you married him?"

"Twenty-seven."

"No kids?"

"No. I don't expect any either. Years ago I told Margaret I'd been happier if I'd been born a boy."

"You have a good life."

"Oh, we make do. Since you found a cattle market for so many of us we do all right, and I appreciate that a lot."

"We all needed that."

"What's she going to call it?"

"I never asked."

"Oh, there is a list a mile long. I liked Adam. The nanny has him?"

"Yes, and Cole and his wife have Rocky."

"That was your daddy's name. I never met him."

"Dad died before we came out here."

"He know you were going to move?"

"He lost his mind, searching for the twins that the Comanche kidnapped, long before the feud started."

"Oh, I never heard that story."

"I took over the ranch when I was sixteen."

"Ouch. No wonder you are such a businessman."

"I complained to my sister Susie —"

"She's up on the Windmill Ranch. We took our cattle up there last year. I met her. She is a busy woman too. With a baby?"

"That's Sis. I complained I never had a chance to be a kid; I had to step into Dad's boots and take over or we'd have perished."

"Here's some apples," Jesus said, coming in and giving her a hat full.

"Oh, now I will really have to go up there and get some."

"Go anytime. Liz welcomes guests even if I am not home."

"You guys drink coffee? Sit down."

"We all drink coffee," Jesus said.

They pitched in and helped her fix the evening meal. Supper was on the table when her men came in. Cecil, her husband, and his brother Burl. Both were well up in their forties; they were as warm as she was about company, and after her fried apples for dessert her husband promised to take her up there for some more.

Chet promised them a beef contract for next year. The next morning before daylight they helped them pack up and go.

"That was the tallest woman I ever met," Toby said when they were well down the Crook Road.

"Chet's first wife was that tall," Jesus said. "Those two were big buddies."

"How long has she been married to him?" Toby asked.

"Maybe four–five years. Around the time I came here. She and Margaret were friends. Cecil had never been married either. They say he followed her around like a starved calf. He even learned how to dance so she'd go out with him. Margaret said he exhausted her and she finally married him. Don't you ever tell anyone this line she told Marge after their honeymoon at Mormon Lake."

"What was that?" Toby asked.

" 'Hell, if I'd known it was that much fun in bed, Marge, I'd been doing it a long time ago. Why didn't you tell me it was that much fun?' "

The cowboys laughed for the next quarter mile.

They reached the ranch road detouring around washouts in the two ruts and downed timber lying across them in the last mile.

"A crosscut saw and two bridges would fix it," Spencer said.

"And we could use a slip to build up the roadbed part," Chet said.

"It wasn't as bad as I remembered it," Jesus said.

"These rotten split-rail fences along this road won't hold much. They could be used as firewood."

"We make our own barbwire at the blacksmith shop at Tom's place. Fence posts are the next item. Raphael might find me some Mexican families that would make them for so much by the post."

"You are going to need a lot of them. Is there juniper close?" Spencer asked.

"There is. It would be better than pine for posts."

They dismounted at the house. Chet wished they'd buried the outlaws farther away from the house, but that was where their graves would be. The front door was still closed. They packed it all inside.

"You need some roof repair. If you have some tin cans we can flatten them. I can stop most of the leaks until you get someone up here and really fix it," Spencer said.

"Good . . . we will do that. A leak can rot out the floors sooner or later."

"Couple of windows will need glass."

"The gunfight did not help that."

"There's a packrat's nest in the kitchen —"

"Don't shoot him."

Chet put his hands over his ears too late.

Toby came out of the smoke-filled kitchen with one fat rat all bloody and torn up. "I guess we won't eat him."

"I don't eat rats," Spencer said.

"Hell, you can't tell them from squirrels." Toby threw the carcass out into the yard.

"Damnit, boy. Go open the back door. That smoke is worse than a pack rat."

Toby went through the haze, opened the back door, and shouted, "Holy shit, there is a rattler out back here long as a rope."

There was another shot and they all ran to see it. Chet saw the snake that Toby held up by his rattlers as high as he could. Its bullet-bloodied head was still on the ground. Big around as Chet's upper arm. He'd never seen anything like it.

"Rattler," Spencer said. "Boy, are you attracting all this zoo stuff?"

"Hell no."

Jesus, his arms folded, stood at a distance.

"We better start looking around. A guy that big has to have a mate that size around here somewhere."

Chet looked all around his circle and gave a shudder.

"Maybe call this the snake and rat ranch instead of rustlers," Spencer said. They all laughed.

"Hell no," Chet said. "It will be hard enough to get a woman to come back here as it is. They damn sure won't come if they think we have a snake pit out here."

"I was just funning. I never thought about it but you're right. It would have shaken a woman if she'd found him."

"My Lord. To get any female to move out here would take some doing anyway."

"I swear, boss, I won't tell the story unless I'm drinking."

"I forgive you. Let's get supper going. We have lots to see."

"The roof fixed, a few windowpanes, and ten buckets of paint and this place would suit a farmwoman. Is the well water all right?" Spencer held out his arms like he was measuring the house with them.

"We drank it last time. Dip a bucket out of it."

Toby dropped the rusty bucket on the chain and then pulled it up sloshing water.

Chet rinsed out an old cloudy-looking beer mug sitting there and then poured some water into the glass. He took a small sip.

"Tastes like it did last time. No dead animals anyhow. We need to bring a couple of sections of pipe and a hand pump. Then plan on a windmill with a house tank on a stand and build a stock tank to catch the overflow."

"Hell, this will be like living in downtown Dallas," Spencer said.

"Lumber for a new outhouse. That one's gone," Chet said, and headed for the barn-like structure. "These corrals all need to be replaced. Ain't one of them of any account that you could drop poles in between the upright posts? That design is not a corral for me."

"You can harvest enough new poles from that hill over there, and drag them over here to make it."

"What is there, sixty acres east of the house to make a hay meadow?" Chet asked.

"You going to mow the sagebrush out of it?" Jesus teased.

"No. That is a grub-them-up job with pick-hoes. Mowing machines cost hundreds of dollars delivered out here. The boys did that up at the top ranch and Shawn says they wrecked them."

"I bet there is more meadow around that corner too," Toby said, pointing to where the opening rounded a corner of timber.

"Tomorrow we ride east and start evaluating the range grass," Chet announced.

"You have started with less," Jesus said. "Why did they abandon it do you think?"

"Say you had a hundred three-year-old steers here even today. Where would you sell them?"

"Chicago?" Spencer asked Jesus. "I see what you say. They came, built a ranch, raised some cattle, looked around one day, and couldn't sell them."

Toby shook his head. "But, boy, with a market you could raise some good beef up here as anywhere in the world, couldn't you?"

"If your wife don't leave you," Spencer said.

"Toby, you know your girlfriend pretty well. Would she stay here?" Chet asked.

"We didn't have any money when my folks were married except day money we made working cattle for someone or whatever, and that was scarce. I dug fence post for ten cents a posthole."

"You think Talley'd stay here?"

"Why not? We'd have food and a little money if we needed it and not be living in a shack. The house fixed like Jesus said would be a palace compared to her folks or our lean-to. My sister, that married David Wayne and moved to Saint David? Down there they had an adobe house, two milk cows, ten hens, and two sows plus twenty irrigated acres. She would not leave him for anything."

"Is there room for another wife to live there?" Spencer asked.

Toby smiled. "She said if he ever did that she'd kill him and I think he believes her."

Toby continued, "I was there when she moved there. I helped him. That adobe house is clean, neat as a pin. His alfalfa is great and they grow gardens of food, otherwise Saint David is the asshole of the world in the damn cactus desert."

"But she has neighbors."

"It ain't like not having enough food or money or a nice place to eat and sleep."

"Toby, we get that house fixed and the well and a new outhouse, I want you to bring her up here. We will have the road repaired — bring her over here and ask her right out if she'd stay here."

"By then we will have all the snakes killed," Jesus teased him.

"Fellows, she will be pleased."

"Would your dad come and help you?"

"Dad's hard-scrabbled all his life. Would he have a place to live?"

"A private room in the bunkhouse we build. We will need that anyway."

"He'd be a fool not to come."

"I mean he'd work for you. I know he ain't a big stout logger. But he's got some years left to work checking cattle, keeping cattle records, and a lifetime of advice that might help you. You have seen his shortfalls and I am not dwelling on that."

"I appreciate your confidence in me. I want you to kick my ass if I am not the best foreman you've got when you come check on me."

Chet ran his tongue on the inside of his lower front teeth. "One more thing. What will you do if she says hell no?"

Toby looked around like it was written somewhere he could read it.

"Take her back to where she would want to be, and then come back and run this ranch. I don't figure anyone will ever again put a ranch like this on a platter for me like you have. I won't blow that chance."

Spencer put his hand on the boy's shoulder. "If you hadn't taken it I gawdamn sure would have."

"I knew that too. The spit was filling my mouth standing here. But I know that woman. She will think we fell into a bowl of whipped cream and strawberries."

"It is going to be winter in six weeks up here. It will be hard to get much done. The iron stove in the house will heat it, but we need Raphael to send up a couple wagonloads of firewood. We can replace the stovepipe. If we move fast we can get it all repaired and supplies in here before it snows, and you two will be comfortable and paint it next spring."

"And get a bunkhouse built so I have some men to help me."

"Spencer, you're the builder?" Chet asked.

"Can we get the lumber up here to build it?"

"We will bust our butts, I bet, to do that."

"We may have to work on the building in the snow."

"I can get some good hands. With a cook and some wall tents with stoves we can do it."

"I can get enough help up here to clear the road and Raphael can get some loads of hay in here for horses. And firewood. Then we'll have the lumber brought here for building. I have pen and paper in my saddlebags. Start a lumber list. They can finish the headquarters interiors later."

"Toby, you're getting us into a helluva race."

Spencer did lots of measuring with Toby recording measurements while Chet and Jesus fixed supper.

Chet came quietly to the living room. "I need that .50-caliber, Spencer. Monica's elk is screaming for a cow elk and is coming this way."

Outside he rested the barrel on the corner of the house, aimed through the buckhorn sites, and when the big bull came into his small view, he squeezed the trigger. First came the explosion — the stock slammed into Chet's shoulder — then the gun smoke. The big bull humped up, tried to turn but hit hard, then collapsed in a pile.

"Whoopee!" Jesus shouted. "Monica has her elk."

"How in the hell are we going to get him out of here?" Spencer asked from the front door.

"Leave anything we don't need to go back and pack the meat on our horses," Toby said.

"Toby, that is why he chose you as foreman of this godforsaken place."

Toby laughed. "Jesus, we better sharpen your knives."

"The food is ready. Go bleed him out.

Then we will figure what else we have to do in the dark." He turned and looked pained at the slipping sun behind his back.

"Oh hell, guys, it isn't that bad."

It was past midnight when they had the last meat cut off the carcass to haul. It took two of them to take the bull's hide and then the head and rack to the barn and pulled them up on ropes so scavengers didn't eat them while they were gone.

Spencer said he had enough measurements to fix the house. They planned to make a rush home. Chet was going to hire Chrystal's husband Cecil to haul the elk meat to the Verde Ranch. They could finish butchering it up there and bring Monica her part of the meat. He needed to get the crew down from Center Point and over there to build the bunkhouse, and some sheds.

By midday they left the bulk of the meat with Cecil and his brother, who agreed to transport it in their wagon. Chrystal claimed some roasts and then they hurried for the Verde Ranch.

They pushed all night and reached the Verde Ranch at sunup the next morning.

Chet met with Tom, who agreed to send a crew with saws and a slip plus a draft team up there to fix the road before the rest arrived. They might fill the washout with logs up to the road for a temporary fix. It made no matter. They'd repair the road to be passable and then work on it.

"I'll send a load of hay along with them. You are serious about this ranch. Who will run it?"

"Toby Evans."

"He's not very old for that job, is he?"

"Tom, he may beat you. He may not but he's gutsy."

"When's he going to be the boss up there?"

"Right now."

"You know some of these guys may not listen to him."

"You better tell them — no, I will tell them. They won't do it but once."

Tom shook his head. "We will have that road open in five days from now."

"Thanks."

"What will you do next?"

"Send Spencer to Center Point and get some men from up there moved down to this new place. And get his needed lumber shipped up there by then to start building. We need some sheds to hold supplies, a bunkhouse for the crew. A meat cooler and a windmill hauled over there along with pipe for it and a holding tank."

"How deep a well?"

"Consider it thirty feet deep."

Tom nodded.

"Hey, I trusted you four–five years ago. An idiot had fired you but I felt you deserved the job. You didn't make any mistakes."

"You have picked many good men. I loved Hampt but I'd never made him a foreman. Damn he's doing a wonderful job. JD is building an empire where he is. Not been my choice. So I may not be the best judge."

"We all make mistakes. But he needs a chance."

"You saw something I missed."

"Little things. Yes."

"I will help him as I do all your managers. I read your notes about the situation at the upper ranch. I met with Drew several times. He never mentioned having to use cross bulls to me."

"I think we scared him into not spending any money. Shawn and Spud will get things under control."

"I will help them all the way."

"Good. And if we can get Toby established over the winter we can get a lot done next year. I need your help and when he asks for help you can give him the right answer."

"I will make Cody a leader too, if he will listen."

"Good. I like him. We can build him a ranch if he matures."

"What else do we need?"

"Support. Toby may need more hay. He will need some saddle horses and some draft horses, harness, buckboards if there are any left. Farm wagons, corral hardware. You know what it takes. He has little of anything but a house and a big rough barn. Oh, he will need barbwire and posts."

"Where are your corral builders?"

"I'll find them. They can build them solid and they work. Cole knows where they live."

"You may burn that Crook Road down with traffic."

Chet was home in two hours. He, Jesus, and Toby rode into the ranch. No one expected them to be back so soon. It was a nice surprise. Liz ran out and asked where Spencer was.

"He went to get the carpenters and craftsmen to go down to Rustlers and build a bunkhouse, some sheds, and do house repairs Toby'll need before the winter comes. I need to talk to Raphael about some things and I will come inside. Tell Monica I shot her an elk. He's coming in a wagon.

Cecil Hayes and his wife will come get apples for hauling it."

"Toby? Toby? Is he all right?" Talley called, sounding upset coming out of the back door.

"I'm coming," he said. "Wait till I get our horses put up."

She held her skirts up and ran for the barn.

Jesus and Chet smiled at her hasty concern.

"What happened?" she shouted, loud enough to make Chet smile even more.

"You what?" she screamed. "You are going to be the new ranch foreman? Oh my God!"

Chet shook his head. That ranch's location would never concern her.

Maybe he picked the right man and that man picked the right future mate.

CHAPTER 27

Things were going fast and furious at the Preskitt Valley Ranch. Toby had a list of window glass sizes, and the hardware Spencer wanted for the job. The various size nails he was to get as well. About midmorning the stable boys hitched a buckboard so Chet and Toby could drive into town. Later they were at the mercantile talking with Ben Ivor in his office.

"What do you need?"

"A wagonload of things," Chet said. "Toby, meet Ben Ivor. Good friend, and he does our hardware business. Leave him the list and we will get what we can haul today and you can come back and get the rest tomorrow."

Chet turned to Ben and said, "Toby is going to run the ranch Bo bought for us. It is up off the Crook Road past the Hayes about ten miles or so."

"Big list of things here. I have most of it

in stock. I'd say if you plan to haul it, bring a wagon so you can haul it right up there . . . Chet?"

"Good idea. Kathrin doing all right?"

"Yes. You know she's expecting again?"

"Well we are too."

"Boy, that's good news. She's doing all right?"

"Yes. She's fine. Excited too."

"They are going to need to build bigger schools, huh?"

"We may have to do that. Tell Kathrin hi."

"She really appreciates you saving her. Hell, I do too. Or I wouldn't have her and my kids."

"Have you started ordering in hay equipment for next year? I want a half dozen mowers and I may need more."

"Hard as they are to get shipped out here, I better get on that now. I bet they sell lots of them, but I am one of their best dealers. They sent me a plaque. I've been going to put it up."

"Congratulations."

"I get an extra five percent discount too."

"Toby and I need to see Bo. You know anyone who sells telegraph systems?"

"Hey, I have a circular on that. It was from Ohio."

"Have you got it?"

435

"Let me look. Drop by later. I will find it."

"I am coming back. I want to read it."

"Come back by. Nice to meet you, Toby. You have a girlfriend?"

"Yes sir."

"Come with me." Outside the office he called to his man Nathan. "Toby here is the new ranch foreman for Mr. Byrnes. Get him a box of chocolates for his girlfriend. You can wait on him next time. He left a big order."

Toby started to protest.

"Never you mind. I want to do lots of business with you."

Chet had joined them and nodded it was all right.

"Thanks."

"Was that bribery?" Toby asked when they were on the buckboard.

"No, that was good business. That box of candy did not cost fifty cents. Your order will cost hundreds of dollars. Merchants ply folks that way. You ever bought groceries and got candy?"

"No, I never bought that much at any one time, but I seen that done before."

"Talley will be pleased you bought her that."

"I will give it to her but I won't say I paid

for it. It was just a bonus I got."

Chet lifted the reins to go to Bo's office. "Being honest don't ever hurt a man."

Toby nodded.

Back at the ranch, they talked to Raphael about securing the order in the wagon.

He agreed that loading and unloading was unnecessary. "I will have a rig and a driver go in tomorrow for it."

"May I ride along?" Toby asked. "I want to be sure it is just what Spencer ordered. He's pretty fussy about things. Besides he really wanted this job."

"Certainly."

"I better go give this candy to Talley before I eat it."

"Sure," Chet said.

"The boy is really concerned about his job?" Raphael asked after he left them.

"I think he's a detail man. That doesn't hurt."

"No. Don't hurt at all. I may need one more *casa*."

"Oh?"

"The young man, Miguel, is courting the girl Lisa you found. He asked me this morning."

"I knew they went riding."

"It won't make your wife angry?"

"No."

"Good. I will work the building in with all the rest."

"We keep growing, don't we?"

"Ah, it is a good place. So many people live what you call hand to mouth."

"Yes. Not only the Mexican people do that. I want a crew to chop sagebrush. Maybe a half dozen young men. I can feed them and provide tents. Pay fifty cents a day. Give them work up there."

"Oh, they would go to work in the winter."

"Think on it. I don't have any shelter right now."

Raphael nodded. "What else?"

"I will need fence posts. Straight juniper ones."

"How many?"

"Let's say, one thousand to start."

"Very many. By springtime?"

"Yes."

"I can find them. But hauling them —"

"Buy two more wagons and tell Frye you need two stout teams. Raphael's Freighting."

He laughed. "I will work all this out."

Chet went to the house for the noon meal. He had the telegraph builders' information that Ben had found for him. He'd not talked to Bo about a surveyor for the place.

They needed to have some property lines

for the fencing crew. Lots to do.

"Lunch is being served," Monica said.

"I am here," he said, washing and drying his hands on the porch. "Where is Liz?"

"She is not feeling good," Anita said from her place. "She said to tell you she will be all right. Just an upset stomach."

"Hold fixing my plate. I will go see her."

He hurried upstairs. She was sleeping on her side. His hand felt for her forehead. Not much fever.

"Oh, you're back?"

"Lay still. What's wrong?"

She sat up with her hands behind her to brace herself. "Nothing. The baby and I have indigestion — that is the word?"

"Upset stomach. Yes. But you have to eat. There are two of you now."

"I will eat. Just having a sick day."

"You aren't better in the morning I'm hauling you to the doctor."

She pulled him down and kissed him on the cheek. "I will be well in the morning."

"You need anything you holler."

"Anita is watching out for me."

He went back down and started eating.

"Well, what did you think?" Monica asked.

"She doesn't feel good. I'll take her to the doctor in the morning if she isn't better."

"I never had a baby. But I have been

around many who have been with child. They have such days, some none, some more sick days."

"She isn't better, I'll load her up."

"Fine."

Somehow this started like a sunny day and a thick cloud had just gone over him shutting out half the light. A foreboding feeling went through him. He closed his eyes for a second. *God, help me. I don't need to lose her.*

He spent the afternoon adding to a list of things he needed done and reading the advertisement on how to connect your town to the nationwide web of wires.

After consideration he wrote a letter to those people — the Cincinnati Telegraph Company. He asked for information and the estimated costs for a four-hundred-mile system.

Then he turned back to the Rustler Ranch project. He needed a surveyor. Bo could find him one. No need to stock the place to start. Had Bo bought anything north of there they could use for a line shack project? Or put a windmill on a dug well and have a tank. Water development would be the key to making it a working ranch. Maybe they could find some seeps to develop into water holes.

He would simply have to find out more about existing water sources. That meant spending days in the saddle. He might have to dedicate some time to doing that this coming winter, but he would have a ranch started and in time a paying proposition. He looked at the addressed envelope to Ohio. And maybe have a solution to the telegraph situation? Toby came by and sat down in a chair close by.

"What's cooking?" Chet asked.

"I didn't mean to bother you. How long do you estimate before we will have cattle on the ranch?"

"I think maybe two years. You need a hay supply first. Hauling hay for horses is one thing. For cattle that is way too expensive. We can clear enough land for hay cutting this coming year and the next year get rain we can stack lots of hay. We have done that elsewhere. But we don't need the cart before the horse."

"Oh, I realize that. Raphael says if I start chopping sagebrush this winter I will have hay to cut next summer — if it rains. That will move the cattle coming up a year earlier."

"That means another bunkhouse?"

"He says tents with stoves would do the men."

"All right, you and Raphael get that crew and a cook. I'll invest the money. I can find tents, stoves, cots, and tables. Let's get Jesus to gather it; he knows the people. We have an open winter you may move up."

Liz was better or acted well enough to come down for supper. She told him to stop worrying about her . . . she would survive.

Spencer came back. The lumber mill thought they had space to cut him enough lumber shortly. Two freighters were hauling the lumber they had that he could use for the start. Those men said they'd haul until the snow got too deep. The crew from Center Point should arrive in one week. Spencer had two more freight outfits said they'd haul some too, and after his inspection thanked Toby for the wagonload of hardware and items needed that were so well tarped down and waiting to be hauled. He gave Chet a new list of more things they would need.

"You hear from Tom about the road repairs?"

"He either has it done or will finish it shortly."

"Thanks, Chet. The construction crew say I get the material to them they will have it done in three weeks."

"That quick?" Toby asked, impressed.

"They work. This is nothing to them. Look what all they built up here."

"We may need to widen that road for those coming and going," Chet said.

"Well," his wife said, pulling him up for supper, "there are no loose ropes around here."

"We are having elk tonight," she announced. "Two *vaqueros* went and got the hide and the head and some of the meat. The man in town who stuffs animals will mount the head, and there is an Indian lady tanning the hide. So by the time the baby comes we will have the head up in the living room and the boss will have an elk skin coat to wear."

Everyone applauded.

"How did you do that?" Chet frowned at her.

"I have people help me when I want a surprise."

"Where is Jesus tonight?" she asked, herding him into the dining room.

"Buying tents and things for all those boys who want to chop sagebrush."

"How many are there?"

"Last count he had was fifteen. We are only taking ten for now."

"What can they clear in a day?"

"Some places where there has been a fire

they can clear two acres a day, or more. Thick patches maybe an acre is all. There are other small trees and stuff that needs cutting down and hauled away."

"Snowy days they can cut up logs and bust them up for firewood for the ranch," Toby said to her.

"Have you heard from the corral builders?" she asked when he seated her.

"No, but Harold Fauk and his family will come through."

"You really liked them when they worked on the stage line setups."

"Yes. They know how to work . . . how to build them stout."

CHAPTER 28

Raphael sat in the warm kitchen sipping coffee with Toby, Spencer, Liz, and Chet. Monica was finishing making breakfast and delivering plates of food.

"You still have coffee?" She checked the foreman's cup.

"I am fine. *Gracias.* I think two loads of hay first. Those teams and horses up there will need more feed than graze. Then two loads of firewood. I will have time to get some grain up there for the animals too. Plus I will have a wagon hauling their hardware and food needs."

"Can you do that?"

"Robert has plenty of hay and firewood for him. We took lots up there this summer, so he is fine. The lower place has good stacks of firewood in place."

"Why did you haul Robert hay?" That was strange to Chet.

Raphael shrugged. "I had the men and

445

teams . . . I hauled it from Camp Verde."

"I have no argument about your men working. Is Victor short on them?"

"He really gets lots of hay put up. Tom even admitted Victor was lots better at farming than he was. My *vaqueros* don't mind hauling it. You said it was all one big ranch."

"All right. We will get snow. Maybe not until later, but we may need to rescue stranded freighters."

"Can they find that place easy?"

"Yes. Tom will have the road open. You know where that friend of Margaret lives. They will point to where our road is at."

Toby jumped into the conversation. "Can we get a sign to put up? That says A CHET BYRNES RANCH, EASTERN DIVISION."

Chet smiled. "And TOBY EVANS, SUPERINTENDENT, under that?"

"I haven't proved that yet."

"Yes, I selected you. The sign painter in town can paint that — get it painted and put up."

"Yes sir."

"Liz can design it for you."

"Thank you, sir."

"When you believe in something you can sure get your back up about it."

"Is that wrong, Chet?"

"No. You will have lots of times when you

have to put your foot down for what you believe. It is how it should be."

"I don't need my name up there."

"If I ride up there and don't know you, who do I ask for?"

"I understand. Thanks, I'm learning."

"Good, now let's talk like friends. You and Talley. What are your plans? Wait. I don't care if you marry or don't — but you are going to be a leader and that sets an example. I don't think I'd be accepted as a leader if I ran around on my wife or we simply lived together."

"Chet, I talked to Dad. We agreed the two of them never got along. He understands I have built a friendship with her since he was married to her — oh, and he likes the idea of the private room for him and a job. If you think people will believe I am not a Christian or a worthy person, then I will talk to Talley. I guess we have been so occupied with being together we may have not thought about how it looked to others. My plans are for us to be married."

"Then if you two plan that — announce it."

"Right now? I don't have the money to buy her a wedding dress and pay for a wedding."

"If you two want to marry, Liz will buy

her a dress that you couldn't afford and the ranch will host the cost of the event."

"You know I almost didn't take that candy at Ben's store. I didn't deserve it."

"Toby, I paid for Hampt and May's wedding and everyone since then. You are part of this team."

"Thank you. Now that you said that, I do feel better about it all."

"When we meet as leaders, you defend what is right in your mind."

"I will, sir. Talley and I will talk. You know I haven't had to make decisions that everyone looked at but me. I am still having trouble believing I need to take charge and to get it right. We'll be here for supper."

"Good. Your decision won't get you fired."

"Thank you."

They shook hands.

CHAPTER 29

"Chet, Ty and Victoria are here," Liz said. "They just drove up in a buckboard."

Chet put the *Miner* newspaper aside. "I'll invite them in."

"What could I serve them?"

"Apple cider. We have lots of it."

"That will work."

He kissed her going by.

Chet leaned out the back door. "I'm home. Come on in. Liz has some cool apple cider."

Ty stopped at the base of the stairs standing behind her. "We aren't interrupting anything?"

"Lord no. Come on. How are things going?"

"Pretty fast. I think we found a place that would suit us."

"Come on in here. Give me her shawl to hang up. Grab a mug and go into the living room. Liz and I were loafing this afternoon.

You found a place you like?"

They sat together on the couch, and Ty sat on the edge to explain. "Yes, we wanted to run some things by you and ask what you think."

"Go ahead."

"The ranch we liked is the Fieldman place. It is in the north end of things. Has thirty acres irrigated alfalfa, watered by two artesian wells. Has corrals and even a barn to store hay, with milking stanchions we would change on the left and horse stalls on the right. There are some half shelters we could use for mares and colts in bad weather. There is a fenced pasture he used for dairy cows. There's a bunkhouse. The house needs some repair and the water system needs to be hooked to the windmill. It is three hundred twenty acres. The price is five thousand."

"Is there any dicker in that price?"

"You mean will they lower it?"

"Like trading for a good horse."

Ty looked back at her.

She held up her hands.

"We haven't asked. What would you suggest?"

"The bank foreclosed on him, right?"

Victoria nodded.

"I think he has tacked the unpaid interest

on the price."

"How much is that?" Ty asked.

"Probably twenty percent."

"A thousand dollars."

Chet nodded.

"What should we offer him?"

"I'd say thirty-five hundred cash. You can always go up."

"I can do that. How will I pay him?"

"Liz, get a check. You write in the amount. I will sign it."

"I put his bank's name on it and the amount?"

"You want a registered clear deed."

"I can request that."

"I am going to give you another check to deposit in your and Victoria's new bank account. This will be to fix the house and your needs to make it a ranch. It will be for three thousand dollars. You will need living expenses and ranch expenses. When it gets down we will replenish it."

"That is a helluva lot of money." She nodded, agreeing with him.

"You have about three weeks to fix a house. But don't let that make you do something you don't want." Chet directed that to her.

"We think we can do this. And we thank you."

"Have fun."

He signed the checks. Ty shook his hand and Victoria kissed him. She also hugged Liz.

They finished their cider and left the mugs on the kitchen table. Liz and Chet walked them to the back door. Chet went with them to the buckboard and sent them on their way. Victoria waved at him, then she settled in close to her man.

"You beginning to feel old?" Liz asked when he returned to the house.

"No, but we sure have young folks around us and another child coming in our life."

"Will you help them get that ranch ready?"

"If they ask."

"Good idea. You have been helping people, I mean really helping young people, with their lives."

"Trying."

At supper, Toby and Talley were there. Anita helped Monica set the table. Lisa came in from helping the ranch women working on the dried brown beans and sacking them. She washed her hands and apologized for not helping Monica sooner.

"You do lots of work down there. You earn your keep around here."

Everyone agreed.

Chet said, "Lisa, I told Raphael this morning to build the requested *casa.*"

"Really?" She rose up and clapped her hands.

"Yes. It will take more time in the winter, but we have the adobe bricks and the rest is close by."

Lisa crossed herself. "Thank you, Blessed Mother."

Toby spoke, "I guess I am next here to tell our plans. Talley and I want to be married when it can be arranged. We don't want to push anyone out. She and I have known each other and we think we can make a marriage work. I asked Liz and she said we could get married in two weeks and not get in Ty and Victoria's way. So I invite you all to come."

"We all will be there," Chet said. They applauded them.

After the meal when he and his wife were alone in the living room, she asked him what he thought was his next move.

"I can't leave here until after the weddings, and perhaps by then, the New Mexico office will have found and arrested Hall. Whatever is the case I want that matter settled. Then solve who hired him and arrest those people. That might be the hardest to do."

"You think he will hire more raiders?"

"No. But he planned the murder of Iris and paid for it. Perhaps not her directly but he sent others there to do that."

"So if they don't get Hall in Mesilla you intend to try and find him?"

"Yes, and bring him to justice."

"I'll pray they arrest him."

"I will too."

Ty was back the next day with Victoria. They looked excited when they drew into the yard. The cool north wind swept Chet's face as he came down the back stairs. He stopped on her side of the buckboard and offered her a hand down.

"Well?"

She turned for Ty to answer him.

"We did better, Chet. We got the ranch for four thousand and Victoria's dad said he'd pay half the money. You only have to pay two thousand. Now, honey, tell him what your mother wants to do."

"Mother has money from her family inheritance. She said that the present house could be my foreman's place to live and is building us a new house. Oh, she asked if you could get the lumber for it. She'd pay for it, but the contractor told her you have it all tied up."

"I'll get that done. You two will really start out great." He turned to Liz standing on the steps wrapped in a wool shawl. "You hear about all the free stuff they are getting?"

"Yes, yes, how nice of them."

"We can make it in the old house because it will take all winter to build the new one," Ty explained as they headed for the back door.

"Well, in case you didn't hear, in two weeks, Toby and Talley are getting married here."

"Liz, you will really be busy. Does Talley have a dress?"

"We are going tomorrow and get it made. May I buy you a dress?"

"I hate to say no, but my mother has spoken to do that."

Liz hugged her. "Darling, I would not get in her way."

"Thanks. But it is great what we are getting together."

"We have hot coffee," Monica announced, setting out cups.

They had a nice meeting and the pair soon ran off to handle more business.

"Well, I bet since you threatened him, they sure put on a new face. Her parents I mean," Liz said.

"Good. He needed one. No, he did do a nice thing for them. They will start out better off than most people. After all, they only have her."

"And you, my love, you have a tribe you are helping get started."

Chet agreed. "Did we pay Ray's tuition plus his room and board?"

"Yes. In his letter he sounded very settled and excited."

"They say that academy in Saint Louis is the best and should get him in a good university. So Ray is with his nose in books. My brother would never understand it. He spent his entire adult life fixing and repairing machinery. He'd get so involved in doing that his wife would cry to Susie that he would never come to bed with her. And now Ty is getting married and starting a horse ranch."

"My husband builds ranches and chases down outlaws."

"We have fun together."

"I did not say we didn't have fun, we do, but heavens it is different from ordinary people's lives."

Toby came in the house. "A hay wagon headed for the ranch broke down. Needs a new wheel. I am going to take two men, jacks, and a new wheel."

"How far away is it?"

"The other side of Camp Verde . . . I'll be

back late this evening."

"Be careful."

"I will be. Where is Talley?"

"She's changing sheets upstairs with Anita."

"I'll go tell her. Don't worry, I can handle it."

Chet shook his head. That boy was going to learn that all the wheels you want to turn might not turn when you need them. At least the surveyor and his two men were up there tying ribbons on property lines.

Next week the sagebrush grubbers were going to be ready to set up camp and tents up there. A dozen boys and their Chinese cook. The boys were all Hispanic from sixteen to twenty years old. Needed work and understood how far away the ranch was, but they'd have four days a month to come back home and raise hell when they were paid. They each had two pairs of long handles and a canvas blanket–lined coat plus gloves that Toby had provided them. And they had their own wardrobe, which wasn't much.

Each one had a hoe and Raphael showed them how to sharpen them. The sharper the easier it would chop off the sagebrush at the base. They also had axes for small trees and larger brush. They were to leave nothing a mower bar would catch on.

Under Raphael's help, Toby made a big older boy named Ronaldo the gang boss. Toby warned him he'd lose his job if he could not keep those boys moving. The job paid a dollar a day and the others made fifty cents. Chet thought they'd done well.

"Toby, they may need protection from a bear or even Indians. I'd arm them or those that know about firearms. A double barrel for Ho So Man the cook and a rifle for your lead man to take along."

"I can do that. I never thought about it, but they could have troubles."

To sleep in they had a large wall tent with a big stove. A second tent was for the mess hall. Jesus had bought the outfit from some logger who quit the business, and it had cost less than a hundred dollars. The cooking utensils, tin plates, cups, and silverware plus washtubs, woodstove, and the large range for the cook. New all would have cost twice that much. Chet knew he got it cheap. The builders had their own setup, which they moved from Center Point to down there.

Chet had made two trips up there to check on things and he thought it all would work. Tom's roadwork would require a bridge later, but they could pass each other coming and going in most parts on the wider road already built.

Since the cut-off sagebrush and bushes would not rot, they'd need to take hay rakes and pile it, then load it on wagons and dump it. Toby agreed and said they'd get that done as well.

Chet received a letter from the U.S. Marshal in Santa Fe that week.

Dear Marshal Byrnes,

I instructed two of my deputies in the Mesilla area to locate and arrest one Gerald Anson Hall to be held for Arizona charges on murder and other crimes. These men are top lawmen and they could not find a trace of such a man by that name or description in the Mesilla area. I am sorry I was not able to help you. All offices in the territory have been put on notice to be on lookout for this man. But at this time he has not been located.

Sincerely yours,
Anthony Diaz
Chief U.S. Marshal
for the New Mexico Territory

"What is wrong?"

"Oh, Liz, the New Mexico marshals could find no trace of Hall."

"But your man said —"

He threw the letter down on the desk. "They might not be able to find their ass either."

"What now?" Liz asked.

"I'll talk to Spencer and Jesus. They may have some good ideas."

"You don't plan to leave before we host the weddings, do you? This week is Ty and Victoria. Next week Toby and Talley. And we planned the Thanksgiving celebration here on Thursday for the ranch people close by."

"It is going to wear you out, girl."

"No, it will keep me from getting depressed. I guess carrying a baby does things to a person that a nonpregnant woman does not feel. I can be up and then feel down. When I am busy I am the happiest."

"I think I understand. Keep busy."

But he was upset. He'd planned to send two of his men to bring Hall back when they apprehended him. Something stunk of a buy-off. It simply was not right. Did they think he would not check on it? That he was so far away he would let Hall slip away and not look further into the deal. *Think again, dummies. Think real hard.* He planned to find and arrest Hall — with or without those

460

marshals and any flimflam deal he'd expose
as well.

Chapter 30

After supper Chet, Jesus, and Spencer were huddled in the small bedroom downstairs for a conference on Gerald Hall. Chet sat on the bed and both men had kitchen chairs.

"You think they got bought off?" Spencer said.

"Yes. He was there dealing faro a month ago. Hall has been working for some influential guys I am sure. A two-bit guy who once ran protection in Fort Worth had no interest in who got a mail contract. But a person who wanted the contract found him and made it worth his while to upset the deal. There's no telling how much they paid him, but when it looked like I might find him they had to hide him or get their tails caught in the door. I think this group thought I was too far away to check it out as well."

"What can we do?"

"Jesus, you have any wedding plans? You

spoke about Thanksgiving?"

He shook his head. "If we need to go down there that is fine. I am taking her to the jeweler and buying her a ring tomorrow. New Year's Day is now when we plan it for. I want to be able to announce it."

"Wow, congratulations, I never thought you'd get it done." Spencer reached over and shook his hand. So did Chet.

"I have to be here the next two weeks for weddings and Thanksgiving, but after that I could join you down there and we can iron all this out. Just be careful and don't get shot or killed. Hall ain't worth that. As Deputy U.S. Marshals you can arrest him and any jail is bound by law to keep him until I get there."

"Who will guard you going down there when you come, Chet?"

"I can ask for Cole's man if he isn't busy."

"Dennis is a good choice," Spencer said.

"Just make sure you get someone to cover your back," Jesus said.

"Oh, I will."

Spencer said, "Jesus, you get her that ring and we can head south tomorrow on the Black Canyon Stage, right?"

Jesus nodded.

"It leaves at midnight and you will have a long ways to go. I know you two can solve lots. I will come after the second wedding. I want him tried for murder in the territory. Send me telegrams of your progress, but be careful. People like him don't play games. He will kill you."

They shook hands and went out to where everyone else was seated.

"Well, what was decided in there?" Liz asked.

Chet smiled. "Jesus has something to say."

"I want to thank you all for making me a part of this family. I came from humble people. Chet hired me to track outlaws and he must have liked what I did. His first wife taught me how to write. No one in my family ever learned how to write. I still write letters for some *vaqueros* to Mexico. I understand bookkeeping and how a business is run. I love my work and I love Anita. She and I want to become man and wife on New Year's Day."

Everyone stood up and applauded. Jesus went over and kissed her. "Thank you all."

The suspense was over. Liz shook her head and whispered, "I may get them all married before our baby comes."

One of Tom's men shot a large elk and he sent half of it up for the wedding reception for Ty and Victoria. The tent was up and cloud cover moved in. Chet decided it might snow some the next day. His two men would be off and gone to find Hall and/or try to solve the mystery of his whereabouts.

They had the cooking fires going for twenty-four hours. But about the time folks began to arrive flakes started drifting down. No matter. They had two big stoves in the tent. The falling white stuff didn't hold back many from attending. Wine and drinks were being taken in an air of friendliness and festive occasion that Chet felt floated around inside the tent.

"Well, how is your new foreman doing?"

"Toby. He is doing fine. The bunkhouse is going up fast. He talked me into another large hay barn being built while they are there. It made sense. The windmill pumps water into the house now, and they can build a holding tank for the excess in the spring. Everything will all need to be painted next spring. And sagebrush clearing is really going good."

"By Christmas they will be done with construction and can go back to the headquarters and finish that."

"Tom mentioned taking some more cattle to Windmill. He worries it might snow a lot this winter."

"I agree. How many?"

"He thinks two months more than are

there now."

"He been over there with cattle for November and has the December–January numbers up there. They have plenty of hay. Yes, let's move February and March up there as weather permits."

"Have you seen Ty's ranch?"

"I looked at it earlier."

"That house her mother is building for them is larger than a hotel. They already have it framed."

"Well, they can go from room to room and feed the fireplaces all day then."

Hampt laughed. "Someone will have to."

"May and I are going to build a wing on our house unless you object. A new baby's coming. Heavens. Lost those two boys and now with the baby will have two new ones."

"I can finance it."

"No, May said we had the money. You do enough for the kids."

"Just doing my part. We have all been blessed in this land. You and I from being some cowboys wondering how we'd take back a ranch I bought and paid for. We have not done bad, ole hoss."

"Hell. You ain't telling me nothing."

"Jesus and Spencer went to El Paso, Mesilla country, to find this Hall who was dealing faro in Mesilla. The U.S. Marshals could not find any sign of him when they went looking."

"What the hell is that all about?"

"You tell me. A man got my address off the poster I guess. Said that Hall was dealing faro and because of the boundary, the Texas Rangers could not arrest him. I wrote Santa Fe to help me. They wrote back that there was no sign of any Hall in Mesilla."

"Is it a cover-up?"

"I don't know. Damn strange. I bet my boys can find out."

"When you going down there?"

"If they have not solved it, I am going down there after Toby and Talley's wedding."

"Let me go with you. We'll kick down some doors and find that bastard."

"I was going to ask Cole's man, Dennis, to go with me. He's been in law work, if Cole can spare him."

"Hell, the three of us can go."

"Hey, love to have you. I want this Hall deal over once and for all."

"If five of us can't settle it, well, it won't be because we didn't try."

"Better tell your wife. She doesn't have those big boys to help her."

"Oh, that big daughter helps her and my hands will do anything she needs done."

"How close is May?"

"February."

"Hell, we aren't back by then we won't come back."

Chet wrote Cole to see if he could spare Dennis. So all he needed was his reply. Liz would be happy if he took Hampt along. He'd stole her heart on the lost herd drive that they made to Nebraska.

Hampt was back in a short time. "She said go help you."

"Get your bag packed."

"What are Ty and Victoria going to do after they get married tonight?"

"Sleep upstairs. Well, if they have time, and go onto their ranch in the morning. They said they had lots to do over there. I think that suits them. They really are very close and I don't think they want to miss anything happening at the ranch."

"May said she heard Jesus and Anita are getting married New Year's Day?"

"That's the plans. He bought her a nice ring before he left."

"Things going on around us like dust devils. Oh hell, we'll get that Hall guy." Snow and the cold wind outside never stopped the activity or the wedding in the tent and then the supper that would follow.

It was May and Hampt's big night along

with Victoria's folks. Ty called May — his mom — and bragged how she put up with two mean boys growing up. She cried like Chet expected — she was the most tender-hearted woman on God's green earth — but Hampt was holding her tightly. If she had not been so well educated those boys would have been dunces. He knew that for a fact. They wouldn't know it for years — but someday they'd realize how much she pointed out to them.

The newlyweds escaped to the house and some privacy. Victoria's mother, Viola, thanked Chet for helping her get the lumber.

"I hear it is a large house."

She smiled. "I only have one daughter. This was the house in Missouri I wanted when we married. Arthur told me bankers don't live in houses that big. I am certain it won't hurt that horse people do, will it?"

"No. Those two are down to earth enough to make it a warm rich place."

"You have done well in this house."

"Yes, I have. Thank you."

"You are very lucky to have Elizabeth. She could treat a king and every cowboy would still love her."

"Viola, I knew that but I never phrased it that way."

"Quite privately, I thank you. We might have lost her. I would have died. You are what people say about you — a caring person."

"Thanks. God bless. I better move around."

Liz said, "The two lovers have already gone into the house. They forgot to ask your blessing."

"I can still do it before they leave tomorrow."

"Don't forget."

"I will try not to. I feel very pleased. Viola thanked me for all I did for Victoria and Ty. And she did it in a very sincere way."

"She has a lot of shell around her that won't let a person in because they may hurt her."

"She likes you."

"I know."

"Come . . . let's dance before you're too big."

They left the spot dancing — no polkas, they were too wild — but the soft Mexican music was easy to shuffle to. God, he loved his woman.

CHAPTER 31

At breakfast he blessed the marriage of Ty and Victoria. They thanked him, hugged everyone, and drove off. The snow was melting under a warmer sun. Nothing could dampen them — they weren't really living in this world but rather walking on top of it Chet decided.

He got the first wire from Jesus.

WE ARE IN MESILLA. DO NOT KNOW A THING.

JESUS

Well, in a little over a week he'd head that way. Hampt was going along and Cole sent a letter saying his man Dennis would be there, that there had been no more raids. Things were going fine. The snow was melting quickly. He hated them going without him but he had work to do, damnit. Signed it Cole and Valerie with a P.S. Rocky said hi.

Chet and Liz attended late Mass, and they enjoyed the returning heat driving home. The remaining snow was gone except in the shade.

"In a week you go to El Paso with Hampt and Dennis to look for this Hall if they don't locate him by then?"

"That animal needs caged. Iris was killed. That woman fed every bum came by and people without means. He also hired those men to kill a driver and the horses. The shooter who tried to kill my men and me. He works for some person or company that wanted that mail contract and he tried to make us fail."

"Hannagen didn't know them?"

"He said he didn't. I don't know the individuals and companies in that business circle, but I find it hard to believe he doesn't know who his competitors are."

"Hall may be hard to find. He must have lived there and has people who will hide him."

"He may be a hundred miles away too. We are going to scour that region and find him."

"I understand that Juárez is a very tough place."

"I would put my men up against a Mexican army. But we will be careful."

"I understand your anger. I simply want you back in one piece." She hugged his arm, sitting beside him. "Both of your boys along with me and the baby coming need you alive."

"I will be careful."

"When you have it solved send me a telegram and come home."

"I promise you I will."

"Good. I won't nag you again."

"That is your privilege as my wife."

"I do not do that. Your safety is my concern."

He nodded. As long as Hall ran free he planned to look for and arrest him.

The whole area between the main house and the outbuildings had been cleaned and readied for the next party, Toby and Talley's wedding, and after that they would have Thanksgiving dinner in the big barnlike hall for the ranch people and close family members. It would hold that size group. The tent would be left up but would not be needed for the Thursday meal.

His people would enjoy the festive occasion after the big apple harvest and summer work harvesting the pinto beans. The peaches picked before that and canning of food all summer so they had them to eat through the winter. His ranch was a community of sharing and helping each other. Most of the men had wives and families. Those children attended school. Six sons worked in the saddle shop. Those boys chopping sagebrush at the east ranch were mostly related to employees who needed work too. Raphael hired many to haul hay, lumber, and feed. They also worked building fences, repairing them, or helping at hay harvest. Raphael, his main man, was the leading man among the Hispanic community. He never took any credit for it. He might even have been the father figure who talked to Anita about setting a date to marry Jesus.

Someone did. Raphael or his own wife? He might never know the answer. Jesus was, to Chet, another son and an extension of his arm.

The day he separated Cargill from Talley at that shack with his rifle, Chet knew his man had stepped in and took charge. The nice Hispanic young man had grown into a no-nonsense leader. If Cargill had not done his wishes he would have killed him and the worthless man needed it. He would bet good money Jesus was rooting out information in Mesilla. Spencer matched him.

Dennis, he, and Hampt would make good support, but those two were tough.

He went to sleep hugging his expanding wife and savoring the event.

Chapter 32

Chet had checked in on the saddle shop. He saw the craftsmanship going into the ones they built and the harness they were making for the stage line. His man in charge, McCully, was a cripple but he looked so much stronger and healthier than when he took him under his wing and set up the shop. His pregnant daughter, Petal, married to one of the saddlemakers, looked much healthier too. The boys working took pride in all their work. He thanked them for all they did.

Bo told him their baby slept all night. They had found a nanny for the boy and would be at the wedding of Toby and Talley. He showed him maps of three homesteads he made bids on. Two of them were closer to the eastern unit, he said.

"Toby could go look at them for you."

"He's just a boy," Bo responded.

"I beg to differ with you. He's smart."

"Sarge will find time. I trust his judgment."

"Why are you such a snob?"

"I would never have hired him to run a chicken ranch for me."

"I hired a damn drunk land agent and then had to sober him up and I did by God. You'd be lying in the alley behind the Palace Saloon freezing your ass off and begging for a drink tonight. Stop the bullshit about Toby. He's a smart young man."

"All right, you win. But he's marrying his own mother."

"Don't spread that around. We all make mistakes. Talley married his father at fourteen. The boy's mother was already dead. Talley and his father never got along. She divorced him and ended up in slavery to Cargill. Did you see her swollen eye? I'd have killed him with my bare hands for doing that to a woman. On top of that he shot an unarmed man who was trying to stop him from hurting her more. Let those two sort things out in their lives. I say they will make a solid family. I thought that about you and I won, didn't I?"

"All right."

"How much private land is for sale around the place Ty bought?"

"I'll look. His father-in-law put up half

the money, didn't he?"

"It shocked me but he did, and her mother had inheritance money to build them a house."

"Have you seen it?" Bo shook his head. "It is not a house but a blooming castle."

"I've seen it."

"What do you need that land for?"

"Oh, his horse business may grow and if he has access to the federal land, or land we own, he could run some cows."

"Thinking all the time how to make money, aren't you?"

"Like you are about real estate sales."

"I will grant you that. Are you partners yet with the stagecoach people?"

"No. I am still looking. You have any money?"

Bo shook his head.

"I got a bid from a company in Ohio to build a telegraph line from Gallup to Hardeeville."

"How much money would it cost?"

"One point two million dollars."

"Forget that and build fires and make signals like the Indians did. Much cheaper. Who in the world has that kind of money?"

"The federal government."

"Let them build it and you manage it for them and do the upkeep. Like when the beavers eat the poles up, you can shoot them."

Chet was laughing by then. "That's all I need."

"Hell, Chet, a beaver couldn't tell a pole from a tree."

He left the office laughing. Why he bet by the time he got back home Bo would have ten sections that were for sale west of Ty's place.

His business done he rode back to the ranch with the sun on his jumper. He felt warm enough. Nice day for now, but it would probably fluff up and snow some more.

Raphael and the stableboy met him in the yard area when he dismounted.

"You need the horse any more today?" the boy asked.

"No thanks, I'm through."

When the boy was gone with the horse, his foreman said, "I know you just went to town and Jesus and the new man are gone on business. But please see me when you need to go anywhere, and I will get a man to go with you. Those were my instructions from your wife, past and present one. I don't want to lose my job. I am too old to chop sagebrush."

"All right . . . I screwed up. I hope you

don't lose your job because I sure couldn't handle the *vaqueros'* women."

Raphael was chuckling. "Are things going well up there?"

"I believe Toby will have lots of meadow-land open for next year. There is lots of grass there now. There were hardly any stray range cattle on the place at all."

"He may have a neat ranch to run for the outfit."

"I think he will be another Hampt in time."

"He won't be that big though."

They both laughed.

The preparation for the wedding and the Thanksgiving meal to follow was the ladies of the ranch operation. Monica made pies, and the slip of a girl he brought back, Lisa, had become a natural leader. And the older women respected her. Her *casa* was coming slower than he thought, but she'd have a wedding some time that winter, he felt certain.

Spud wrote him letters. Shawn wrote him about progress. They had four local cowboys hired who were out on the range with Spud catching unbranded calves and working them. Spud or Shawn rode with them each day and made additions and corrections to the log entries.

Tom had told them to castrate the long-horn bulls and they had all but two done. Those were probably both real wild and Tom was going to ship them more than enough Hereford bulls to replace them by springtime. The womenfolk were doing well.

JD's wife, Bonnie, wrote them she was definitely pregnant again.

Liz had little sickness and he felt maybe the spell was over. She was growing in size. One Wednesday, Valerie, Stella, and Rocky arrived. Cole's man Dennis Crain brought the three down. Cole was not having problems but thought he better stay on the job. Victor, Rhea, his nanny, and Adam came and Susie with Sarge and their boy joined them.

Sarge said he felt he needed that month's cattle drive off to come and be with family. His man could handle it. Tom and Millie had a meal down there for the crew. And later that morning Toby and Talley drove in.

The weather held above freezing for the wedding. He offered a blessing for the couple that was staying in the Brown Hotel because of the possible weather — but that was a secret.

A few days later it was Thanksgiving. Everyone was still there.

Chet asked grace before the meal started.

He thanked them all for being there and how this day had been designed to thank God for their harvest and their living in a country free of oppression.

They had everything a person could imagine on the food table from Mexican, elk, beef, and pork. Potatoes white and sweet plus rice and gravy. Canned sweet corn, green beans and hot peppers, *tortillas* both flour and corn, biscuits and corn bread. Monica's pies were on a separate table. Coffee, hot and cool tea, apple cider, milk, and water to drink.

Chet decided everyone ate until they near busted. His wife beamed like she was thoroughly pleased with how it went. Lisa and three of the wives made sure all the children were fed. McCully, Petal the saddlemaker, and her man came late, but were seated and there was enough food that they had all they could eat.

"How much has this grown since you started?" his Liz asked him.

"Maybe doubled. But they are the best outfit in the world."

"Raphael told me he chewed you out about going to town without a guard and it would not happen again." She was laughing by then.

"He wasn't lying either."

"When you first met him he wasn't the boss here, was he?"

"No, two white men were the ones. They got killed over by Bloody Basin. Monica led the charge for him to be the foreman. I never admitted to her she was right."

"Well now, we just get cleaned up and you go south."

"Yes. I better go play with my sons."

"They have grown every time I see them."

"Ours will too."

"I had not thought about that, but you are right."

The living room floor was alive with balls and dolls along with the ranch toddlers who all were overseen by three teenage girls and Stella Riviera, Rocky's nanny. They didn't need a daddy; they were busy playing.

The party went on into the night with the little ones sleeping on blankets while the teens and parents danced to the ranch musicians. He and Liz excused themselves and went to bed.

The next day, Dennis Crain arrived and Chet and he prepared to leave to meet up with Jesus and Spencer. May had caught some kind of bug and Hampt hated to leave her. Chet reassured him the four of them could handle the matter and shook his hand.

He and Dennis took their bags, rifles,

saddles, and, by buckboard, they went to meet the midnight stage. Liz rode with him and saw him off. It was hard for him to kiss her good-bye.

There had been no wires to tell him of any success, and Jesus would have notified him in time if they had their man. He wired them and mentioned a time when they might arrive — when they got closer he'd know for sure and wire them again.

He'd gotten Dennis a wool blanket to use going off the mountains to Hayden's Ferry. As the only passengers he thanked him for thinking about him and curled up to sleep. For Chet it was in and out, but he woke up and relieved himself at the Bumble Bee horse change.

Crain and Chet had their first chance to talk about the mission. Chet went over all the problems he blamed on Hall. When they had changed stages at the ferry, he continued the rest of the story, so by the time they rocked by the Casa Grande ruins, then thought to be from when the Aztecs were there, Dennis had the whole story.

"So no one knows who hired him?"

"Not unless Jesus and Spencer found something out. A man wrote me he was dealing faro in Mesilla, New Mexico, and that the rangers couldn't go over there to arrest him. I sent U.S. Marshals after him. They said no one knew where he went."

"Damn, that is weird, Hannagen not knowing. You know most times people like the head of the stage line know who bid against them."

"Told me he had no idea who he bid against."

"Why don't you inquire at the postal department in Washington, D.C., and tell them it involves a criminal case and you need to know the names of those bidders?"

"I never thought of that. Yes, I can do that. Thanks. Two brains are better than one. I guess it never entered my mind. Oh, along with a stage line, I have been thinking that we need a telegraph wire up along that route so we know what is going on. Later we'd have it for the rail service too. It is four hundred miles. I got my first bid last week. Guess what they want to do it?"

"A hundred thousand?"

"No. One point two million."

"Hell, you could pave the whole road with bricks for that."

"I'm working on a way to string one."

"Man, that would sure help us on security. But that's why you want it. You know it takes days to get the word if we have a wreck."

"I know. This is the last stop before Tucson. Pachuca Peak Station. We better use the facilities."

"Yes. Hey, thanks for the blanket. I don't need it today down here, but it was handy coming down. Where do we go from Tucson?"

"There is a stage from there to Lordsburg just over in New Mexico. Another over to Deming and that is the end of the rail line that goes to El Paso. We'll get off in Mesilla at the Texas border."

They ate some beans wrapped in a flour *tortilla* that a Mexican woman served them. She made the *tortillas* fresh and they ate them swaying in the coach with the driver cracking his whip and heehawing his two teams. Plenty of dust coming inside the stage and hot air as well.

"You lost your wife you told me?" Chet asked.

"She was fine one day and the next dying. Ruth was the light of my life. She taught me how to read. I had little schooling and it never seemed important until I realized, in law work, they didn't hire the best man — they hired the best man that could read."

He shifted his position when they hit a bump in the road. "I met her in a railroad camp. She was a shady lady. Her husband died and she had no trade so she did that. I was just a big galoot in those days. Riding along, I saw her walking under a parasol down the tracks, I guess going to go to the store. They had one in a tent. I swung that pony around and tracked her, trying to get her to talk to me. Boy I was talking to the wind.

"She stopped and haughty as hell she said, 'Mister, I am a whore and I work in that tent marked Sadie's Palace. For five bucks every thirty minutes I will talk or entertain you there.'

" 'Sounds reasonable. I'll be by to see you.' I tipped my worn-out gray cowboy hat at her and went to win some money at cards in another saloon tent. I was damn lucky and won three hundred dollars with four queens in my hand. Dumb me . . . I thought they were her and that was why I was so lucky. I talked to her one night at ten bucks an hour for six hours.

"The next night I spent the same amount. But I convinced her that night, I was not after her body but all of her."

"You were determined. Go ahead."

"She asked what would I do?"

"I said I would get a job as a lawman."

"She came back with the fact that I told her I couldn't even read."

"I told her I would learn how. I'd get a wagon, team, and camping gear and we will find a job I could handle. I'll find a preacher and marry her."

"She agreed?" Chet asked.

"Yes, and we were married and lived on wild game going west. I got a job stacking buffalo hides. Three drunks came by and started a fight with my boss and his buyer. I stepped in and knocked two of them out by slamming their heads together and kicked the gun out the third man's hand. They couldn't believe I did that. The boss gave me twenty dollars and told me his buddy, Wild Bill Hickok, was a marshal in Abilene and that he thought he could use me. He wrote a letter.

"It is a long ways from Fort Dodge to Abilene. Ruth was afraid I'd not get a job when we got there. Wild Bill hired me and I worked for him two years, and by then I could read a book. She taught me all about money. I moved down the line to Wichita. I could also handle a crowd, catch a thief or crooked dealer. The cancer took her like a prairie fire. Doctors wrung their hands. I held the loveliest woman in my arms every night — when I lost her I cried myself to sleep."

"My friend, I have had losses like that too.

I thank God every day I have Elizabeth."

"Cole told me all about that. He told how you shipped Valerie to Preskitt from Tombstone and he later courted her. Also he agreed, when he knew my story, that he'd be in the same shape as I was if he ever lost her."

Chet just nodded. Since it was a four-hour wait for the Lordsburg Stage, they had time to eat so they went to a Mexican restaurant he knew for lunch. The time passed fast and they saw they were going to be real crowded in the stage for the east. Two peddlers, a woman in her thirties, with the two of them all shoehorned in the coach. Chet asked the driver to let him ride on top. There was no shotgun guard. He agreed and that left Dennis with the woman to talk to and Chet to listen to the driver's laments about being underpaid and saying how his wife shared her body with other guys he knew when he was away on stage-driving business.

They made it to Benson without him falling off. The salesmen departed there and Chet told the driver to have better luck in the future. After a meal from a Chinese's cook, Chet, Dennis, and Virginia — the lady still riding with them — headed for Lordsburg. Chet introduced himself. The lady was a widow with a ranch east of there, and her foreman was coming to get her. She had four hundred head of mother cows and the T-Bar-K Ranch brand. It was off to the mountains north, and Dennis had told her he would like to stop and see her spread on his way back.

"Since I don't know when that will be, I will wire you when I can make it if that suits you?"

"Of course. That would be fine. Mr. Byrnes, you are a legend in Arizona. I have read lots about your law work. Dennis said that was where you were going now. To arrest a man evading the law."

"We hope so, ma'am."

"No, no ma'am. I'm Ginny."

"My wife and workers call me Chet."

"Dennis said you had just built a stage line."

The conversation ran on while they were crossing the *playas* that spanned both sides of the road, looking like great lakes but only inches deep. Chet noted when they parted from her in Lordsburg that her foreman had dressed up to meet her and had a coal-black team and coach. She kissed Dennis on the cheek, told him to come see her, and shook Chet's hand.

Back in the coach he asked, "Interested?"

"If nothing is pressing coming back, I

490

would like to visit her."

"You better do that. It would beat eating beans from a can by yourself."

They made Deming and all the noisy steam engines hooking cars on switches and whistling like they had nothing better to do.

If stages bucked, then train cars jerked. They were six plus hours at twenty-five miles per hour from Mesilla. It was ten o'clock at night when the black porters put their bags, saddles, and guns off onto the wooden deck. Jesus and Spencer were there with a buggy to haul them to the hotel.

"Anything so far?" he asked them.

"We got our first real lead today. We are going to see about it tomorrow."

"Is it where he might be?" Chet asked.

Jesus looked at Spencer.

"We've been bribing people to learn all we can. This is the damndest place to find out anything. There must be some tough influence coming over from Juárez with strong arms. But we have a lead to see about tomorrow. The guy expects fifty dollars if we learn what we want."

"Good. Dennis and I need to eat, get some sleep, and breakfast. Then we can join you."

"We have all that handled," Jesus said. "How is everyone at home?"

Chet handed him a long letter from Anita. "The rest are fine."

Jesus smiled.

The next morning they went and had breakfast and then took a taxi to the address the snitch gave them. They told the taximan to wait. No one had any idea it was a funeral home. They went inside and, in Spanish, Jesus spoke to the first man who met them.

The man said he had no idea what they wanted and told them they must talk to the boss. A large man greeted them in his office. His name was Brazos and he wondered what they wanted from him.

Jesus told him in Spanish they were looking for Gerald Anson Hall.

The man smiled and spoke in English, "Oh, he died a few weeks before and he was buried."

"Did they bury the right man?" Chet asked.

"Oh yes, *señor.*" And he opened a drawer and handed him a good-size picture of a man in a coffin. He was wearing a suit.

"Is this him?" Chet asked, not having ever seen a picture of Hall.

"Oh *sí.* They had to have picture of him."

"What for?"

"I guess to collect the reward from Riley."

"That is why you have his picture?"

Brazos shrugged. "Two pictures do not cost much higher than one, and the *hombre,* he paid me for both of them. So I kept mine."

"Did he die of natural causes?"

"Oh yes. He had three bullets in his heart."

Chet shook his head. "They killed him. And collected a reward, right?"

"Oh, I heard later they paid five hundred dollar for him dead."

"Can you tell me who killed him?"

"No. He might kill me."

"Can you tell me who wanted the photograph?"

"Philippe Romulus."

"You guys know him?"

"He is a thug here in Juárez," Jesus said.

Chet put a hundred dollars American on the man's desk. "He works for who?"

The man held his hands up about the money. "I can't take that."

"Two hundred?"

"No."

"Three hundred for the name of the man he works for."

"Sam Riley."

"The man who paid the reward?"

Brazos nodded. "Have a nice day, *señor.*"

Outside and getting into the taxi to go

back to Mesilla, Chet asked, "Who is Sam Riley?"

"Big businessman on the U.S. side of the border."

"You guys suspect him?"

"No. We never had this much information before," Jesus said.

"There are two taxis following us," Spencer said.

He directed their driver, "Go down the alley and stop at the other end to block them. You two slip out so they don't see you, and when they both stop you cover them from behind."

Dennis and Spencer slipped out and their buggy went on between piles of rubbish. Soon both rigs turned and rushed down the alley.

"Get down, driver. They may shoot at us," Chet told the man.

"Sí, señor."

Chet and Jesus with guns ready faced the oncoming wagons. The men in them threw up their hands. The other pair had the second occupants covered.

They were made to stand facing the wall and tell their names, which meant nothing to Chet. He drew out the youngest one and took Jesus's big knife to hold close to his face.

494

"Tell me where your boss is at right now or lose your ears."

"At his *casa*," came the answer. "It is on the Bishop Road past Reale."

"Jesus, you know where that is?"

"Yes. What color is his house?" Jesus asked the shaking boy.

"Verde."

"Get back over there," Chet told him.

He spoke to his other men. "Spencer, you and Dennis pay these other drivers to go on. You hold this bunch here for an hour. Then meet us you know where."

"We can do that." Spencer had disarmed them and made them squat down at the wall.

Jesus and Chet hurried the taxi driver to the place the boy told them. Chet told him to park around the corner. The *casa* was a big two-story house turned into an uptown restaurant downstairs.

They swept into the interior and someone shot at them from the balcony.

Jesus returned fire while Chet covered the room. Nothing but screaming women workers and white shirt waiters in the place. The room was filled with spent gunpowder. Chet and Jesus rushed upstairs and faced a man aiming a gun at them. He hesitated a second and Jesus shot him. They flew to the end of the hall and found a window where a man was escaping, having jumped down and was now running away.

They faced each other and both said, "Sam Riley. He's going to warn him."

At full speed they ran back through the gun smoke–filled room, took the stairs two at a time, found the driver, and were headed for the American side, where Jesus said Riley had an office.

"He has a business on the second floor in the Texas First Bank Building," Jesus said.

His U.S. Marshal badge shown had opened the U.S. customs gate quickly for them to go back. The clogged streets slowed them, but when they arrived at the bank, Chet showed the bank guards his badge. Instant entry, up the stairs and at his opened door, the man's secretary looked stone-faced at them. They went straight by her with their guns drawn.

The desk was empty and so was the open safe behind it.

She mumbled, "I don't know where he went. I spoke to him not ten minutes ago."

Chet looked at Jesus. "The train depot."

Jesus agreed.

The driver charged off with them for the train depot.

"You've seen him before?" he asked Jesus.

"Yes, we followed him some for two days and learned nothing. He is five-eight. Blond hair. But how did he know that we were on to him?"

"Damned if I know. But things are unfolding. I think your investigations made him uneasy, and he thought we have more evidence than we had, so he was prepared."

"You think the information we need was it in the safe?"

"That and money. He didn't leave it for us to find."

"Pull right," Jesus told the driver. "That's him running down the platform with two suitcases."

The driver whipped the horse to go faster. Chet was standing up using his right hand on the shade brace to steady himself, ready to jump from the coach if they got close enough for him to pounce on Riley.

The man started to veer away but too late. Chet made a lurch forward . . . caught him with his arm wrapped around his head. He sent the man and his two suitcases in what he later described as an ass-over-teakettle wreck on the train platform.

Thank God Jesus covered him before he could get up.

Women were screaming. Men stood back bug-eyed and aghast.

"Nothing wrong here. U.S. Marshals arresting a felon."

"What in the hell is going on here?" An Irish cop with a billy club joined them.

"Nothing, officer. I am a U.S. Marshal and I am arresting this man —" He'd forgotten his name.

"Sam Riley," Jesus said, and winked at him.

"Thank God you remembered what he looked like."

"I want a lawyer."

"Pard," Chet said, removing a small pistol from inside Riley's jacket. "Those people in hell, well you know how hot it is down there? Well I am going to tell you they want cold water. You can go to hell to get your lawyer, like they can get water."

Chet opened the first suitcase and closed it before the loose currency blew away.

The second one contained papers and ledgers. He had lots to go over.

"What'cha be doing with him, Marshal?" the policeman asked.

"Lock him up in a tight cell. No bond. The charges are murder as well as night riding against innocent people."

"You know the routine?"

"I will be there and file charges."

"And I be thanking you, sir."

"You have kids?"

"Five of them."

"Buy them some new clothes." He stuffed two twenties in the man's pockets.

"And may the good Lord smile on you and your generosity."

They loaded the money and the other suitcase in the Juárez taximan's rig and went to the hotel. The cases were sent up to the room and Jesus with them. Chet stayed and talked to the driver.

"You own this rig and horse?"

"I only wish, *señor,* I did."

"You have a wife?"

"Sí."

"You treat her well?"

"I have little money. We never fight. I have three children."

"If you owned this horse and buggy could you make more money?"

"Ha, the man, he wants a hundred and fifty for him. I asked him one day."

"What is your name?"

"Antonio Stephens."

"I am Chet Byrnes. We will be partners. I will give you the money to buy this outfit. You will keep and feed the horse. You will keep all the money but for me put ten pesos in the church poor box each year from my share."

"Are you serious? Ten pesos?"

"Here is my money. One, two, three hundred dollars."

"Why pay me so much?"

"Someday you might buy another horse and buggy and hire a driver and put ten more pesos in the box for me."

"*Señor,* I am about to cry. Why do this for me?"

"You never backed down or ran away. We'd never have arrested this man if you hadn't cared for us. Don't get drunk on my money. Buy one horse anyway. And kiss your wife and children for me."

The man smiled through his tears and held up two fingers. "I will have two carriages next time you come to Juárez, Chet Byrnes."

He turned in the dusty hot street and looked up. Jesus was in the hotel window and nodded to approve whatever he did for the man. Now he would write a wire to Elizabeth and tell her it was over except for his torn pants and his slightly wrenched knee, this time from the wreck on the platform. A boy would take his wire to the telegraph office and she'd know he would be coming home soon.

CHAPTER 33

In the hotel room, the four men had a bottle of whiskey open and some red wine Jesus was drinking. They looked relaxed sprawled out on the furniture in the living room portion of their suite of rooms.

Chet poured some whiskey into a glass and raised a toast. "Get your glasses up. For some run-of-the-mill cowboys we didn't do too badly today. If no one has a claim on the money I want it split between the three of you. You risked your lives coming down here and found Hall and the man who hired him. I believe all that money is ill-gotten gains and we will stick to that story."

"How much is there?"

"You will count it, put it in a bank vault, and we will wait to see what happens. Toast to the four of us."

The whiskey was sharp. And it cut lots of Texas dust out of his throat. He washed it down with a pitcher of water. Damn that stuff was tough. It had been years since he tried any, and that would not happen again for another long time.

They began counting the money. Chet under a lamp started to read the ledger entrees. He went forward several pages and stopped at a note that listed a monthly supplement to Rod Carpenter — five hundred dollars. Son of a bitch, Riley was paying him well to not do anything almost a year before Hannagen hired Chet and the ranchmen to build the stage stops.

He began to pay Hall about the same time that same amount a month. And Hall reported paying men he hired for their labor it said. But Chet would have bet some were dummy expenses that Hall made up. Then each time he showed Hall paying a hundred bucks a man, Chet could bet he got to keep what he did not pay out. That on top of his wages.

"Sent the money by Wells Fargo — charges," he read out loud.

"What was that?" Spencer asked.

"He shipped money somewhere and I think he erased the sender. Damn, I may have to go over this a dozen times. This guy shipped money to someone. All of this is a mess, but Hall collected all fees whether he paid them or not."

"What else?"

"I am going to get a real auditor to look at all of this, and hopefully he can make something out of it."

"How soon can we go home?" Dennis asked.

Chet smiled at the man. "You will have time to stop and see Virginia."

"You object to it?"

"No. Just wondering."

"Might be what I need or don't need. You never know."

"Take a couple days with her — whatever you need. We made a major breakthrough here and even your boss won't believe what we found, money aside. Hall is pushing up daisies. The next guy is going to jail for a long time. And we know now why we had no help from Gallup."

"Cole will stomp his boots when he hears that. He thought Carpenter was lazy and dumb. All the time he was on the take to drag his feet."

"Who gets the reward for Hall?"

"You guys are counting it right now."

The next two days he spent gathering evidence that the prosecutors requested so Riley could be charged as an accessory to the crimes committed. The federal prosecutor's office found several other crimes he had been involved in, in the ledgers.

The office told him they considered the money unclaimed ill-gotten gains and it should go to his deputies. Of course Riley's lawyers protested, but their client faced even more charges so they dropped any claim. Most of it was small bills, but it amounted to over five thousand dollars a man. The money was then sent by Wells Fargo to Tanner at the Preskitt bank to be recounted and applied equally to their new or existing accounts.

Dennis left early to stop and visit Virginia. Spencer and Jesus stayed to help Chet finalize the case. He'd sent Hannagen a wire saying Carpenter would be arrested shortly for his part in the crimes. The response was another apology and a question as to why Pinkerton didn't find any of this out.

Chet had no answer. Riding home via train and stage, Jesus asked Chet if he would help him find a ranch he could run cattle on and get a good foreman who would work for him.

They were due to get into Tucson that night and Chet watched the thick forest of *saguaros* that clad that part of Arizona, going by the stagecoach window. He had no idea the amount, but he knew Jesus had never spent any of the reward money he had gotten over the years he worked with Chet. It was in the bank.

"Where would Anita like to live?"

"In a nice house. Not big as the Preskitt ranch but a nice one. I want her to meet more people so she can exchange ideas and share things. She's worked for Elizabeth so long, she steps back instead of forward. We talked about it. I was like that when you chose me. I didn't want to offend even the outlaws. I saw myself doing that. Now I don't hang back. I am one of your men and I need to be a part of them."

"You know the day I saw that?"

"No."

"When you drew your rifle and made Cargill move away from that woman."

"It was my place to do that."

"I can't tell you what to do about Anita, but you have moved her to accepting you as a husband. You need to take her more places. That may help."

"I will. But my job is your safety too."

"Unless Spencer finds himself a woman —" Chet said, looking at him.

"Damnit. I am looking. But I am getting more fussy by the day about getting the right woman."

They laughed.

They arrived in Tucson. There would be a

three-hour wait for the stage to the ferry. They ate supper at another restaurant that served barbecue. A well-dressed black-haired woman who looked familiar to Chet arrived with a man in very expensive clothing.

"Know him?" Chet asked the guys after they were seated across the room and out of view.

The two shook their head.

Spencer said, "I ain't that rich but what about her?"

"You don't want her?" Jesus said under his breath.

"Who is she?"

Jesus did not answer them right away. When he did it was in a whisper. "She was the woman messed up Reg. Her name is Jeannie Downley and she has a big place up by Hackberry. I don't know if she's married to that rich guy, but I saw her twice before."

"How do you know so much?" Chet asked.

"She turned my head one day and this old cowboy along with me said, sit tight. She'll drive you crazy like she did poor Reg."

"I'd like to be made crazy," Spencer said.

Their waiter came by and Chet asked him who the well-dressed man was.

"Lane McClure. He owns a big ranch

south of Tombstone. He has places in Texas too. She's not his wife. I don't know if he has one — but her name is Brinkley Stone. Her daddy has a big ranch north of Oracle and a big house up on Mount Lemon. She lives with her father."

"Those two come in often?"

"I think, when he is back here in Arizona, he brings her here. He goes back and forth between here and Texas."

"Thanks . . . we wondered." Chet turned and said, "Now you know. What do you think, Spencer?"

"Probably something to look at and not touch."

Chet caught the wary shake of Spencer's head, knew how he felt, and couldn't do a damn thing about it.

"Fellows, I am anxious to get home. It is going to be Christmas shortly."

"She busy filling your stockings while you are gone?" Jesus asked. "Spencer, I have not told you but that first Christmas with Chet was the damndest one I ever had."

"Liz is doing almost all of it."

"Reckon I'd get a good woman in my stocking if I asked for her?"

Chet shook his head. "I doubt it."

"All I'd like is to have a nice-looking woman, not some teenage girl. I don't want a fat one or a real skinny one."

"Spencer, you are going to have trouble finding one period," Jesus said, frowning at him.

"We better step up our walking if we want a seat on that coach."

"You know something we don't, Chet?"

"Remember I rode up with the driver clear to Benton going east."

They sped up and found seats. No other passengers but hours later, when they stopped at Papago Wells where the road went west to Yuma or north to Hayden's Ferry and onto Preskitt, they gained a young woman passenger headed north.

Chet thought about himself making the run with Margaret when he and Heck first came west on that trip. Rebecca Franks made conversation with all of them, but she and Spencer hit it off. She asked him about his work. That led to his job as a marshal and what it pertained to. She obviously found him very interesting.

The way things went Chet would have bet he might have found her interesting enough. It was dark when they arrived in Preskitt. She stood on her toes and kissed Spencer on the cheek, thanking him for loading her things into the buckboard he had asked to borrow to deliver her to a Preskitt address.

Liz was waiting in a second buckboard with a ranch driver. Jesus got into the front of that second buckboard, while Chet got onto the second seat sitting close to Liz. They headed off to the ranch.

The next morning Chet didn't see Spencer until midday.

"How was last night? And now you know where she lives?"

"Yes. I'm not familiar with town street addresses. I was a cowboy before down on the Verde and never came to town much. When I did I was in the Palace and other water holes. You know that two-story house of ill repute on Mountain Street?"

"Yes."

"That's where she was coming to work."

"You didn't make her a better offer?"

"You know you could've knocked me over with a feather. She kissed me, again, asked if I wanted to come in. I said no, I better get back."

"You need time off?"

"I do. I'll be back when I can. Damnit. Why do women make things so damn hard?"

"Where was Spencer going?" Jesus asked him as they watched him hurry off.

Chet shook his head. "He better tell you."

"That woman?"

"Yes, but that's all I know."

Jesus went on up to meet with Anita at the house.

Toby came over and reported they had poles cut and were ready to build corrals. The sagebrush cutters already had fifteen acres chopped, raked, and ready to mow next spring. He was hoping for lots more.

Chet told him that Harold Faulk said in a letter he was coming and would be there by Christmas to build the corrals needed. He did some for a big ranch after he left and needed the work. He, his wife, and big kids really worked hard. He told Toby to keep cutting poles.

"Talley left you yet?"

"No sir. She's not a quitter."

"I didn't think so either."

Someone else drove up. Chet rose to see who it was. He went through the kitchen with Toby on his trail.

"Why Chet, it is Spencer and a woman. Do you know her?"

"Yeah, we met. Toby, you sound like, despite the winter, you are gaining ground. Kiss your wife and hug her for me."

"I will. I'm heading home."

He said hi to Spencer and the woman. Toby waved, climbed on his farm wagon loaded down, and shook the reins to the

Belgium team. The other two came up the stairs. He welcomed them inside.

"We'd like to talk to you and Elizabeth," Spencer said.

"I'll get her. Come on in the living room and have a seat."

Liz frowned at Chet when he found her and told her Spencer and a woman with him wanted to talk to them. "I'm coming."

Seated in the living room, Spencer told Liz how they met on the stagecoach and they were talking about marriage. But they wanted to know some things.

"Rebecca worries people won't accept her because of her past if we get married. She's been working in a house of ill repute. I took her out of it. I told her we were not looking back, we were looking forward. She fears she must hide her head in shame."

"I wish Valerie was here. That is Cole's wife. My husband put her on a stagecoach and sent her up here to work in a café. She is as respected a woman as any I know — she is raising Chet's son Rocky. Raise your head as his wife. If you feel more solid, go to church with him or any of us. I won't tell you that some people may not want to stone you, but the Bible says you are forgiven."

"Where should we live, in your opinion?"

"Cole and Valerie lived in town when they

were married. I am certain we can find a rental house and get you set up."

"I kind of wanted to be away from people."

"Rebecca," Chet said. "Maybe work for Jenn in town at her café. Meet people and make yourself not outgoing but interested in their lives and they will accept you."

"If you don't want to do that we can offer you a room in my house until you marry. Most of the girls come here do what they can to help, but it is not a slave camp. You two can meet in the house but I expect a holding hands sort of stay. I am not a prude but I offer it only as your choice of shelter before you marry him."

"Spencer, did you expect this?" she quietly asked.

"Yes. I knew they're damn good people and they've been helping lots of lost people, and I want you in a place where no one challenges you or makes you do things you don't want to do."

"Do you have a wedding date chosen?" Liz asked.

"Is in a month all right?" she asked him.

"I can wait that long. I'll find us a warm rent house meanwhile so we can go there when we become man and wife."

Liz told her, "Get your things. We have a

hot water system with a boiler to bathe with and lots of things hotels don't have, we do."

Rebecca was crying. Liz went to her and Spencer knelt on the other side of her. They were going to be all right.

Chet had more bids coming in the mail on the telegraph system and they were getting cheaper. They were all still way too high but who knew. The stage line was running smoothly. Shawn, in his letter, said they were about to finish up the branding and things were swell on the mountain. Lucy felt great.

There was Christmas and two weddings coming up — Spencer and Rebecca's and on New Year's Day, Jesus and Anita's.

He had lots of blessings in his life.

ABOUT THE AUTHOR

Author of over 85 novels, **Dusty Richards** is the only author to win two Spur awards in one year (2007), one for his novel *The Horse Creek Incident* and another for his short story "Comanche Moon." He was a member of the Professional Rodeo Cowboys Association and the International Professional Rodeo Association, and served on the local PRCA rodeo board. Dusty was also inducted in the Arkansas Writers Hall of Fame. He was the winner of the 2010 Will Rogers Medallion Award for Western Fiction for his novel *Texas Blood Feud* and honored by the National Cowboy Hall of Fame in 2009.

The employees of Thorndike Press hope you have enjoyed this Large Print book. All our Thorndike, Wheeler, and Kennebec Large Print titles are designed for easy reading, and all our books are made to last. Other Thorndike Press Large Print books are available at your library, through selected bookstores, or directly from us.

For information about titles, please call:
(800) 223-1244

or visit our website at:
gale.com/thorndike

To share your comments, please write:
Publisher
Thorndike Press
10 Water St., Suite 310
Waterville, ME 04901